GRAY
APOCALYPSE

GRAY
APOCALYPSE

James Murdoch

DEMAND
PUBLICATIONS
SEATTLE

Murdoch, James A.
    Gray apocalypse / by James A. Murdoch.
    p. cm
    LCCN 2008926546
    ISBN-13: 9780966443097
    ISBN-10: 0966443098

    1. Extraterrestrial beings—Fiction. 2. Human-alien
encounters—Fiction. 3. End of the world—Fiction.
4. Science fiction.   I. Title.

PS3613.U6945G73 2009   813'.6
                    QBI08-700052

Cover layout by Bob Aulicino
Cover art by Kaiser Valshon

Demand Publications
2608 Second Ave., Suite 2450
Seattle, WA 98121

To my Tasha

Prologue

July 16, 1954

*T*o say this was a momentous day would be an understatement. I had a private lunch with General Twining who briefed me on the preparations still needed before work can begin on the underground facilities in New Mexico, Utah, and Nevada. These will be the exclusive locations for the collaborative arrangement with the entities, and they will be permitted no other bases from which to operate.

Following lunch, Foster Dulles joined me in the Oval Office for a meeting with Admiral Roscoe Hillenkoetter, Dr. Vannevar Bush, Dr. Detlev Bronk, and, of course, General Twining. We went over the main points of the agreement and discussed once again the arguments for and against the arrangement. The discussions were only a formality since the decision to go forward with the program had already been made. As foremost members of the joint committee assembled by President Truman to investigate the alien presence and examine recovered artifacts, they were invited to witness the signing of the executive order initiating a collaborative arrangement with these beings from another world.

All of these men are outstanding Americans who have devoted years of their lives to studying the nature of the alien phenomenon, and they therefore understand this action for what it is—a leap of faith. Can we trust these Breeder Grays, as General Twining is in the habit of calling them? They are similar to us only in that they are nearly as tall as we are and walk on two legs. It is impossible to know much more about them other than the fact that they possess the ability to communicate by telepathic means and have technical and scientific know-how that is beyond our ability to understand. They come and go in our airspace at will, and we are unable to stop them. They take people aboard their craft for "biological study," they say, and there is nothing we can do to prevent them from so doing.

Because of their capabilities, I don't believe there is an alternative. It was Truman's policy to engage unidentified flying objects in aerial combat. But it was, as General Vandenberg once remarked, like sending flies to take on eagles. The loss of men and materiel was tragic and staggering. Despite the loss of hundreds of pilots and planes, we were able to bring down only a few of their craft. And those that fell from the sky were knocked down by accident, as when they inadvertently flew into the path of advanced radar systems being tested at White Sands.

What these creatures want is to be free of harassment by our armed forces. They wish to continue their study of the human race in a peaceful, orderly, and secret fashion in order not to create panic if the truth about their presence were known. They have agreed to turn over to us the identity of each and every person they use for their study so that we may monitor them to ensure they have not been harmed. In exchange, the aliens are willing to share technology with us. The abductions are an activity they are engaged in anyway, and we are powerless to stop them. This collaborative arrangement will give us, if not control, at least some degree of oversight.

I made this decision with considerable hesitation. But given the circumstances, I believe it is the best course of action. I agree with General Twining's assessment: Access to these exotic technologies will give our best minds a chance to unlock their secrets and, in time, perhaps will allow us to achieve technical parity. If it later turns out the intentions of these creatures are hostile, at least we will be in a better position to defend ourselves.

Maintaining secrecy is of utmost importance, of course, as it is imperative our enemies do not learn of the technical and scientific advantages that we achieve through this collaboration. My order continues the secrecy protocols established by Truman, but places responsibility for security at these facilities directly with the joint committee, though under the supervision of the NSA.

The important questions are still there and may go unanswered in my lifetime. Did we make the right decision? Will humanity truly benefit from this? Will the arrangement allow America to remain strong enough to fulfill its mission of spreading its ideals throughout the world?

I proceed with the leap of faith that this was the right thing to do, but if the agreement turns out to be a mistake, then God help us.

—From the diary of Dwight D. Eisenhower

Chapter 1

Alamogordo, New Mexico, 58 years later

*T*he naked ceiling bulb snapped on, flooding the subterranean cell with harsh light that stung Michael Kendon's eyes. They had left him in total darkness for more than an hour, and the sudden brightness hit him like the slaps and punches they had rained on him during the interrogation.

They're coming!

He tensed as he listened for boots marching down the wide tunnel that led to his cell. Either they were going to drag him out for another round of questioning about the breakout of the captive research staff, or they were going to bring Meller to him.

If they brought him, there was still a chance, however slim, that he could finish what Meller had started.

They had taken him from an adjacent cell an hour before, just after Kendon's interrogation. Kendon could still hear his cries as Bogdan and his security goons marched him away: "Listen to me. You're being used! They're going to kill you, too. Everyone!"

For the last hour, Kendon had been visualizing what they were doing to him, and it made him feel sick. He knew their methods. He had been raised from childhood as one of them, as an agent of the security directorate, as one of the keepers of the secrets of the Collaboration.

A well-built man with the rugged face of a soldier, Kendon kept his eyes squeezed tight until they adjusted to the light, then he looked around the cell—a twelve-by-fifteen room carved out of solid granite. Across from him was a metal door mounted on enormous hinges. He hadn't been told where he and Meller had been taken, but from the network of unfinished tunnels and chambers he had seen, he was certain they were at Alamogordo, one of the oldest of the Collaboration bases.

A few minutes after the cell light flicked on, Kendon heard the march of boots. The sound grew louder until stopping outside the massive door. Seconds later, the locking mechanism released, and the door swung open.

Bogdan, the security director for all of the New Mexico facilities, was standing between two guards. Kendon felt his heart sink when he saw Meller stretched out on his back. It didn't look like he was breathing, but if they brought him there, it had to mean he was still alive.

Bogdan had a lot at stake in bringing Meller to him. Were he successful in recovering the one-one-five pod that Meller and his research group had escaped with, and were he able to locate the weapon it was destined for, Bogdan would end up as security chief for the joint committee that would rule over the half-million people who were to survive the asteroid impact in special underground facilities.

Bogdan's brute tactics hadn't worked on Meller. Now he had to hope Kendon's soft approach would.

"Put him in there with the other traitor," Bogdan ordered.

Kendon suppressed the burst of hatred that gripped him as they dragged Meller in by his arms. Fingernails were ripped from one of his hands. Blood was clotted at the bridge of his nose where the sutures had ruptured, exposing the surgery he had done on himself to get rid of the implant.

The bastards! They punched him there on purpose.

A tall thin man who had once been Kendon's mentor, Bogdan

was from the Bosnian crèche of 1972 and had been groomed from an early age as an assassin. It was known throughout the security apparatus that he had personally eliminated forty-two squeaks—people who had dared to talk to the outside world about the Collaboration.

Keep the presence of the Breeders and their clones and their hybrids a secret by whatever means! That had always been the Directorate's primary mandate.

After glaring at Kendon for a moment, Bogdan marched out of the cell, followed by the two guards. The door swung shut with the fierce clang of metal on metal.

When the sound of boots faded, Kendon leaned back against the granite wall. He couldn't bear to look at Meller. His tortured body was clear evidence of what the plot to defeat the Breeder agenda had come to: nothing. After all those years of secret effort and quiet hope, it was a complete failure.

When he saw Meller finally stirring, Kendon forced himself to slide across the cold floor and leaned over him. He brushed back a strand of white hair that had stuck to blood on Meller's forehead and stroked the older man gently on the cheek.

After a minute, Meller's eyes quivered open and flitted back and forth to take in the cell. His face at first was filled with terror, as if believing the torture was about to resume, but then he recognized Kendon. "Those people are animals," he groaned in a barely audible voice.

Meller's body began to tremble, and Kendon wished he had a blanket to throw over him. "I can take some of the pain away. Do you want me to?"

Without waiting for an answer, Kendon put the palm of his hand gently over Meller's ripped fingers and felt the familiar flow of healing energy. It was an ability he had possessed ever since he could remember.

After several minutes, he said, "Does that help?"

"Yes."

Kendon formed the word "whisper" with his lips. Meller blinked his eyes rapidly to show he understood.

Leaning close, Kendon said in a low voice, "What did you tell them about me?"

"They wanted me to implicate you."

"Did you?"

"I told them you didn't have anything to do with the resistance because no one trusted you. You were kept in the dark about the real purpose of the one-one-five pod. It was an experimental upgrade for our antigravity reactors. That's all you were told about it."

Kendon looked at Meller's hand and felt anger building in him. "They'll do anything to get that pod back," he said.

Meller tried to get up on one elbow, but then fell back. His voice a whisper, he said, "I almost told them. The pain was too much. If they'd kept it up, I think I would have talked."

"You're the only one left who knows. Jenara is dead. He threw himself out of the helicopter when they were bringing him back. Menkin is dead, too. They broke his neck. Everyone is dead except for you and me."

"We didn't get beyond Texas. Other than me, no one was able to get rid of his implant in time. That's what gave everyone away. We never had a chance to get the pod to the weapon. They were able to zero in on us."

Meller had once drawn Kendon a sketch of the weapon, a cannon-like affair that was designed to be powered by the same exotic element that fueled the Breeder ships. It was designed to discharge a gravity beam powerful enough to deflect an asteroid the size of the one the Breeders were now hurtling at the world.

"The human race is finished," Meller groaned. "The Breeders and their damned hybrids now own this planet."

Kendon shook his head. "It's not over yet. I have an escape plan, but I have to know where you hid the pod and where the weapon was built."

Meller remained silent. He scrutinized the puffy cut above

Kendon's eyebrow, then averted his eyes. Meller had never told him everything, only enough so that at the final moment he could enable the breakout. It had been painful for Kendon not to have Meller's full trust, but he understood: Though he had turned against the Collaboration and had secretly joined the resistance, he was still an officer in the intelligence wing of the security directorate. He was still a man who had once been part of assassination teams that hunted down and killed defectors and terminated squeaks.

"They have you like they have me," Meller said. "You don't have any way out of here, either."

"You have to trust me."

When Meller fell silent again, Kendon pressed on, his voice full of urgency. "We only have three days left, Donald. The asteroid is going to strike Sunday night. Your weapon is the only hope."

Three years before, Kendon had infiltrated Meller's research group posing as a captive engineer transferred from one of the Nevada bases. The idea was to ferret out dissidence among the captive technical staff and prevent sabotage. By then, Kendon was already a defector in his heart, and when he learned the truth about Meller's work, he kept it to himself. Instead, he became a double agent, secretly plotting an escape so that they could break out with the powerful energy device and get it to the weapon Meller had built in secret years before when he was still free to come and go from the Collaboration's underground research facilities, before the Directorate sequestered all of the contract workers.

Kendon had made the mistake of revealing his true identity to Meller. If he had kept it to himself, he would have been as trusted as the other conspirators.

"You shouldn't have kept me out of the escape. If you had allowed me go with you, none of you would have been captured. I have the skills that would have prevented it. I am your only hope now. I have to know where to find the pod, and I have to know where the weapon is."

"You told them you could get it out of me," Meller said. "You worked out a deal with them. That's why I was brought to your cell."

"I convinced them you would die before revealing anything, and that I could get it out of you because you trusted me. Once I know, then I can escape. I could escape anyway. I've had a plan worked out for a long time. But what good would it do if I don't know where to locate the pod and your weapon? The asteroid will kill everyone on the surface, me included."

When Meller didn't say anything, Kendon continued: "This is what you worked for all these years. If I am able to get free, I can make it happen. I can reach the weapon. I can deflect the asteroid. I can defeat the Breeders."

Meller scrutinized Kendon's eyes. Finally, he whispered, "I'm sorry I didn't trust you more."

"Tell me what I need to know."

Meller's eyes flitted back and forth, as if to see if anyone was listening. "I can't tell you exactly what you want to know. What I can tell you is that Puerto Ricans are smart people. You can count on it, especially in the southwest. But to find the one-one-five pod and the location of the weapon, you have to get to my daughter first. I've told you enough about her. It should be easy for you to find her."

"What does she have to do with it?"

"She doesn't know that she knows, but she does."

"How do I get her to talk? She doesn't know me. She hasn't seen you for ten years. For all she knows, you died a long time ago."

"Virginia Woolf. Tell her it has to do with Virginia Woolf. Her books meant a lot to my daughter. When you tell her the name, she will be able to lead you to the one-one-five pod and the beam weapon."

Kendon shook his head in disbelief. "You've got to be more specific. There's too much at stake."

But Meller had gone quiet. He raised his hand and with his bloodied forefinger touched the bridge of Kendon's nose.

Kendon understood. His own implant was still embedded in the cartilage. Now more than ever there was a need for caution. Like the other conspirators, he had become a master at controlling his mind, at shrouding his thoughts within a center of whiteness, but what if he slipped? The Breeders read mental imagery like humans read books. The name of a long-dead English writer wouldn't conjure up any images, not for them.

All that Kendon really knew about Laura Meller was that she was a physician at a children's hospital in Austin. Meller had once shown him a photograph of her, and he could picture her in his mind. He struggled not to think of her, but to let her blend into the whiteness that kept the Breeders from knowing his thoughts.

"When you find my daughter, I want you to give her a message from me."

"I will do whatever you ask," Kendon said.

"Tell her how I wish I could have been with her all these years. I want you to tell her how much I have always loved her."

Kendon had forced himself not to think about the implications of getting them to bring Meller to him, but he could no longer avoid it, and it made his stomach churn. He shifted his torso to ensure his body was between the ventilator and Meller. If there was a surveillance camera, it had to be hidden behind the ventilation cover.

"They've agreed to hold you until they get their hands on the pod. Then you will be spared."

"But you don't intend to give it to them."

"No."

"You know what that means. I'm sure you've analyzed if from every angle."

Kendon felt light-headed, and he thought he was about to pass out. A stabbing pain gripped his chest, and his hands became unbearably hot.

His voice wavering, he said, "Yes."

Meller showed Kendon his tortured fingers. "I don't want to die the way they will make me die. What if I talk? You know they will do everything possible to make me talk. Then all that we've worked for will be for nothing."

As soon as Bogdan realized Kendon had deceived them, he would drag Meller back to the interrogation room. Meller would be subjected to the most barbaric and grotesque torture, with stimulants injected into him to prolong his life until they learned what they wanted to know. The Directorate would then beat Kendon to the one-one-five pod.

Meller said, "I want you to be the one to do it, Michael. You told me you know how to do it so it doesn't hurt so much."

Kendon stared at his hands. They were trembling. He closed his eyes in an effort to escape, if only for a brief moment, but he was immediately thrust even more deeply into the hopelessness of their situation. The same images that had been intruding into his head ever since his arrest appeared again. It was a vision of an enormous spacecraft hovering above and behind an asteroid the size of a mountain. Thin, pulsing beams flashed from the spacecraft, striking the asteroid. The spacecraft was nudging it, altering its trajectory so that it would impact Earth. The details of the elongated spaceship and the cratered asteroid were so clear that Kendon doubted the vision was the product of his imagination. It was if he was watching it up close, as a spectator of impending destruction.

Kendon opened his eyes to free himself from the vision and looked down and Meller. He realized that the taut lines of Meller's face had eased, and he was staring at Kendon with the calmness of someone who had come to terms with his fate.

As if by their own volition, Kendon's hands moved over Meller's mouth and he pressed down hard, but after a few seconds, he jerked his hands away.

"Do it!" Meller said.

"I can't."

"Do it."

"I can't bring myself to hurt you."

"Do it out of mercy. I beg you."

Kendon felt his head was about to explode, as if all of the neural connections of his brain were in revolt. He waited for Meller to exhale, then covered his mouth with his right hand. With the thumb and forefinger of the other hand, he pinched Meller's nostrils together. He propped his forearm on Meller's ribcage and pushed down with all his weight to keep him from drawing in air. It took all of Kendon's strength of will to continue, a will steeled by the knowledge of what was in store for the world if he failed.

Even as life was draining from him, Meller managed to keep his eyes focused on Kendon's. But soon, Meller's chest began to heave upward as his body became desperate for air. A minute later, his body went limp.

Memories of the three years he had spent with the scientist and his research group flashed through his mind. Taken from an Eastern European orphanage when he was only three years old, Kendon had never known a family; he had never experienced a mother or a father, or brothers and sisters. Meller's captive research group had become his family. The scientist had become like a father to him, and now he had taken his life.

Kendon never realized he could hurt so deeply. He struggled to suppress the pain. He knew he could not allow himself to feel. To feel was to betray.

He breathed deeply to suppress his emotions, and he forced himself to clear his mind of every thought. Soon, his mind became a landscape of whiteness, as blanched and empty as an expanse of Arctic snow.

When he was sure that life had gone from Meller, he pushed himself to his knees and grabbed Meller by the shoulders. He shook the body and shouted as if in panic, "Meller, what's happening? What's the matter with you?"

He cried, "Guards! Guards!" while pressing frantically with both of his hands on Meller's chest. He shouted for the guards again and began a pretense of mouth-to-mouth resuscitation.

When the guards burst into the cell, Kendon said, "He's had a heart attack. Get a medic!" He slid back against the granite wall, horrified by what he had done.

The guards were young, from one of the Moldavian crèches. They looked at each other with indecision, then turned toward the sound of boots clicking in the corridor.

Bogdan strode into the cell. He stood there a moment before nudging Meller's torso with his foot. He turned to Kendon. "Explain."

"His heart gave out. I told you to soften him up for me, not to kill him. You were too rough on him."

"Did he talk? That's all that matters."

Kendon shrugged. "I need a smoke."

"For your sake, Arkasha, he better have talked," Bogdan said, calling Kendon by his Belorussian crèche name.

Bogdan reached into his pocket. He tossed the pack to Kendon—unfiltered Russian Prima cigarettes that were popular with many of the intelligence agents. The cigarettes, along with their first names, were their only connections to their Eastern European origin.

Kendon tapped out a cigarette, leaned forward for Bogdan to light it, and inhaled deeply. He had given up smoking years before, but he was now in the grip of a furious craving. He held the smoke in his lungs for as long as he could stand it, then exhaled slowly. He stared at the amber end of the cigarette and allowed himself to think about the one-one-five pod they were so eager to retrieve: a million megatons of energy contained in forty-two pounds of the same exotic element that enabled the Breeders to travel the galaxy, packaged in a five-foot long, blood-red cylinder. It was the only power in the universe that could keep the huge asteroid from bringing about the end of the human race.

He dropped the mental guard of whiteness and let his mind broadcast the image of the pod, red and menacing, buried deep in a cavern under a foot of stinking guano at the base of a huge, glistening stalagmite.

He looked up at Bogdan and smiled.

"I know where he hid the pod."

"Where?"

"I will take you there."

Chapter 2

*T*he tour bus from Boqueron High School was already half an hour late, and Eric Tepler, the resident astronomer at Cabo Rojo Observatory, was getting impatient. All week long he had been looking forward to giving students from the nearby high school a tour of the remote lighthouse-observatory and an opportunity to peer at the heavens through the telescope.

Earlier that week, he had given a lecture to the tenth-grade science class about his work detecting Near Earth Objects—potentially hazardous asteroids and comets. The observatory, atop what had once been the tower of a lighthouse, had been set up exclusively for that purpose. Following the lecture, he had invited the entire class to visit.

But where were the students, their parents, and the teacher? The distance between the seaside town of Boqueron and the cape was only ten miles. What could be holding them up? he wondered. Gabriela Estrada, the teacher, had promised him the group would arrive at the agreed upon time.

"*A las siete en punto*," she had added for emphasis, at seven o'clock sharp.

He wondered if the bus had gotten a flat tire, or had veered off the road and was bogged down somewhere in the salt marshes that separated the isolated cape from the mainland. Normally, he wouldn't care if they were late. He had grown used to the easygoing pace of Puerto Rican life, and even he was now occasionally late for appointments. But over the last twenty-four hours, his world had dramatically changed. He had made a sensational astronomical discovery, and he was planning on using the student visit to make it public.

Shortly after nightfall the previous day, he had detected "The Big One," as he tagged it. He had only been able to observe the object for two hours, but his preliminary calculations told him he was onto something huge. If his numbers were correct, it was an asteroid five or six miles in length and three or four miles wide, a mass of stone the size of Mount Everest floating toward Earth through the dark currents of space.

His calculations showed it would pass within four lunar distances of Earth on Sunday night—a mere million miles. Following standard procedure, he had e-mailed his data to the Minor Planet Center in Cambridge, the clearinghouse for such information. The MPC would post the data in its daily electronic circular, thereby alerting a network of observatories around the globe to the discovery. Other astronomers would then confirm the find and add it to their tracking and data-gathering routines.

There couldn't have been a better time for the high school science class to visit. But where was the bus?

The young astronomer stood at a window of the converted lighthouse, now equipped with a dome where the beacon used to be. He ran his fingers through his unruly brown hair and stared at the dirt road that snaked through the salt marshes, hoping to catch a glimpse of the bus.

But still no sign of it. *Nada.*

Frustrated, Tepler sat down at the battery of monitors next to the telescope and called up the sequence of photos taken the night before. His heart began to beat faster when they appeared on the screen. They were images only a highly trained specialist could decipher—enhanced photos showing a streak of light across the heavens that stood out against a background of motionless stars.

He grinned and shook his head in amazement that it hadn't already been detected. "This is really going to interest her," he thought, a picture of the teacher forming in his mind. "In fact, this is going to interest a lot of people."

The object would be observable that night at about the same time he had found it the night before, around eight o'clock. Mentally, he worked out an agenda: When the students showed up—if they showed up—he would toss out a few questions to see how much they remembered from his lecture. Maybe he would give them an idea about the mechanics of NEO detection as a way of building up to his discovery. Finally, at eight o'clock *en punto*, he would announce his find and then show the asteroid on a monitor mounted above of the telescope's control panel. They would be able to see it in real time, as the humongous object hurtled through space toward Earth.

Another ten minutes went by before he finally heard a motor. He rushed to the window and saw a yellow school bus struggling up the steep road, its engine straining and its headlights blazing. The driver tooted the horn.

"Finally!" Tepler said to himself.

The young astronomer raced down the spiral staircase of the tower two steps at a time. When the bus pulled up, he was already standing by the wrought iron gate.

He put on a pair of glasses and straightened them as the bus came to a stop. Except when reading finely printed scientific texts, he really didn't need glasses, but he kept a wire-rimmed pair in his shirt pocket to wear in public because he thought they made him look more like a scientist than the reclusive hippie that people sometimes took him for.

The bus was packed with students and parents, most of them staring up in awe at the dome. To his dismay he couldn't see the teacher.

The bus door swung open, and the driver said, "*Señor* Tepler,

I'm sorry we're late. There was a bad accident outside of Boqueron and the highway was blocked."

Tepler brushed back his hair and put on a welcome smile as fifteen students and nearly a dozen adults filed out. He recognized most of the students and remembered some of their names. Finally, he saw Gabriela. She had been sitting behind the driver and had waited for everyone else to get off first.

When she stepped down, Tepler felt a tug in his heart that was both painful and exquisite. Ever since taking the position at the remote cape, he had led the life of a hermit scientist, and the isolation had become unbearable. He was eager to get a life apart from his work. Behind the decision to invite the class to the observatory was a desire to get to know Gabriela. He had met her only two weeks before when he gave a talk about his work to the Boqueron Rotary Club. She was in the audience and came up to him afterward to invite him to speak to her science class. He felt attracted to her, especially when he learned that, in addition to being a high school teacher, she was an accomplished violinist. Classical music was one of his passions.

Gabriela smiled and held out her hand. "I am very sorry, Dr. Tepler. You were so kind to invite us, and we've repaid your kindness by making you wait."

Tepler took a deep breath and tried to act cool and casual. All that day, he had been analyzing the look that had passed between them when they parted earlier that week at the high school. It was a much longer gaze than would have been expected between a man and a woman who were only being polite to one another.

He shrugged and said, "It's not a problem. The telescope only works after dark anyway."

Gabriela was a young woman of quiet energy, with fair skin, black hair, and dark Latin eyes. Fortunately for Tepler, she spoke English fluently, as did her most of her students. His Spanish was good enough for him to handle most day-to-day situations, but he still felt more at ease expressing himself in English.

She looked up at the dome. "My students are very excited. It's all they've talked about the entire week. I've been looking forward to this, too. I've wanted to visit ever since the observatory was built, but I've never dared go beyond the sign at the bottom of the hill."

Tepler nodded. A private foundation with headquarters in New York had purchased the lighthouse more than a decade before and had spent millions of dollars to convert it into an observatory. Five years earlier, when the conversion was completed, the foundation hired Tepler to run the facility. Signs were posted everywhere saying, "Restricted Access. No Admittance Without Proper Authorization."

Tepler turned to the students and their parents, who had congregated in front of the bus. "You couldn't have come at a better time. I've got something important to show you—an exciting discovery that will utterly amaze you and show you what my work is all about and how important it is."

The group followed him into the huge main building, a massive structure with three-foot thick exterior walls, twenty-foot high ceilings, and arched interior doors twelve feet high. At one end of the main room was a short flight of stairs that led to the tower.

With the astronomer leading the way, the visitors went up the narrow spiral stairs of the tower in single file, more than two dozen pairs of shoes clattering simultaneously on the metal steps.

As he led the way up, Tepler explained that with the exception of the thick walls, nothing about the forty-foot high tower was the same as the original. The lighthouse tower, visible for miles around, had had been gutted, and the interior was now filled mainly by a thick metal cylinder that supported the heavy telescope and the observation deck.

Inside the small observatory, the parents squeezed against the walls of the dome, the children in front of them. Many were staring up at the horizontal slit of the dome to see where the squat green telescope was pointing. Others, including Gabriela, were looking at the telescope.

Tepler stood next to the instrument with one hand on top of the forked mount that gave the telescope the look of an immense amphibian. He patted it like he would a pet and said, "Ladies and gentlemen, I would like you to meet my good friend, The Frog."

As he surveyed the group, he saw smiles popping up. "I won't bore you with the technical details, but believe me, The Frog is a powerful tool. It can reach far into the solar system to spot distant comets as they streak across the heavens."

He looked pointedly at Gabriela. "I made a discovery last night that I'm eager to share with you. But first, with your permission, I would like to see how much your students remember from the lecture the other day."

"They will be more than happy to answer your questions," she said.

Tepler surveyed the faces of the students. "Okay, who can tell me the difference between a comet and an asteroid?"

Several hands shot up. Tepler pointed to a tall girl standing to one side of Gabriela. He remembered her name was Rosalia and that she had asked most of the questions when he visited her class.

"Comets are covered with ice and other volatile materials and leave a bright trail across the sky when they are on their way to the sun. They come from far out in the solar system," the girl said. "Asteroids are mostly made of stone and they don't leave a trail. Most of them orbit the sun in an area between Mars and Jupiter called the asteroid belt. But some have different orbits and can come near Earth."

"Very good, Rosalia!" Tepler said.

Gabriela caught the girl's eye and nodded approvingly.

"Now," Tepler continued, "who can tell me about the ones that come close to the Earth and why we should be interested in them?"

A dark-haired boy with a lopsided grin pushed his hand half-way up. Tepler pointed to him.

"Some of them are big and could destroy life on earth if they hit. That's why we should watch for them. And then zap them with a rocket."

"Has our planet ever been hit by one?" Tepler continued.

Half the students raised their hands. A girl, the shortest of the class, said, "A huge asteroid caused the end of the dinosaurs sixty-five million years ago," she said.

"Where did it hit?"

"Off of the Yucatan peninsula of Mexico. It left a crater more than a hundred miles across that can be seen in satellite photos."

"How do we know that it caused the disappearance of the dinosaurs? What was the clue that tipped off scientists that there was a connection?"

Rosalia jumped in. "Iridium deposits. Iridium is an element that's rare on Earth, but not in asteroids. Scientists found thin deposits of iridium all around the world and learned they were formed sixty-five million years ago, the same time the dinosaurs disappeared."

"Who can tell me about more recent asteroid strikes?" Tepler said.

The boy with the lopsided grin raised his hand and said, "In Arizona, there's a crater a mile in diameter that was caused by an asteroid fifty thousand years ago."

Tepler looked approvingly at all the young, eager faces. Two years earlier, with the reluctant permission of the trustee, he had started giving lectures in nearby seaside communities like Boqueron and La Parguera, and in the city of Cabo Rojo ten miles inland. Hitting the lecture circuit was a way of getting relief from the forced isolation at the cape, but it was also good public relations. The lighthouse conversion had irked a lot of people. Though it had been decommissioned for decades, it was part of the history of the region and part of the landscape, so not everyone was pleased to see a glimmering dome where a beacon used to be.

For the benefit of the parents, Tepler went over the main points of the talks he had been giving. Straightening his glasses, he described the dark scenario of an asteroid hitting Earth at a speed of twenty miles per second, but he pointed out that such a catastrophic event was highly unlikely in the foreseeable future.

"Depending on its size and where it struck, it could destroy large areas of the planet, or even bring about another mass extinction, as happened to the dinosaurs. But this time the extinction would be of human life. However, if it were detected sufficiently in advance, it would be possible with today's technology to deflect it. But to be able to defend our world, we have to know it's there, which is what my work is all about."

"How much advance warning is needed?" one of the parents asked.

"A minimum of two years," Tepler said. "But the more time the better."

Gabriela raised her hand and asked, "Isn't it true there are limits to the size of asteroids that you can find?"

Her question was a prompt, since she already knew the answer from the talk he had given at the Boqueron Rotary Club.

"Most of the efforts now going on worldwide are focused on large near-earth objects with a size of a kilometer or greater," he said. "There's no telling exactly how many of them are out there, but the working estimate is about a thousand. We've only detected three-fourths of them to date. A few we know of are five, six, or even seven miles in diameter. The reason we're focusing on the larger asteroids is because they're easier to detect, and they're the ones that could destroy most, if not all, of humanity."

"But aren't the smaller ones dangerous, too?" a parent asked.

"Absolutely," Tepler said. "Just a few years ago, an asteroid a thousand feet in diameter came within fifteen thousand miles of Earth. If something that size were to hit, it could wipe out a country the size of Spain. That would be catastrophic, for sure, but it wouldn't bring an end to the human race. Astronomers have in fact detected thousands of smaller asteroids, but they're harder to find because of their size. We need better technology to fully catalog them, including space-based observation platforms."

Tepler was always aware the idea of an asteroid hitting the earth could cause anxiety in people, particularly in people with vivid imaginations. And so he quickly added, "But even an impact from a smaller one is unlikely in the foreseeable future. There's no need to worry. Are there any more questions?"

He looked around the room, then glanced at the clock. It was eight o'clock. When it was clear no one had a question, he said, "I have an announcement to make. Last night, just after sunset, The Frog and I discovered what I am calling "The Big One," an asteroid five to six miles in length, maybe three to four miles in width. That puts it in the top percentile of known asteroids in terms of size. Imagine Mount Everest streaking through space at the speed of twenty miles *per second*. What's even more interesting is that in only three days it will swing close to Earth on its way toward the sun."

He watched the reactions of the students and adults. Some of the students formed the word "Wow!" on their lips and looked at one another. The parents stared in silence.

Tepler stepped up to a chalkboard he had set up on an easel and quickly sketched the sun, the Earth, and The Big One. He drew arrows to show the asteroid's trajectory back toward the sun, then drew another set of arrows to show the orbit of the Earth around the sun. The path of the asteroid nearly intersected with that of Earth.

"At this moment, The Big One is six million miles away from us and is closing in at 72,000 miles per hour. I was only able to observe it for two hours, but that was enough to calculate that it's going to cross earth's orbit in three days at four lunar distances, about a million miles. That's not far on the cosmic scale—only a stone's throw. But for us, it's far, far away."

He looked slowly around the room. "I've sent the data via email so my colleagues around the world can confirm my calculations about the size, speed, and orbit of the object. Outside the astronomical community, no one has heard about this yet. I am making this public to you first."

Gabriela said, "Thank you for sharing this with us, Dr. Tepler. I hope you receive all of the recognition you deserve for your discovery."

Several of the parents also congratulated him and broke into applause. Tepler smoothed back his unruly hair and made an exaggerated bow.

"Thank you, thank you," he said and raised his palms to quiet everyone down. "For years to come, The Big One will be known only by a code name—the year of discovery followed by a few letters and numbers signifying things of interest only to astronomers. But eventually, when its orbit and characteristics are fully understood, it will get a permanent name. Since you are the first to learn of the discovery, I'm going to take suggestions from you."

He picked up a piece of chalk and pointed to Rosalia, the first student to raise her hand.

"Phoebe, after the Moon goddess."

Tepler thought about it and then nodded. "One of the moons of Saturn is called Phoebe, but that doesn't mean we can't call our asteroid Phoebe."

He scribbled the name on the board. More hands shot up. He quickly compiled a list of fifteen names. One student scored laughs by suggesting "Big Bang;" another when he said, "Choo Choo, after my dog."

Tepler approached the computer monitor and swiveled it to face the group. He hit a few keys on the keyboard, and an image of a long faint streak appeared. He tapped the screen with a pointer.

"What you are looking at is The Big One, also known as Phoebe, Big Bang, Choo Choo, and twelve other incredibly ingenious names, as it appeared last night. As Rosalia noted earlier, asteroids don't leave a streak like comets do. This image appears as a streak because it's a composite of the images that The Frog captured of its trajectory over a period of two hours. The streak shows the distance it covered during that brief time, 144,000 miles."

Tepler waited a moment while the students and their parents moved forward to get a better look at the monitor.

He continued, "Since last night, The Big One has had the opportunity to travel nearly two million miles. Because its orbit can be predicted with reasonable accuracy, I programmed the telescope to pick up on it, and you will see on the monitor what the telescope sees," he said, tapping the screen.

He sat down in front of the monitor. His fingers poised over the keyboard, he turned to look at the students. "Are you ready?"

The students had pushed closer to him to look over his shoulders, and the parents had also crowded forward.

In a showman's voice, Tepler said, "Then here it is! The Big One!"

He typed in the command, pressed "enter," then stood out of the way to give everyone a better view of the monitor.

A few seconds later, Rosalia said, "Where is it? I don't see anything."

Tepler leaned toward the screen and examined it for a moment. "That's funny." He tapped the screen with the pointer. "It should be right here."

He looked again closely, but he still couldn't find the asteroid. He felt a rush of embarrassment. All that build-up and now he couldn't find it. In an assured voice, he said, "Just give me one little minute. I'll fix that."

He sat back down and checked the alignment of the telescope, thinking that perhaps one of the visitors had accidentally bumped it out of position. But it was still firmly locked on target, aiming exactly where the huge asteroid should have been. He zoomed out to show a broader area and was heartened when the familiar image of the asteroid appeared. But after scrutinizing the screen for a minute, he suddenly felt a chill grab him at the back of his neck. The asteroid was not where it was supposed to be. In fact, it was way off course.

"That's not possible," he said out loud.

"What's not possible?" Gabriela asked.

"Something's wrong here," Tepler said. "Bear with me for another minute. I need to do some checking."

His fingers worked the keyboard furiously. For the next few minutes, the screen was filled with esoteric mathematical symbols. He entered a series of numbers, and a computer-generated image of the asteroid's path in relation to Earth appeared on the screen.

As he contemplated the image, Tepler felt himself getting weak. "This isn't possible. This can't be," he kept saying to himself.

He cleared the screen so no one could see what he had just seen. He stood up to face the group, but felt his legs getting wobbly and dropped back into the chair.

Gabriela edged her way through the children and placed her hand softly on his shoulder. "Are you all right, Eric?"

"Yes, yes, I'll be fine. I made an error in my calculations, that's all. I'm going to need to do a lot of checking. In fact, I'm going to have to get busy. Immediately. I'm sorry."

He didn't want to tell them about what he had seen. He needed to be certain. He had to check and recheck the data, and then alert the network so that other telescopes could be trained on the object. He didn't want to create a worldwide panic, but if his calculations were correct, then two things were certain. Some time over the last twenty-four hours, the trajectory of the gargantuan asteroid had changed dramatically. Somehow, it had been deflected from its original path, and now an asteroid capable of wiping out all of human life was on a possible collision course with Earth.

An image flashed through Tepler's mind of September 11, 2001, and of hijacked airliners crashing into the World Trade Center. The ramifications of that event had been staggering. Now a tragedy of infinitely greater magnitude could be only three days away.

Tepler looked up at all the bright faces, at all of these eager children who were only beginning to dream big dreams. He looked at the parents, who had already realized some of their dreams and had brought children into a world they were certain would go on and on. He looked into Gabriela's eyes. She was leaning over him, and her face was melting with concern.

He had been planning that evening to invite her out to dinner. He wanted to ask her when he was at the high school, but they never had a moment to themselves. Tonight, when the tour of the observatory was finished, he intended to walk with her to the bus and take advantage of those parting moments to ask her out. He knew a restaurant in La Parguera with a view of the small mangrove islands that dotted the bay and the iridescent water the region was famous for on moonlit nights.

Now it all seemed meaningless.

Gabriela stepped behind his chair and put her hands on his shoulders. Her hands were soft and reassuring.

She said to the students and their parents, "I'm sorry, but I don't think Dr. Tepler is feeling well. We'll have to call it a night."

Chapter 3

The Black Hawk helicopter skimmed over the desert, barely a hundred feet off the ground. Kendon stared out of the window and watched the mesquite bushes whiz by below, fast and mesmerizing like a rewinding film.

He had known about the asteroid for years, but now that it was about to strike it seemed unreal that the world could come to an end, that even the desert landscape below him would be wiped away.

Eliminating the human race and every vestige of its civilization had always been the Breeder objective, Kendon knew. The asteroid would clear the way for implanting the world with their hybrid creation. Now only he was left to prevent a universal genocide, and he could not afford to make a mistake. Even thinking about his plan could bring about defeat. He tried to cleanse his mind of anything but the image of the one-one-five pod buried in a cave.

He tried especially not to think about the backpack.

It was hidden under a foot of guano at Carlsbad Caverns, at the base of an enormous stalagmite. He had buried it there years before while on the last hunter-killer mission he had undertaken to liquidate some foolish contractor who had dared to talk about what he knew: in his case about a super-advanced nuclear boring machine used to create tunnel networks between Collaboration facilities. Following the killing—a murder disguised as suicide—Kendon had stuffed the backpack full of everything he would need if he ever got brave enough to escape from the secret underworld.

The image of the backpack wanted to erupt into his mind, and he fought to keep it from his thoughts. Instead of the backpack, he labored to imagine the blood-red one-one-five pod.

Red, red, red, a metal cylinder five feet long.

Yet there was danger even in deliberately projecting a false image because it gave them an opening into him, a psychic wedge that could allow them to probe deeply into his mind.

When it became too difficult for him to sustain the image of the cylinder, Kendon retreated into a storm of whiteness. That had been one of Meller's discoveries: A mental landscape of brilliant whiteness blinded the Breeder mind that attempted to penetrate it, like a blizzard would a skier. Kendon imagined a blizzard below, the desert swept by furious white snow.

As he gazed out of the window, he could feel Bogdan staring at him. The security director was strapped in a seat across from him, a triumphant gleam in his eyes. As the Black Hawk skimmed the desert floor, the staring became more and more intense, and it felt to Kendon like a fist beating down on flesh.

Finally, he heard Bogdan's voice rise above the roar of the helicopter, reaching him through the blizzard:

"You don't fool me, Arkasha."

Kendon continued looking out of the window, immersed in his blizzard, ignoring Bogdan.

"You were one of them."

Kendon was wearing the dress grays and the knee-high black boots of a Directorate intelligence officer, the insignia of his rank of major on his high collar. He had insisted upon his innocence, and therefore his right to wear the uniform.

He replied without looking up from the window, "It's in your nature to be suspicious. You suspect everyone. If you had the power to act on your suspicions, half the security staff and three quarters of the technical and scientific personnel would have been liquidated by now. Fortunately, you don't have that power."

He knew Bogdan had nothing to go on. When the escape of Meller and his people was discovered, they had arrested Kendon at his living quarters without warning or explanation. The arrest was inevitable, and he was resigned to it. He was determined to reveal nothing and knew he would probably end up being tortured to death.

They had taken him away in a black Nomenklatura bus—one of the thousands of windowless mobile prisons that were now rounding up "the people of the list," the roster of five-hundred thousand people who were to survive the asteroid impact along with the members of the Collaboration and its security apparatus. He had ended up in the underground interrogation room at Alamogordo.

Despite the beatings, he had admitted nothing. None of the other conspirators had denounced him, and there was no one left to implicate him in the resistance. Most of the rebels had killed themselves before being captured, or had died fighting, and Meller had died under Kendon's hand.

"You were among them for three years," Bogdan continued, "among those traitors. It was your role to uncover dissidence and identify traitors. You were close to Meller. You should have been onto his plot a long time ago. The fact that it happened is the evidence that you were a part of it."

"I've proven myself to the Committee again and again," Kendon said. "My record speaks for itself. The undercover role was my own idea. I pushed for it. I trained for it. Now it's going to pay off."

Kendon had come up with the undercover idea as a way of breaking free of his role as assassin. Though indoctrinated with the idea that it was an act of loyalty to kill the disloyal, he had quickly sickened of killing and had sought a way out by proposing the idea of going undercover in key research labs staffed by captive scientists and engineers.

He made a sweeping motion in the direction the helicopter was heading. "Very soon, you will have the one-one-five-pod."

"I know you were one of them," Bogdan repeated.

Reaching into an inner pocket, Kendon pulled out a document. He unfolded it and held it dangling between two fingers.

"It doesn't matter what you think. What matters is what the Committee thinks. I've been exonerated."

"You've been given an opportunity to save yourself. Nothing more. It all depends on whether or not we retrieve the pod."

It was a game of who was using whom. The agreement was just a piece of paper, and Kendon knew it meant nothing. It wouldn't stop a single bullet. If they were to recover the one-one-five pod and the forty-two pounds of ununpentium it contained, Bogdan would not hesitate to put him in front of a firing squad—right there in the caverns.

Ununpentium—Element 115. It was an exotic element from galaxies millions of light years away that powered the fabulous ships of the human-sized Breeders and the smaller Clones. Meller had figured out how it could be turned against them. Were the Directorate to recover the red pod, the only chance left to defeat the Breeder agenda would be lost.

Kendon again formed a mental image of the five-foot cylinder. *Deep in an underground chamber, next to a massive stalagmite, under a foot of guano.*

Meller had been a spelunker in his younger days, back when he was still free to come and go from Collaboration research facilities. He had explored some of the lesser-known caverns at Carlsbad and had told Kendon about a concealed entrance at one end that led to a network of bat caves, in an area not open to the public.

That was where Kendon had stashed the backpack, planning on recovering it if he was ordered to go above ground on another assassination mission. It was an escape kit that contained a change of clothes, phony ID, a semiautomatic pistol, ammunition, a length of climbing rope, binoculars, bundles of dynamite, a lighter, a remote detonator, a screwdriver, a flashlight, and $32,000 dollars he had stolen from ATMs.

It also contained the indispensable surgical kit he would need to self-remove the implant. After escaping, getting rid of the implant was the priority. It emitted a signal unique to the carrier, coded to the DNA. Even though he had become a master at blocking the Breeders from penetrating his mind, he knew they could always track him through the implant signals. There was no getting away from the Breeders without getting rid of the T-shaped device.

Again, he fought against the image of the backpack that tried to break into his mental landscape.

Red, red, red, a blood-red cylinder five feet long.
Whiteness. Blizzard. Blindness.

The Black Hawk climbed above the Guadalupe Mountains as it approached Carlsbad Caverns. Bogdan handed Kendon a microphone to guide the pilot.

Kendon pressed it to his lips. "Fly over the tourist entrance. From there, follow the mountain ridge southwest for two miles."

The pilot flew along the ridge as closely as he had earlier skimmed the desert floor. Soon, the helicopter reached a fold in the mountain where the ridge ended. As the helicopter hovered, Kendon caught a glimpse of the two escort helicopters, each carrying a dozen black-clad Directorate troops.

The pilot looked back at him and nodded when Kendon pointed straight down. As the helicopter descended, Kendon eyed the three guards strapped in at the other side of the compartment, the ones who were going with them into the cave. They were dressed in black uniforms and wore the burgundy beret of assault troops. Two of them had dozed off, their heads rolling with the motions of the helicopter. The other stared straight ahead. They were husky men with flat, empty faces. Kendon presumed they were from Harsh Meadows, a subterranean facility in northern New Mexico where children who were physically strong but mentally dull were raised—the gooney crèches, as they were termed.

The Black Hawk settled in a swirl of dust a hundred yards from the hidden cave entrance. Bogdan snapped his fingers for the guards to exit first. Before jumping out, they grabbed the stash of shovels, flashlights, and lanterns.

The two other helicopters landed nearby. Armed with M-16s, the troops leaped out the instant the Black Hawks touched down. With torsos bent, they fanned out from under the whirling blades and quickly secured the canyon.

Kendon jumped out of the helicopter and stared in the direction of the mountain. Fifty feet above the canyon floor was the hidden entrance that had once been used by miners who extracted guano from the bat caves to sell as fertilizer.

Bogdan, in his gray dress uniform, seemed hesitant to dirty his spotless boots, but after a minute, he got out and said, "Okay, where is it?"

Kendon pointed to the steep, rock-covered slope. "We're within a hundred yards of the cave entrance. Meller said it's up on the side of the canyon on the right side of the fold, under a formation of boulders. Have them search up there."

Bogdan barked at the guards: "Find the entrance." Turning to Kendon, he said, "The Committee will be pleased when we've recovered the ununpentium, but I'm not going to be satisfied until I know what it was to be used for. It had to be for a weapon of some kind."

Kendon shrugged. "What does it matter? Without the pod, how can it work? You've inventoried the stock. The pod contains the only ununpentium that's still not accounted for."

As chief of nuclear research in charge of a program to upgrade the power output of the Collaboration's anti-gravity reactors, Meller had almost unlimited access to the super-heavy element.

Kendon knew that as part of the original Collaboration agreement, the Breeders had consented to share technology with Americans and had turned over a number of functioning spacecraft, but they had never lived up to their promise to reveal the science and technology behind them. The Collaboration, therefore, had initiated a reverse-engineering program at Dulce, an underground facility in the mountains of northwest New Mexico connected by high-speed transit tunnels to Los Alamos.

Under the guise of research, Meller had secretly created the pod with the sole purpose of powering the beam weapon he had created in secret prior to his captivity.

If only Meller had trusted him enough, Kendon thought. If only he had allowed him to be part of the actual breakout. Meller was an engineering genius, but he was not someone capable of leading the resistance in its final and most challenging phase. If Kendon had been with them, the one-one-five pod would already be mated with the weapon, poised to take on the asteroid as it approached Earth. Now he had a mountain of possibly insurmountable challenges ahead of him.

From the slope, one of the guards shouted. "I've found it. A cave entrance!"

Kendon and Bogdan hurried to join them.

"That's got to be it," Kendon said with feigned excitement when they reached the familiar rock formation, hidden in part by desert brush.

He had to stoop to get under the rocky ledge that stuck out over the entrance. Once inside the cave, he was able to stand up straight. He made a show of shining his flashlight down the narrow passage. "It's steep," he shouted over his shoulder. "It looks like it goes down pretty far."

"Let's find that damn pod and get the hell out of here," Bogdan said. He ordered one of the guards to remain at the cave entrance, then pointed to the other soldiers and said, "You two come with me."

Kendon grabbed one of the shovels. Flashlight in one hand, shovel in the other, he led the way. Each of the guards carried a lantern and a shovel. The passage was narrow and meandered downward for a hundred yards. At several turns, the cave walls squeezed together. Kendon and Bogdan didn't have any trouble slipping through, but the beefy guards had to suck in their chests.

The ground, the walls, every surface was covered with a slippery, brownish-red substance with a pungent odor. One of the guards, whose angry eyes seemed out of place on his round baby face, slipped as he climbed over a boulder.

"What the hell is this stuff?" he said.

"Guano," Kendon said.

"What's that?"

"Bat shit."

When the tunnel leveled off, they found themselves in a large chamber with a formation of stalagmites in one corner that reached upward to the icicle points of a dozen stalactites. Kendon shined his flashlight at the jagged ceiling. It was covered by thousands of small brown bats. Disturbed by the intruders, a few of them flitted around the chamber before finding another place to hang.

"Don't worry, they don't bite," Kendon said, but then realized he had made a mistake. How would he know they don't bite?

The chamber broke off into two more large tunnels. As he led the way, Kendon said, "Meller told me to take the one that goes to the right. At the end will be another, larger chamber. That's where the pod is supposed to be buried."

The tunnel went down steeply, with boulders to climb or stalagmites to skirt. There were bats everywhere. A few flew close to their heads, angry at being disturbed. Soon they were in a chamber half the size of a football field, with a ceiling fifty feet above the uneven floor. The ceiling was covered with ancient stalactites, all of them coated with bats, tens of thousands of bats.

Kendon shined his flashlight around the chamber, stopping at a stalactite formation that hung three-quarters of the way down from the ceiling. It was a collection sharp icicles the color of dirty snow that had coalesced around a thick, longer stalactite that almost touched its counterpart, a massive formation jutting ten feet from the ground like a petrified tree stump.

On the opposite side of the formation was the narrow opening of a tunnel that led further into the caves, toward the main tourist caverns a mile away. At the time he buried the backpack, Kendon had explored the tunnel and knew where it led. It was his path to freedom.

Only three yards from the tunnel opening was the backpack, buried under six inches of guano. Kendon kept Bogdan and the guards away from that side of the stalagmite by pointing with his flashlight to the ground on the opposite side.

"The pod is supposed to be buried somewhere around here, about three or four feet away from the base," he said, pacing back and forth.

He stopped and planted his shovel in the guano, releasing its pungent fertilizer smell. "You dig here," he said to one of the guards. He walked a yard further and said to the other guard, "And you dig here."

The big men obediently set their lanterns to one side and sank their shovels into the guano. Kendon walked away from them, stopping where the backpack was buried.

"It could be anywhere along the rim. I'll dig here."

Bogdan stood to one side, closer to the guards than to Kendon, and watched eagerly to see what each scoop of guano revealed. With the pod in his possession, he would be assured of a future as security director over all of the surviving humans. But he also had a personal stake in recovering the pod. Early in Kendon's Directorate career, Bogdan had been Kendon's mentor and had supervised and sometimes accompanied him during his hunter-killer forays into the upper world. Not only had Kendon betrayed the Directorate and the Collaboration, he had betrayed Bogdan.

If they were actually to find the pod, Bogdan would return trium-phant with the one-one-five pod in his possession, while Kendon's bullet-ridden body would be left in the cave to rot.

"If you hit something hard, that has to be it," Kendon said as he dug down to the backpack.

The guano had the consistency of topsoil and crumbled easily. Kendon quickly uncovered the top of the backpack, which he had wrapped in plastic to keep the moisture and corrosive guano out. He pushed the shovel through the plastic and exposed the flap of the backpack, but stopped when Bogdan shined his flashlight at him.

"What have you found?" Bogdan demanded.

"Guano and more guano."

Kendon moved two feet closer to the guards and started dig-ging anew. When Bogdan stepped toward him, he threw a shovelful over the backpack.

"You two," Kendon said to the guards. "Do like I'm doing. Clear away six inches, then sink the shovel in to see if you strike some-thing solid."

They imitated him. Soon, the guard with the baby face said, "Hey, I hit something hard."

Bogdan stepped up beside him. "Dig faster!"

Their backs to him, Kendon quickly scooped guano way from the backpack. Finally, he knelt down and loosened the cover straps. He glanced nervously toward the guards, who had dropped to their knees to get a better look.

Bogdan demanded, "What have you found?"

The guard dug further, then scooped out more guano with his hand. "It's a goddamn rock," he said finally.

Turning toward Kendon, who was clearing guano from the backpack, Bogdan said, "What about you?"

"The same. A rock." Kendon was on his knees, but straight-ened up and pointed. "Dig closer to the stalagmite."

The cover straps were freed. When the guards resumed dig-ging, Kendon looked away for an instant to slide his hand into the backpack. He remembered leaving the gun on top of the clothes. His hand found it, but just as his fingers closed around the grip, he felt the cold metal of a gun barrel pressing against the back of his head.

"That doesn't look like a rock," Bogdan said. He pressed the gun harder, forcing Kendon's head to bend. "Open it up!"

"This must be part of what they buried," Kendon said. "The pod has to be near here." He gripped the gun with one hand. With the other hand, he grabbed a handful of guano.

"Is that so?" Bogdan sneered.

Kendon spun around, throwing the fistful of guano into Bogdan's face. Bogdan fell backwards, his eyes stinging. He fired wildly and screamed, "Shoot Arkasha! Shoot that goddamned traitor!"

Kendon rolled to one side and leaped to his feet. The guards grabbed for their weapons, but were slowed by the snap-down flap of their holsters. Kendon fired two quick rounds at the closer of the two, the one with the baby face. One bullet hit him in the shoulder; the other tore through his throat. The second guard tried to leap to one side, but Kendon fired two more rounds, hitting him in the chest.

The gunfire stirred the bats into a frenzy. Thousands broke loose, emitting desperate squeaks as they flew wildly around the chamber.

Kendon swung his gun toward where Bogdan had fallen, but he had managed to escape. With two quick rounds, Kendon blasted the lanterns, plunging the cavern into total darkness. Grabbing the backpack, he scampered behind the stalagmite, near the small tunnel opening and his path to freedom.

Two shots rang out. The bullets ricocheted off the cavern wall behind him.

"You're not going to get out of here alive, Arkasha," Bogdan raged from somewhere in the darkness.

"Come and get me," Kendon shouted back.

"You don't have a chance, traitor. My men are on the way."

Kendon knew that in only a few minutes, assault troops would pour into the chamber, and if he didn't seal the entrance, they would soon catch up to him. He reached into the backpack for one of the dynamite bundles—three sticks wrapped together—and a cigarette lighter. He had packed the dynamite to take care of any number of contingencies, but he had not foreseen this one.

He wondered where Bogdan was. He listened, but he couldn't hear movement. If he could get Bogdan to shoot again, the muzzle flash would give him away. He turned on his flashlight and tossed it several yards near where the guards had fallen.

Bogdan fired at the light. The muzzle flash came from about seventy feet away, near the tunnel they had followed to the bat chamber.

Kendon lit the dynamite fuse with the lighter, creating a feeble aura. Bogdan fired three times toward the light. The bullets slapped against the massive stalagmite, missing Kendon's head by inches.

When the fuse had only a few more seconds of burn time, Kendon lobbed the bundle in Bogdan's direction like a hand grenade, then dove into the small tunnel opening, dragging the backpack behind him. The explosion ripped through the chamber, causing hundreds of stalactites to drop from the ceiling like sharp knives. The bats that survived the blast swirled frenetically. Deprived by the fierce concussion of their radar, they crashed into walls and into cavern formations. Kendon stood up in the darkness and was pelted in seconds by a dozen bats. One struck him on the forehead, another above his right ear.

He felt sorry for the bats. He had just done to them what the Breeders were about to do to the human race: He had destroyed their world.

Gun in hand, hunched over to avoid the bats, Kendon found his tossed flashlight and swept the light around the huge chamber. The two guards, one lying face down and the other on his side, were half-buried in rubble. He searched for Bogdan, but couldn't find his body. He was certain he couldn't have had time to reach the safety of the entrance. He had to be buried somewhere under broken stalactites, crushed beneath their weight.

In the distance, Kendon heard Directorate soldiers calling out to one another. One of them shouted, "Hurry! This way."

Climbing over debris, he went back to the backpack for another bundle of dynamite, then made his way back to the main tunnel and crammed the dynamite into a fissure. He lit the fuse. By the time it exploded, he had already recovered his backpack and had ducked into the safety of the small escape tunnel. Nevertheless, the concussion from the blast was powerful enough to fling him face forward.

He could picture the cavern entrance collapsing into a pile of rubble. If he was lucky, it would be sealed completely, and it would take the soldiers hours to dig through.

With only a flashlight to guide him, he ran as fast as he could down the narrowing tunnel.

Chapter 4

The Breeders were nearby, mentally and physically. Kendon could feel it. Mentally, they had been near through the thoughts and emotions of Bogdan and the two guards. They couldn't see directly through human eyes, but they could determine the progression of events by tapping into the mental imagery of their human surrogates.

With the spikes of fear and the sudden cessation of thought, they would have concluded the three humans were no longer alive. But they knew Kendon was alive, and they had to know he had gone deeper into the caverns, too deep to follow through the implant. His was a mind too powerful for them to penetrate, but it was housed in a body that could be tracked once it was back on the surface, thanks to the implant.

Kendon was certain the Breeders were physically close, too, waiting for the moment he emerged.

How he despised them! As he descended deeper into the caves, he could feel their coldness, colder than the blizzards that swirled in his mind. He could picture them, the heads large in relation to their bodies, with dark, elongated eyes that revealed nothing. They had super intelligence and magical technology, yet they were spiritually sterile. They were the living dead, devoid of emotion, with a compulsive genius for evil.

He remembered what Meller had said: "They tricked us into a secret collaboration by appealing to our desire for power. They promised us advanced technology and through it supremacy in the world."

It was a clever ploy to distract the childish humans: Give them toys to play with, lock them into an arrangement where they could be easily controlled and monitored, and then, at the appropriate time, eliminate them.

The best that the collaborators could then do once they grasped the truth was to extract an agreement whereby a list of people including the intellectual and political elite and former abductees would be spared. In the post-asteroid world, the Committee would control what was left of the human race through the Directorate, through people like Bogdan. A three-tiered hierarchy would be established: Breeders, Clones and hybrids, and then the surviving humans.

Bogdan had once summed up the rationale for the collaborators to submit to the annihilation scheme: "There's nothing we can do to stop the Breeders, but at least *we* will still be alive."

To Kendon, it was clear the remaining humans would merely serve as a genetic resource to further the Breeder goal of perfecting the hybrid race, and they would provide a labor pool to restore the world and implant the flora and fauna from the Breeders' home planet.

"Who would want to survive?" Kendon had asked. "Once our usefulness is exhausted, do you think they will put us in zoos?"

"We have our plans," Bogdan replied.

Kendon was burning with a desire to get rid of the implant. It was task number one of a long list of tasks that he needed to accomplish. He found a crack in the cavern wall to wedge in his flashlight. He stripped off his uniform and put on the jeans and red plaid shirt he had stuffed in the backpack.

He got out his surgical kit and injected himself in the bridge of his nose with a local anesthetic. But the light from the flashlight was insufficient for him to perform the surgery—it cast too many shadows from his fingers. He realized he would have to find a place within the tourist area of the caverns to extract the implant— perhaps an office, or a bathroom, some well-lit location that he could temporarily secure.

As he made his way through the rock-strewn tunnels he became more cautious, certain the anesthetic would soon affect his coordination. He feared slipping down a sheer rock wall, or falling into one of the numerous crevasses, each a death trap for the unwary.

He knew he was getting close to the main caverns when the tunnel widened and he heard the faint echoes of chatty, happy voices—tourists. The closer he got, the brighter the light in the distance became and the louder the voices. He was pleased, in part because he was nearer to his goal, but largely because the sounds dispelled the oppressive and frightening aloneness he had felt in the deepness of the caves.

Up ahead was the natural opening to the Carlsbad Caverns. From the helicopter, it had looked like a huge crater in the desert. Meandering pathways had been built so visitors could hike down to the cavern floor two hundred feet below the entrance. He knew there was another entrance a mile away where a seven hundred and fifty foot elevator shaft brought visitors from the surface to one of the deepest and largest of the cavern chambers. The caverns reminded him of Dulce and Pie Town and Harsh Meadows and all the other underground facilities he had known, where long shafts led to complexes of chambers carved out of solid rock, some as huge and sprawling as a modern shopping mall.

Kendon made his way toward the light and was soon near the foot of the natural entrance. He was in a restricted area that the trails bypassed, hidden in the darkness behind a stalagmite formation. If it weren't for the implant, he could readily escape by walking up the trail to a parking lot where it would be easy to steal a car.

Keeping in the darkness, he watched the crowds walking down the zigzag path from the entrance high above. He brushed himself off, then tucked in his shirt and waited for an opportunity. He was confident he could easily merge into the crowd and transform himself into just another tourist.

Groups of people were sauntering down the trail, mostly families: mothers, fathers, and children. Kendon was moved by the sight. Every time he had gone to the surface world on a Directorate mission, he would see mothers and fathers and their children, and, invariably he would feel an ache in his heart at the glimpse of a life he had never known.

On the trail not far from him, he saw two fair-haired boys who had run boisterously ahead of an attractive woman with her hair in a ponytail. She was pushing a stroller with a toddler in it and was unable to keep up with the boys.

"David! Gregory!" she said firmly, "don't get so far ahead."

The boys stopped running and waited for her to catch up. Behind her was a man about her own age who had stopped to wait for an older couple with gray hair and friendly faces. The younger man smiled at them while they caught up. Kendon deduced the relationships: The older ones were the parents of the man, grandparents of the children, and father-in-law and mother-in-law of the woman who was pushing the stroller and trying to keep the two energetic boys in line.

A family!

Kendon stared them, hungry for their experience.

He saw another group, mostly adults, obviously from a tour because of their numbers, start the descent down the winding trail. Kendon thought he could easily join them as soon as they reached the bottom, but he felt an electric jolt when he spotted two black-clad soldiers at the top of the trail. They were holding M-16s and were looking down into the cavern. Some of the tourists glanced warily at the machine guns.

Kendon became alarmed. Were the troopers about to descend

into the caverns? He had to think fast, but not like a fugitive. He had to see the situation as a Directorate agent would see it. If they were acting on their own, they would surely go after him in the caves. But more than likely the Breeders were controlling the search, indirectly through their interface with the Committee, so the soldiers would be instructed to remain on the surface. They would wait for Kendon to emerge in order for the Breeders to pick up on the implant signal and pinpoint his location.

Kendon waited for an opportunity, which came when the soldiers turned abruptly to look in the other direction, as if someone had called them. It happened just as the family he had been observing reached the stretch of trail close to where he was hidden. With the backpack slung casually over a shoulder, Kendon ambled toward the trail, one hand loosely holding the strap. He nodded familiarly to the older couple and walked briskly to get in front of the stroller. As he did, the toddler dropped a squeaky rubber duck. Kendon scooped it up and handed it back to the child.

"Thank you," the woman said.

The thought that he had just killed three people made him feel unclean, unworthy to be in their presence. He stepped up his pace to get ahead of them. He kept thinking they didn't have a clue that in three short days it would all end, that a power beyond their comprehension was plotting their demise.

He began steaming inside at the thought that it wasn't right for people like that to die. *Who do those goddamned creatures think they are that they can do such a thing to people like this and to their world?*

Kendon became furious at the thought of the Breeders, but then he became furious at himself for letting his emotions get out of control. The anger could break through his mental shield and give him away. He breathed deeply to calm himself down, to restore the shield, but the image of the young family stayed in his mind.

He said in a low voice, *I will succeed. I will save you.*

He kept repeating it to himself, as an incantation that accompanied each quick step.

I will succeed. I will save you.

He followed the trail through the softly illuminated caverns. The trail wound through one grand chamber after another, descending gradually another five hundred feet over the course of a mile. He walked quickly, almost at a sprint, passing groups of people.

As he went by each group, he repeated to himself, *I will succeed. I will save you.*

Finally, Kendon came to the rest area in one of the huge chambers, which had a snack bar and tables. He searched the area for black uniforms, but there were none. On one side was the elevator, and a group of tourists was waiting for the doors to open to take them back to the surface more than seven hundred feet above.

He looked around for a place to extract the implant and saw the men's room. It was brightly lit. Several men and a boy were standing in front of urinals. Kendon scrubbed his face with warm water and then lathered it with liquid soap from the wall dispenser. He took his time washing up, waiting for the restroom to empty. When it looked like there was no one left, he stepped over to the door and searched his backpack for the screwdriver. With a powerful slam of the palm of his hand against the end of the plastic handle, he rammed the screwdriver deep into the keyhole. With one twist, the door locked.

He propped the backpack on the counter next to one of the sinks and took out the surgical kit. He lined up the instruments on a paper towel—a scalpel, a retractor, tweezers, gauze, a suturing needle and thread, a flesh-colored bandage, and the syringe he had used to inject himself with the anesthetic.

Under the bright light of the fluorescent lamps overhead, Kendon touched the tiny red point left by one of the injections with the tip of the scalpel. He sank the knife in. Fighting a feeling of revulsion, he made an incision three-quarters of an inch long. He cut again laterally at the top and bottom of the first incision. Blood trickled down his face and dripped off his chin into the sink.

At first, he didn't feel anything, but as he probed with the knife, he touched ragingly sensitive nerve endings. He took the syringe and gave himself another injection.

It took all of his strength of will to continue cutting into his nose. He understood now why the resistance had failed: It was a superhuman task to violate one's own flesh, to mutilate oneself. It was only the thought of the enormous importance of the task ahead of him that pushed him to continue. Using the retractor, he pulled the flesh to one side and exposed the cartilage. Blood dripped down his fingers, and he felt like he was going to vomit.

Just as he was about to resume probing, he heard a toilet flush. He groaned. He should have searched the men's room more carefully. Out of the corner of his eye, he saw a slender, middle-aged man with thinning hair come out of the end stall and walk toward the line of sinks. Kendon turned his head slightly to look. The man was reaching for the faucet, apparently unconcerned about him.

Kendon looked back at the mirror. He tried to act as if nothing unusual was occurring and wondered how to deal with the man. He would have to tie him up and gag him. He heard water flowing at the far sink, and then he heard an uncertain voice say, "What? What's the matter with you? Did you fall?"

Without looking away from the mirror, Kendon said, "There's something lodged in the cartilage. I'm trying to get it out."

"I'm a dentist, but I have medical training. Maybe I can see what the problem is and call the paramedics for you."

Kendon turned to look at him. He was a pleasant looking man with a polite smile.

"You've done surgery?" Kendon said.

"Yes."

"Good. Help me out. In the cartilage is T-shaped metal object.

I've exposed it, but I'm having trouble extracting it. You need to dig around it on the sides."

He realized he must look frightful. Blood dripped from his chin, and his hands were smeared red. He extended the scalpel to the dentist.

The man looked down at the line-up of surgical instruments, and the expression of his eyes changed from Good-Samaritan concern to fear. He backed away.

"Listen, I don't know what's going on here. I . . . I don't do surgery in a men's room. I'll go to the help desk and have them call for paramedics."

The dentist backed up toward the door. The screwdriver was still in the keyhole. When he reached for it, Kendon grabbed his gun from the backpack and sprinted over to him. He put the gun to the back of his head.

"I wouldn't do that if I were you."

The dentist turned around. His eyes were bulging. "Hey, listen, I didn't come in here to cause anyone any trouble. My wife and kids are waiting for me at one of the tables outside. Let me go back to them."

"I don't want to hurt you, but I will if I have to."

He motioned with the gun for the dentist to go back to the sink. It was easy for Kendon to read the man's face. It said he was dealing with a lunatic, and he had better play along.

Back at the sink, Kendon handed him the scalpel. "I require your assistance. There is a metallic device in the cartilage, and it has to come out."

The dentist reluctantly took the scalpel. "Okay, whatever you want. But do you have to keep the gun pointed at my stomach."

"Yes."

"Whatever you do, please don't shoot me. I have a wife and two children and they need me."

"If that thing doesn't come out of my nose, something very tragic is going to happen that will cost you your life and the lives of everyone you love. And it won't be my doing. I would explain it to you, but you wouldn't believe me."

Kendon lowered the pistol so that it pointed at the floor.

"Okay, okay," the dentist said. "If you want me to remove it, I will. But I can't do anything with you standing like that. You have to lean against the wall so that your head has something solid to push against."

Kendon complied.

"Where is it?" the dentist said.

With his free hand, Kendon pointed to an area just below the bridge of the nose.

"Lift the flap of flesh and you'll see it—a straight line a quarter of an inch long."

"What is it?"

"An implant. A tracking device."

The dentist didn't seem to be listening any more. He had quickly turned professional. Kendon studied the dentist's light brown eyes as he probed around the sides of the implant with the tip of the scalpel.

"This is going to hurt," the dentist said.

"I don't care. If you knew what was at stake, you would get it out as quickly as possible."

The dentist began slicing the hard cartilage around the implant. When he dug deeper, Kendon thought his head was going to explode. The more the dentist probed with the scalpel, the more his head pressed hard against the wall. The pain became so intense he groaned.

"I told you it was going to hurt."

"Keep going," Kendon said through clenched teeth.

The dentist cut under the implant and lifted it slightly. But it wouldn't come free. He grabbed the thin forceps from the counter and squeezed the tip around the object. It was all Kendon could do not to scream.

"Take it out!"

The dentist tugged on it like it was an infected tooth, twisting it slightly, then pulling more, wiggling it, then twisting and pulling again.

Just when Kendon thought he was about to pass out, the dentist exclaimed, "I've got it!"

He showed Kendon the end of the forceps. Kendon took several deep breaths and then laughed giddily. At last, he was free of it.

"You've just saved the world," he said joyfully. "Now, sew me up."

The dentist expertly closed the wound with small, tight stitches. As he worked, Kendon began to see things about him. He didn't know what to make of it. He could see things about the dentist's life as clearly as if he had been present when they happened.

When the stitching was done, Kendon washed the blood off and applied a flesh-toned bandage over the wound. It hid the wound well.

"Am I free to go now?" the dentist asked.

"Not quite. We have a security matter to resolve."

"My family is waiting outside. They're probably very worried about me."

Kendon washed the implant and held it up. "If I told you this was manufactured on a planet forty light years from here, would you believe me?"

The dentist stared at him and said nothing.

"If I told you alien beings inserted it in my nose when I was twelve years old, would you believe me?"

The dentist shrugged his shoulders.

"If I told you these same beings are planning on bringing an end to the human race this coming Sunday, and that I am the only man on Earth who can stop them, would you believe me?"

The dentist smiled involuntarily, as if to say he was prepared to believe anything as long as he got out of the men's room alive.

"You see the problem?" Kendon continued. "The reason I was

in this bathroom cutting myself open is impossible for you to believe."

Kendon scrutinized the dentist's eyes and sensed that he was at least willing to listen. He went on: "Up on the surface are two dozen men wearing black assault uniforms who are looking for me. They know the truth about what I am telling you. If they get their hands on me, they will kill me. And if I die, I guarantee you that in three days you and everyone on this planet are going to die, too."

"What exactly is going to happen on Sunday?"

"A very large asteroid has been diverted, and it is going to hit somewhere in the Caribbean Sea some time after dark Sunday night. There won't be any place on Earth to hide. The destruction will be universal."

The dentist shook his head, as if he'd just heard the whopper of the century.

"Look, Mister, you haven't harmed me. There's no reason for me to say anything to anyone about this. I was glad to help you out."

Kendon closed his eyes and again saw things about the man. He wondered if being freed of the implant had triggered something in him, or perhaps it had unblocked a natural ability, like the healing power of his hands.

He said, "Your name is something like Holiday. No, I'm hearing the name Halloway. Philip Halloway. Your wife's name is Eileen."

"How could you know that?" the dentist said.

Kendon put his hand up to quiet him and closed his eyes again. "When you asked her to marry you, you were on a sailboat. You rented it for the occasion. It was in the evening, a cool evening on a lake. The sailboat had symbolic importance for you. It had to do with the adventure of joining yourself to another person in marriage. You were married in New York. You have two brothers and one sister, and they all have children. You get together often. You are a close family."

Kendon opened his eyes. The dentist was staring at him differently than before.

"How do you know all of this?"

Kendon looked at the man for a moment and said softly, with all of the feeling he could muster, "You love them above all else, don't you Philip?"

"Well, of course I do."

"Then take me seriously. Everything I've told you is true, as true as what I just told you about yourself."

Halloway nodded. "I've promised you that I won't say anything about this."

Kendon could not detect any duplicity. He sensed that the dentist was a man of his word. "I am going to let you go back to your family, but I will need one more favor from you, Philip."

"And that is?"

"I need you to go with me up the elevator to the main lobby. Out in the parking lot, there's likely to be one or two Black Hawk helicopters and the men in black uniforms that I was telling you about. I need to know how many there are, and where they are. And if you see anything unusual up in the sky."

"This is all very strange," the dentist said, but in a tone that sounded like he would do as he was asked.

"You can't imagine how strange."

Kendon cleaned up the surgical equipment and stuffed everything back into the backpack. He wrapped the implant in tissue paper and dropped it in his shirt pocket. As long as it was free of his body and body fluids, it was inert. He turned the screwdriver to unlock the door, then yanked it free.

Several men had been waiting to get in. They stepped aside to let Kendon and the dentist get by.

"Watch out for the door," Kendon said. "It'll jam on you if you're not careful."

He followed the dentist across an open area to the tables. An attractive woman was sitting at a table with a boy and a girl.

"Phil, where have you been?"

"I'm really sorry, Eileen," Halloway said. "This gentleman had a serious medical emergency, and I helped him. Bad gash on the nose."

She looked up at Kendon and smiled. He liked how she looked. He liked how the children looked, too.

Kendon tapped the bandage. "It was very kind of your husband to help me."

"Listen, honey, I'm going to go up the elevator with him to make sure he gets out of here all right, then I'll be right back. I promise."

She looked disappointed.

"Daddy, I want to see the Big Room," said the boy. "When are we going to see the Big Room?"

"Give me ten minutes."

The dentist picked up an Indiana Jones hat from middle of the table and plunked it on his head. "Time for an adventure," he said.

Kendon walked with him to the elevator shaft. While they waited, he glanced casually around the rest area to be sure no one in a black uniform was there. When the elevator opened, a dozen people came out.

Kendon and the dentist were the only ones going back up to the surface. "The people in black are not legitimate authority," he said after the elevator began the long ascent. "They provide security at the underground bases where the aliens operate from. I know, because I used to be one of them."

"You've seen these aliens?" Halloway said.

"Yes."

"What do they look like?"

"There are two kinds. One is just like the popular descriptions of them. They're small and childlike, with gray skin. They have large heads relative to their bodies and enormous eyes. They have three-lobed brains and they smell bad, like ammonia. The others are about as tall as humans with grayish-blue skin and more angular facial features than the little ones. They're the ones in charge. Mentally, they are extremely powerful and can exert control with their minds."

Halloway was blinking a lot. Kendon realized it was too much for him to absorb. After staring at him for a moment, Kendon said, "I liked your family."

Halloway smiled.

"You're lucky to have a family. I was taken from an orphanage in Eastern Europe when I was three years old, and I was raised in subterranean bases in New Mexico and Nevada. I've spent most of my life underground. The same is true about the people who are hunting for me."

"Why are they after you?"

"I have access to something they want, something that can prevent what's going to happen on Sunday."

The elevator door opened on the lobby of the visitor center. Kendon glanced around and didn't see any of the assault troops inside, but he could see two soldiers in the parking lot near the curb. Halloway saw them, too.

"Go out there and walk to a car somewhere in the middle of the parking lot. When you get there, search for your keys, then act frustrated like you can't find them and come back here. Look around, but don't be obvious about it."

The dentist was out of sight for several minutes. Kendon finally saw him walking back at a brisk pace, but then the dentist stopped and looked up at the sky. Other people in the parking lot were looking up, too. Some were pointing.

A few minutes later, Halloway came back into the lobby, looking nervous, almost hyper. He whispered rapidly, "I counted twelve men in black uniforms and saw only one helicopter. It's near the road. Two of those guys are standing next to the main exit of the parking lot. They're stopping the cars that are leaving and asking questions. The others are in the parking area in groups of two or three, mostly on the right side of the parking lot."

"You were looking up at the sky. Why?"

"I heard some people say, 'Look, UFOs!' So I looked up to see what they were talking about."

"What did you see?"

"What they were pointing at."

"What did they look like?"

"They were lenticular in shape, bright, and silvery. They didn't move."

"How many?"

"At first three, then five more appeared. They came out of nowhere."

Kendon took the implant from his pocket. "That's where this came from."

"Why don't you get rid of it?"

"I intend to. But I need it to create a diversion."

Halloway looked around the lobby, then out to the parking lot, then at Kendon. "Listen, now I believe what you told me. I want to join you. I have a stake in this, too."

Kendon smiled. "Have you ever stolen an automobile?"

"No."

"Have you ever killed anyone?"

"No."

"Then you would only get in the way."

He put his hand on the dentist's shoulder. "You have a family waiting for you. Spend your time with them. For the next three days, don't leave them. Not even for a second. If I fail, you will never have a chance to be with them again."

Halloway took off the Indiana Jones fedora and pulled a pair of sunglasses from his pocket. "You need to disguise yourself better. Wear these."

Kendon put the hat on. With the dark glasses, the hat, and the change of clothes, it would be hard even for someone who knew him to recognize him.

The dentist nodded approvingly.

"Thanks," Kendon said. "If I'm successful, I will look you up one day. I want to know your family. Then I'll tell you everything. *Everything*. I give you my word. It will be my way of thanking you."

Walking reluctantly back to the elevator, the dentist waited with a dozen other people for the doors to open. Kendon felt remorse when he saw Halloway's drawn face and sagging shoulders. He realized he had burdened him with a terrible knowledge. As the elevator doors closed, the dentist smiled weakly and gave Kendon a thumbs up.

Word about the UFO sighting had spread, and tourists were pouring out of the lobby to look. Some were smiling and pointing excitedly, as if they had just spotted someone famous. Others had taken out cameras and camcorders and were aiming them at the sky.

Kendon calmed himself with deep breaths. He strengthened the whiteness in his mind by turning it into a blizzard. Shielded, he searched through a trash can for a plastic bag. He found one and took the last bundle of dynamite from his backpack along with a small, remotely controlled fuse. Carefully, he pushed the fuse into one of the sticks and dropped the bundle into the plastic bag. He took the screwdriver from the backpack and slid it into his trouser pocket.

Out in the parking lot, Kendon mixed with the tourists and, like them, stared up at the sky. He counted eight disks. Two of them he recognized as Breeder command ships from their size and the circle of multicolored lights flashing around the directional pods. They were about half a mile up and off slightly to the south. Kendon slung the backpack over his shoulder and made his way to a row of cars in the middle of the lot, stopping occasionally to make a show of looking up at the disks.

As he walked between two rows of cars, he casually dropped the plastic bag full of dynamite to the ground and sauntered toward rows of cars parked the farthest from the soldiers. He strode up to an older blue Ford Bronco, as if he owned it. With practiced speed, he rammed the screwdriver into the lock and opened the door. He repeated the maneuver with the ignition switch.

The Bronco started right up.

Kendon pulled out his gun and chambered a round. He put the pistol on the seat next to him and took out the detonator. He looked back to where he had planted the dynamite. No one was within fifty yards of it.

Slowly, he backed out of the stall and drove up behind several cars that were waiting to exit the parking lot. Two Directorate soldiers were letting vehicles pass after looking in and asking a question or two.

Kendon checked again to be sure no one was near the dynamite. Certain the area was clear of people, he hit the detonator button. Instantly, a huge fireball erupted in the middle of the parking lot, tossing several cars into the air. The gas tanks of two of the vehicles exploded. Flames and black smoke swirled high into the sky. All of the Directorate soldiers, including the two controlling the parking lot exit, ran toward the explosion.

Kendon honked to get the vehicles in front of him to move, but one of the drivers had jumped out to see what had happened, blocking everyone else. Driving around them, Kendon turned onto the road and sped toward the main highway. In the rearview mirror, he could see the plume of black smoke rising high into the sky.

Not far up the road, at the intersection with the main highway, was Whites City, a tourist stop with curio stores and a gas station. After parking at the back of the station, Kendon dug into the backpack for the surgical kit and took out the syringe and the bottle of anesthetic. He emptied the bottle and squeezed the remaining liquid out of the syringe. He slid the needle into a vein in his forearm to draw blood, then squirted the blood, his living energy, into the bottle.

His mind wrapped in the security of a blizzard, he waited for an opportunity. It soon came in the form of a semi-truck that was inching up to the road, about to turn right and head south on Highway 180, the road to El Paso and the Mexican border.

Kendon drove up behind the truck. He removed the implant from the tissue paper and dropped it into the vial of blood, then screwed the cap back on. Just before the truck lurched onto the highway, he jumped out of the car and dropped the bottle into a niche in the back of the trailer.

The implant was coded to his DNA. It needed his life force to function. It was now re-activated—pulsing and giving away his position.

The truck slowly roared onto the highway, diesel smoke spewing from its vertical exhaust pipes. With a fading roar, the truck soon disappeared down the road.

Kendon raced a few miles in the opposite direction and turned onto a ranch road that led to the foot a steep hill. He scrambled to the top and stood on a rocky outcropping. He searched the sky and felt his heart leap when he saw the alien formation: All eight disks were slowly moving southwest, in the same direction as the truck.

He recalled the inscription found on the archway of the control room of a Breeder Gray command ship that had been downed during the pre-Collaboration era, when Americans had challenged the alien presence militarily. It was written in hieroglyphic-like characters. Someone had taken a photograph it and it ended up in Directorate intelligence files. Cryptographers were eventually able to decipher it. The inscription turned out to be a boast: *"We are gods! We create, we rule, we destroy!"*

An image formed in his mind of a Breeder, its destructive intent clear in its cold eyes. He clenched his fist and shook it at the sky. He roared, "I am Kendon! I am human! I will defeat you!"

He shouted it again and again, louder each time, with a furious energy that rose up from his solar plexus and exploded from his throat.

He scrambled back down the hill to the stolen Bronco, and

soon he was shooting along the highway in the direction of Texas, feeling exhilarated at his freedom. He had never felt anything like it before. It was a wonderful sensation of buoyancy, as if he had just made it to the surface of an ocean, and at last he was able to breathe.

Memories of his past flashed through his mind—first of a boy named Arkasha who was grabbed from an orphanage in Belorussia so long ago. And then came a surge of memories of that lonely boy being raised in a distant land to carry out an agenda forged by a group of men who were terrified by a reality beyond their comprehension.

As he drove down the road, he remembered the evils he had committed in the name of that agenda: the murder of dissidents who had dared to speak about what they knew of the secret world. They had tried to warn of things that were almost impossible to believe. They had sounded the alarm, and for that they were condemned to die. For that they were hunted down and killed.

It was a sordid life he had been forced to lead, and at last he was able to leave it behind in the rubble of a demolished bat cave.

Arkasha was dead!

Kendon was born!

He had always felt that he had a special purpose. Even when he was young and in the grip of the Collaboration's relentless indoctrination he had felt he was different. He became convinced of it the day he understood the unusual nature of his hands.

They were healer hands, not the hands of a killer.

The sky was clear, the sun was shining, a refreshing wind was blowing in his face.

With joyful abandon, he kept shouting, "I am Kendon! I have a purpose! I will fulfill my purpose!"

Chapter 5

Tepler worked the entire night checking and rechecking his data. Long before the first rays of dawn washed out the stars, he was convinced there was no escaping the evidence: An asteroid the size of Mount Everest had in fact changed course, and it was on a possible collision course with Earth.

"How did it change trajectory?" he wondered. "Was it struck by another asteroid?"

And, more importantly, "What is the probability of impact? Five percent? Ten percent?"

He was bothered that he couldn't come up with answers. He was even more disturbed when he checked his e-mail and found that the data he had sent the night before to the Minor Planetary Center had bounced back. He sent it again, but it was immediately returned marked "undelivered." He couldn't understand why his e-mail wouldn't go through. Barring a simultaneous discovery by other astronomers, it meant that no one else knew about The Big One yet.

He grabbed the phone and called the center. He could usually get someone on the line at night, but the only response was a recorded voice telling him to leave a message. In desperation, Tepler called one of the University of Arizona observatories at Kitt Peak where he had done post-graduate work.

Brian Bencomo, an astronomer he had worked with, answered. "Hey, Lone Ranger," he said, using the nickname Tepler had acquired from being the sole astronomer at Cabo Rojo. "What's up? You getting all lonesome out there?"

Tepler was used to the bantering. Most of it was good-natured, but he knew that a lot of people would love to have his job, given the location and the advanced telescope at his disposal. The foundation trustee occasionally dropped hints about job queries from other astronomers. Tepler always had some good quips to respond to the bantering, but tonight he wasn't in the mood for jokes.

He said, "Listen to me closely, Brian. Something's wrong. I've detected an object that's less than three days from a possible collision with Earth. What's really screwy is that when I first detected it, the orbit was different. It was going to miss by a million miles, but now it's heading our way. I've checked my data again and again. The orbit definitely changed from one day to the next. It must have been hit by another asteroid."

"I presume you e-mailed your data to MPC," Bencomo said, referring to the Minor Planetary Center.

"I did. Twenty-four hours ago. I was expecting half a dozen confirmations by now, not to mention some telephone calls to congratulate me."

"And the e-mail was returned to you undelivered."

"Yeah, I just found that out when I checked my mail. Then I called the center, but I couldn't get through to anyone."

"We've had the same problem. Their server's down or something."

"And their telephones? Brian, this thing needs to be confirmed, and fast."

"We've got the telescope set up for a run. It's a project that's been scheduled for months. We're just about to get going."

"Interrupt it. This thing is big, maybe six miles in length and three or four miles in width. If it hits, it's going to be K/T all over again. There won't be a Kitt Peak anymore. In fact, there won't be anything left anywhere."

"There can't be any objects of that size out there that we don't already know about."

"I thought so too, but I have the evidence."

"Jesus, my reputation will go down the drain if there's something wrong with your data, Eric."

"It's *my* reputation at stake, not yours. I've gone over the calculations again and again. I want you to check it out for yourself."

"All right, e-mail me the data. I'll see what I can do."

"Forget e-mail. I'm going to give it to you over the phone. You need to look at the object *right now*. Don't put it off. You'll get a good idea what I'm talking about after you've tracked it for a couple of hours. Then check out my data from the first night. I guarantee you're going to have chills up and down your spine."

Tepler gave him the numbers, celestial coordinates that would allow Bencomo to pinpoint the object.

"I'll get back to you as soon as I can," Bencomo said.

"Don't bother with e-mail. Call me."

After hanging up, Tepler plunged back into his work. The asteroid's path had changed sometime after dawn Thursday morning and before nightfall when Gabriela and her students arrived for the tour. He guessed from the deflection angle it was sooner in the day than later. The only plausible explanation was that it had been struck by another large object, and the kinetic energy of the impact had caused it to career like a billiard ball from its previous course.

Asteroid-to-asteroid collisions were not unheard of. He thought of the images beamed back from the Galileo spacecraft of Gaspra in 1991 and Ida in 1993, both behemoth main belt asteroids in safe orbits between Mars and Jupiter. They were the first asteroids ever photographed close up and showed the scars of countless impacts.

Armed with a hypothesis, Tepler turned his attention to finding evidence of a second asteroid and examined the sequence of images one more time, beginning with the ones he'd taken the first day.

After an hour of careful scrutiny, he discovered something that he hadn't noticed before—a streak of light in the vicinity of the asteroid. The streak was exceptionally faint compared to The Big One, but he could see it in all of the images taken the first night. It appeared to be approaching the larger asteroid.

"That's got to be the impact asteroid," he said to himself.

He visualized a smaller asteroid slamming into The Big One at a sharp angle, its rocky material being swallowed up by the larger object. That was all that would be needed to alter the larger asteroid's trajectory.

But if that were the case, the streak should now be gone. However, as he studied the most recent images, he was stunned to see the streak was still there. He wondered if it was a smaller companion asteroid traveling in the same direction. But how could it continue to follow after the larger body altered course? Only one of them would have been impacted.

"This doesn't add up," he thought.

Three hours after his call to Kitt Peak, Tepler got a call back from Bencomo.

"Good work, Eric."

"Pretty scary stuff, huh?"

"Everybody here's either in denial or having a panic attack. We've gone over your data. The orbit of the asteroid was definitely altered. Your idea that it was hit by another asteroid is the only possible explanation."

"I'm not so sure anymore. I've gone over everything again, and I found a second object near it. It was in the images I took when I first discovered the asteroid. I figured it was the impact asteroid, but it's still there even after the other one changed course," Tepler said.

"Yeah, we see it, too."

"What do you make of it?"

"We don't know," Bencomo said. "Right now, we're focusing on pinning down the new orbit."

Tepler gave him his estimate of the impact probability

"After we got your information and tracked it for an hour, I thought maybe one in ten, too," Bencomo said." But after tracking it for a couple more hours, we would put it more like one in five."

"We need to go public with this."

He could picture Bencomo shaking his head. "I've had a discussion with Spacewatch people about it. Nobody's going to shoot you or throw you in jail if you send out e-mails and make phone calls to everyone you know, but it's better to wait. We don't want to create a worldwide panic. We need to get input from JPL and NASA. They've got the heavy artillery. They'll be able to nail this down better than we can and make an accurate prediction. Then and only then should anyone go public with this."

"I guess you're right," Tepler said wearily.

The young astronomer was finding it difficult to think clearly anymore. During the last twenty-four hours, he had only had a few hours sleep. Caffeine and adrenaline had kept him going, but fatigue was catching up to him.

"How long do we give them?" Tepler said.

There was a pause. "We've been trying to get someone at JPL and NASA for the last couple of hours, but no luck. I don't understand it. I've never had any trouble before connecting with someone there—day or night."

"What's the problem?"

"I don't know. All we can do is keep trying. Once they swing into it, it's probably going to be their call about how to handle it. My guess is that the decision to go public with it will end up in the Oval Office. Of course, you will get credit for the discovery."

Somehow Tepler wasn't excited about the idea of being the first to discover the end of the world was at hand. All he could think about now was getting some sleep. After hanging up, he took a long look at The Frog, shook his head, and said, "Good night, little buddy."

He was eager to drop into bed. He trudged down the spiral stairs, dragging his shoulders against the steel cylinder. Fatigue made him clumsy, and he nearly tripped over a metal plate that was leaning against the wall at the base of the staircase. Irritated with himself, he bent down to move the plate back against the cylinder where it belonged so that he wouldn't trip over it again, but then he stopped. The rectangular plate was the cover for an opening at the base of the enormous cylinder, apparently an access panel. Fighting a desire to head straight for bed, Tepler stooped under the stairs to look through the opening.

Two years before, out of curiosity to see what, if anything, was inside the massive cylinder, he had removed the panel and discovered a sophisticated mechanism that had no apparent connection to the telescope or to the observatory. Just inside the panel opening was an empty tube about five feet long and a foot in diameter that extended horizontally from the opening to the center of the cylinder. At the far end of the tube was a lever. A year after making the discovery, his curiosity piqued once again, he had pushed the lever forward with the end of a broomstick to see if he could determine its function. And then something amazing had happened: The immense cylinder had briefly come alive. For about ten seconds, he could hear mechanisms in the interior of the cylinder. The hollow tube had rotated several degrees up, as if it was being pulled up into the center of the cylinder. But the energy draw on the observatory's electrical system had been too great, and the lighthouse's main fuse had switched off. After finding the fuse box and flicking the switch back on, Tepler found that another amazing thing had happened: The tube had returned to its starting position.

He had repeated this experiment on several occasions. The last time, instead of going to the fuse box to restore power, he had gone back up to the observation deck and was astonished to find a transformation had occurred there as well. The telescope had partly swiveled to one side, exposing a deep chamber below. A cannon-like tube had begun to emerge from the floor, but was frozen in place by the power failure.

When he restored power at the fuse box, all of the transformations reversed. The telescope was back into its normal position, the floor was solid once again, and the five-foot-long hollow tube behind the access panel was once again back in the horizontal position.

He had been too unnerved by his discovery to experiment with the trigger mechanism again. It was clearly something he wasn't supposed to know about, otherwise he would have been told about it. Fearing for his job, he never mentioned anything about the discovery in his monthly "State of the Observatory" reports to the foundation, as the trustee termed them.

As he peered once again through the access door at the empty horizontal tube, he said out loud, "Something is supposed to slide in there, but what?"

Too fatigued to think any more about it, Tepler dragged himself to his bedroom and let himself fall backward onto the comfortable mattress.

In less than a minute he was deep asleep.

Five hours later, Tepler was wakened by the sound of banging on the thick wood of the front door. He heard a woman calling his name. Startled, he sat up and looked around, barely remembering where he was. "What! Who's that?" he said in confusion. He looked at the digital clock in front of the lamp on the night table. It was already half past noon.

"Eric! Eric!"

He recognized Gabriela's voice. He pushed himself off the bed and stumbled through several rooms to get to the front door, almost tripping in his rush. Before getting to the door, he saw Gabriela through a window. Her hands were cupped to her mouth, and she was shouting up in the direction of the tower.

He tucked in his shirt and ran his fingers through his unruly hair before swinging the heavy door open. The bright sunlight stung his eyes. He leaned casually against the doorframe, his eyes squinting from the brightness.

"Did I hear you say Eric? I do believe there's someone here by that name."

He fought off a yawn and rubbed his eyes.

Gabriela smiled, but then realizing she had awakened him, she became embarrassed. "I thought you were up in the observatory. If I had known—"

She looked as lovely as she had the night before, wearing a white blouse with ruffles and a gray skirt, her dark hair tied back in a bun.

He yawned and stretched. "No school today?"

"I left early. I had to see you."

He couldn't think of anyone else in the world he would be more pleased to see. He had briefly forgotten about the asteroid, but seeing her at his door reminded him of what he had found the night before, and he began to feel the same dread he had felt then.

"I was worried about you, Eric. Something happened last night. I wanted to make sure you're all right."

He stared into her dark brown eyes and wondered if he should tell her. She was going to hear about it soon anyway. If it wasn't already in the news, it would be later.

Tepler led her into the cavernous main room that he had furnished comfortably with colonial-era sofas, armchairs, and tables. The walls were decorated with paintings of bearded Spanish noblemen. What caught Gabriela's attention was his collection of classical music on CDs and LPs. He gestured for her to sit in one of the sofas, but instead she ran her fingers across some of the CDs, smiling appreciatively when she came to a collection of violin concertos.

He remembered that she was a violinist. There was nothing he would have liked better than to talk with her about music and find out about her music background, but now was not the time. He stared at the wood floor for a moment and wondered how to tell her about the asteroid. He decided to stall for time.

"I have something to show you, Gabriela, something very important, but I need to get my brain up to speed. I'm going to shower, get a change of clothes, and then we'll go up to the observatory." He pointed to the audio equipment. "If there's something you want to put on, please go ahead. The acoustics in this building are fabulous."

He stood under the hot shower wondering how to tell Gabriela that her life and the lives of everyone she loved could end in a couple of days. Maybe he should simply show her his findings and let her come to the realization of what it meant on her own.

The sleepiness and tension drained from him by the hot water, he dressed in casual slacks and white cotton shirt and went to join her. He found her in the kitchen, standing with her back to him, busily putting some grilled ham and cheese sandwiches and a pot of coffee on a tray, unaware of his presence. She had put on a recording of Josef Hassid, an LP Tepler had not listened to in years, and the profound sadness of a truncated life filtered into the kitchen.

He gazed at Gabriela for a moment and wished he had met her years ago. Her face brightened when she turned and saw him. She pointed to the tray. "You need to start your day with a solid lunch."

He took the tray. "Come with me."

They went up the spiral staircase to the observatory and sat by the workstation in front of a row of monitors. A speaker brought the music from the phonograph downstairs to the observatory.

"I don't know why I chose something so sad," Gabriela said. "I saw it and remembered how he died so young."

"Maybe it's your intuition picking up on what I want to show you," Tepler said.

As he ate one of the sandwiches, Tepler ran his fingers over the keyboard and called up the same images he had shown Gabriela's class the night before. On a separate monitor, a computer-generated image showed the asteroid's trajectory in relation to the Sun, the Earth, and the Moon.

"Something happened last night that you should know about. You're going to find out about it soon, so I may as well be the one to tell you."

He pointed to the screen. "This line shows the asteroid's path when I discovered it two nights ago. It shows that the asteroid was going to miss the Earth by four lunar distances—a million miles."

He hit some more keys and another line showing the asteroid intersecting with Earth was superimposed on the first line.

"Why are they different?" Gabriela asked.

"Sometime yesterday morning, the asteroid changed course, and now it's heading for Earth."

He scrutinized her face and noted a look of alarm.

"Are you sure?"

"I've gone over the data a hundred times."

Gabriela stared at the floor and was quiet for a moment. Finally, she said, "I can see now why you acted the way you did last night. I'm glad you didn't say anything to the children."

"It's not certain the asteroid will hit us. There's maybe one chance in five it will. Other observatories are working on it. I'm waiting for a call from Kitt Peak. Hopefully, we can get a better idea of the situation."

"How can an asteroid change direction?"

He explained the collision theory and called up the pockmarked images of Gaspra and Ida. "They slam into each other once in a while. Depending on the size, speed, and angle of impact, an asteroid, even one as big as this, can get knocked out of its orbit."

He was surprised how calm Gabriela appeared. She stood up and walked to a window that looked out on the Caribbean. She stared out the window for a while, then turned to him. "I have prepared myself a long time for this moment, Eric. I've known since I was a young girl this was going to happen."

He shook his head as if not understanding.

"It was predicted. Here in Cabo Rojo."

"I've been here for five years. I've never heard anything about it."

"Nobody discusses it any more. It had to do with UFOs, abductions, and so forth. For a few years, everyone talked about it, but there was a lot of ridicule, and stupid, mean tricks were played on people who claimed they had seen flying saucers or that they had been abducted. My uncle was the one who made this prediction. Cruel things were done to him. No one talks about it anymore."

Tepler leaned back in his chair. He had never bothered with the subject, dismissing accounts of aliens and abductions as modern mythology, a testimony to the creative power of the collective human imagination. He thought about such things like a scientist: Intelligent life was likely elsewhere in the universe, but the distance between stars was so great that interstellar travel was impossible. Therefore, there couldn't be an alien presence on Earth.

"What did he base his prediction on?"

"He said he was taken aboard a spaceship and that beings that resembled humans showed him the future. They showed an asteroid hitting the Caribbean Sea just southwest of Puerto Rico. He was told that another alien race was going to make it happen."

"When was this supposed to occur?"

"They told him the world had fifteen years to prepare. It was a warning so that the human race could to do something about it."

"And how long ago was this prediction made?"

Gabriela thought for a moment, as if trying to remember dates and times. "I was ten years old at the time. I am twenty five years old now."

Tepler shook off the chill that ran up and down his spine. He snapped up the phone and dialed Bencomo's number. When he got a voice mail message, he hung up. He checked his e-mail. About fifty messages were waiting for him. He scrolled through. All of them were from the night before, the last having been sent just after he last spoke with Bencomo. That didn't seem right. He tried answering several e-mails, but within seconds, they bounced back.

He looked up nervously at Gabriela and picked up the phone again. He speed-dialed several astronomers, but he either got busy signals or voice mail. After three more tries, he finally got through to Bencomo.

"Where is everyone?" Tepler said. "The Internet's down. Nobody's answering the phone."

"I don't know. We haven't been able to get through to anybody either. I tried all morning to contact JPL, Arecibo, NASA. But there's no answer."

Bencomo's voice sounded strained and frightened, just below the threshold of hysteria.

"Is everything all right, Brian?"

"No, not really."

"What's the matter?"

"I don't know what the hell is going on, that's what's the matter."

"What about an announcement. When are we going public with this?"

"We're not."

"Says who?"

"Some people came by here who said they were federal agents. They said we should keep a lid on this for a day until the government could assess the situation better. We don't want to create a panic."

"People need to know," Tepler objected. "There's a four out of five chance this event won't happen, but if it does strike, at least they would be able to spend their last days with the people closest to them."

"We've narrowed it down to one in two chances. If it misses, it's going to be by a hair."

"A lot of people could be saved even with only a couple of days notice."

"Eric, you know the scenario as well as I do. The molten ejecta from an impact like that would go suborbital and spread around the globe. It would rain molten rock. Most of the landmass of the world would end up incinerated. Soot and dust would block sunlight for years. The tectonic configuration would likely change. You would have masses of land rising above water and others going under. Whoever survives the initial impact would die eventually from starvation or disease. Better if people didn't have any warning at all."

"Not if it struck in deep ocean. It would cause global tsunamis and kill everyone in coastal areas. But even with only two days notice, tens of millions of people would have time to flee to higher ground."

"We've determined the time and location of impact. If it strikes, it's going to fall near you, just off the south coast of Puerto Rico on Sunday night at about eight thirty five. The water there is relatively shallow, so you would have a triple effect: tsunamis, superheated steam, and molten ejecta. It would be a repeat of the K/T event, only this time it would be humans disappearing from the face of the earth instead of dinosaurs."

The phone still jammed in his ear, Tepler looked at Gabriela again. She was scrutinizing his face, listening closely to the part of the conversation she could hear. Her face grew gloomier, a mirror image, he realized, of his own face.

"There's still a chance it will miss," Tepler said.

He felt his voice straining, just like Bencomo's voice was straining, against the rising angst.

"If the deviation was caused by an asteroid collision," Bencomo continued, "then there's still a chance it will miss. But what if the deflection wasn't caused by a collision with another asteroid?"

"What other explanation is there?"

"Take a good look at your own data, Eric. Look at the streak. Take a good, hard look."

"What am I going to see?"

Bencomo ignored the question. "And one more thing. People are disappearing. I've heard that men in black uniforms and flashing Office of Naval Intelligence badges took everyone from the Minor Planetary Center. They said it had to do with national security and took them away in black buses. Watch your back, Eric."

The phone clicked off.

Tepler slowly put down the receiver. Gabriela had quietly moved from the window and was sitting beside him. She put her hand over his, and they looked at each other for a long moment without speaking.

Forcing himself to calm down, Tepler said finally, "That was Brian Bencomo, an astronomer at Kitt Peak. He asked me to take a closer look at the asteroid images. He didn't say what I would find, but I got the idea it would explain why the asteroid changed course."

He called up the most recent of the asteroid images and pointed to the streak.

"What is it?"

"I don't know. When I first detected it, I thought it was the impact asteroid. But it's still visible even after The Big One changed course. It changed course, too." He tried blowing the image up more than before, but the enhancements washed out the image. He remembered that UPS had delivered a package two days earlier with a state-of-the art enhancement program developed by NASA. The trustee had balked at the cost, but had finally caved in. It took half an hour for Tepler to install it and learn the essential commands, but soon he was at work bringing the streak to life. The NASA program made logical guesses and filled in the image so that it could be blown up much more than with conventional programs.

Soon, a blurred but distinct image emerged. The streak was long, tapered at the ends, with a bulge in the middle, an object easily a third of a mile in length and several hundred feet thick in the middle.

Gabriela gasped. "That looks like a flying saucer!"

Tepler had formed the same idea, but he didn't want to say out loud what the evidence showed. It was too bizarre. It meant that an enormous spaceship caused the asteroid to deviate from its course.

"They want to destroy our world, just like my uncle said."

Tepler turned slowly to look at Gabriela, who was transfixed by the image.

"I want to meet your uncle."

Chapter 6

During the few years they worked together, Donald Meller had talked so much about his daughter that Kendon felt he already knew her. Meller had once shown him a college graduation photo of him and Laura standing in front of an ivy-covered wall. She was wearing a blue gown and mortarboard with a tassel dangling on one side. She was pretty and had her father's intense, intelligent eyes.

He had never seen the photograph again, but the image of her was burned into his mind, along with Meller's recent words: "She doesn't know that she knows, but she does."

He had to get to Austin as quickly as possible and check the telephone directory for her name, but he didn't believe he would find a point of contact other than the children's hospital where he knew she specialized in pediatric cancer.

Would she be there when he arrived?

Kendon wished the Bronco could fly, but eager though he was to get to his destination, he kept to the speed limit. He was driving a stolen automobile, and he had to be careful not to get stopped. He was certain the theft would have been discovered by now and reported to the police.

Even before getting out of New Mexico, he had a close call when a state police car followed him for several miles. It could

have been coincidental, but it made him nervous to have the police vehicle so close behind him. The patrol car finally turned off
on a side road.

Kendon was happy the trooper hadn't stopped him; he didn't
want to take an innocent life.

It was clear he had to get another car. When he reached Semi-
nole, the first Texas town after crossing the state line, he found
a used car lot. He parked the stolen Bronco in a neighborhood a
few blocks away. From his hunter-killer days, he still had a phony
Arizona driver's license under the name Michael Jones, and he
used it to buy a silver Jeep Cherokee that he paid for in twen-
ty-dollar bills, part of the stash of stolen ATM money in the
backpack. The salesman at first balked at the cash transaction,
but rushed the paperwork through after Kendon slid an extra thousand dollars across the desk.

Kendon realized he looked and acted suspicious. His clothes
were rumpled and smelled of guano. The wound from the removal of the implant, though partially mended from self-healing, was
still evident. During the drive out of New Mexico, he had kept
the palm of one hand over the bridge of his nose. The surgical
wound had begun to shrink, but he knew it would take a lot longer before the mysterious energy flowing from his hands could make
it disappear completely.

Feeling more secure in the new car, Kendon drove to Big
Springs where he got onto the Interstate and the herd safety of
the stream of vehicles.

Just before reaching the freeway, Kendon spotted two black
Nomenklatura buses, windowless except for the driver's compartment. They were speeding in the opposite direction, and Kendon
presumed they were full of captives being transported to one of
the underground facilities in New Mexico. He pulled over to the
curb when he saw a red sedan chasing the long, powerful buses.
The driver was honking furiously and was shouting, "Stop! Stop,
you goddamn kidnappers!"

The driver, a middle-aged man with a gray beard, swerved in front of the lead bus and slammed on the brakes, as if hoping to force it to stop, but the bus rammed the car without slowing down, tossing it to one side like a toy. Jumping out of the wrecked vehicle, the man ran into the middle of the road to block the second bus. He was waving his arms, shouting, "Let them go, let them go! Please, let them go!" Instead of slowing, the bus barreled down on him, and he jumped out of the way barely a second before being run over.

Following the buses were two black Humvees. They skidded to a stop next to the wrecked sedan. Black-clad Directorate soldiers jumped out and beat the man to the ground with truncheons. After snapping handcuffs on him, they shoved him into one of the Humvees and sped away.

By then, a dozen people had come out of stores and shops and were staring with mouths open.

The incident had begun and ended in less than a minute. The spectacle infuriated Kendon, and he wanted badly to intervene, but he knew there was nothing he could do. All he could do that would make a difference was to find the one-one-five pod and the beam weapon and defeat the Breeders and their genocidal scheme.

He put the car in gear and raced to the freeway.

Six hours later, after getting gas in Abilene and buying a road map and taking shortcuts along rural backroads, he finally reached Austin. It was already nine o'clock in the evening, and it was dark out and cool. Kendon wasn't certain of the exact time of asteroid impact, only that it would occur in the evening on Sunday, some time after dark. He felt chilled when he realized an entire day had already gone by since he was in the cell at Alamogordo with Donald Meller, and now only two days were left to locate the one-one-five pod and get it to a weapon hidden somewhere in Puerto Rico.

He stopped at a telephone booth and flipped through the directory, but he did not find an entry for Laura Meller. At a convenience store, he asked for directions to Children's Hospital and found it easily. He doubted she would be there, but he was confident someone at the hospital would be able to contact her.

He wondered what kind of a reaction he would get. She hadn't seen her father in ten years. He had vanished from her life without explanation, without even saying goodbye. She would want to know how he knew him and what he knew. But how much could he tell her without sounding like a lunatic? She wouldn't know anything about the shadow intelligence agency and the underground world it kept secret. He was a complete stranger with an even stranger story.

He parked the silver Cherokee on a side street. Before getting out, he removed everything from the backpack except for the automatic pistol and an extra ammunition clip. With the backpack slung over his shoulder, he strode into the hospital lobby. Seated behind a computer monitor at the reception desk was an elderly man with a frail body, white hair, and a helpful expression.

"I need to see Dr. Laura Meller. It's extremely urgent," Kendon said.

The man moved the mouse next to the keyboard and squinted as he examined the screen. He looked up at Kendon with watery blue eyes. "I'm sorry. It doesn't look like she's in, but she's scheduled to be here in the morning. Would you care to leave a message?"

"No. It can't wait. It's extremely urgent for me to talk to her."

"Is this regarding one of her patients?"

"No, it's about her father, Donald Meller."

The receptionist picked up the telephone and nodded to him. "I'll call her ward."

He talked for a minute, repeating what Kendon had told him. After hanging up, he said, "The head nurse will contact Dr. Meller and relay your message. If you want, you can have a seat over there." He pointed to the lobby chairs.

While waiting, Kendon became uneasy. He was in public, exposed to scrutiny. It was possible the Directorate, as a last resort, could manipulate upper-world police into conducting a manhunt for him. He had to be careful and get what he needed from Laura Meller as quickly as possible and leave.

He wished again Meller had trusted him enough to include him in the escape. If he had been with them, he wouldn't now be searching for Meller's daughter at a hospital in Austin, with only two days left, worried about being identified and wondering if there was still any hope.

After a fifteen-minute wait, Kendon heard the receptionist calling him.

"Sir!"

He was holding the telephone receiver up for him. Kendon walked to the desk and took the phone.

"This is Dr. Meller," the voice said. "I'm told you want to speak to me about my father."

Her voice had a hesitant, suspicious tone to it. The voice swiftly brought him back to the bizarre reality of the situation. He could picture Meller the night before, his fingernails ripped out, his face battered, pleading for death.

"My name is Michael Kendon. I worked with your father."

"I don't know who you are."

"Your father worked for Bach-Merling as a nuclear engineer. I know him because of that."

"He disappeared ten years ago. Bach-Merling has denied he ever worked for them."

"But you know that he did, at least until ten years ago."

"Yes, that's true."

"It's very urgent for me to meet with you. I spoke with him yesterday. He ask
ed me to contact you."

"You mean he's alive?"

Kendon could hear her weeping. He pictured in his mind those final moments, how Meller's eyes had held his until life drained from him. Now he was talking to the daughter of a man he had to kill.

Kendon's head began to hurt. He couldn't tell her the truth. He rubbed his forehead and said, "I have a lot to talk to you about. But I can't talk over the phone. It's too complicated. Where can we meet?"

She was silent for a moment.

"I'm sorry. Give me your name again."

"Michael Kendon."

"Wait for me in the ward, Mr. Kendon. I'll tell them you're coming up. Give me half an hour to get there."

Chapter 7

Kendon sat in the small waiting room feeling upbeat that he was at last a step closer to the one-one-five pod, but he wondered about Virginia Woolf. What was the connection between a long-dead British author and the power unit for the beam weapon?

After ten minutes of restless waiting, he got up and stared out of the window at the electric glow of Austin. He was moved by the nighttime beauty, but in his mind the city view was soon overlaid by the image of an asteroid hitting Earth at an incredible speed, sending a blast of vaporized sea in every direction at a thousand miles per second. He could see its searing force tearing through the city followed by a deluge of molten rock.

The image was too painful to sustain. He turned away from the window and walked up and down the corridor to work off the tension the waiting was causing him. As he paced back and forth, he peered into the private rooms. Through one of the doors, he could see a young girl lying on a bed, the covers pulled up to her neck. She was completely bald, and at first he thought he was looking at a large doll. Her eyes were closed, but her lips were pressed tightly together and were moving. Her face was flinching, and he understood she was struggling against pain.

When he saw that no one else was in the corridor, Kendon

stepped into the room and sat quietly in a chair next to the bed. He stared at the girl, at the dark circles under her eyes and at the teddy bear next to her cheek. He guessed she was six or seven years old.

She sensed his presence. Her eyes opened, and she turned her head toward him.

Her voice weak, she said, "Are you a doctor?"

"No, just a friend."

"You smell funny."

Kendon looked down at his clothes and smiled.

"That's from the guano."

"What's that?"

"Bat droppings. I was in a cavern this morning, Carlsbad Caverns."

"Did you see bats?"

"Millions of them."

"My mommy said she'll take me there when I get better."

"Are you in pain?"

"Yes. The nurse gave me my medicine, but it still hurts."

"What's the matter with you?"

"I have a brain tumor."

Kendon felt a wave of sadness. So young and already suffering so much. He forgot about the impending doom and even his reason for being at the hospital. He looked at the palms of his hands, then rubbed them together slowly.

"What's your name?"

"Molly."

"I know how to take the pain away, Molly. Do you want me to?"

"Oh, please, it hurts so much."

He placed his hands over her forehead. "Did they tell you where it is?"

"On the left side, in the middle."

He positioned his hands and kept them there gently. She was

looking up at him. Her eyes were brown, and he thought he detected a gleam of merriment, like they were playing a game.

"I want you to close your eyes and imagine it going away. Imagine it shrinking slowly until it disappears. Can you do that?"

"I think so."

After a few minutes, Kendon began to see things about the girl, just as he had seen images about the dentist earlier that day at the caverns. A picture formed in his mind of her in a playground holding a large ball and throwing it, then another of her in a yard playing with a dog, tossing a stick and laughing when the dog retrieved it. He could see her in the hospital room with people he understood were her parents. He sensed their sadness and their efforts at cheerfulness when their hearts wanted to break.

The girl's eyes were closed, and Kendon wondered if she had drifted into sleep, but after ten minutes she opened them and said, "I got it to shrink down to the size of a pea."

Kendon smiled. "That's great. Make it go away completely. Use the power of your mind to make it go away. You have that power."

"It doesn't hurt anymore," she said.

"Molly, listen to me. I have to go soon. But someone else could do this, you know. Like your parents, or one of the nurses. Tell them what to do."

He kept his hands on her head for another ten minutes. He felt his hands growing hot and moved them an inch above the girl's head. He focused all of the resources of his mind on the tumor. His mind became a scalpel, and he imagined cutting the tumor out and then holding it in the palm of his hand. He imagined throwing it hard like you would throw a stone, far off into the distance where it could do no more harm.

A minute later, he heard a voice at the door.

"Mr. Kendon?"

He looked up. At the door was an attractive woman wearing a white physician's coat, tall and with brown hair down to her shoulders, looking exactly like the graduate in Meller's photo, but older. He could vaguely see Donald Meller's features in her face, particularly in the shape of her eyes. She was looking at him inquisitively, and he realized he wasn't supposed to be there.

"Molly and I are old friends," he said.

"He took the pain away, Dr. Laura. With his hands."

The woman stepped up to the bed and pulled the blanket up to girl's chin. "I'm glad to hear that, Molly. Where are your parents?"

"They went to get something to eat."

"Good. You rest, and I'll check on you later."

She turned to Kendon, who noticed her eyes were reddened, as if she had been crying.

"Please come with me," she said.

He followed her down the corridor and was taken by her confident bearing. They went into a small office that was lined with books and publications. A window gave a view of the landscaped hospital grounds.

"Please, have a seat."

On her desk was a large purse. As soon as she sat down, she pulled the purse onto her lap and eyed him closely. He realized his appearance was suspicious, dressed as he was in rumpled clothes that smelled of guano. He made a gesture toward his clothes and shook his head. "I literally had to crawl through a cave to get here."

"I hope this isn't a joke, Mr. Kendon. I haven't seen my father in ten years, and then out of the blue I get a telephone call from a complete stranger telling me he saw him just yesterday. I suppose you can imagine how I feel."

Kendon grappled with how to proceed. If he told her the truth bluntly, she wouldn't believe a word of it and would likely call hospital security to have him thrown out.

"I know that when you were growing up you were very close to your father. He told me a lot about you. It was very painful for him not to be with you."

"Why didn't he call me?"

"I don't have good news for you. Your father died yesterday. I was with him. Before he died, he asked me to find you. He wanted me to tell you how much he loved you. Those were his last words."

He watched her struggle to control her emotions. "Where was this?"

"In New Mexico, near Alamogordo."

"Why wasn't I contacted? I would have gone there to be with him."

"He wasn't allowed contact with the outside world."

"By whom? I don't understand what you're talking about."

"Your father was involved in highly classified research, initially through Bach-Merling. At some point he came to know too much and was held against his will, along with many other scientists and engineers, in secret facilities in New Mexico. He spent the last ten years of his life hundreds of feet underground in a facility in northern New Mexico. He was a captive. That's why you didn't hear from him."

"This is a free country. How is that possible?"

"It's not as free as you think. There's a dark side to it that's not under the control of your elected officials. The democratic part of your political system doesn't know anything about it."

"And you, what was your role in this? Are you a scientist?"

"I was with the security apparatus."

"You mean like a guard?"

"As an intelligence officer."

"How did my father die?"

Kendon struggled with how to tell her enough to obtain her help without having to admit that he himself had killed her father. He realized she would need a lot of preparation to understand.

From the moment he first saw her, he had been getting strong impressions from her. It seemed that all he had to do now to learn about people was to be in their presence, and he would pick up mentally on things. It had just occurred with Molly, and now images were filling his mind about Laura Meller. He sensed above all tragedy, and not just the tragedy of her father's disappearance. There was another: She had been married and her husband had died. Kendon had the impression he had killed himself because an image of a gun formed in his mind. He became certain her husband had committed suicide with a gun, but the image he was picking up on had more immediacy. He suddenly realized Laura was thinking of a gun—a gun that was in the purse on her lap. He pulled his backpack up from the floor onto his lap and felt the bulge of his semiautomatic pistol.

He continued, "Your father escaped four days ago with other scientists and engineers. I helped them escape. All of them made it out of the facility and dispersed, but within a few days, they were located. The ones who didn't die resisting capture either committed suicide or were tortured to death."

Laura shifted slightly in her chair. Her face had hardened. She shook her head in disbelief. "If what you're saying is true, then why don't you go to the police?"

"They don't have any way to get into such facilities, and it's not something they have the power to deal with."

"None of this sounds plausible," she said. "How did you get out?"

"I escaped this morning. I'm being hunted, and if I'm caught I'm going to be killed, just like the others."

With an air of casualness, Laura opened her purse and reached inside. Kendon whipped out his pistol just as she leveled her gun at him. They aimed at each other across the desk. He felt mildly amused, pleased by her spunk, but he could tell she was frightened because her hand was trembling.

"You've never killed anyone, Laura, but I have. I had to kill several people this morning. That's how I escaped."

"You are known as Arkasha," Laura said coldly.

Kendon was stunned. "How do you know that?"

"They had your picture on television. They gave your name and your alias. They said you murdered two men at Carlsbad Caverns this morning, two federal agents."

Kendon nodded. It made sense. The Breeders had to know by now he was no longer implanted and that they and the Directorate had been fooled. It made sense to use upper-world resources to capture him. The Directorate had channels it could use to pass on the location of the bodies and provide the information about Kendon needed for a manhunt. Once he was in police hands, it would be easy for the Directorate to grab him.

But only two dead? He wondered about the numbers that were reported. Did it mean that Bogdan had survived, or one of the gooneys?

He said, "Why did you come here to meet me? Why didn't you go the police?"

"I wanted to know why you called me. I wanted to know what you know about my father."

Kendon thought about it for a moment. He was sure she hadn't alerted anyone, so he wasn't in immediate danger of capture. He had to earn her trust.

"How about if I give myself up to you?"

"That would be the right thing to do."

"I want something in return. I want you to listen to me. If you don't believe what I have to say to you, then call the police. All I ask is that you listen."

Laura didn't respond. Kendon lowered his gun, gripped it by the barrel, and handed it to her.

"Take it. I surrender."

She shoved it into her purse, but kept her pistol pointed at him.

"Talk," she said.

"Your father said to ask you about Virginia Woolf. He said her books meant a lot to you when you were young."

Kendon studied Laura's reaction. He knew he had touched something deep in her because he could see mental images the name evoked—a room with a roll-up oak desk and a black and white portrait of a woman with an anguished face on the wall above it. He saw a man who was thin, handsome, and intense. Kendon had the impression the man was her husband and that he was a poet. He was certain he had hit a psychic motherlode.

"Go on," she said.

"That should convince you that I knew your father. How many people in your life know about your interest in Virginia Woolf?"

She shrugged. "Dozens."

He recited two short poems of hers, one light-hearted and witty that she had called *Butterfly Moon*, and another that was dark and brooding: *Hero for the Damned*.

"How do you know those poems?" she demanded. "They were never published."

"Your father used to recite your poems from memory. He was very proud of you. There is no such a thing as literature in the underground. I found them very beautiful, so I memorized them."

He had not intended to flatter her, only to speak the truth, but he realized she was pleased by the fact that he knew the poems by heart.

He closed his eyes. He began to see more about her. The relevant experiences coalesced around poetry, including the tragic experiences. Soon, he saw the image of Breeder eyes, large, dark, and chilling.

So, the Breeders were part of her tragedy!

With his eyes still closed, he said, "You were married to a poet. It was blissful at first, but it turned tragic. You were experiencing abductions, a series of them. Your body was being used to create a hybrid creature, half-human, half-alien. Your husband realized this was happening, but he could do nothing to protect you. What they were doing to you annihilated him as a man. He fell into a depression, then one day he killed himself."

Tears formed in Laura's eyes. "How do you know any of this? Not even my father knew. It started after he disappeared."

"It's coming from you, Laura. You are telling me."

"I haven't told you anything."

"Not consciously."

She stood up. "I don't want to hear any more of this. Please leave. Just take your gun and leave."

"It's because of what they did to you that I'm here. There's a way to stop them. Your father found a way, but he died before he could carry out his plan. No one else is left to fight them. It's up to you and me now."

"Everything you're saying is nonsense."

"Really? When they brought you to a brightly-lit room and had you hold an infant, you knew it wasn't totally human, but you knew it was yours. Was that nonsense? Why don't you tell me about that, Laura? Tell me what you thought about and what you felt when you were holding that half-human creature that you knew was yours."

"Maybe I should shoot you just to make you shut up."

"If you do, you're going to die in two days."

"You're insane."

"There are millions of those half-human creatures now. Enough, in fact, to replace the human race, and that was always the intention behind the abductions. It's going to happen on Sunday. They've diverted an asteroid so it will hit Earth and bring an end to the human race. Unless we stop them, Laura, you and I. Your father created a weapon to deal with it. Part of it is in your possession, only you don't know you have it. Virginia Woolf is the key to finding it. That's what your father told me before he died."

Laura's breathing had become rapid and shallow. Still holding the gun, she squeezed her hands against her ears. The phone suddenly rang. She grabbed it as if it was a lifeline to the sane world. She listened without comment and nodded, then slowly put the receiver down. She looked for a moment at her gun, then at Kendon.

"What did you do to Molly?"

"You mean the girl in the ward?"

"Yes."

"I felt sorry for her. All my life I've been able to heal with my hands, so while I was waiting for you, I tried to help her."

"She has an inoperable brain tumor. This morning she could barely stand up. At the most, she has a month to live. That was a call from the nurse. She said Molly is jumping up and down on the bed and acting like a naughty child. She says she won't stop until she sees you again."

Laura put the pistol back into her purse and pointed to the door. "Walk in front of me. I haven't made up my mind about you yet."

As they walked down the corridor, Kendon noticed a group of people at the far end of the ward in the waiting area. They were standing at the windows looking up at the sky. Some were pointing. One was a nurse who turned and motioned repeatedly to Laura to join them, but Laura pointed at Molly's room to show where she was going.

The girl was jumping up and down on the bed and was holding her teddy bear as if dancing with it. A man and a woman were there, who Kendon guessed were Molly's parents.

"That's him, that's the man who took the pain away," Molly said when she saw Kendon.

Kendon winked at her. The dark circles were gone from under her eyes, which now sparkled with vitality. She threw her arms out for Kendon to hug her. The woman was dabbing tears from her eyes and the man was grinning.

"I don't know what you did to her, mister," the man said with a drawl, "but I sure want to thank you."

Laura got Molly to sit on the edge of the bed. With a thumb, she raised her eyelids and examined her eyes. She took her pulse and with a stethoscope listened to her heart.

She said to the parents, "Her energy level is perfectly normal. We'll do some testing to find out exactly what's going on here."

Turning to Kendon, Laura said, "Maybe I *should* take you seriously."

Kendon nodded and pointed to the door. When they were out in the corridor, he said, "What does Virginia Woolf mean to you?"

She was quiet for a moment, then said, "When I was growing up, we lived in the countryside. I was fond of her books. One of them is called *A Room of One's Own*. I liked to write poetry and stories, so my father fixed up my room with an antique writing desk. It was near the window and had a view of the hills. That's where I wrote, in a room of my own."

"We need to go there. Do you still own the property?"

"It's part of a trust, but essentially I own it. I often spend the weekend there. It's not terribly far, only an hour's drive from here."

They were interrupted by the nurse who had been staring out of the waiting-room window.

"Dr. Meller! Dr. Meller! Come here. You've got to see this."

Kendon and Laura went up to the window and peered up where the nurse was pointing. High in the night sky were bright disk-shaped lights that were hovering at an altitude of about three thousand feet. Kendon counted twelve in all.

"What are they?" Laura asked weakly.

"What do you think?"

"I don't want to think."

Kendon pulled her away from the window. He touched the bridge of her nose.

"You're implanted. When you were first abducted, they embedded a device that works like a transmitter so they know where to find you when they need you again."

She became panicky. "Don't let them take me. I don't want to go through that again."

"They've linked us together. They're after what I'm after."

"I can't run. No matter where I go they'll know. You need to get out of here. I'll draw you a map."

"No," Kendon said, with enough vehemence for the people at the window to turn and look at them. He lowered his voice. "Block it from your mind. The implant also helps them penetrate your mind if they want to. Don't let any images form in your mind. Think white, think bright. Keep repeating that to yourself. Imagine a ball of white light."

She closed her eyes. "Okay, I see a ball of white. Now what?"

"We have to get you X-rayed. If you have an implant, it has to be removed. We don't have much time.

"Then let's go down to radiology," she said.

Kendon picked up on the panic in her voice and took her hands. "I promise I won't let anything happen to you."

They rode an elevator one floor down. As it descended, Laura gave Kendon his pistol back, which he shoved into the backpack. They followed a yellow line down a corridor to the radiology room.

"I don't know if anyone's on duty this late," she said.

A short, stocky man in a white lab coat was seated at a workstation. He stood up when they entered.

"I'm glad you're here, Morgan," Laura said. "I need an X-ray of the bridge of my nose. It's urgent."

"I don't think I'm authorized to do that, Doctor."

"I'm authorizing you."

Kendon smiled politely but firmly at him and nodded. "It can't wait."

"What's the problem?"

Kendon said, "I suspect she has something right here at the bridge of the nose, embedded in the cartilage. Probably T-shaped. Of unknown material, possibly metallic. We need to know for sure if it's there. We need at least two images—one from the top, one from the side."

The technician shrugged. He pointed to the table. Laura lay on her back. He swung the arm of the machine over her and made some adjustments, then slid a large, thin cassette underneath the table. Kendon joined him in the adjacent room, behind a leaded glass window. After clicking the X-ray machine, the technician returned to the room to turn her on her side for a second X-ray.

Kendon, meanwhile, found an office with a window and scanned the sky. He could see three of the disks. He was sure the others were still up there, but the building blocked his view.

He felt them probing, trying to enter his mind, but he was able from years of effort to create a mental shield. He was shrouded in white, living in the center of a blizzard. He felt secure mentally, but he also felt the beginnings of panic: He was certain they or their surrogates were going to make a move of some kind. Time was running out.

He rushed back to the radiology room just as the technician finished processing the X-rays. The X-rays were digitalized and were displayed on a large monitor.

The technician pointed to an object. "Is that what you mean?"

Laura's face whitened. "It's been there all this time, and I didn't know."

Kendon said, "It has to be removed immediately. Who's here who can do surgery?"

The technician said, "I ran into Dr. Urquidi ten minutes ago in the corridor. He said he was visiting a patient."

Laura picked up the desk phone. "Which ward?"

"Orthopedics."

She punched four buttons and waited. It took a minute to connect with the other doctor. "Dr. Urquidi? This is Dr. Laura Meller. We have an emergency. Can you meet me in surgery immediately?"

She was gripping the receiver so tightly her knuckles whitened. Her ear pressed to the receiver, she bobbed her head up and down as she listened and said finally in a frustrated voice, "I don't have time to explain over the phone. Just be there. I repeat, this is an emergency."

As they rushed out the door, Kendon grabbed the technician by the arm. "I need your help. Come with me."

The surgery ward was on the same floor as the cancer ward. They were in the operating room in two minutes.

Kendon said to Laura, "White out your mind. Think white, think bright. Don't let anything in your mind betray what we're doing."

A half a minute later, Dr. Urquidi, a thin-faced man with an arrogant expression and cold eyes, entered. He stared at Kendon, Laura, and the technician.

"And what is the nature of the emergency, doctor?" he said.

She called up the X-rays on the surgery room monitor and pointed to the implant.

Kendon said, "You've got ten minutes to take it out."

"What are you talking about?" the doctor huffed. "This doesn't look like an emergency, and I don't have time for this right now. It needs to be scheduled."

Kendon grabbed him by the arm and walked him to a nearby office with a window. He pointed to the sky. "You see those lights? They're alien spaceships. They're after Dr. Meller, and they're after me. That T-shaped object in her nose is an implant, a tracking device. They put it there. It has to come out."

The doctor struggled to break free of Kendon's grip. "This is ridiculous," he said.

Kendon whipped the gun out of the backpack. He put the barrel to the doctor's head. "And what about this? Is this ridiculous?"

"Just who the hell are you?"

"If I told you, you wouldn't believe me."

Still gripping his arm, Kendon marched the doctor back into the operating room. Laura had already positioned surgical instruments, a suturing kit, a vial of local anesthetic, and a syringe on a stainless steel tray next to an operating table. She had taken her doctor's smock off and strapped a green garment over her clothes.

She looked with surprise at Kendon's gun. The technician was staring at it, too, his mouth wide open. He glanced nervously at Laura.

"Are you doing this under duress?" Urquidi asked her.

"Yes, but not from him." She pointed to the sky. "From them."

She lay down on the operating table. "I'm ready, Dr. Urquidi. Please proceed."

Kendon released his grip on the doctor and said, "Skip all the pre-operation stuff. There's no time. Just start with the local anesthetic."

"I want to know what this is all about and why you need to point a gun at me," the surgeon said.

"I'll tell you all about it while you work." Kendon shoved the gun into his belt and turned to the X-ray technician. "I want you to extract blood from her. Enough to fill a vial."

The surgeon quickly prepared the anesthetic and then made injections on both sides of the bridge of Laura's nose. As he became engrossed in the work, the arrogance was replaced by a look of cool professionalism.

Kendon stood behind Laura, his hands smoothing back her long hair. He cupped her face between his hands and leaned close. He whispered, "Your father was a great man, Laura. You have his greatness in you."

She closed her eyes. Kendon said softly, "Think white, think bright. Think of a ball of whiteness growing and filling the room. It has warmth and nothing can hurt you when you're wrapped in its warmth."

He repeated it in a soothing voice until he could see she had slipped into a state of deep relaxation.

"The anesthetic hasn't had time to work," Urquidi protested.

"She won't feel anything," Kendon said. "Go ahead."

After a glance at the X-rays, the surgeon made two small incisions and quickly exposed the cartilage. After he rinsed and scraped, Kendon could see a thin metallic line.

"That's an alien implant," Kendon said. "It was manufactured forty light years from here."

As the surgeon cut into the cartilage around the sides of the object, Kendon gave a brief account of the alien presence and their ultimate objective, a narrative in short, declarative sentences, each with the impact of a hammer blow. He told them of the approaching asteroid and that it had been deliberately diverted to strike the world.

As he spoke, he watched the surgeon's face. Urquidi said nothing, but he began blinking more rapidly and his breathing quickened. The X-ray technician, who was standing nearby extracting blood from Laura's arm, turned pale.

Soon, with the help of a thin, curved forceps, the surgeon extracted the implant. Kendon took the vial, now full of Laura's blood, and handed it to him.

"Drop it in here. It needs the body fluids of the host to work."

After the surgeon dropped it inside, Kendon screwed the cap on and handed it to the technician. "Not of word of this to anybody. We have a way of defeating the asteroid. If we fail because you've told somebody about what's happened here, I guarantee you that in two days you and six billion other people are going to be dead."

The technician's lower lip was trembling. "What do you want me to do with this?"

"Get to your car and drive to the nearest truck stop. Plant it on the back of a large transport truck. The aliens are smart, but they're not that smart. They will follow the truck."

The surgeon quickly sewed up the incisions and cleaned the blood from Laura's face. A minute later, she sat up, a small bandage over her nose. She seemed dazed. Kendon took the green gown off her and led her by the arm.

The surgeon stepped back to let them pass. He didn't look either of them in the eyes.

"Good luck," he said almost inaudibly.

They rushed down the hallway to the elevators, but after pressing the button, Kendon said, "Forget the elevator. Which way to the back entrance?"

They went down a staircase, then followed a wide corridor that led to another hallway. Soon they were outside the building, walking toward the parking lot. As they got near, Kendon spotted the X-ray technician. He was struggling to get away from three tall men in long black coats who were wearing sunglasses even though it was nighttime. Next to them was a long, sleek limousine-like vehicle that wasn't quite touching the ground.

"Who are they? Are those the agents you were telling me about?" Laura said in a frightened voice. "What are they doing to Morgan?"

Kendon pulled her by the arm across the street. They rushed down a side street to his Jeep. He opened the passenger door and pushed Laura in, then jumped in on the driver's side and started the motor.

As he sped away from the hospital, Kendon said, "Those aren't Directorate agents. They're hybrids. They're taking Morgan away and very soon they'll know everything."

"Are they going to hurt him?"

"Yes."

"Oh, my God," she said, shaking her head. "Can't we do anything to help him?"

"No," Kendon said. "Now, which way do we go?"

Chapter 8

Tepler and Gabriela searched for her uncle at the marina at La Parguera, a fishing village ten miles north of Cabo Rojo. On a landing next to wooden boats painted in combinations of bright red, green, yellow, and blue were three fishermen mending nets. Their faces were weathered, and they were wearing blood stained cotton shirts with buttons missing.

Tepler and Gabriela walked up to them. "I'm looking for my uncle, Miguel Estrada," she said.

"You mean *El Mudo?*" one of them said without looking up from the net. "I saw him go out in the morning. He should have been back by now."

"How is the catch?" Gabriela asked.

"Yellowfin. Good size, but not much."

They spoke in the rapid, familiar Spanish of Puerto Rico, with clipped words that always made Tepler strain to understand. But he had picked up enough to know that Gabriela's uncle no longer kept his boat at the marina, but down the road at a mangrove shack where he lived.

"I know where it is," she said.

Tepler drove slowly down the road, bordered on one side by mangrove thickets that grew out of the water along the shore. The other side of the road was lined with modest pastel-colored homes.

"Why do they call him The Mute?"

"That's the nickname they gave him when he stopped talking fifteen years ago."

As they got closer to her uncle's home, Gabriela said. "This is why I came back to Puerto Rico, Eric. This is why I gave up my music studies. It is because of what is happening now."

"I don't understand," Tepler said.

"I was studying violin in New York. I had a scholarship, but then I came back. At first, it was because my father fell ill, but I ended up staying. I knew in my heart my uncle's prediction was true, and I felt I had to be here because of it. Somehow, it was important for me to be here for this."

She had taken up teaching to help support her family, gave violin lessons on the side, and occasionally performed in local concerts. When she mentioned a performance a year earlier in Mayaguez, he said he had gone to it and remembered seeing her, and he recalled thinking at the time how talented she was—and incredibly beautiful!

She pointed to an opening in the mangroves. Tepler pulled off the road and stopped at a flimsy gate that blocked a sagging plank walkway over the water of the mangrove thicket. The walkway led to a two-room shack where her uncle lived. It was built over the water on pilings, with a corrugated iron roof that extended over a narrow porch.

They sat on a bench next to the front door and waited for her uncle to show up. All Tepler could see were wide channels formed by mangrove islands. Other shacks were nestled here and there at the edge of the islands. It was a beautiful and calming setting, and he wished he was experiencing this moment with Gabriela under different circumstances.

While they waited, Tepler's mind drifted to thoughts about death. He had first experienced the shock of death with the loss of his parents. His father, a hypnotherapist, and his mother, a high school teacher, had died seven years earlier when a drunk driver broadsided their car at an intersection. Though he had seen them lying in coffins, he still could not fully grasp that his own end would come one day. He couldn't truly imagine himself no longer existing—death happened to other people.

All that had changed in the last day, particularly in the last few hours, when primal fear gripped him in his guts, chest, and throat. He felt like he was in a bad dream where he was stuck in the middle of a road and a huge truck was speeding toward him. No matter how hard he struggled, he couldn't get out of the way.

Tepler stood up and looked at the sky. In his mind, he could see the immense ablative flame that would appear the moment the asteroid penetrated the Earth's upper atmosphere. He knew that if he were able to see it, he would have at the most six more seconds to live: five seconds before impact, and one second before the blast vaporized every molecule of his body. He began to feel dizzy and thought he was going to vomit.

He felt Gabriela's hand slide into his. He turned to face her and he could see that she was thinking the same thoughts. They threw their arms around each other, and he felt her warm tears soaking through his shirt. After a few minutes, the fear that had gripped him slipped away and he felt calm again. He thought that if he was going to die in two days, he hoped it would be while holding her.

As he felt her soothing warmth, the image of the lighthouse-observatory and the huge cylinder came to mind. He wondered if he should tell her about his discovery. He wanted to whisper to her that it had to be a weapon of some kind, a weapon to use against the asteroid, but he decided against revealing anything until hearing her uncle's story. Perhaps some piece of information, some detail, would emerge that would explain what was inside the cylinder. If there was a connection, perhaps there was hope. And if there was hope, then he would share the hope with her.

Before long, they heard the buzz of an outboard motor. In the distance, Tepler saw a small boat heading their way. Soon he could make out the red and yellow hull of a low-slung wood boat, a design typical of the fishing boats of the region. A slight, older man was seated next to the outboard motor.

"That's Miguel," Gabriela said.

They waited on the porch for the craft to drift up to the shack. Tepler was surprised by how old Gabriela's uncle appeared. He was short, thin, and stooped, and he was wearing a grimy blue baseball cap. Three yellowfins were at the bottom of the boat.

Miguel at first seemed not to notice them. He tied the boat to a metal pole jutting from the water next to the porch, then he looked up at Gabriela.

"*Hola, Tío*," Gabriela said, a warm smile brightening her eyes.

The man's face was deeply lined and dark brown from a lifetime in the sun, but his lower face was lightened by several days' growth of white beard. His hair was white and tousled where it stuck out underneath the blue cap. He seemed confused at first by their presence, but then he said Gabriela's name as if just recognizing her. He smiled and asked about her mother. He didn't once look at Tepler.

"*Tío*, this is my friend, Eric. He is the astronomer at the lighthouse. He has something very important to talk to you about."

Miguel looked at him for the first time. The fisherman's eyes were deeply set, and Tepler could see fear and mistrust in them. They were the eyes of someone who had been deeply hurt and who was afraid of being hurt again.

The old man nodded slightly, but didn't say anything. He held up the palm of his hand as if to indicate he needed to finish something. He waddled to the center of the boat, picked up one of the yellowfins, then waddled with it back to the porch and slid it onto the floor. He repeated the maneuver twice more and climbed agilely to the porch. He unlocked the door and bent down to pick up one of the yellowfins. Tepler stooped down and grabbed the remaining two just under the tail. He estimated each weighed between forty and fifty pounds.

The room served as a kitchen, living room, and workshop. Miguel pointed to a deep sink, and Tepler dropped the fish in. The old man offered him a towel to wipe his hands and said to Gabriela, "What do you wish of me?"

She hesitated a moment before answering. She took his rough hands into hers and said, "We have come here to tell you that you were right about the asteroid, *Tío*. It's coming, just like you predicted."

After blinking a number of times, the old man said, "How do you know this?"

"Eric discovered it. He showed me the images he took with the telescope, and then I told him about you."

Tepler balled his right hand into a fist, held it in the air, and then smashed his fist into the palm of his other hand. "That's what could happen in two days. Gabriela said you knew about this fifteen years ago. It's very important for me to ask you about it."

The old man seemed confused. He pointed to the fish. "I have to take these to the market."

Tepler had noted a twitch to the man's left eye the moment he stepped out of the boat. The eye began twitching again rapidly.

"I don't remember much anymore," Miguel said.

"Please, *Tío*," Gabriela said. "Please talk to him about it, for the sake of your sisters, your brothers, for everyone's sake." She pointed to Tepler. "He is a good person. He is respectful of you. He is not going to hurt you."

Tepler realized the uncle had likely repressed much of the memory because too many painful things had happened to him as a result of speaking about his experience. But nothing important is ever truly forgotten, Tepler knew. His father had shown him how repressed memories can be resurrected and had taught him the technique.

Tepler smiled at him warmly. "Okay, so you don't remember. But I want the fish. I'll buy the entire catch. Can you gut them, de-bone them, filet them?"

"If you wish."

Next to the deep sink was a cutting table. Tepler sat with Gabriela at a small dining table while the uncle set to work carving up the fish.

The room was humble but neatly kept. The walls were wain-scoted in turquoise, the upper wall in yellow. The ceiling was made of thick beams overlaid with water-stained plywood. A large rug covered the wood planks of the floor. In one corner was a stand with a crucifix, a statue of the Virgin Mary, and votive candles. With intense focus, Miguel slit the fish open and cleaned them, then carved them into steaks. When the cutting was done, he took out a block of ice from a freezer, broke it up with an ice pick, then packed the cuts in plastic bags with chipped ice.

When he was nearly finished, Tepler got up and stood closely behind him. He put his hand lightly on the man's shoulder and said softly, "Where were you when they abducted you, Miguel?"

The old man's hands were busy scooping ice into one of the bags. Tepler was watching his hands. As soon as he asked the question, the hands stopped scooping and hovered just above the ice, trembling slightly.

"On the road to La Parguera, late at night."

"What were you doing there?"

"I was coming back from Boqueron, from visiting my sister, Gabriela's mother."

"What did you see?"

"A brilliant light. At first I thought it was a truck coming up the road. But the light came from above."

"And then?"

"And then I was in a room and there were other people and they told us about the asteroid."

"What else did they tell you?"

"I don't remember."

"How long were you there?"

"I don't remember."

"What did they look like?"

"Not like the gray ones. They were tall. They had fair hair."

Tepler left his hand on the old man's shoulder. "I have a way to help you to remember, Miguel, a way to relax you so that important memories can come back. And it only works with very special people who have very special things to remember. Do you want to try?"

The fisherman glanced at Gabriela. She smiled warmly at him, then stood up and pushed her chair close to him. The fisherman sat down with his hands in his lap.

Tepler had sensed the fisherman was basically of a warm and trusting nature and would be easy to hypnotize. He sat in another chair directly opposite him, their knees almost touching. After putting him through a series of relaxation routines, it took Tepler only ten minutes to lead him through the several stages of hypnosis into a deep trance.

Miguel sat in the chair, his body slightly slumped, staring ahead of him. His eyes seemed glassy.

To prove to Gabriela her uncle was indeed in a hypnotic trance, Tepler asked him to place the fingertips of his hands together, showing him what to do. Then he said, "Your fingers are attracted to each other like magnets, Miguel. Powerful magnets. They're stuck together and no matter how hard you try, you can't separate them."

Miguel struggled, but couldn't break his fingers apart. His face had a look of wonderment.

Then Tepler said, "Blow on your fingers now. When you do, they will come apart."

Miguel blew on them, and they came apart.

"Very good," Tepler continued. "I want you to close your eyes because now we're going back to that night on the road, Miguel, the night you saw the bright light."

The old man began the tale of the abduction by recalling that the light was no longer hovering, but was on the road, blocking him. "I am afraid . . . I see two men . . . I think they are Swedish. They take me by the arms. They are not speaking, but somehow I hear them say not to be afraid, that no harm will come to me. We walk into the light. It is a large vehicle and we go through a door without walking. They take me to a room where there are other people. I am sitting in a chair for a long time and I think we are moving but I'm not sure. After a while, they bring someone else into the room, a man, and they make him sit down."

"Why do you think the people who brought you aboard are Swedish?"

"They are tall. They have fair hair. They are very beautiful and have soft features, almost like women, but they are men."

"How are they dressed?"

"In suits, silver suits that fit tightly to the skin."

"I want you to look straight ahead of you, Miguel. What do you see?"

He blinked a few times and seemed to be pondering what was before his eyes. "I see a table, dark gray, but without legs. It's round. Behind it I don't see anything."

"Above the table. What do you see?"

"The same thing, but upside down, about the height of a man above the bottom table."

"Other people are in the room," Tepler continued. "Which side of you are they on?"

"On both sides."

"I want you to look at the ones on the right and describe them."

Miguel strained to turn his head, but was unable to, almost as when he was trying to pull his fingers apart but had been told he couldn't.

"I can only see what is in front of me," he said.

"You saw people when you were brought into the room. What do you remember about them?"

"They look like they are Puerto Ricans. One man I think I have seen before, a taxi driver in Boqueron. I don't know the others. Two women and three other men."

"Where are the beings that brought you aboard?"

"I don't see them."

"Do they come back?"

"Two of them but not the same who brought me in there. One of them is speaking. I see his lips move and he speaks in Spanish, in high Spanish, *Castellano*. His voice is very beautiful and the sound makes me think of poetry."

"What is he saying?"

"He is saying to watch the table, and he is telling us what is there."

"Are you watching the table now?"

"Yes."

"What do you see?"

"I see images that are moving like they are real but I can see through them . . . I see things I don't understand . . . I see animals I have never seen before. It is where they are from, their planet. There are trees but they are different, very big like in a rain forest. They live under the ground, in the side of hills, not on the top of the ground, to preserve the beauty of the surface."

"Does he say anything about your planet, about Earth?"

"He says there is danger. In the future, an asteroid will strike near Puerto Rico. I see an image of Earth and I see the asteroid hitting it. I don't want to look, but I can't close my eyes. It creates fires everywhere and the air is filled with smoke."

"Where?"

"All over the planet."

"Does he say when this will occur?"

"In fifteen years."

"Why is he telling you this?"

"He says that it doesn't have to happen. It will only happen if we let it happen."

"Is something causing the asteroid to hit Earth?"

"The Breeders."

"Does he say who they are?"

"Not in words. I see an image of them on the round table, and I understand they are called Breeders, and that they will make it happen. I don't like their eyes."

As he spoke, his body tensed up, and his eyes showed fear.

Tepler said, "What else are you told about these Breeders?"

"The blond one says that they cannot interfere except to warn us, and that it is up to the people of this world to prevent it from happening."

"How can we prevent it from happening?"

"He doesn't say. He says we must tell others about what we have been shown. If we do, then heroes of the human race will step forward, and they will be able to prevent it. That is why we are being shown these things. We must warn the world of what is to come."

"Have you seen these creatures other than in the image?"

Miguel's eyes began to flutter. Tepler realized he had made a mistake. He had changed tenses and had shifted Miguel's attention away from what was occurring aboard the spacecraft.

"Never mind," Tepler said hastily. "We don't have to talk about the Breeders right now. What other images are you being shown?"

"None."

"What happens after that?"

"I am on the road again. I go back home."

Tepler glanced at Gabriela. She was listening with rapt attention, her eyes not quite focused, as if living in her mind what her uncle was describing. But then she noticed that Tepler was looking at her. She was about to say something, but he put his index finger to his lips and shook his head. He made a gesture of writing, and she scribbled something on a piece of paper and handed it to him.

"Ask him about the flying saucers he saw coming out of Bahía Sucia. And the creatures he saw near there."

He nodded to her. He knew the bay. It was near Cabo Rojo.

Tepler said, "I want you to go back to the time you saw something coming out of the water at Bahía Sucia."

He waited a moment for the answer, but Miguel didn't say anything. Tepler realized the fisherman had simply followed instructions and had mentally gone back to the incident, but he had not been asked anything about it yet.

"Where are you when you see it?"

"In my boat. I am fishing and I see something big leaving the water."

"What is it?"

"It's a large spaceship. It is round and it flips once when it comes out of the water and flies away fast, straight up in the air."

"How big is it?"

"Thirty or forty meters across."

"Are there more?"

"Yes, another one comes out of the water. It does not do a flip like the first one, but rises straight up. A lot of water is swirling underneath it."

"What do you do then?"

"I'm afraid and head for the shore. I get out of my boat."

"What do you see?"

"Creatures. They come out of the brush where the sand starts."

"What do they look like?"

"At first I think they are children because they are small and skinny. But their heads are very big and their eyes are very big, too."

"How many are there?"

"Three, I only see three. They see me and then they run back into the brush."

"How are you feeling?"

"I am very frightened. I get back in my boat and leave."

"Have you seen creatures like that again?"

"No."

"Are they like the ones that you were shown when you were taken aboard the spaceship."

"No, those were bigger, taller, with stronger builds. These are smaller, like skinny children with very long arms."

Tepler leaned back and wondered where to go with the questioning and if it was necessary to continue under hypnosis. The abductees had been given a highly specific warning of a disaster that Tepler knew for a fact was about to happen, and they had been given instructions to tell the world about it. From what Gabriela had told him, he knew her uncle had made the prediction public and had suffered ridicule. He would certainly remember those events without the aid of hypnosis.

Tepler decided to bring him out of the trance. If necessary, he could always re-induce the hypnotic state. He leaned toward the fisherman. "Miguel, I am going to count to five and then clap my hands. When I do, you will feel refreshed and relaxed, and you will have a strong desire to talk more about yourself with me. You will see me as I am, your friend, someone you can trust. Do you understand what I'm saying?"

"Yes."

"And if you hear me say, 'It never rains in May,' you will once again relax deeply and hear only my voice. Do you understand?"

"Yes."

Tepler counted to five and then clapped loudly. Miguel came out of the trance with a startled look, then smiled when he saw Tepler and Gabriela.

"That was very interesting, *Tío*," Gabriela said.

He was still reserved, but not as suspicious as before. He went to the refrigerator for a Fanta orange soda that he poured into three glasses. They drank the soda after clinking glasses. Without being prompted, Miguel began talking about the sequel to the abduction. Because seven people in all were taken aboard the craft and heard and saw the same things, he was confident he would not be alone in talking about it. He went to the local newspaper, and the story came out with his photograph. Soon after, a television station interviewed him.

But everything started to go wrong at that point. Despite his claim that he had not been alone, no one else stepped forward. He tracked down the taxi driver in Boqueron, but the man denied he had been abducted or knew anything about the asteroid prophecy. Only one person, a woman from La Parguera, claimed to have seen a strange light hovering above the highway the night of the abduction, but her credibility was demolished when it turned out she had an arrest record for theft.

The fisherman became quiet again. Tepler understood he was a simple man who had experienced extraordinary things. The questioning had pushed him back into painful memories, and Tepler began to fear he was losing him.

"Did anyone take you seriously?" Tepler asked.

The old man said finally, "A scientist. One scientist from the United States. I don't remember much anymore. He came here," he said and pointed to the room.

"What did he want to know?"

"About the prophecy."

"Why did he want to know this?"

"I don't remember."

Tepler felt an electric jolt in the back of his neck. Was this the vital link to the observatory and the hidden weapon? He didn't want to ruin it by pushing too hard. He forced himself to calm down. He looked toward the window and said in a casual tone, "Do you know, Miguel, that it never rains in May?"

That was all it took for Gabriela's uncle to fall back into a trance. He sat quietly with his hands folded in his lap and stared ahead of him, not blinking even when Tepler snapped his fingers in front of his eyes. Gabriela smiled in amazement.

"We're getting close to something important," Tepler whispered to her.

Again Tepler sat across from the fisherman, their knees almost touching. He leaned forward slightly and said, "Miguel, I want you to go back to the time when a scientist comes to visit you. Tell me about the scientist."

Miguel stared straight ahead, as if looking through Tepler. He said, "I'm coming back in my boat with two small yellowfins and a barracuda. I bring the fish in and I hear a knock on the door. A tall man is there, about my age, an American. He says that he saw a television program about me and he wants to ask me about it."

"What do you say to him?"

"I tell him that it is painful for me, and that I don't wish to speak about it anymore."

"Does he leave?"

"No, he says he knows about such things. He knows about the Breeders and he is worried that they cannot be trusted. He wants to hear about the asteroid prophecy."

Tepler said, "Good. Now I want you to tell me everything that happens with the scientist, everything he says and everything you say."

Gabriela's uncle complied, in slow speech, without the need for much prompting. Tepler could see from his eyes he was once again with the American scientist, as if it was happening right then and there. Tepler got the impression the scientist had also used deep relaxation techniques on the fisherman in order to draw out details. The scientist was particularly probing about the connection between the Breeders and the asteroid and had elicited more details about them than Tepler had. At one point, the fisherman told the scientist, "The blond ones say the Breeders have the ability to control an asteroid and they will make it hit Earth."

It was clear the scientist was very interested in the timetable for the event, but Tepler couldn't obtain anything more than the number the fisherman had already told him: fifteen years.

"Does the scientist say something can be done about the asteroid?"

"He says that a weapon can be built, and he knows how to do it."

"Does the scientist tell you his name?"

The old man paused. "He says his name is Donald Meller."

"What more does he say to you?"

"He tells me that I will forget that he has been here so that no one will know he has talked to me. It would be dangerous for me to remember."

Tepler's head was spinning. He was eager to rush back to the observatory with Gabriela. He had to take a closer look at whatever it was underneath the telescope, to try to unfold it completely. Then he could get a better idea if it was truly a weapon. If so, maybe he could get it to work.

His mind was racing out of control. He breathed deeply to calm down. He had to free Gabriela's uncle from the trance and then enlist her help at the observatory.

"I'm going to count down again, Miguel, and at the end you will feel refreshed and relaxed. When you hear me say, 'The sky doesn't have to fall any more,' you will yawn and say, 'It's time for me to go to bed.' You will have a long and refreshing sleep. When you get up in the morning you will feel happier than you have ever felt before."

After he came out of the trance, Miguel looked at his niece and said, "Was I helpful, Gabriela?"

She threw her arms around him. "You were wonderful, *Tío*."

Tepler, who had begun stacking up the bags of ice-packed fish on the counter, said, "You have no idea how helpful."

When the old man wasn't looking, Tepler slipped all of the money from his wallet under one of the votive candles. It was three times more than what they had agreed on.

The fisherman was fidgeting with his baseball cap, not knowing what to do with himself. Tepler smiled and said the words that would put him to sleep, "Do you know, Miguel, that the sky doesn't have to fall any more?"

The old man stretched and then yawned. "It's time for me to go to bed."

Tepler put his hand on the fisherman's shoulder. "You want to know something?"

The old man looked at him sleepily.

"You're a hero, Miguel. A true hero."

The fisherman smacked his lips, yawned again, then walked slowly toward the bedroom. His eyes were barely half open, and Tepler knew that in a minute he was going be in a deep sleep.

With Gabriela's help, Tepler lugged the bags of fish to his truck and stacked them in the back.

"You were very kind to my uncle," she said. "I appreciate that."

"I wasn't exaggerating. He *is* a hero."

"Did he tell you what you needed to know?"

"Yes."

As he held the passenger door open for her, she touched his arm and said, "I would like to stay with you, Eric, but I think it would be best for me to go to my family now."

Tepler nodded. "I think so, too. But there's something extremely important I need to show you first."

Chapter 9

The sun was still blazing over the Caribbean when Tepler and Gabriela got back to the observatory. During the short trip between the fishing village and Cabo Rojo, he resisted the desire to tell her what he had found in the cylinder, deciding it was best to wait until she could see for herself.

Once inside the main building, he led her to the tower and rapped his knuckles on the huge cylinder.

"When I began working here five years ago, I thought this was the support for the telescope and that it was a nifty thing to wrap a metal staircase around, but there's more to this cylinder than meets the eye."

He crouched under the metal stairs, nearly bumping his head, and removed the heavy metal plate. "I found this access panel two years ago, and when I took it off I discovered something inside that doesn't have anything to do with the telescope." He shined his flashlight into the opening. "Look at this, Gabriela."

She moved closer to him to see inside. The flashlight illuminated the five-foot-long hollow tube. "What is it?"

"Do you remember what your uncle said about the scientist who visited him, Donald Meller? He told your uncle that a weapon could be built to deal with the asteroid? This could this be it, Gabriela. This could be Meller's weapon."

Gabriela's face brightened. "What makes you think it's a weapon? All I see is a hollow tube."

"There's more to it, a whole lot more."

He shined the light on the trigger at the end of the tube. "My guess is that the tube holds whatever powers the weapon. When it's slid all the way in, it pushes up against a triggering mechanism, then whatever is inside this big cylinder comes to life." He told her about his unsuccessful efforts to unfold the device. "It draws on the observatory's electrical system, but it overloads the circuits. I've only been able to get it to come out part of the way."

He picked up the sawed-off broomstick that he had used before. He reached in and pressed the end of the stick against the trigger.

"Watch this."

When the lever was pushed forward, a whirring sound emanated from within the cylinder and the tube began to slide smoothly forward and then upward. But then the power failed, and they were in the dark.

"See what I mean? If we turn the power on again and if nothing's pressing against the trigger, the tube will slide back down into its original position. But if something is still pressing against the trigger, the tube will continue moving upward into the cylinder, into the vertical position."

He pointed to the spiral staircase and said, "There's more to see upstairs."

They clambered up to the observatory and found that the telescope mount had slid to one side, partly exposing a hole in the floor. Gabriela looked confused. "What's down there?"

"Under the floor are gears that drive the transformation. If we can keep power going to the cylinder, the telescope will move to one side completely, and a cannon-like tube will emerge from below. I've been able to uncover the hole completely, but I haven't been able to get the cannon to come very far out. Once the tube at the base of the cylinder turns up into the vertical position, I can't reach the trigger any more."

They went back down the spiral staircase, their shoes clattering on the metal steps. Kneeling next to the opening, Tepler pointed the light at the trigger. "The trick to getting this thing to unfold completely is to keep the trigger engaged," he said.

Gabriela took the flashlight from him and peered inside. "What about a rope? If we can loop it around the trigger and through the back of the tube, then we could keep the trigger engaged by pulling on the rope."

She made a tugging motion with her hands.

Tepler looked inside. At the back of the tube was a set of concave bars, about six inches behind the trigger mechanism.

He nodded. "That might work if I can get it through those bars."

With a pair of pliers, he wired a metal hook to the end of the broomstick. He found a roll of cord in the storeroom and cut a length of it, then tied the end into a hangman's noose. Getting the noose around the trigger was easy, but it took half an hour of muscle-cramping maneuvering to thread the other end of the cord through the concave bars and haul it back to them. Once the end of the cord was in his hands, Tepler pulled on it lightly. It stiffened, and the levering action snapped the trigger forward.

They both broke into smiles and said simultaneously, "It works!"

Tepler led Gabriela to the circuit breaker panel, mounted on the wall of a utility room in the main building. He tapped a double switch with his forefinger. "This is the one that controls the power to the observatory. When I tell you to, switch it on."

Leaving Gabriela at the circuit-breaker panel, Tepler returned to the cylinder access hole. He tugged on the cord and shouted, "Flick the switch on."

The power surged and the cylinder came to life with the sound of hidden gears engaging. The tube slid farther toward the center of the cylinder and angled farther upward, then the power failed again.

"Wait a few seconds, and flick the switch on again."

By pulling on the cord, Tepler kept the tension on the lever. A few seconds later, the power went back on and the tube slid farther inward. After ten tries, the tube had gone into the vertical position and had begun to rise into the cylinder. Over the next fifteen minutes, they went through the procedure at least a dozen more times. Finally, Tepler couldn't hear any more movement inside the cylinder. Whatever was in there must have completely deployed.

Gabriela called out from the circuit-breaker panel: "What do we do now?"

Tepler was eager to run up the stairs to the observatory, but he called to Gabriela to join him at the stairs and gallantly motioned for her to go up first.

His jaw dropped when he saw the transformation. The cannon-like tube had thrust up from the floor and was nearly touching the underside of the dome. It was about three feet in diameter and twice as long as the telescope, painted the same frog-green color.

The cannon had locked into place next to the telescope. A panel with an array of controls and monitors had also emerged from the floor and had snapped into position next to the telescope monitors.

They walked around the imposing device, observing it from every angle.

"It sure looks like a weapon," Gabriela said.

"Maybe it's a particle beam weapon," Tepler said, "Or a laser, like in those Star Wars projects they used to talk about in the 1980s."

Tepler sat at the control panel, the cannon looming above. The observatory's electrical system seemed adequate to power the panel as well as the telescope controls and monitors. As Gabriela looked over his shoulder, he turned the control monitor on and typed in various commands.

"I think I can figure out how to make it work, but nothing is going to happen without a power source."

After fifteen minutes of playing with the keyboard controls, Tepler's face lit up. "This is amazing. The weapon controls are integrated with the telescope controls. The telescope is the tracking and aiming device."

He turned the telescope on and quickly realized the deployment had caused the instrument to go out of alignment. He felt frustrated that he wouldn't be able to re-calibrate it until after dark. He closed his eyes and imagined the faint glow of the asteroid, an innocent-looking speck hurtling through universe darkness—a speck that had traveled nearly a million miles since they last observed it, a million miles closer to impact.

"All we need is power. Then it's a matter of aiming and firing."

"Where could the power source be?" Gabriela said.

"Donald Meller has to be behind this. We need to find out who he is and where he is."

"Do an Internet search. He's a scientist. There should be something about him," Gabriela suggested.

"I would, but the Internet's down. There's no e-mail, there's no anything."

She thought for a moment and said, "It doesn't make any sense to build something like this and not have the power to make it work. If it's what fits into the tube, then it has to be a cylinder about five feet long. Maybe it's hidden in the building somewhere."

They searched the observatory, but when it was clear there wasn't anywhere to hide such a device, they went down to the base of the tower. The walls of the tower were solid stone and the floor concrete, ruling out the lighthouse tower as a hiding place.

With exhausting thoroughness, they went through each room of the main building, searching the historical rooms, the office, and even Tepler's living quarters for a secret hiding place. But again they found nothing. Frustrated, they went outside and searched the grounds. The lighthouse had been built on a limestone bluff, with brush growing between cracks in the rock. After a systematic search, they gave up.

A cool breeze came off the Caribbean Sea. They walked to the edge of the bluff and watched the crash of waves against the cliffs below. Tepler knew about the caves down there. He had explored the shoreline at low tide and found several with entrances that were concealed at high tide, but with chambers inside that always remained above the water line. He had explored them all, and had never seen anything in them other than moist rocks and slippery algae.

Tepler picked up several stones and threw them toward the sea. "I feel like I'm missing something, but I don't know what it is."

They went back to the observatory and once again he studied the sequence of the most recent asteroid photographs. It was like watching a grim executioner on his way to the death chamber.

Tepler thought about the terms of his employment contract and the rules restricting visitors. Now it became clear why he had to be the only astronomer and sole occupant of the building and why money was never budgeted for support personnel: It was to keep the secret, and it struck him now as obvious that he had been hired as a caretaker.

A foundation had built the observatory, but he had never been able to find out anything about it other than it was the funding source for the lighthouse conversion and that it oversaw the operation of the observatory. It was called the Third Alternative Foundation—TAF for short. Tepler had never thought about the name before, but now he wondered what it was supposed to mean. A trustee at a bank in New York City disbursed the funds and supervised the facility. Did the trustee have any other role? Who set up the foundation? Tepler wondered. And where did the money come from?

He slapped himself on the forehead. "Gabriela, how dumb can I be? I know how to find out about Donald Meller."

He grabbed the phone and punched in a New York telephone number.

It was a number that he knew by heart.

Chapter 10

Kendon sped along the highway, scanning the skies for any
thing unusual. As the city lights faded in the distance, he
told Laura about the extraordinary power contained in the one-
one-five pod and explained the technology behind the gravity beam
weapon.

"When it's inserted into the weapon, it provides the energy to
make it work. Like a battery."

"What does the pod look like?" Laura asked.

"A red cylinder, five feet long, a foot in diameter, but larger at
one end."

Laura was leaning back in the passenger seat, one hand over
her forehead. Kendon liked the way the light from street lamps
danced on her face, lighting up and then shading the features of
her eyes and cheeks.

"I don't believe this is happening," she said.

"I don't either. How do you feel?"

"No pain yet. It will take a couple of hours for the anesthetic
to wear off."

"I have painkillers, antibiotics, and anti-inflammatories in my
backpack, but you won't need them. Once we get to a safe place, I
can heal you quickly, just like I did to Molly, just like I did to
myself."

"They know we're together. I have a house in Austin. Is that where they'll search?"

"You can count on it. The Directorate will find out everything about you. Who owns the house that we're going to?"

"It's part of a trust. A few years before he vanished, my father put everything into a trust fund, so the property can't be directly traced to me."

"It used to be in your father's name?"

"And in my mother's."

"They might send someone to search it. We can't stay long. We have to find the pod fast and get out of there."

"And if we find it, where do we go with it?"

"Your father said something about southwestern Puerto Rico. What is there about Virginia Woolf that could tell us where to go in Puerto Rico. Did she live there?"

"No, I don't believe she was ever there."

"What are the other books she wrote?"

"There was *Mrs. Dalloway, Jacob's Room, The Waves, Orlando,* and several others."

"Is there a town called Dalloway in Puerto Rico?"

"I doubt it."

"How about Orlando?"

"Maybe."

"What else did she write?"

She strained to remember. "I think I know which book my father was referring to: *To the Lighthouse.* Puerto Rico is an island, so it has to be ringed with lighthouses."

"That makes sense," Kendon said. "A lighthouse would be a clever place to hide a weapon like that. A lighthouse somewhere in southwestern Puerto Rico. There could be a half-dozen lighthouses in that region, but at least we know where to start looking."

He drove for another fifteen minutes, then glanced at the dashboard clock. It was nearly eleven o'clock. He had been running on adrenaline for the last twenty-four hours, and he was beginning to feel exhausted, but he knew he had to push on.

He looked over at Laura. She had nestled back in the passenger seat and seemed to be asleep. Kendon didn't want to disturb her. She needed to rest, which would help the healing process.

Keeping his left hand on the steering wheel, he gently covered her wound with his right hand and tried mentally to direct the flow of energy, but he had trouble keeping his mind focused. His thoughts were consumed with bitter memories of the underground life that had been imposed on him, a life that kept its existence a secret only through the creation of a ruthless security system of which he had been a part.

After they were on the road for more than half an hour, Laura stirred. Kendon pulled his hand away.

"Your touch is so soothing," she said.

"The healing works better with two hands. We'll do more later."

She turned the overhead light on and removed the bandage while looking in a pull-down visor mirror. "The swelling has gone down. How do you do that?"

He shrugged. "It's an energy that comes out of my hands. That's all I can tell you about it. I found out I had this ability when I was about seven or eight years old, but I learned to keep it to myself."

"I can't tell you what I would give to have an ability like that, to cure children like you cured Molly. I fund a research institute that investigates alternative cures, and all along everything I've been looking for is in your hands."

She looked in the visor mirror again. The only traces of the surgery left were two thin lines of stitches. She patted some makeup over them.

She turned toward him. "What do you think?"

He grinned. "You're pretty good at making things disappear yourself."

After a few minutes of silence, Laura said, "Where did you get a name like Arkasha?"

"It's Russian. I was born in Belorussia. All I know is that I was in an orphanage somewhere near Minsk. My real first name is Arkady, but I'm called by the diminutive, Arkasha."

"Do you know anything about your parents?"

He shook his head. "I don't even know my true last name. When I was three years old, I was taken by the Directorate to the United States, and I was raised in one of the underground facilities that I've been telling you about. I was given an English name. Your father knew me as Michael Kendon, but to everyone in the Directorate, I was Arkasha of the Belorussian crèche of 1977. We always referred to one another by our crèche names."

"I'm afraid I don't understand," Laura said.

"The Directorate doesn't recruit adults. It recruits two-, three- or four-year old Slavic children, both boys and girls. They scout orphanages for healthy children who are brought here, maybe fifteen hundred every year, from different Eastern European countries to be raised in a controlled environment in various underground facilities. The children are grouped together initially by their country of origin into nurseries identified by nationality and year of formation. We retain our given first name, and we speak the language of our country of origin until we are in our teens. Only then are we taught English, and then we are triaged onto career paths based on aptitude."

"Weren't you taught anything about America?"

"Not until later. We were indoctrinated with the idea that we were part of an elite force created to shield the Collaboration from the world, that we were in America but were not a part of it. We were raised to be loyal to the Committee and to the goals of the Collaboration. None of the Directorate people have any connection with America. Absolutely no family ties here and nothing is traceable even in the birth country. Our father is the Committee, our family is the Directorate, our nation is the underground."

Kendon wanted to tell her more, but he knew she wouldn't be

able to understand how someone could be raised to kill. Over the decades, hundreds of people—maybe even thousands—had been killed for the crime of talking about the Collaboration. They had taken oaths of silence and had been given warnings and incentives. But still there were contractors, scientists, engineers, and technicians—not to mention the occasional Directorate agent or soldier who defected to the surface world—who talked about what they knew. Most of it was too bizarre to be believed, but it was always seen as a serious breach of security. He had been raised with the belief that it was an act of loyalty to kill the disloyal, to track down and dispose of anyone, no matter how limited their knowledge, who dared to speak about what they knew. They had to be eliminated, for the sake of the Collaboration and to serve as a warning.

"Who makes up the Committee?" Laura asked. "Are they from Eastern Europe, too?"

"No, it's made up of military officials of the highest rank, and of powerful industrialists, politicians, and bureaucrats. They rotate in and out of your government. They are always in control. No one outside of their small group knows the truth about the Collaboration."

Laura shuddered. "How frightening."

"It isn't easy to break free of the kind of indoctrination I was raised with. I had a very confused mind until I met your father."

"How did you get to know him?"

"I infiltrated his research group, posing as a captive nuclear engineer transferred from one of the Nevada sites. His was the most important of the research groups at the Dulce facility, and the idea was to determine if there were any security problems. The Committee was worried about acts of sabotage, escape attempts, even outright rebellion."

"I don't understand why was my father held captive."

"Years ago, the Collaboration decided to force thousands of contract workers into captivity in order to keep better control over its secrets. The captives were kept in line through threats to kill their families."

Laura said, "When my father disappeared, my mother and I tried for years to find out what happened to him. We even hired private investigators and pulled political strings in Austin and in Washington, but that didn't get us anywhere. We found out that his official records had been expunged. It was like he had never existed."

Kendon said, "Most of the time, people above ground were led to believe their loved ones had died in accidents here or overseas while taking part in activities involving national security and that there weren't any recoverable remains. The families were compensated, memorial services were held, but these people are actually still alive in secret facilities."

After several more minutes, Laura pointed to an exit. Kendon peeled off the highway and drove down a farm road through tree-covered hills.

"Two hills, two vales, and we're there," she said.

Ten minutes later, Kendon turned onto a gravel road that led through a canopy of trees to an immense, darkened house. He had never seen anything like it. Even in the dark it was imposing. Kendon stopped in front of a rounded portico upheld by white pillars.

Laura rummaged through her purse for keys. They walked up marble stairs to an enormous ornate door that Laura unlocked and then pushed open. When she switched the lights on, Kendon was stunned by the lavishness of the interior: French doors, curved staircases, ornate balustrades, parquet floors, crystal chandeliers, and statues and paintings everywhere.

All that Kendon possessed were the clothes he was wearing, the contents of the backpack, and a gun. He could not imagine someone having so much, particularly Donald Meller. He knew Meller only as a brilliant scientist and engineer and as a man with an engagingly humble way of dealing with people.

"This is where my father lived before he disappeared," Laura said with a sweep of her hand.

Kendon felt his heart swelling. He raised both arms and gestured toward the high ceiling. "How could Donald Meller have only one child if he lived in such a house? This is a house that needs the voices of a dozen children."

"Big families are no longer the norm. There was only me."

"I have trouble seeing your father in a palace like this."

"It wasn't very important to him. It was important to my mother."

"Is she here? Am I going to meet her?"

"She lives in Europe. In Rome."

He peered through one of the French doors, which led to a study and, through it, to rooms deeper in the house.

"It's obvious that you are a wealthy woman, yet you continue to work."

"I didn't earn any of this. My father made an enormous amount of money from inventions he patented, and he had a lot of luck with investments. I felt I should give something of myself, so I became a physician."

Kendon was dazzled by her looks. She stood in the middle of the foyer with easy posture, wondrously female. For the first time, he became self-conscious of his shabby appearance, of the tousled hair, the two-day growth of beard, and the rumpled malodorous clothes spotted with guano.

At the thought of guano, his mind snapped back to their purpose for being there. "Where is the room you were telling me about?"

Laura pointed toward the top of the stairs. As they marched up the curved staircase, Kendon let his hand slide on the varnished banister. He kept looking around in awe. At the top, Laura walked down a wide corridor and opened a door. "A room of one's own," she said as she stepped inside.

It was a large bedroom painted in pastel blue with a four-poster bed, a built-in bookcase, and a dresser with a large oval mirror—the room of a teenage girl. Next to a window was a roll-up desk, and on the wall was a portrait of Virginia Woolf.

Kendon's heart sank when he looked around the room. It seemed like an unlikely place to hide a million-megaton pod. He was certain it wasn't in the room, that they had misinterpreted Meller's clue. While Laura searched the closet, Kendon dropped to his knees to look under the bed.

"It's not in here," Laura said from the deep closet.

"It's not here either," he said.

Kendon felt a spike of panic, the same fear that had tried to erupt with paralyzing force several times that day. He breathed deeply and let the image of brilliant whiteness fill his mind. Soon he was calm again, breathing evenly, able to think clearly.

"Your father could have been alluding to the house, not necessarily to your room.

"Then let's search the entire house," Laura said.

Methodically, they searched first the upstairs rooms, then downstairs, and finally the basement. Kendon looked for every conceivable hiding place, for secret doors and sliding panels, but he gave up when it was clear the one-one-five pod wasn't in the house.

Kendon said, "Your father hadn't been here for ten years. How could he have gotten into the house?"

"We always keep a key for the back door buried in the garden."

"Show me where."

He grabbed the flashlight from his backpack, and they went through the kitchen to a back entrance. He followed Laura along a brick path to a garden surrounded by bushes. It was exceptionally dark and only glimmers of moonlight broke through the black clouds that covered most of the sky. In the feeble light, Kendon could make out a large yard, some sheds and other structures, an outline of trees, and a hill rising up on one side.

Laura pointed to a niche between two rocks. Kendon shined

the flashlight on the spot and squatted down. The ground was undisturbed. He scraped the earth with his fingers, and after digging down three inches, he unearthed a plastic bag with a brass key in it.

"Unless he had another key, he didn't go inside," Kendon concluded.

"I think I know where it is," Laura said.

She pointed to a dark structure a hundred feet behind the house, in front of a cluster of trees. Kendon shined the flashlight on it.

"It's a cedar playhouse my father built for me. I used to sit in it even when I was a teenager and write. It has a window with a view of the hills. I remember how I loved the smell of the wood. It was a private little place for me, like my room, but cozier."

They walked briskly across a lawn and then followed a gravel path to the building. Kendon pushed the wood door open. Garden tools were propped up against the farthest wall; along another wall bags of fertilizer and compost were stacked.

The tools were covered with cobwebs, but Kendon noticed the dust on the compost bags had been disturbed. He handed the flashlight to Laura and with two hands began moving the bulky sacks. While lifting one of the compost bags, he spotted something long and round pushed up against the wall.

"Shine the light down there."

The bright beam lit up a red cylinder, five feet long and a foot in diameter.

"That's it!" Kendon said excitedly. "That's the one-one-five pod."

He got down on his knees and slid his hand over the cold metal of the cylinder, savoring his first victory: Step one had been achieved. The ununpentium hope for the future of the human race was at last in his hands.

He looked up at Laura. Tears were flowing down her face. He thought at first it was because they had finally located the pod, but he quickly understood it was because of her father. He had been there only a few days before, alive, and she hadn't been able to be with him again even though he'd been so close.

Kendon put his arms around her. "You stay here," he said softly.

He sprinted to the front of the mansion for the Jeep, drove along a gravel road, and stopped in front of the playhouse. He flung the back door open.

Inside the playhouse, Laura was shining the flashlight on another object half-hidden between the one-one-five pod and the wall. She pointed with the flashlight. "What's that?"

Kendon rolled the one-one-five pod away from the wall to free the object and lifted it up. It appeared to be a weapon of some kind, the size and length of a bazooka with a box-like center. As on conventional firearms, a grip with a trigger extended down from behind the box. On the top was a carrying handle that also served as a sighting mechanism. Extending down from the end of the barrel was another shorter grip for steadying the heavy weapon.

"Your father told me about a miniaturized version he had been experimenting with. Maybe this is it."

When he examined the weapon, he discovered it had two intensity settings controlled by a switch. He flicked the switch, and a small red light flashed on. He heard a slight whirring noise inside. He stepped outside the playhouse and pointed to the hill.

"What's up there?"

"Trees and boulders."

Kendon pointed to a tree in the distance, halfway up the hill, about four hundred yards away, feebly illuminated by moonlight shining through a break in the clouds. He stepped a few yards in front of Laura, aimed, and pressed the trigger, but nothing happened.

He examined the weapon again. While flicking the intensity setting back and forth, he saw the red light change to green. The moment the green light went on, an arc of turquoise energy the shape and size of a large umbrella flowed out of the barrel.

"What's that?" Laura said.

"I don't know."

Kendon pressed the stock of the weapon against his shoulder and aimed at the tree. When he squeezed the trigger, a thin turquoise beam shot from it, lasting the length of time his finger pressed on the trigger.

Instantly, not only the tree but also the entire hillside exploded, sending tree fragments, stones, and dirt hundreds of feet into the air. They had to take cover in the playhouse to keep from being hit by falling debris.

"I'll be damned! And that was on low intensity," Kendon said.

"What was that blue streak?" Laura gasped.

"A focused gravity beam. This is the miniature version of the weapon your father created to deflect the asteroid. It doesn't even have a thousandth of the power contained in the one-one-five pod."

He turned the weapon off and gingerly put into the back of the Jeep. Together, they lugged the red cylinder out of the playhouse and slid it into the back of the vehicle.

"We can't risk staying here much longer," Kendon said. "We'll grab some things from the house and get going. You need a change of clothes, things like that. Whatever food is in the refrigerator, we'll take it with us."

They rushed back to the house, but Laura stumbled while running. Kendon helped her to her feet. Kendon rummaged through the kitchen while Laura ran upstairs. The sight of food made him realize he hadn't eaten for almost a day and he was ravenous. He stuffed his mouth with cuts of salami and cheese while filling the backpack with canned food. He found some plastic bags and emptied the contents of the refrigerator into them.

By the time Kendon finished, Laura was back in the kitchen dragging a large suitcase. She was dressed casually in jeans and running shoes.

Just as she came into the kitchen, Kendon heard a familiar noise somewhere in the distance. It was the unmistakable sound of helicopters approaching. "Black Hawks! We have to get out of here—now!"

He grabbed the suitcase and the backpack, and Laura scooped up the plastic bags. They ran to the Jeep, threw everything inside, and jumped in.

"The helicopters are approaching from the front of the house. Any other way out of here?"

"There's a dirt road behind the trees that cuts through a pasture and leads to a farm road."

Laura pointed to an opening between the trees. Kendon started the vehicle, but kept the lights off. He drove through the opening, then turned the motor off and slowed to a stop without braking, fearing the taillights would give them away.

He jumped out. Through the trees, he saw two Black Hawk helicopters swoop in low. One landed at the side of the house while the other remained in the air, hovering just above the roof. A searchlight swept across the grounds as a dozen Directorate troops jumped from the first helicopter. The soldiers quickly fanned out, surrounding the house.

Kendon slid back into the Jeep. With the lights off, he drove down the dirt road, trying to see what he could in the rear view mirror. Laura turned in her seat and got on her knees to see better.

"They've got infrared," he said. "All they have to do is look in our direction and they'll see us driving away."

They hadn't gotten three hundred yards when the helicopter that was hovering over the mansion swiveled abruptly in their direction, like a predator sensing movement in the brush. It remained in place for a moment, then flew slowly toward the line of trees.

"Oh, my God, they're coming!" Laura screamed.

Kendon grabbed the beam weapon and leaped from the car. He flicked the switch on just as the helicopter flew slowly over the treetops. The helicopter's searchlight swept across the pasture until it reached Kendon and then stopped, bracketing him in blinding light. The whump of the rotor blades became deafening.

Kendon began sweating. They were out in the open with nowhere to run. The red light of the weapon remained on. He realized he had flicked the switch to the full-power setting, and it occurred to him that it might take longer for the weapon to warm up at that setting. He flicked it to low intensity just as a voice from the helicopter barked in Russian over a loudspeaker, "Drop your weapon, Arkasha."

Kendon recognized the voice of Dimitri, the pilot who had flown him and Bogdan to Carlsbad Caverns. Through the trees, Kendon could see the second helicopter lift off from the mansion grounds, leaving the Directorate soldiers behind. With an aggressive turn, it climbed above the house and swooped in his direction.

The red light turned green.

Kendon pulled the weapon to his hip and squeezed the trigger. The turquoise beam struck the Black Hawk under the pilot compartment, and the helicopter exploded into a tremendous fireball. Kendon jumped to one side as a flaming fragment shot toward him, striking the ground where he had been standing.

He jammed the stock into his shoulder and aimed at the second helicopter. It swerved evasively, but not quickly enough to avoid the turquoise ray. The beam caught it on the underbelly, and in an instant it exploded, lighting up the surroundings like a flare.

Kendon had seen a dozen Directorate soldiers on the grounds. They had to be around the mansion or even inside by now. He yelled to Laura, "Don't look back."

He aimed the weapon at the house and squeezed the trigger. The line of trees separating the grounds from the meadow exploded first. The beam caught two of the soldiers out in the open, and they vanished as if they had never been there. Everything the beam touched exploded. Room by room, the elegant manse blew apart, the rubble thrown miles away by the kinetic fury of the beam. In ten seconds, nothing remained.

Kendon shoved the weapon into the rear of the Jeep next to the one-one-five pod. His mouth was dry and his hands were shaking as he started the vehicle and jammed it into gear. Laura was doubled over, her arms clutching her belly. Kendon became alarmed, thinking maybe a helicopter fragment had hit her.

"Are you hurt?" he said.

She shook her head. "No, I feel sick."

He drove was fast as he could along the rutted road. They were both jostled in their seats.

"We don't have much time. In twenty minutes, this place is going to be crawling with assault troops. We have to get back to the highway."

"How many men were in those helicopters?"

Kendon noted that her voice was full of anger. "I don't know for sure. They can carry twelve to fourteen in each, including the pilot and copilot."

"Now they're all dead. Just like that."

"I don't think any of them survived. I couldn't let them. Even the ones on the ground could alert their commanders. This place would be swarming with soldiers before we could get away."

"And the house? My home—my father's home. How could you?"

"They were inside. I had no choice."

Her voice became low and scornful. "How do you feel about killing all those people? How do you feel about destroying everything that was dear to me? Does it make you feel good?"

"What I feel isn't important. You have to keep one thing in mind, Laura. If there is no future, the past has no meaning. In less than two days from now, if we're not successful, six billion people are going to die. The world as we know it will cease to exist."

"This is sick."

"Yes, but you and I didn't create the sickness. We are only re-acting to it."

"I feel like jumping out of the car and running away."

"You're free to do as you wish, but I would prefer for you to stay with me. I don't want to go through this alone. You give me strength. You give me hope."

When he reached the highway and merged into the traffic, he looked over at Laura. She was squeezed against the door, as if to put as much distance between them as she could.

He could hear her weeping softly.

Chapter 11

Weariness was digging deeply into Kendon's bones. After driving for half an hour, he got off the highway and parked down the road, away from the bright lights of gas stations and motels. They were at least twenty miles from the wrecked mansion, safe from the Directorate, safe from the Breeders—at least for the moment.

Kendon glanced behind him at the blood-red one-one-five pod and at the mini-beam weapon. He was elated to have the one-one-five pod, but he was thrilled about the portable weapon. If it hadn't been for Meller's foresight in creating a shoulder-fired version, it wasn't likely they could have escaped. Meller had planned it better than Kendon had realized, but would Meller have been capable of shooting down helicopters and killing people? Was that why the escape ultimately failed? Because Meller couldn't bring himself to kill? Meller had a fabulous weapon in his hands, but he was a scientist, not a warrior; a creator, not a destroyer. He had misjudged himself, and it brought him down.

Laura stirred from her fetal position against the passenger door. She sat up straight, reached into her purse for a tissue and blew her nose. "I'm sorry about the outburst. It's just that a few hours ago, my life was moving along just fine, and then you showed up and turned everything upside down."

"I understand."

"Where are we?"

"I don't know. I got off the highway. I was falling asleep."

"Do you want me to drive?"

"I don't know where we're going. We need an airplane, which means we have to find an airport."

"Every big town has an airport."

"I'm too tired to think straight. We need to rest and then figure out exactly where in Puerto Rico we have to go. We'll have to wait until the morning to find an airport."

Laura pointed to the motels back up the road near the highway. "I can get a room."

"It wouldn't be safe to stay in one of those. My face has been all over the news. Probably you've been on the news, too. We could be recognized."

In the days when he had been on Directorate missions, the hunter-killer agents had made use of rundown motels owned by immigrants who spoke little English. They were happy for the business and never asked questions. He started up the Jeep and drove down the road, away from the highway.

"Where are we going?"

"We'll find some out-of-the-way place."

As they drove, Laura pulled down the visor mirror and examined the bridge of her nose. She shook her head. "I still can't believe it. All that time and I didn't know an implant was there."

"They kidnapped you and used your body for reproductive purposes without your consent. They've done it to millions of women. If they were subject to your laws, they would all be in jail."

"I'd love to see those bug-eyed creatures behind bars."

"I'm going to do better than that. I'm going to drive them off the planet."

Inflammation had set in again, causing redness that had spread to her cheeks. She noted it in the mirror and frowned.

"I'll take care of that later," Kendon said.

After a moment, Laura said, "You asked me what my thoughts were when I was holding the child. That's something I've asked myself for a long time. I know I felt sorry for it because at first I thought it was autistic. They all seemed that way, but I finally understood it was more like they were emotionally muted. I knew somehow they will never feel as intensely as we do. I also realized I was being used more than just physically. They were using me emotionally as well. They wanted the child to bond with me, and me with the child, to see if it could become more emotionally responsive."

"Did you bond with it?"

"No. Once I understood what they were doing, I refused to hold it. They had violated me physically, against my will. I couldn't accept the emotional violation."

"That was brave. How is it you remember so much?"

"I was having time-loss experiences and strange dreams. I saw a therapist. Much of it came out through hypnosis."

"Other than for cross breeding, they don't have any use for humans. To them, we're creatures driven by instinct and emotion. We are irrational, unpredictable, and bellicose, and we can't be trusted. The Breeders are devoid of emotion as we understand it. They live in their intellects, almost like computers."

He told her of the Breeder boast found inscribed in their ships: We are gods. We create, we rule, we destroy.

"They created the hybrids to get something of both. The hybrids have a third brain lobe that gives them strong mind-to-mind abilities. But they have less of a sense of their individuality. They have hive mentalities. What one thinks, they all think. Because of that they're easier to control."

Tears flowed down Laura's cheeks. "When I was holding it, I knew it was from me, but it wasn't me. It wasn't human."

"They punished you for defying them. They caused your husband to kill himself. They made him see his impotence. They pushed him into despair and planted the idea of death in his mind. All he did was to pull the trigger."

"How could you know this?"

"It's all there. I can see it like in a book. It was after you defied them that your husband killed himself, isn't that true?"

She buried her face in her hands. "Yes," she said.

"They're evil, Laura, totally evil."

After driving for five miles, Kendon found a drab L-shaped motel on the outskirts of a small town. A red neon sign in the office window said "Vacancy." Five vehicles were parked in front of rooms with orange-red doors. The fewer the vehicles, the fewer the eyes, Kendon thought.

Kendon glanced at the dashboard clock. It was already past midnight. He turned into the parking lot and looked into the office. A man wearing a green turban was seated behind a counter, watching television. A satellite dish was mounted on the rooftop above the office.

He would have preferred to send Laura to get the room, but the swelling around the bridge of her nose and the line of stitches made her identifiable. Worse yet, her eyes were red from crying.

He parked and went in. The television was tuned in to a foreign program with folkloric music and dance. The clerk, a middle-aged East Indian with a trim black beard, sunken cheeks, and dark circles around his eyes, tore a registration form off a pad and slid it to him.

Kendon had seen a sign with the town's name, Madison, among a forest of campaign posters. He wrote the name "Michael Madison," made up an address in Austin and handed it back.

The clerk looked at it and said, "How many people?"

"Two. I need a room with two beds."

"Your driver's license, please."

Kendon shook his head. "I'm sorry, I lost my wallet."

He pulled some bills out of his pocket and slid fifty dollars across the counter.

"I have to see ID."

"Here's my identification." Kendon slid another fifty-dollar bill across the counter.

The clerk looked at him coolly and did not reach for the money. Kendon pushed a third fifty-dollar bill to him.

"That's all the identification I have."

After hesitating a moment, the clerk lifted a key from a panel of brass hooks and tossed it onto the counter.

A couple of minutes later, Kendon backed the Cherokee several feet from a door where the motel wings joined. He moved his backpack, the valise, and the bags of food to the room, then took out the beam weapon while glancing around the courtyard to see if there was movement at any of the windows.

He was strong enough to move the one-one-five pod by himself, but it was bulky and the last thing he wanted to do was to drop it. He slid the red cylinder out as far as it would go without it tipping forward. Laura took one end and they carried it into the room, then put it down between the two beds.

The room was clean but shabby, with cigarette burns along the edge of the night table. A TV with a cable connection sat on the dresser, and a wobbly table with two chairs was pushed up against the window. The carpet bore the traces of decades of visitors.

Laura stood next to one of the beds and looked around the room with astonishment, as if she had just landed on another planet. Kendon felt sorry for her. She was a wealthy, accomplished woman, and he had brought her to this low place. She was right when she said he had turned her world upside down.

She looked down at the red cylinder and sighed. "I never imagined I'd end up sleeping with a nuclear bomb."

In the crude light of the room, Kendon could see the inflammation had spread. He regretted not letting the surgeon follow proper hygienic procedures when he forced him to remove the implant, but there hadn't been enough time.

Laura took a small mirror from her purse, examined her nose, and frowned.

"Does it hurt?"

"It's starting to."

Kendon took out the vials of antibiotics, anti-inflammatories, and painkillers from his backpack. "My hands or these. It's your choice."

"I've seen what you can do with your hands. What do you want me to do?"

"Just lie down and get comfortable."

He felt dizzy from fatigue. He went to the bathroom and splashed cold water on his face, then hot water, then cold water again. He stared at himself in the mirror. His eyes were bloodshot, and a two-day growth of beard darkened his face. Even to himself he looked like a fugitive.

Laura was stretched out on her back, her hands over her stomach. Kendon first sat on the bed, but then decided it would be easier on his knees. He knelt next to the bed and made her shift closer to him. He liked the expression on her face, a mix of dignity, intelligence, and softness.

"Just relax and let your body sink into the mattress," he said as he covered her eyes and most of her nose with his hands.

For half an hour, he spoke to her soothingly, creating imagery to guide the healing: of cartilage growing, of tiny blood vessels regenerating, of skin renewing, of the death throes of unwanted bacteria, of the mind performing heroic deeds at the microscopic level.

As he knelt beside her, he couldn't keep the thought of Donald Meller out of his head. It seemed like ages ago, but only thirty-six hours before his hands were positioned over Meller almost like they were now over Laura. Once again, he was in the underground cell; once again he was hurting, hurting like he had never wanted to hurt.

Ever since he was little, he had realized the suffering implicit in the ability to feel and that attachment exacted the heaviest toll. As he grew up in the emotional void of the underground, he had learned to keep his feelings for others in check, not to form attachments, to be mistrustful especially of friendship. Directorate training was designed, in part, to foster emotional isolation, and those like Bogdan who achieved the greatest separation also achieved the highest positions within the hierarchy. But the power of his feelings had always been there; he could never crush them completely. And when he came to understand the truth about the Collaboration, it had liberated not only his mind, but also his ability to feel. With the truth came a rush of attachment, first to the cause, then to the quiet conspirators who formed the core of the resistance, and then, above all, to Meller. But with attachment came suffering, and with caring came pain.

As he tried to drive those memories from his mind, he felt Laura's eyes fluttering under his hand. He pulled his hands away. She opened her eyes wide and looked at him.

"You're thinking about my father."

"How do you know?"

"I saw things in my mind."

"Like what?"

"It was vague, but I could see that you were hurt, both of you."

She touched the moistness on his cheek. "Your tears are for my father."

He nodded.

"You loved him like he was your own father."

He nodded again and squeezed his eyes together in a futile effort to suppress the feelings. Killing her father had been an act of desperate mercy. The corrosive sickness of the underworld was such that there was no choice. He and Meller knew it, but that didn't make it any less painful.

Kendon wanted badly to tell Laura what really had happened, but he held back. It would be too much for her. He hoped that she couldn't see it in her mind.

After a long silence, she said, "Whatever you tell me now, Arkasha, I will believe it. Whatever you say has to be done, I won't question it."

"I am Michael now. Arkasha is no more."

He examined her wound. Like a doctor, he pressed the base of her nose where the inflammation had spread earlier. The swelling and redness were gone. The coagulated lines from the surgical incisions had thinned, but not enough yet to remove the stitches. He placed his hand over the wound again. "You're making good progress," he said.

She lay comfortably, her hands still folded over her stomach. After about ten minutes, she said, "Please tell me more about my father."

Kendon didn't want to talk about him. If he did, one thing would lead to another, and she would press him to explain how he died.

"You need to focus your mind on your wound. The healing works better that way."

"Your hands do the work. I want to know about my father. Please tell me. About his work. About everything."

"If I told you everything, I don't think you would understand."

"Leave out what you don't want me to hear."

His knees were starting to ache from kneeling. Fatigue was making him feel woozy. He sat sideways on the floor and propped his elbows on the mattress. He gazed at the profile of her face.

"You are the beauty and I am the beast," he said. "That is the answer to all of your questions."

"Are you?"

"Yes."

"Why do you say that about yourself? You're not a monster."

He was silent for a moment. Finally, he said, "To become someone in the security apparatus, you have to prove yourself by killing. The mission of the Directorate is to keep the secret, and anyone who speaks about the secret is killed. In the name of the Collaboration, I hunted people down, and I killed them. We called them squeaks. I personally murdered three in cold blood, and I had a role in the death of several others."

"But you left that behind you."

Kendon thought about the caverns, then about the mansion and the helicopters and the men who were in them. He realized that many more people were likely to die before they were able to get to their still unknown destination. No, the killing wasn't over.

The energy pouring from his hands soothed Laura, and she slowly drifted into sleep, her faced relaxed and composed. When he finally removed his hands, he could see only stitches along the bridge of her nose. Not a trace remained of the surgical cuts or the inflammation.

He continued the healing for another half an hour, thinking of the irony that a killer could be a healer, a healer a killer. He had not chosen to be either, but it was his fate to be both.

He gazed at her. When her father had talked about her, he had tried to imagine Laura Meller in his mind, but he had been unable to conjure up an image of a woman untainted by the Collaboration experience. He had never imagined that one day he would know her. Now she was there before him, dragged into the consequences of the Collaboration by her own fate.

He felt a stirring in his heart, and he realized he loved her and that he had been in love with her ever since the day Meller showed him a photo of her.

He leaned close and kissed her lightly on the lips. "We will defeat them, you and I. It is our destiny."

Chapter 12

Kendon was stirred from sleep. Doors opening, doors closing, bright light seeping through his eyelids. He had been dreaming of being chased, but now he couldn't remember by whom or why.

For an instant, he didn't know where he was. He stared at the water stains in the ceiling. He looked to the left and to the right, then threw off the covers and sat up abruptly. It took half a minute for the sleepy blur to leave his eyes and for him to focus on the shabby motel room.

Laura was in the bathroom, completely dressed, and was combing her hair. He could see her through the half-open door. She glanced at him without stopping the combing and smiled.

"Good morning."

"What time is it?"

"Nine thirty."

He bolted to the front window and lifted a corner of the curtain. The parking lot was drenched in sunlight, blinding him at first. Only two vehicles other than his were still in front of the rooms. He ran his fingers through his hair. "I should have been up a couple of hours ago."

"You needed to sleep."

"We don't have any time to lose. We need to get an airplane, and we still have to figure out where in Puerto Rico we need to go."

"I got you something to eat. And a change of clothes." She pointed to her bed. She had laid out a pair of khaki trousers, a blue polo shirt, undergarments, and socks.

"Where'd you get those?"

"I borrowed some of your money and went shopping. And then I got something from a deli for breakfast and some sandwiches for later."

Kendon smelled food and looked around to see where the aroma was coming from. On one of the chairs was a plastic bag with two Styrofoam boxes inside. Laura removed the boxes and placed them on the table.

"That wasn't a good idea. What if they've got you on the news? They know you're with me."

She put a pair of sunglasses on and posed like a fashion model. "No one could recognize me. I looked like ten other women I saw in stores. What do you think?"

"You look remarkably like Laura Meller wearing sunglasses."

"If anyone is looking for me, they'll look for someone with a bandage over her nose."

He took the sunglasses off her and examined the bridge of her nose. He couldn't see any evidence of the surgery.

"I took the stitches out myself and then covered up the tracks with makeup. I don't know how you did it, but it healed completely last night. There isn't a microbe left to make it flare up again."

She pointed to the trays. "You need to eat."

They sat down at the rickety table. Kendon had hardly eaten anything since his arrest. He wolfed the food down, then eyed her plate. She had barely touched it.

"I've already eaten," she said.

She slid the plate toward him. He ate everything on her plate, too.

"That was good, but we can't take any more risks," he said after gulping down a small carton of orange juice. "We've got a lot of canned and bottled food from your house. We'll have to make do."

He pushed away from the table and grabbed the portable beam weapon that was propped up against the wall. While Laura gathered things to leave, Kendon looked for a way to disassemble the weapon, but it appeared to be solidly built. He found a screw at the base of the grip and loosened it. Inside was a small round battery. He dropped it in the palm of his hand and showed it to Laura.

"This provides the initial energy to activate the fuel, and then the reaction becomes self-sustaining. When the trigger is pulled, a miniature accelerator bombards the fuel with protons."

He replaced the battery and turned the weapon on. He flicked the switch to low intensity and counted the seconds before the red light switched to green. He tried it with the high-intensity setting, too. To achieve low power, the weapon needed six seconds to warm up; for full power, ten seconds.

When the green light went on, the same parabolic turquoise glow that he had noticed the night before emanated from the barrel, extending several feet. The glow was fainter than it had been at night, but it was still noticeable. He discovered it was forceful when he swiveled the weapon: When the outer edge of the parabolic field came in contact with the curtain, it threw the fabric violently to one side, shredding some of it.

He flicked the switch to the "off" position, and the parabolic field vanished.

"What's the fuel?" Laura asked.

"Ununpentium."

"What's that?"

"On the periodic table it would be element 115."

"The last time I looked, there were only one hundred and three elements."

"It doesn't exist naturally on Earth, but it does in other parts of the galaxy. A lot of the commerce of the universe involves Element 115. It's the gold of the universe."

He knew they needed to get going, but he couldn't resist the urge to show her what ununpentium looked like. He put the beam weapon down and stepped over to the one-one-five pod that was still on the floor between the beds. He lifted it onto one of the beds, the head extending beyond the edge. He gripped the carrying handles welded to the head and strained to turn it.

"Do you want to see what ununpentium looks like? Believe it or not it's orange."

Laura stepped back, alarmed. "Isn't it radioactive?"

"No, it's stable, but the physics at that level of atomic arrangement is really strange. It only emits energy when bombarded by protons. The beam weapon is basically a particle accelerator, and the proton bombardment it generates causes the release of gravitational energy. The technology amplifies and focuses it."

He carefully removed the twelve-inch diameter head. Extending several inches from the exposed top was a pointed dark orange object. The tip was needle sharp, but widened in slim pyramidal form the farther it went into the red cylinder.

"The rod weighs forty-two pounds, almost twenty times the amount of ununpentium in the reactors on Breeder ships. It contains the equivalent of a million megatons of potential energy that can be converted into a focused gravity beam. That's what it will take to divert the asteroid."

Kendon screwed the head back in place.

Laura extended her hands to show the length of the one-one-five pod. "It's so small."

"Your father began working on the weapon fifteen years ago. He had the beam part of it fully designed even before he was confined to the underground. Construction was already underway. Something like that would cost a fortune, Laura. Where could he get that kind of money?"

"How much money are you talking about?"

"Tens of millions of dollars."

Laura thought for a moment. "You saw the house. My father was very wealthy. He could have paid for it himself. In fact, that would explain a lot. Our family life fell apart because tens of millions of dollars disappeared."

As Laura continued, Kendon felt a build-up of excitement: "Fifteen years ago, he was worth $150 million, at least. He had a magic touch for making money even though it didn't mean anything to him. But over the course of five years, about half of that vanished. His long absences had already caused a strain between my parents, but the money was the final blow."

"Did he explain what happened to the money?"

"Only that it went into a research trust fund. He offered to create an irrevocable trust for half of the remaining assets, including the house, in my name and in my mother's name. That's what happened. It's all in a trust. My mother lives off of it. I use my share to fund cancer research."

"Who controls the money?"

"A trustee at a bank in New York City."

"Maybe he knows something. Whoever controlled it may have disbursed funds for the construction of the beam weapon. We have to contact him."

Kendon peered out of the window at the sun-drenched parking lot. Only one car was left other than the Cherokee. "But we can't call from here," he said. "The first thing we do is to get out of here."

He went into the bathroom. He was eager to take a shower and change into something that didn't have the fertilizer smell of guano. He allowed himself five soothing minutes of hot water cascading down his face and shoulders.

As he stood in the narrow shower stall, he heard a voice and thought it was Laura saying something to him from the other room. But then he realized she had turned on the television to a news channel. They had to know what was on the news. Surely there was something about the helicopters. He wondered if anything had been announced about the asteroid. How could there not be? With so many telescopes in the world searching for asteroids, surely an astronomer somewhere had detected it. He dressed in the khaki trousers and dark blue polo shirt Laura had bought him. The shirt fit snugly around his broad shoulders.

Just as he picked up the electric shaver Laura had left for him on the sink, he heard her cry out, "Michael, come here. You need to see this."

Laura was sitting on the bed next to the one-one-five pod, her eyes riveted to the television. A news report showed what little was left of the mansion. The reporter said, "Federal investigators are sifting through the wreckage of two Black Hawk helicopters that apparently exploded in midair here late last night, five miles outside of Larabee in Texas Hill Country. Investigators say the helicopters were engaged in a search for a suspected terrorist and believe they were downed by shoulder-fired missiles. It is unknown at his time how many people were aboard the helicopters, but authorities say there were no survivors."

The reporter went on: "The remains of the helicopters were scattered on an estate that authorities say belongs to Dr. Laura Meller, a pediatric physician at Children's Hospital in Austin. The property is the location of the historic Larabee mansion, which was entirely demolished. Authorities are baffled by the fact that debris from the mansion was discovered miles away. Dr. Meller was last seen Friday night in the company of a suspected terrorist who authorities believe was involved in the murder of two federal security agents at Carlsbad Caverns Friday morning."

The TV screen was filled with the photograph of Kendon that had been taken for his Directorate security badge. A video surveillance photo was shown of him in the hospital lobby carrying the backpack. A blowup showed him in profile.

The voice continued: "Authorities are seeking this man in

connection with the downed helicopters and the death of the two security agents. Michael Kendon is believed to be a pseudonym of Arkady Semyonovich Vitrikov, a Russian with suspected ties to Chechen rebels. Federal sources say they fear he may be in possession of stolen nuclear materials. He is armed and is considered extremely dangerous."

Kendon was standing next to the bed, his mouth wide open. He repeated the name slowly, syllable by syllable. "Arkady Semyonovich Vitrikov."

Laura looked up at him. "Is there something you're not telling me?"

"I just learned who I am—my father's name is Semyon Vitrikov. So, the Directorate had that information all along."

"I mean about the Chechen terrorist connection."

"That's nonsense. It's a lie that the Directorate is spreading through their federal connections. There's nothing new in that. They've been lying about the alien presence for the last seventy years. All it means is that they haven't been able to capture me on their own, so now they're hoping someone will recognize me and turn me in. They want me badly, and they want the one-one-five pod even more."

"What do we do now?"

Kendon peered through the curtain. "Did they show you as well?"

"No, they only gave my name."

Kendon noticed a cell phone next to Laura. The flap was up, and the phone was lit up.

"Did you just call someone?" he said in a worried voice.

"Yes, I called the hospital. I left instructions for Molly and some of the other children under my care."

"Did you talk to anyone?"

"No, I left a voice mail for the head nurse. I told her not to worry, that I'd be by later today. I can throw up smoke, too."

"That part is okay, but you just gave our position away. It's easy to locate someone from a cell phone. They know we're connected. By now, they would have worked up a comprehensive profile on you, and they'd know about your cell phone and would be monitoring it."

"They can do that?"

Kendon grabbed the cell phone from the bed and turned it off.

"It's my fault. I should have warned you. We have to get out of here fast. All they need is a few minutes of talk time to figure out where we are."

They scurried around the motel room, stuffing everything indiscriminately into bags.

Kendon opened the front door. The back of the Cherokee was only a few feet in front of the door. As Laura handed him things, he tossed them in the back. They lifted the one-one-five pod and slid it into the rear. He put the portable beam weapon in last, pushing it near the front seat.

As Laura put her sunglasses on, Kendon said, "Walk naturally to the passenger door. Face the door while you wait for me to open it. Don't look around, and don't act nervous."

Kendon strode to the driver's door, unlocked it, and slid in. He reached across to unlock the passenger door. Laura climbed in. He drove to the street, stopped, and turned left toward town. Only a quarter of a mile from the motel, he saw lights of police vehicles flashing. In the rearview mirror, he could see more flashing lights coming from the opposite direction. He had no way of knowing if they were converging on the motel or if the police action was unrelated to them, but he didn't want to find out. He pulled the portable beam weapon forward so that it was between him and Laura.

He drove into an older neighborhood lined with trees and two-story homes, and drove along narrow residential streets until reaching the center of town. Soon they reached the main road through the commercial district.

"Is the trustee's telephone number stored in your cell phone's memory?"

"Yes."

"Do you know it by heart?"

"Yes."

He drove through town looking for a place to dispose of the phone. At the edge of town was a two-lane bridge over a wide river. Kendon slowed as he drove onto the bridge.

"Give me the phone."

He lowered the window. When he was in the middle of the bridge, he swerved into the left lane up close to the guardrail and tossed the cell phone into the river.

On the other side of the bridge was the two-lane road going out of town, heading in the opposite direction than they had come in the night before. It was dotted with the same election campaign posters. The sun was still rising and blinded him. To the left was the river that at times was close to the road and at other times farther away, hidden by trees.

"Keep an eye on the sky," he said.

"You mean they can still track us?" Laura said, worried.

"It's possible they've identified this vehicle. If the guy who sold it to me saw me on television, he would have talked. So they would know what I'm driving and the license plate number and the name I used. If they were able to pinpoint us through the cell phone at the motel, they could at this very moment be looking at satellite images of the vehicles parked there. They can track post time and real time. That means they can follow us." He pointed upward. "Look, not a cloud in sight."

He put his hand on hers. "I know it's hard on you, Laura. But just imagine the alternative."

"Can't we just convince people about what's going to happen and get them to help?"

"If your government made an announcement about the asteroid, then sure, we could get plenty of people on our side. But without a statement from a credible source, who would believe us? We would be taken for crackpots."

"There has to be something about it in the news."

She turned the radio on and searched through channels for a news station. It was all music, advertising, talk shows, and paid political announcements. Finally, she found a news channel. Again, Kendon was the focus of the reports, but nothing was said that hadn't been covered in the TV news. There was nothing about the asteroid.

Kendon drove through the countryside, not quite sure where they were but certain they were heading east because he was driving into the sun. They kept listening to the news, hearing the chatter of people who didn't have a clue that their end was imminent.

They drove by meadows, rolling hills, expanses of trees, cows looking up at them, horses galloping in pastures, and modest farms with red barns and silos. They saw the sun sparkling on the river and the blaze of autumn leaves. The land was so beautiful it made Kendon ache inside.

As they drove, they heard something that hadn't been reported yet—the "black bus conundrum." Federal authorities were investigating reports of black buses carrying off thousands of people across the country. The report said that most of them were leaving voluntarily, heading for "conferences."

"There were some reports, however, that people were being dragged from homes or businesses and forced onto the buses," the news report said. "While attempting to stop the buses, the police have been ignored or confronted by men in uniform driving black Humvees who showed identity cards of the Office of Naval Intelligence or the Federal Emergency Management Agency. However, federal authorities say they have no information about the buses, but are investigating."

"They're Nomenklatura," Kendon said.

"I don't understand."

"It's a Russian word the Collaboration adopted that refers to the list of people who will survive. They're being rounded up and taken to underground facilities. Most of them don't know they're on the list."

The windows were open. Laura reached for the radio to turn up the volume, but Kendon suddenly grabbed her hand.

"Listen."

"What?"

"Helicopters."

Laura looked out the window.

"There are two of them, up high, behind us."

Kendon swerved off the road and bounced down a slope into a clump of trees just as three rockets hit the road where they had been. Shrapnel tore through the trees above them. The helicopters swooped low overhead.

Black Hawks.

Kendon reached across and opened Laura's door. He took her sunglasses and put them on. He pointed to a shallow gully where a clump of trees grew around some boulders. "Run! Fast! Get low behind those boulders and cover your head."

As she jumped out, he grabbed the beam weapon and switched it on to low intensity. He climbed up to the road, counting, "One . . . two . . . three . . . "

He could hear the helicopters but he couldn't see them. They had swooped ahead a quarter of a mile and had risen high in the sky to put the sun directly behind them. He knew the tactic: Make sure the sunlight is in the enemy's eyes. They were positioning themselves for the kill.

" . . . four . . . five . . . six . . . "

Kendon jammed the stock of the beam weapon to his shoulder just as he heard the swoosh of rockets launching, maybe six of them. The green light switched on. He couldn't see anything in the blinding sun, but he pulled the trigger anyway. He waved the beam weapon up and down, side to side, painting the sky with fierce energy and heard three explosions, then two more. A sixth rocket exploded in the air only fifty feet from him, flinging hot shrapnel at him, but the lethal fragments were deflected by the faint turquoise glow that spilled from the barrel of the weapon.

He kept sweeping the sky in the direction of the sun until he heard an explosion and saw a fireball that for an instant blotted out the sun. The remains of a flaming helicopter dropped straight down, a sprinkling of fire from the sky.

The second helicopter fired its rockets then veered away. Kendon couldn't see the rockets. With methodical fury, he swept the sky with the turquoise beam. Five of the rockets blew up, but a sixth hit the ground in front of the boulders where Laura had run, exploding with a tremendous roar.

Kendon groaned. He couldn't see Laura. Was she injured? Had she been killed?

He aimed for the second helicopter. It had swung out of the sun, and he could see it clearly as it tried to get away. The back half of the helicopter exploded when the turquoise beam caught it in the tail. The rest of the helicopter spiraled down, trailing black smoke, and crashed at the side of the road.

Kendon ran toward the boulders. Laura was huddled between two of them with her arms covering her head. For a instant, he was sure she had been hit, but he didn't see any blood. He pulled her to her feet.

"Are you okay?"

"Yes."

They jumped into the Cherokee, and Kendon drove down the road in the direction of the wreckage. It was in flames and billowing plumes of dark smoke. Cows were trotting away from a nearby pasture that had caught on fire.

Kendon drove slowly around the debris. He could see an arm dangling from the broken cockpit window and the crest of a black helmet.

"That was your baptism of fire," he said, knowing the experience had been traumatic for Laura, but also transforming.

He sped down the road. Neither of them spoke. After a while, he glanced over at Laura. A lock of hair had fallen down to her cheek, and there were smudges of dirt on her forehead and chin.

Her eyes were closed. Her lips were trembling.

Kendon marveled at how beautiful she looked.

Chapter 13

*F*or a frantic half hour, Tepler tried to contact Mortimer Barclay, the trustee who had hired him and who oversaw his activities at the observatory, but the New York City office number kept ringing without switching to voice mail or to an answering service. It was only midafternoon, but it was Friday and everyone who could get away with it was already heading home.

As he worked the telephone, he kept staring in amazement at the transformed observatory, now a battle station and the only defense against an imminent global disaster.

He remembered Barclay telling him, in his habitual supercilious voice, that he lived in the Hamptons. He tried directory assistance, but was told there were no listings for the name. Finally, he called the bank's customer service number. After some verbal sparring, he was able to get connected to someone in the trustee's department. He managed to get a private cell phone number, but when he dialed, he only got Barclay's voice asking the caller to leave a message.

As he waited for the beep, he pondered what message to leave. Should he tell him about the asteroid, or only give a vague warning of a looming catastrophe if he didn't call back? Should he mention the name Donald Meller, or wait until he had the trustee on the line before disclosing anything about the scientist? Barclay had always been difficult to deal with. He decided it would be prudent to keep the message vague.

When he heard the beep, Tepler said forcefully, "Mr. Barclay. Eric Tepler. I have to talk to you about something connected to the observatory. It is extremely urgent. It is, in fact, a life and death situation. I can't tell you more until I'm able to speak to you in person. Please call immediately. I repeat, this is of extreme urgency."

He repeated his cell phone number twice and slammed the phone down. He ran his fingers through his hair and paced back and forth as he tried to think about what to do next.

"Maybe other astronomers know about Donald Meller," Gabriela suggested.

He flipped through his files for telephone numbers and dialed a dozen, but all he got was voice mail. He called several numbers at nearby Arecibo and was connected with voice mail there, too. He tried accessing his e-mail, but the server was still down.

"What the hell is going on?" he groaned.

He wondered if the phone and e-mail services were being deliberately cut off so that news about the asteroid wouldn't spread. He looked out the observatory window at the limestone expanse of the grounds and at the uneven road leading through the salt marshes to the observatory.

"Maybe we should get out of here. Bencomo told me to watch my back. He said people are disappearing."

"What did he mean by that?" Gabriela said, suddenly alarmed.

"People are being taken away in black buses. Some time in the last twenty-four hours, men in black uniforms rounded up everyone at the Minor Planetary Center in Cambridge. Now I can't get through to JPL or NASA or to any of my colleagues at Arecibo. Have they all disappeared, too?"

Tepler thought about his options and realized there weren't many. He would have to use other means to investigate. After thinking about it, he said, "I'm going to drive up to Arecibo to find out what's going on."

"I want to go with you. We can drop by my house first so my parents won't worry about me."

He wanted her to be with him, but he didn't know what to expect at Arecibo. "I don't think that's a good idea. I might be getting you into something I can't get you out of."

"It hardly matters anymore."

"It matters to me. It's much better for you to be with your family."

He could read from her face she was torn with conflicting emotions. If she stayed at home, she would have to share the terrible knowledge. How do you tell everyone you love their lives could end before the weekend is over?

He pointed to the weapon, which was so imposing that it dwarfed the telescope. "We can't leave this deployed."

It took them twenty minutes of flicking switches to get the bizarre machine to uncouple from the telescope and, amid the whirring of hidden gears, sink back into the cylinder. When it was hidden again, Tepler found it hard to believe the weapon had ever been there. The huge squat telescope sat alone in the center of the observatory, pointing innocently at the sky through the opening in the dome just as it had done for the last five years.

Gabriela lived in the seaside town of Boqueron, ten miles north of the cape. Tepler followed her in his truck. She lived on a tidy street with walled entrances hiding shaded courtyards and ornate two-story homes. A few blocks away was the bay, with picturesque boats moored in front of quaint homes and shops.

Tepler followed Gabriela through a gate into a courtyard. A dozen festive people were sitting around a long table on which trays of food and drinks were set out. They all cheerfully greeted the newcomers and motioned for them to join in. Several people urged Gabriela to get her violin.

A slender, well-dressed woman Tepler took to be Gabriela's mother came up to them and gave him a gracious smile.

Gabriela said, "This is my friend Eric Tepler, the astronomer at Cabo Rojo."

"Welcome to our humble home. Please join us," Maria said.

Tepler was introduced to all the aunts, uncles, cousins, and friends of the family. Several said they had heard of him. Most of them spoke to him in English, but as soon it was clear he spoke Spanish, the conversation flowed in the native tongue.

One of Gabriela's cousins was wearing Army fatigues. Tepler learned his name was Nestor Estrada, a lieutenant colonel in the Puerto Rico National Guard and commander of an infantry battalion that had just been called up. He was on his way to the armory and had stopped in to say goodbye.

When Tepler asked about the reason for the call up, the colonel replied, "I don't know yet. I'm flying to San Juan later for a briefing."

Tepler made a heroic attempt to match the cheerfulness. He had always liked the eagerness of Puerto Ricans to turn every moment into a celebration. In normal times, it would be fun to be there, but now he wanted desperately to leave. The chasm created by his secret knowledge separated them, and he knew his strained efforts at friendliness could never bridge it.

Finally, he got up to leave, explaining apologetically that he had to get to Arecibo. Everyone understood that it had to do with his work and told him they hoped to see him again. Gabriela accompanied him to the street.

The conflicting emotions appeared again in her face. "I have to tell them about the asteroid."

"I understand. I think they should know."

"Should I tell them about the spaceship?"

"They wouldn't believe you."

"I won't tell them about it then, or about what we found underneath the telescope."

"It's best not to talk about the weapon. If you say anything about the asteroid, be sure to say it's not certain it will strike. There's still a chance it will miss. You wouldn't be lying. If I can figure out how to make the weapon work, maybe I can deflect it."

He started to go, but Gabriela put her arms around his neck and hugged him. Her closeness was electric and he kissed her passionately.

"I'm sorry I didn't get to know you sooner, Eric."

"I've been wanting to tell you the same thing."

"Please promise me something," she said. "If nothing can be done to prevent the impact, I would like you to be with us. It wouldn't be good for you to be alone. We will hold hands. We will pray. I will play the violin."

He imagined her playing the violin as the asteroid is closing in, her face defiant, her hand feverishly working the bow, her fingers dancing over the strings. The image appealed to him. It would be a grand parting gesture, a cultivated finger in the air at whatever evil was behind the asteroid.

Gabriela had tears in her eyes. Tepler felt his eyes moistening, too. He squeezed his eyes shut and nodded. "It's not going to come to that. There's still hope."

It was a two-hour drive to Arecibo Observatory, the huge radio telescope run by Cornell University. Tepler drove east to Ponce, then turned up the four-lane highway that went north over the central mountain range. The telescope was deep in the mountains ten miles from the main highway. He had been there a dozen times and knew some of the data analysts and program managers. He had always been impressed by the facility and the sophisticated planetary studies carried out there. Arecibo staffers, in turn, knew the capabilities of the Cabo Rojo telescope and were always amazed that there was only a single astronomer.

On the way up the mountain road, Tepler passed slow convoys of black buses, with black Humvees driving ahead and behind.

The Humvees were full of men wearing black uniforms and purple berets, and they were holding machine guns. They glared at him when, while passing, he looked over at them.

Near the crest of the mountains, he turned onto the road leading to the observatory. The road ended at a guarded entrance, but a hundred yards in front of the guardhouse, two black Humvees blocked the road. Six men wearing the same black uniforms and purple berets he had seen earlier stood with machine guns. He couldn't see any of the usual security guards at the gate.

At first, Tepler didn't know whether to turn around or to continue on. He decided to drive up to the blockade. As he approached the uniformed men, he waved and broke into a broad smile, then asked in Spanish if it was still possible to get to the facility. When none of the armed men answered, he asked again in English. Two of the men said something in a language he didn't recognize, and all of them laughed derisively.

The soldier who seemed to be in charge said, "Do you work here?"

He had Slavic features and cold gray eyes. Tepler didn't see insignia on the shoulders or lapels of the uniforms, only a nametag that said "Misha."

"No, I'm on my way to San Jose. I've heard of the observatory and I was hoping it was still open today for tours."

"It's closed. Permanently."

Several of the men laughed. Tepler noticed the soldier move his finger to the trigger of his machine gun and saw the soldiers behind him stiffen.

Tepler feigned surprise. "Really? Did they give up the search for extraterrestrials?"

The gray eyes grew colder. The soldier pointed the machine gun at Tepler's chest. "You ask too many questions. Go back the way you came. We better not see your face around here again."

"Who the hell are those people?" Tepler wondered as he sped

away. He had never seen uniforms like that before. It was clear they weren't from Puerto Rico.

After following the winding road for a quarter of a mile, he drove his truck off the road into the jungle underbrush, deeply enough so that it couldn't be seen from the road.

The observatory was surrounded by jagged hills three to four hundred feet high, covered by dense jungle. Tepler followed a trail through a valley. He knew from previous visits that one of the hilltops north of the radio-telescope dish had been leveled to create a helicopter landing pad. He headed for it.

He was soon at the foot of the helipad and had an unimpeded view. The telescope was unmistakable—a thousand-foot dish built over a depression in the ground, surrounded by mountains. The huge radio-receiving antenna was suspended hundreds of feet above the dish, and the two suspension towers jutted high above the rain forest like a misplaced bridge.

Tepler looked for the research facilities, but he could only see the visitor center and the parking lot. The administrative buildings and research facilities were out of view behind another pointed hill covered with lush foliage, but he knew that roads connected the facilities to the dish.

In the parking lot below were two black buses and four black Humvees. A few minutes after getting to the helipad, Tepler saw men in black uniform march a line of men and women to the buses at gunpoint, at least a hundred people. They were being forced onto the buses, some pushed, some pummeled, some with a rifle muzzle at the back of the head.

Before they were all on the bus, he heard gunshots in the distance, single rounds and then the tat-tat-tat of rapid fire. He heard shouting and more gunshots. In the valley below, a chubby man with a white shirt and yellow tie was running frantically through the brush near the edge of the dish. Tepler recognized him as one of the project managers, but only remembered his first name, Bernard.

Three of the black-clad men were close behind him. One of them knelt, aimed, and fired. The project manager threw his arms up and fell face forward. The three men walked up to the sprawled body, and one of them fired a burst of rounds into the man's back.

Tepler felt an explosion of rage. He wanted to burst out of hiding and stop the outrage, but he was keenly aware that if he gave himself away, he would suffer the same fate.

He was about to slip down the hill and backtrack to his truck when he heard a helicopter arriving. He slid under the brush and froze, his face squeezed to the ground, as a Black Hawk helicopter landed on the helipad. Two men wearing gray, foreign-looking uniforms and black berets stepped out and walked to a boulder at the edge of the helipad, barely ten yards away from him.

One of them had a radio and spoke into it in a language Tepler didn't recognize. It sounded Slavic, like the language he had heard earlier at the Arecibo entrance. In his student days, he had known Russians and could recognize the language. He was sure they weren't speaking Russian. Maybe Bulgarian, or Serbian, or Croatian.

They stayed for five minutes and then got back into the helicopter, which took off. A few minutes later, Tepler heard more gunfire in the distance, this time a prolonged clatter of several machine guns firing simultaneously. Not long after, four black-clad men carrying assault rifles ran down the road that led from the administrative building to the parking lot and jumped into the Humvees. The two buses and the escort of Humvees sped out of the parking lot and soon were out of sight.

Tepler hid until he was certain they were gone. He made his way down the mountainside to the parking lot and walked cautiously up the road to the administration building. From a distance, he saw what all the shooting had been about, but he didn't believe his eyes until he was up close: Slumped against a blood-splattered wall were the bodies of eleven men and three women. He went from one body to the next, hoping to find someone alive.

Three of the men were security guards, their white shirts splattered with red. In the middle was a frail, gray-haired woman with glasses that were cockeyed on her face. Her back was slumped against the base of the wall, her head bent to one side. Five red blotches marred her flowery silk blouse. When Tepler saw her arm move slightly, he knelt next to her. He recognized her as one of the office workers and straightened her glasses.

"Who were they? Why did they do this?" Tepler asked.

She half-opened her eyes and tried to speak. Her pale blue eyes reminded him of his grandmother. He touched her lips with his fingers. "Tell me who they were. Why did they this to you?"

Her lips quivered. He leaned close her to listen, but just as he did her eyes closed and her head fell forward.

Panicking, he raced back to his truck, first along the edges of the parking lot, then following the shoulder of the road to the guard shack, ready to leap into the brush if he heard voices or the approach of a vehicle. From the main gate, he surveyed the road but couldn't see the Humvees that had blocked the entrance earlier.

With his body half bent, he ran along the roadside and finally reached his truck. He drove with silent fury back toward Cabo Rojo, grinding his teeth and wondering what to do. He wanted badly to report the massacre to the police, but he feared being detained for questioning.

Who the hell were those men? Why would they kidnap or murder the entire Arecibo staff?

He knew with certainty now that it wasn't safe at the Cabo Rojo observatory. The killers must have it on their hit list. As he sped down the highway to the coast, he remembered that he had neglected to replace the access panel to the cylinder. If they searched the observatory, they could find the weapon. He had to get there before they did and screw the access panel back in place.

He didn't want to believe it, but the evidence was overwhelming, and he couldn't shake the idea from his head: *The men in black uniforms have to be involved. They want the asteroid to hit.*

As he barreled down the coastal highway toward Cabo Rojo, he tried calling the trustee but got voice mail again. He left another urgent message, then dialed Gabriela's number and groaned when she didn't answer. A few seconds later, his phone rang. It was Gabriela, apologizing because she hadn't been able to pick up the phone in time.

"Gabriela, something terrible has happened." He told her what he had seen at Arecibo.

"Oh, God, no! Who could do something like that?"

"I don't know. Everything about it was strange. They were dressed in black uniforms and they were speaking a language I didn't recognize."

He suggested she call the police, but to leave him out of it. "Call from a pay phone. Make it anonymous. And make sure you don't leave any fingerprints. That way you're out of it, too."

"What are you going to do?"

"I've got to get back to the observatory. I forgot to screw that access plate back in. If they get into the building, I don't want them to find the weapon."

"Come here after you've done that."

"I've got to keep an eye on the observatory. There's a cave in the side of the cliff where I can hide. You can't see it if you're looking down from the top. I'm going to grab a sleeping bag and some food and stay there."

"Be careful."

"Have you told your family about the asteroid?"

"No, not yet. They're having such a good time, I can't bear to tell them. But tonight, after everyone is gone, I will tell my mother. I will ask her what to do."

By the time Tepler got back to the cape, it had already been dark for more than two hours. He stopped when he got to the salt marshes to see if there was any movement at the observatory, but he couldn't detect anything suspicious.

Instead of following the road up the hill to the observatory, he drove along a rough dirt road that led to an inlet at the foot of the bluff. After parking the truck, he followed a steep path to the observatory, careful not to make noise. He was satisfied no one was there when he saw that the huge entrance door was intact. If they had been there, they would have had to force the door open.

After letting himself in, Tepler locked the front door and threw the deadbolt. He was about to turn the lights on, but stopped when he realized it would broadcast his presence for miles. He rummaged through a drawer for a flashlight and made his way through the main room to the tower. Beneath the spiral staircase was the telltale access panel propped up against the wall. The twine he had used earlier to snare the trigger was still on the ground, along with a pair of scissors and the sawed-off broomstick. He cursed himself for his carelessness as he re-inserted the heavy metal panel into the cylinder and screwed it into place using the scissor blade as a screwdriver.

He cleaned up the floor, but now the panel stood out as if it had a flashing neon sign hanging over it saying, "Here it is! Here it is!"

From a storage room underneath the tower, he hauled parts of the old lighthouse beacon and piled them up in front of the panel. When he was satisfied it was well hidden, he rushed to the kitchen for food to take with him, then ran to his bedroom for a sleeping bag and other gear. He put on a windbreaker and dropped the cell phone into the upper pocket.

Just as he stepped out of the bedroom, Tepler heard the straining motors of four-wheel drives. He rushed to a window that faced the access road. A sickening feeling clutched his stomach and throat when he saw three Humvees coming over the crest of the bluff.

He rushed down the short flight of stairs to the storage room, which had three narrow windows almost at ground level that gave a view of the cliffs and the sea. He opened one of the windows and wondered if the opening was large enough for him to crawl through. He pushed his gear through first and pulled himself forward, but just as he poked his head through, he saw headlights. One of the Humvees had driven to the backside of the observatory, cutting him off. He slid back inside and watched the headlights indirectly, observing how they lit up the low brush that covered part of the grounds. The lights stopped for a moment, swung away, then disappeared.

Tepler heard pounding on the front door, on the opposite side of the building. A harsh voice shouted, "Open up! Police!"

He stuck his head through the window again and couldn't see the Humvee. The pounding on the front door started again, with the same aggressive command. He squeezed himself through the window, grabbed his gear, and scurried to the wrought iron fence that surrounded the observatory. He threw everything over the iron bars and climbed over.

From there, it was fifty yards to the edge of the cliff. Bent over to use the brush as cover, he made his way slowly toward the cliff. When he was half way, he heard a motor starting. Headlights went on, bracketing him in blinding light.

A voice shouted. "Hey, you! Stop, or I'll shoot!"

Dropping everything, he raced for the cliff, running faster than he had ever run in his life, his arms pumping like a sprinter nearing the finish line.

There were treacherous rocks at the foot of the cliff, not far below the surface. He knew the tide was in and that in the upward sweep of the waves, the rocks were deeper in the water. If he could fling himself out far enough and if he could catch the upward sweep, maybe he had a chance to survive the fall.

Fifty feet to the edge, forty feet, then thirty feet.

The Humvee bounced over the rough limestone toward him. The voice again ordered him to stop.

Twenty feet, ten feet.

A machine gun ripped loose. A line of bullets splattered the ground two feet to his right, spitting up dirt and limestone.

Only five more feet to go. He didn't have to stop. All he had to do was to fling himself over the edge.

Another burst of machine gun fire ripped through the darkness. Just as he leaped into the emptiness, he felt flaming metal tear through his right shoulder.

He knew he couldn't control the fall. All he could do was to curl his body up and wrap his arms around his legs with his head pulled up against his knees.

A tightly wrapped ball of searing pain, Tepler tumbled down and down, into the crashing water.

Chapter 14

The first thing Tepler saw when he resurfaced were the splashes of bullets slapping the water twenty yards from him. He had hit the foamy water at the exact moment it swept back from the cliff, and he was dragged outward by it. He had stayed underwater until his lungs nearly exploded, ignoring the sting of salt water in the raw flesh of the shoulder wound as he kicked wildly and stroked furiously to get as far away from the cliffs as he could.

When he came up for air, he could see the killers at the cliff's edge. Three of them were firing down into the water while a fourth was shining a powerful light. Tepler sank back under and swam farther out, hoping the water would shield him from the bullets if they had spotted him. After a minute of struggling against the resurging sea, he broke to the surface again. The shooting had stopped; the men had disappeared. He wondered if they decided he had been killed by the fall and his body dragged out to sea.

It didn't look like anyone could survive such a plunge. Even he was amazed he was still alive.

He dove again under the water and swam away from the coast, furiously kicking and stroking the water with his one good arm. A hundred yards from the cliffs were huge cragged rocks that jutted out of the water. After ten painful minutes of swimming, he reached the largest and grabbed onto the cold, barnacle-covered surface. Every move caused excruciating pain in his right shoulder. With an upsurge of the sea, he was able to pull himself inside a wide fracture. It was cold and jagged, but at least he was out of view of the cliff and sheltered from the blows of crashing water.

He slid his hand under his jacket and probed the gunshot wound. The entry hole was small, but the exit wound was bigger and the skin and muscle were shredded. Despite the stabbing pain and the sting of salt water, he was thankful it hadn't been worse. The bullet could have shattered a bone, which would have made it impossible for him to swim.

"Who the hell are those people?" he kept wondering. "Why are they so keen on killing or kidnapping astronomers? It doesn't make any sense. What stake could they have in the end of the world? The asteroid is going to kill everyone, them included."

The cell phone was still in the upper pocket of his soaked windbreaker. He tried to turn it on, but it wouldn't work. He wanted badly to call Gabriela to tell her what had happened, and he still desperately needed to contact Mortimer Barclay to find out about Donald Meller.

He had to get to Boqueron, but he had no choice now except to cling to the rock until the first light of dawn. He stayed wedged in the fissure the entire night, sleeping a few minutes at a time, feeling stiffness and a dull, throbbing pain set into his right arm. He wondered if he would be able to swim back. When it started to get light out, he lowered himself into the water and pushed off toward the bluff.

He swam on his back, kicking with his feet and backstroking with his good arm. On the north side of the observatory bluff was the inlet to a small bay with a sandy beach where he had parked his truck the night before. He swam to the beach and made his way to his truck. He was tempted to get in and drive to Boqueron, but he was certain the truck would give him away. He knew he could also be detected if he walked along the dirt road, so he opted to wade through the knee-deep water of the salt marshes, concealing himself behind shrubs, to get to the paved road a mile north.

It was getting lighter out. Before reaching the paved road, Tepler spotted the headlights of several vehicles. He splashed deeper into the salt marsh and knelt behind dense bushes until they drove by. More black Humvees, four of them.

A moment later, he heard a helicopter. He hid in the brush as it flew low overhead. It was the same kind of helicopter he had seen at Arecibo. He watched it set down on the flat of the bluff not far from the observatory, landing a minute before the column of Humvees arrived.

Had they discovered the weapon? Tepler wondered. Why else would a helicopter land there?

Once the Humvees were up the hill, he sloshed through the thick, salt-heavy water. The stench from the marsh choked him, and the salt-laden air burned his wound as much as the seawater had. Finally, he made it to the road and followed it, passing occasional houses and stores. He decided against banging on doors for help. Someone might call the police, and he couldn't risk the chance of being detained.

After walking for half an hour, he heard a car coming from behind him. Was it another Humvee? He hid behind a wall, but by the time he was satisfied it wasn't a Humvee, it was already too late to flag it down. Ten minutes later, he saw another vehicle coming from the other direction. It had only one headlight, and that one jiggled. As it got closer, he could see it was a pickup truck. He stepped a few feet into the asphalt lane and waved, his injured arm dangling uselessly. The truck slowed, moved to the other lane, and drove around him. The driver, an older man wearing a straw hat, glared at him.

Tepler realized how frightful he must look. His hair wasn't wet any more, but it was tangled and his clothes were rumpled. The truck accelerated and drove away. But fifty yards up the road, it stopped abruptly and then backed up. The driver lowered his window.

"You need help?"

"My arm's hurt. I need to get to Boqueron."

"Car accident?"

The man looked genuinely concerned, but Tepler didn't want to reveal too much. One question would lead to another. He pointed to his shoulder. "I got banged up pretty bad."

The driver leaned over to push the passenger door open, and Tepler slid in. The Samaritan turned the truck around and headed north toward Boqueron.

Tepler looked nervously out of the rear window at the observatory. The dome stood out in the faint early light. He could make out the outline of the Black Hawk, but the observatory was now too far away to see the Humvees parked in front.

"I know where the hospital is in Boqueron. I will take you there."

"Thanks, but I know some people in town. I have to get to them."

They drove a few miles without speaking. Up ahead, Tepler saw the headlights of several vehicles traveling close together. As they got closer, he saw that the headlights were high up and more widely spaced than with conventional vehicles. He slid down in the seat and covered his head with his good arm to act like he was sleeping. The Humvees zipped by without slowing down. As soon as they disappeared down the road, he straightened up and looked through the rear window. They had to be going to the observatory. There was no other place for them to go.

He noticed the driver looking at him.

"Those are bad people," the driver said.

"What makes you say that?"

"They're taking people from their homes all over Puerto Rico—San Juan, Punta Santiago, Caguas, Ponce. They take them away in black buses that don't have windows. I heard that they took people from the Arecibo observatory. The police went there because they heard some people were killed, but they didn't find anything. Just cars in the parking lot, but no people."

"What's going on?"

The driver shrugged.

"Why don't the police stop them?" Tepler asked.

"They tried, but they say they are Naval Intelligence or some other American agency, and the police don't interfere. I think they're afraid."

The old man drove slowly, but Boqueron wasn't far and they were at the outskirts of town in fifteen minutes. As they drove into the center of town, the driver said, "I've seen your picture in the newspaper. You are the astronomer at Cabo Rojo."

Tepler nodded.

The driver motioned to Tepler's arm. "They tried to get you, too, didn't they?"

They were only a few blocks from Gabriela's home. Tepler pointed to an intersection, and the driver pulled over. Tepler thrust his right hand out, wincing at the pain the movement caused. The driver squeezed his hand.

Tepler said, "It's not safe to talk. Don't say anything about this to anyone."

The man nodded. "God be with you."

The town was coming to life. Several cars drove down the street. People had come out of buildings and were walking briskly along the sidewalks. A bus was idling at the opposite corner.

Tepler walked stiffly a few blocks to Gabriela's neighborhood and soon was at her gate. He pressed the button mounted in the center of blue floral tiles. He peered into the courtyard, but he couldn't see a hint of movement in the house. He pressed the bell again. A minute later, the front door opened. Gabriela's mother peered out, squinting to see who was there.

Tepler waved at her and said in Spanish, "*Señora*, I'm sorry to wake you up so early. It's an emergency. I have to see Gabriela."

A minute later, Gabriela ran to the gate. She was wearing a light-blue robe. She swung the gate open and put her hand to her mouth when she saw his arm.

"Eric, what happened to you?"

"I got shot. They took over the observatory, the same ones who killed those people at Arecibo. I barely got away."

"When did this happen?"

"Last night, just after I got back to the observatory." He gave her a clipped account.

"It's a miracle you survived. God was watching over you."

They went into the kitchen. With Gabriela's help, Tepler tried to take off the windbreaker, but it was impossible to remove it from his wounded arm. The blood had dried, gluing the jacket and his shirt to the torn flesh.

Gabriela's mother came into the kitchen. Tepler instantly knew she had been told about the asteroid: At the garden party the evening before, she had been spirited and vivacious. Now her face was weary and sad, and he guessed she hadn't slept at all.

"Mama, get a pair of scissors."

Maria came back a minute later and stood quietly as Gabriela cut off the sleeves of the jacket and shirt. While she was snipping off the lower sleeve, Gabriela's father, Marcelo, came into the kitchen. Like Gabriela's mother, he looked somber. He nodded at Tepler and stood silently with his wife while Gabriela worked.

Soon most of the material was off his arm. Gabriela soaked the remaining cloth with warm water to dissolve the coagulated blood, and before long she was able to peel off what was left of the fabric. Tepler had been bearing the pain ever since plunging into the sea, but he had to grit his teeth as the fabric came off to keep from screaming.

He could tell from their faces they didn't like what they saw. He looked, and he didn't like what he saw either: The bullet had ripped through the shoulder muscle, and there was a gaping hole where the bullet had exited. His entire shoulder and part of his chest were now purplish blue.

"Who could have done such a thing?" Maria said.

"We need to get you to the hospital," Gabriela said.

Tepler shook his head. "They have to report gunshot wounds to the police, and I could end up being detained a long time for questioning. Is there a doctor who could fix me up and keep it quiet, or a nurse?" he said.

Gabriela's parents looked at each other and began discussing people they knew. "Salvador, he has a nephew who's married to a nurse," Marcelo said.

"But they're in New York right now," Maria said.

They named various people, thinking hard to remember names and relationships. Finally, Marcelo picked up the phone and made some calls.

Half an hour later, a man came into the kitchen carrying a black bag. He was short and thin, with wire-rimmed glasses and a pleasant smile. His name was Dr. Hernandez. His smile vanished when he examined Tepler's arm.

"I can patch you up, but if you want to repair the muscles and minimize scarring, you're going to need specialized care."

Tepler nodded. "I'll have to make do with the patchwork for now."

The doctor injected a local anesthetic and spent half an hour cleansing the wound and stitching it up, first the shredded muscle and then the skin. When finished, he covered the wound by wrapping gauze around Tepler's upper chest. He gave him plastic vials of antibiotics and painkillers. "I'll check up on you later," he said as he was leaving.

Gabriela fetched one of her father's shirts and helped Tepler put it on. She combed his long brown hair and stepped back to see how it looked. He liked the pampering, but he wished the circumstances were different.

Gabriela's parents had left the kitchen when the doctor began working on the wound, but came back in after he was gone. They sat at the kitchen table. Gabriela's father was holding his wife's hands.

Tepler said, "Gabriela told you about the asteroid?"

"Yes."

Maria began weeping and leaned her head against her husband's shoulder.

"I asked Gabriela not to tell you everything. There's a lot more to it. And there's hope."

He explained that the asteroid had changed course, and that it looked like an enormous spacecraft had diverted it. He told them about Donald Meller and the weapon hidden beneath the telescope. "The power source for it has to be out there somewhere. He wouldn't have built something like that without the fuel to make it work."

Gabriela's mother shook her head sadly. "No one believed my brother about being taken aboard a spaceship. Everyone thought he was crazy. I have to confess that I didn't believe Miguel, either."

It was already nine o'clock. Tepler wondered if the trustee had gotten his message and had tried to call back. He took the cell phone out of the upper pocket of his ripped windbreaker and tried turning it on, but the seawater had ruined it. He had never set up a password to access his voice mail from another phone so he couldn't check for messages. He told Maria and Marcelo about the trustee.

"He's our only link to Donald Meller."

Gabriela volunteered her cell phone.

Tepler dialed and waited tensely for an answer, hoping he wouldn't get voice mail again. It was the first time in five years he was eager to hear the condescending voice of the trustee.

On the fourth ring, Mortimer Barclay answered.

"Oh, it's you, Tepler. I don't appreciate being called on my private line."

"Did you get my message?"

"Yes, and I called you last night, but I didn't get an answer. It must not be such a life and death matter after all."

"Mr. Barclay, I'm going to be as brief as I can. On Thursday, I discovered an asteroid the size of Mount Everest. It's been confirmed now by other observatories."

"That's what you're paid to do, isn't it? To find asteroids? Congratulations."

"It's heading for Earth. It will strike tomorrow night"

"I'm not in the mood for jokes, Tepler."

"I'm not joking."

"I haven't heard anything about it on the news. Something like that would go public."

"What is there about the observatory you haven't told me about, Barclay?"

It was the only time he had ever addressed the trustee like that, using only his last name. His voice dripped with anger and impatience. For years, out of a desire to keep his job, he had swallowed his pride and had put up with the trustee's unpleasantness. But keeping his job was the now least of his concerns.

"What is there to tell you, Tepler?" the trustee huffed. "It's equipped with a telescope. You were hired to run the facility and conduct research into so-called Near Earth Objects. It was all spelled out in the contract."

Tepler couldn't conceal his anger. Almost shouting, he said, "I'm asking you to tell me the truth about the observatory. It has another purpose, doesn't it?"

"I don't care for your tone, young man. If you're not careful, I will hire someone else to run the facility."

"You're not going to be hiring or firing anyone. Tomorrow night, you're going to be dead."

"I don't believe anything you're saying. I can tell you've been out drinking, and now you're seeing pink asteroids. I don't see any reason to continue this conversation."

"I wish you we here in this room with me. Let me describe what you would see: There are four people sitting around a kitchen table. Three of them are friends of mine who know they could die tomorrow night and don't want that to happen. I am holding this phone in my left hand because I have a bullet hole in my right shoulder. Last night, some people in black uniforms took over the observatory and shot me as I was trying to get away. Hours before that, they massacred fifteen people at Arecibo Observatory and took everyone else away in windowless buses. I saw the bodies, Mr. Barclay, and they weren't pink."

There was a silence at the other end of the phone. "I don't quite get it, but I'll take your word for it."

"Who is Donald Meller?"

Barclay was silent again for a moment. "How do you know that name?"

"You wouldn't believe me if I told you. But if he's got something to do with the observatory, I need to know. It would explain what I found under the telescope."

"And what is that?"

"The telescope is sitting on top of a massive cylinder. Inside the cylinder there's some kind of weapon. If it's what I think it is, it was intended to be used against the asteroid."

"I don't understand anything you're saying."

"Listen to me closely. Fifteen years ago, a fisherman from this area predicted an asteroid would strike. He was taken aboard a spacecraft and was told about it. He was instructed to make the prediction known to world. He did, and as a result Donald Meller visited him and learned some interesting things that were never made public, such as the fact that an alien species with no fondness for the human race was planning on diverting the asteroid and that it would happen this year. Not long after that, the Third Alternative Foundation that you represent purchased the Cabo Rojo lighthouse and converted it into an observatory, and I believe into a weapon as well—Donald Meller's weapon."

"You're talking about things I don't know anything about."

"Are you saying you don't know Donald Meller?"

"I didn't say that."

"Does he have something to do with the observatory? Yes or no?"

"Yes, actually. He started the foundation. He provided the funds, the construction plans, everything. The foundation was created as a vehicle for building and operating the observatory."

"And as trustee, did you oversee the construction?"

"Yes, I did."

"Then you saw the construction plans?"

"I did. He told me it was some sort of experimental facility. He gave me detailed plans, and I followed through. The central column that you referred to was built in New Jersey by an engineering firm he owned. It was flown to Cabo Rojo aboard a cargo plane, and it was lowered into place by helicopter. The telescope was installed over it. When it was completed, you were hired to run the observatory."

"And baby-sit the facility."

"I believe you were hired in part as a custodian, yes."

"I have to get in touch with him."

"I'm sorry, but I haven't seen or heard from Donald Meller in ten years. "

Tepler felt like he had been punched in the stomach. "You mean you don't know how to contact him?"

"He has disappeared. For all I know, he's dead. He was working for a defense contractor in New Mexico, Bach-Merling. Then he was never heard from again. Bach-Merling denied he ever worked for them, but I know that's not true. He had even been on their board of directors at one time."

"Was there anything else he had you oversee, such as building a fuel source for the experimental facility?"

"I don't know what you mean. The observatory is powered by the local electrical grid. I know because I pay the utility bill every month."

"The weapon needs a different power source, probably nuclear. It's some kind of a Star Wars weapon—laser or particle beam, something exotic like that, but it won't work without an independent source of energy—a powerful one."

"I wish I could help you, but I truly don't know anything about it."

"There must be someone who knows."

"Well, he does have a daughter, but she's a pediatrician in Austin. I don't believe she knows about the research trust fund. Dr. Meller's instructions were to keep it secret, even from his family."

"She still might know something. How can I reach her?"

"I will try to get in touch with her. It happens I manage a separate trust fund for Laura Meller and her mother, and I speak with Laura from time to time. Give me your telephone number."

Tepler gave it to him and said, "Do you know how fast an asteroid travels?"

"No, I do not."

"This one's moving at 72,000 miles per hour. It will hit tomorrow night at eight thirty-five, Puerto Rico time, off the southwestern coast of Puerto Rico. That doesn't give us much time, Mr. Barclay."

"I will see what I can do."

Tepler pushed the "Off" button and looked around the table at Gabriela and her parents. For their benefit, he summarized the part of the conversation with the trustee they were not able to hear.

"There's hope. All we can do now is wait," he said.

Gabriela reached across the table for his hand. "We should pray for God's help."

When it came to religion, Tepler was an agnostic, but he had always been respectful of other people's beliefs. He took Marcelo's hand on one side, and Gabriela's on the other, and they formed a circle of tightly clasped hands.

They sat there, their heads bowed, their eyes closed, searching for words to express the inexpressible.

Chapter 15

The river road was open to the skies, with an occasional stretch covered by a canopy of trees. Kendon knew that without cover they could not escape the cold, technical eyes of the satellite. The satellite accomplished what the implant had done, pinpointing his location.

He could now feel the familiar mental probing, like fingers slithering into his skull. He resisted by creating a swirling blizzard in his mind and wrapping himself inside a cocoon of whiteness. Laura also needed protection against the psychic intrusion. As he sped down the two-lane road, he guided her deeply into her own mental sanctuary.

"They can't control you if you don't let them. They can't know your thoughts if you hide them in brightness."

She was staring straight ahead, her lips squeezed together. Kendon could sense her determination, but he knew it wasn't enough to hide behind a mental shield. They were being hunted, and his senses were fine-tuned to pick up on anomalies. He hadn't seen any other vehicles for miles, so he was certain the road had been blocked ahead. No one was getting through.

He feared more than anything running into a roadblock set up by local police who had been manipulated into believing he was a terrorist. How would he deal with them? He knew there could be only one way. He would have to sweep them away with the beam weapon.

More likely, they would drive into a Directorate ambush. Because he could think like them and plan like them, he was sure the Directorate had positioned commandos somewhere along the road, men armed with machine guns and an eagerness to be the ones to kill the traitor Arkasha. He and Laura would be shredded the instant they drove into the trap.

Every few miles, the river came into view. It flowed in the same direction they were traveling.

"If we are where I think we are, I know of an airport," Laura said. "It's about thirty miles downriver."

"That's great, but we can't stay on the road."

They came to another stretch of tree-canopied road that appeared to go on for miles. Once under the protective cover, Kendon swerved without warning off the asphalt onto a dirt lane. The river was a quarter mile away. Through the trees, he could see a scattering of cabins, some small and dilapidated, others larger and better kept.

He drove fast over deep, water-filled potholes. Laura looked at him quizzically.

"What do you know about the river?" Kendon said.

"It flows south and eventually empties into the Gulf of Mexico. Downriver is Clifford, where the airport is."

"They've set up an ambush on the road. We have to find a boat."

The dirt road ended in a thicket of trees with autumn foliage overhanging the river. They got out and looked at the swirling water. The river level was high, swollen by recent rain, and the narrowest the river appeared to be was about fifty feet.

"If we stay under the branches, they won't be able to see us," he said as he pointed to the sky.

The cabins were spaced far apart, between thick growths of river trees. Kendon broke into two garages without finding a boat.

At a third cabin, they found a canoe mounted on the wall of a storage shed, but a canoe would be too tricky to maneuver, and he couldn't risk capsizing and losing the portable beam weapon and the one-one-five pod.

Kendon knew that theft went against everything Laura believed in. He had watched her reaction as he forced his way into the garages. Each time, she had closed her eyes and bowed her head.

"We don't have any choice, Laura. The rules have changed."

Finally, they found a larger cabin built on concrete pilings. From the look of the grounds, no one had been there recently. Underneath the cabin was a garage and storage shed. Kendon picked open the padlock, and inside the garage, on a trailer, was a twenty-foot aluminum boat with a small outboard motor. Paddles and life jackets were hanging from the wall, and sleeping bags and other camping gear were on shelves. In a corner, he found a five-gallon can half full of gas.

He was surprised when Laura pulled the sleeping bags from the shelf and tossed them into the boat.

"The rules have changed," she said.

Kendon found fishing rods and a fisherman's hat in a corner and threw them into the boat, too. Fortunately, the trailer and boat were light enough for them to pull. They tugged the trailer out of the garage and guided it down to the water, then he backed the Cherokee down to the boat. The one-one-five pod, their sacred cargo, fit easily in the center. Once everything was transferred to the boat, Kendon drove the Cherokee into the garage and locked the door.

Before leaving, they went up to the cabin. Kendon forced the door open and spotted a wall-mounted phone in the kitchen. His face brightened when he picked up the receiver and heard a dial tone. "We're in luck. What's the trustee's number?"

He dialed and waited for someone to answer, but only got voice mail. He handed the receiver to Laura. With his prompting, Laura said, "Mortimer, I have to talk to you. I don't have a cell phone, so I'll try to call you later. Stay by your phone. This is extremely urgent, more so than you can possibly imagine. In case you've heard news about me being kidnapped by terrorists, I want to put your mind at ease. It's completely false. Please tell no one that you've heard from me."

Kendon searched the cabin for anything usable. From a bedroom, he grabbed a floppy straw hat and several olive drab military blankets. In the kitchen, he found carving knives and took the sturdiest.

"We've been here too long already," Kendon said. "We have to get out of here."

Before getting into the boat, Kendon pushed the trailer into the water until the current grabbed it and dragged it under. After climbing into the boat, he threw the blankets over the one-one-five pod and set up the rods so that it looked like they were out fishing.

With the angler's hat jammed on his head, he started the small outboard motor, but then shut it off because it made too much noise. He loosened the swivel screws and pushed down on the motor so that the propeller came out of the water. He handed a paddle to Laura. "We have to do it the hard way."

They paddled away from the riverbank far enough to catch the current, but close enough to stay beneath the foliage of overhanging trees. Laura knew how to handle a paddle. As she rhythmically stroked the water, she gazed pensively at the trees and at the occasional cabin on the opposite bank. She was wearing the floppy hat, and Kendon liked how the dappled light that came through the leaves fell on her shoulders but not on her face.

They traveled several miles in the easy current. Up ahead, the land on the other side of the river flattened, and the trees along the river thickened. Kendon wondered if they had bypassed the road ambush, but as they floated with the current he began to feel vaguely uneasy, that going any farther would be a mistake. He tried to visualize a setup, and he became alarmed when an image came vividly into his mind of snipers lying in ambush along the riverbank.

He spotted an opening in the dense river foliage, apparently the mouth of a creek. Huge cypresses with exposed roots emerged from the water. Once into the creek, they were hidden from the river. They dragged the boat onto the bank between two trees.

In a whisper, Kendon said, "I need to check the road and the forest up ahead. I could be gone half an hour. No matter what, stay here."

She took out her pistol. He gave her his gun, too. "You know how to use these. Only shoot if you have to defend yourself."

"I don't want to stay here alone."

"You don't have the training. If there's someone out there, you'll give us away." He grabbed one of the carving knives he had taken from the cabin. "Your father entrusted me with your life. I'm not going to let anything happen to you."

Knife in hand, Kendon slipped into the forest, noiselessly moving between trees and through underbrush, ignoring the sting of nettles on his face and hands. Years before, he had fled his murder-filled career path to become an undercover researcher in the laboratory where Donald Meller worked with a mission of detecting dissent and conspiracy. Now he was back in his original element and it felt natural, as if there had never been a break with the past.

With predator stealth, he made his way through the forest toward the road. He knew he had come close to the road when he saw a break in the treetops. Every few feet, he paused to listen. Soon, he heard voices, and as he drew nearer, he was sure they were speaking Russian.

As he got closer, he heard them hurling juvenile insults at one another back and forth across the road. *They think they own the road, so they've let their guard down.*

Kendon slipped back into the forest and worked his way farther up. Finally, he was able to see the two-lane road. On the other side was a meadow that went up a hill and ended at the foot of a low cliff. A Black Hawk helicopter had landed far back, barely visible. Positioned along the sides of the road were four Directorate soldiers. One was lying behind a .50-caliber machine gun; the others were armed with M-16 rifles.

Crouching, he made his way back down toward the river, moving with even greater caution than before. Two or more commandos would have been dispatched to watch the river. The woods sloped downward, a matrix of trees, boulders, underbrush, and shallow gullies. On the trip down the river, he had noticed at some places how the forest sloped gently to the water; at others, it ended at a bluff with a sheer ten- or twenty-foot drop to the river.

If he were the one watching the river, waiting for the kill, he would position himself on one of the bluffs.

It took all of Kendon's skill to avoid making any sounds as he crept through a low gully. Before reaching the river, he sensed a presence. He crawled up to a thicket of bushes and peered through. Standing on a boulder at the edge of a bluff was the black-clad figure of a Directorate soldier who was looking upriver through binoculars, an M-16 dangling from his shoulder.

Kendon couldn't detect anyone else. He maneuvered around the brush and crawled up the shallow gully, gripping the knife in his right hand. *Stay there, don't move.*

Just as he was about to close the gap between them, the soldier lowered the binoculars and turned his torso slightly to speak into a shoulder microphone. Kendon froze. The soldier was in his late teens or early twenties, about Kendon's size and build, with a crew cut. His purple beret was stuffed in his belt.

Kendon heard him say in Russian into the microphone, "The river is clear."

And then a less audible voice came from the shoulder microphone: "We know they turned off the road. TAC 4 is searching. You and Viktor are to remain in place. If you see a man and a woman in a boat, shoot to kill."

The soldier again raised the binoculars to his eyes. He had to be the spotter for the other sniper, for Viktor. Kendon looked everywhere but couldn't detect the second sniper. He had to be on another bluff farther north, closer to the creek and Laura, because the forest thinned out in the other direction and sloped down to the river.

Fifteen yards separated Kendon from the soldier. He wished he could make his body float through the air like he had done many times in dreams. He crawled half the distance under the cover of trees, bushes, and depressions in the forest floor. The last five yards was open ground, and the only cover he could count on was the murmur of the river.

Stay there, don't move.

The boulder the soldier was standing on jutted four feet from the ground. Half crawling, Kendon slipped up behind him. With viper speed, he grabbed the soldier's boots above the ankle, yanking them furiously backwards. The soldier fell flat on his face against the hard edge of the rock as Kendon pulled him to the ground. He had hoped to land him face down, but the commando twisted his body furiously so that when he hit the ground he was on his back. His face full of fear and rage, he kicked his feet free of Kendon's grip and squirmed to loosen the rifle from his shoulder, but Kendon grabbed a rock and slammed it down on his head, then hit him a second time. He shoved the carving knife into the soldier's throat just below the Adam's apple. With two hands gripping the handle, he pushed the blade in until it was stopped by a vertebra, and then he pressed harder until he severed the spinal column. The head fell back, the body went limp. The small mouth and large gray eyes were still wide open, as if in amazement. It was a round face with soft Slavic features, the face of a boy.

The shoulder microphone squawked, "Volodya. What's going on?" the voice said in Russian.

Kendon pressed down on the transmitter button. "I'm taking a piss."

"If they get by us because you're taking a piss, I will shoot you myself."

"Fuck your mother."

Kendon quickly stripped the body of the uniform and boots and changed into the uniform. It was an almost perfect fit—even the boots and the beret were right. He slung the rifle on his shoulder and headed north, walking nonchalantly through the trees, scrutinizing every possible ambush site.

A hundred yards north, he saw a human shape lying under a bush facing the river, a sniper rifle cradled in aim. Kendon could easily have shot him, but even the crack of a single round would carry to the road.

Kendon walked noisily toward the prone figure. When he was ten yards away, he said loudly in Russian, "Hey, where the fuck is Volodya?"

He kept walking nonchalantly toward the prone figure, one hand on the rifle strap. The sniper turned to look, his face showing surprise. Kendon didn't like the face. It was narrow, with dark eyes, dark eyebrows, and a cruel curl to the mouth, giving him a look more of craftiness than intelligence.

Viktor jerked his thumb in the direction Kendon had come from. "Over there. Who the hell are you?"

"Nikolai. TAC 4. We just arrived. My orders are to relieve Volodya."

Kendon slipped the rifle from his shoulder and held it loosely to his side.

Viktor jumped to his feet, his dark eyes glaring. "I have not heard such orders."

He glanced at the name on Kendon's uniform, which read "Volodya."

The sniper was about to press down on his shoulder mike when Kendon swung rifle butt upward, catching him under the chin and flinging him onto his back. Kendon raised the rifle butt to smash it down on the sniper's head, but Viktor managed to deflect the blow with his arm and roll over. He was agile, on his feet in a second. The look of surprise had vanished, replaced by a clever smile. He touched his bloodied chin, then moved one hand toward the shoulder mike.

Kendon aimed at his chest. "Put your hands in the air."

The clever smile turned into a friendly smile. "Are you going to shoot me? They will hear it and come for you, Arkasha."

"I am Nikolai."

"You are Arkasha."

"How can you know who I am?"

"Everyone knows who you are. You are famous."

Viktor's eyes shifted from side to side, as if looking for an escape.

Kendon said, "You were waiting for Arkasha. You were going to shoot Arkasha. That's why you are here."

"No, it's not true. Volodya and I, we had a pact. We like what you are doing. We want you to succeed. We don't want the world to be destroyed. We were going to let you pass and tell them we didn't see you."

The shoulder mike was plugged into a receiver clipped to the belt. "Unplug the shoulder mike," Kendon ordered.

"I will, but please don't shoot me. I'm your friend. I want to join you."

He reached for the cord, turning slightly. But instead of pulling the cord, he grabbed his side arm.

Kendon fired a single round, sending the sharp crack of a report through the woods. The bullet ripped into Viktor's chest, flinging him backward to the ground. Kendon rolled him over. With his knee on the back of the neck, he yanked Viktor's head back, breaking his neck.

He turned him face up again just as the shoulder microphone barked, "Viktor, report."

Kendon imitated Viktor's voice. "Nothing to report."

"There was a gunshot."

"No, it was a big tree branch that broke. It almost fell on me."

The shoulder mike of Volodya's uniform crackled, "Volodya, report."

Kendon tried to imitate a softer voice, "Nothing to report, Commander."

"What happened to Viktor?"

"A branch broke from a tree, and it fell on his head. But he's got a rock where a head should be, so he's not hurt."

There was a brief pause, as if the commander was assessing the communication. Then the voice said, "Proceed as before."

Kendon stripped off Viktor's uniform and boots, dragged the body to the edge of the bluff, and pushed it over. It splashed into the water and was quickly caught by the current, bobbing like a piece of driftwood as it headed downstream.

Backtracking, he returned to Volodya's body to retrieve his clothes. He knelt beside the young soldier's body, staring at his face and thinking what a shame he had to die. Like Kendon, he had been taken from an orphanage too young to have a choice in the matter and had been raised in an unnatural environment. It was the face of someone who had not yet been completely corrupted by the Collaboration experience.

Kendon couldn't stay there long. He rolled the body over the edge of the bluff. It splashed into the water face up, and Kendon watched it float into the current.

He gathered up his clothes and made his way back to Viktor's position. Using his shirt as a makeshift bag, he stuffed in Viktor's uniform and the berets and side arms of the dead snipers. He slung the rifles over his shoulder and made his way, bag in hand, through the forest toward Laura and the boat.

He had told Laura he would be gone for thirty minutes, but he must have been away at least twice that long. He became worried about her. Running half bent and using brush and gullies for cover, he finally reached the creek. Cautiously, he looked over the edge of the embankment and saw the boat.

He said in a low voice, "Laura, it's me!"

The small boat was where it was supposed to be, but Laura wasn't there. He felt a burst of panic. He searched inland as far as the road, then backtracked to the boat. There was still no sign of her. He peered under the blanket, hoping she had hidden there. The portable beam weapon and the one-one-five pod were there, but she was not.

While he was still bent over the boat, he heard a menacing voice behind him. "Don't move."

He put his hands in the air. He slowly turned. Laura was pointing the pistol at his chest.

"Laura, it's me. Don't shoot!"

She lowered the gun and ran to him, throwing her arms around him. "Oh, Michael, I was so worried. I heard a shot. I thought something happened to you."

"I ran into some trouble."

She stepped back and stared at the black uniform. "You left as Michael and came back as Arkasha."

"I left alive, I came back alive." He showed her the sniper rifle and the M-16. "They were waiting for us. If we'd gone four hundred yards more, we would have been picked off."

"What do we do now?"

He lifted the end of the blanket. "Get under. We have to get out of here."

Laura stretched out on the floor of the boat next to the one-one-five pod, and Kendon covered her with the blanket. He threw the bundle of clothes in and stashed the sniper rifles next to the portable beam weapon. Splashing through the cold water, he guided the boat into the current then climbed in. He looked up at the sky and was glad to see clouds had moved up from the south and the sky was now covered over. Once in the current, he slid under the blanket, ensuring Laura was in the center of the boat with the one-one-five pod protecting her on one side and his body on the other.

"We've got to be careful," he whispered. "I could go back and take them all out with the beam weapon, but then the Directorate would know we're here, and we would lose our advantage. Right now, they're looking for us up at the cabins. It will take them a while to figure out what happened."

The shoulder microphone on Viktor's uniform came to life. A voice speaking Russian said a few crisp words and the name Viktor. Kendon grabbed the microphone from the pack of clothing. He pushed the button and answered in Russian, but in a voice different from his own. Then he released the button. The speaker said something more in Russian, and the microphone went silent.

"What was that about?" Laura whispered.

"They wanted an update from Viktor, the sniper. So I gave them an update—no change, all calm, nothing to report."

They were face to face, with faint light coming through the blankets but enough to see. When he pulled his hand away from the microphone, he slid his hand onto her hip. She pulled closer to him. Her body was warm, soft, and comforting, and he pulled her tightly against him. He didn't want the closeness to end. Earlier, when she had thrown her arms spontaneously around his neck, he had felt at first a sharp emotional stab. Never before that he could remember had anyone hugged him or shown him such unreserved affection. In the underworld, humans had become as cold as the Breeders. He wanted to stay in that position forever, next to the warmth of this woman.

As the boat drifted, Laura gazed at him. Her eyes were probing, but he felt they were accepting, despite everything. He felt he could tell her anything now, even about what had happened to her father, and she would understand.

The boat floated downstream for ten minutes before scraping against something. Kendon sat up. They had drifted to the other side of the river and had brushed against a boulder, and now they were drifting near a tree that had half-fallen into shallow water along the riverbank. As he dug the paddle into the water to steer the boat back into the swift current in the middle of the river, Kendon spotted a body that had been trapped by the tree. The chin was caught in the fork of a branch, and the body was being tugged in the direction of the current. Water was breaking over the face and feet.

Laura had sat up and had grabbed a paddle, too. Kendon tried to distract her by pointing to something on the other side of the river, but she saw the body. She put her hand over her mouth.

"His name was Volodya. I was sorry about him. The other one, no one will ever miss him."

Laura looked down and shook her head softly, her face anguished. Kendon pointed to the confiscated rifles.

"I understand," she said almost inaudibly.

Kendon surveyed the river downstream. The trees had thinned out along the river plain and there wasn't much foliage to hide under, but the sky had clouded over. Despite their technical sophistication, high-resolution satellite cameras were useless when the clouds were thick.

The current had taken them several miles south of the ambush site. Kendon wondered if the Directorate had discovered the snipers were missing yet. He hadn't heard any more radio transmissions, but that didn't mean anything except that he and Laura needed to cover as much distance as quickly as possible. Once the Directorate commanders knew they had been duped, they would search downriver. He and Laura still had a long way to go before reaching Clifford and its airport.

He started the outboard motor and accelerated into the swift current. He surveyed the skies, then pulled the beam weapon close to him so that the grip was within reach. With the motor pushed to its limit, they traveled at least ten miles in thirty minutes.

The skies stayed clear of threats, but Kendon wondered for how long. Surely they would have found the Cherokee by now and the trailer he had ditched in the water, and Directorate troops would have gone looking for the snipers and not found them.

On the west side of the river, the land was getting hilly again, and the trees along the river thickened. Up ahead, the river narrowed.

Laura shouted, "I see rapids up ahead."

Kendon grabbed the binoculars. Boulders jutted from the river, and the water sluiced between them. It was a wide enough gap to maneuver through, but what was on the other side? How far did the rapids go?

Kendon lowered the binoculars. "We can't risk capsizing and losing the one-one-five pod. We have to go around the rapids."

The river was speeding up dangerously. Kendon veered the boat into calmer water near the riverbank, then drifted toward the boulders. When they could go no farther, he jumped into the water and dragged the boat onto the rocky bank under the cover of low tree branches. He stripped out of the sniper's black uniform and put on a denim shirt and trousers Laura had packed. After pulling the boat into the brush and covering it, they climbed up the hillside to get a better view downriver.

Kendon was glad they hadn't continued on the river. Through the binoculars he could see that the rapids went on for a quarter of a mile. In some places the water was dangerously turbulent, enough to capsize a small aluminum boat or smash it against the boulders.

For the first time, he felt on the verge of despair. For every step forward, they seemed to take two backward. Only fifteen miles farther south was an airport and the airplane they needed to get to Puerto Rico, but now their only objective was to avoid being torn to pieces by raging water and to keep from falling into the hands of the Directorate. It was already late afternoon, the day before the asteroid would hit. Even if they managed to get airborne, they still didn't know exactly where in Puerto Rico they had to go.

Kendon tried to hide his feelings, but Laura seemed to pick up on them. She looked at him sternly. "The binoculars, please."

He handed them to her. She looked down river and then in the direction of the road, hidden by a thick growth but only several hundred yards away.

"The way I see it, we have two options," Laura said firmly. "We can hike to the road and flag down a car. I think I could convince someone to cooperate with us. Or, we carry everything downstream, including the boat, and then we continue down-river. Sooner or later we'll get to Clifford and the airport."

Her confidence was like a tonic. He knew they had to push forward no matter what. He had more at stake now than ever before. He had Laura, and he didn't want anything happening to her.

They hiked up the hillside to the road, but kept cautiously back under bushes. They waited for fifteen minutes, but not a single vehicle went by. Finally, they heard a motor in the distance.

"Wait here," Kendon whispered.

He crept slowly to the shoulder of the road, careful to stay behind the cover of bushes. Coming up the road from the south was a black Humvee, followed by another. He slid back down to Laura and pulled her low to the ground.

"Humvees."

The vehicles grew louder as the whine of the powerful motors penetrated the forest. Soon they were at the road above them, driving slowly as if patrolling. They kept on going.

As soon as the Humvees were out of sight, Kendon and Laura hiked back to the boat.

"They control the road. That leaves us only the river," he said.

It took two exhausting hours going back and forth under the cover of the trees. On the first trip, carrying the lighter gear, they explored a path through the ravines and underbrush of the forest. On the next, they carried the weapons and the outboard motor. The boat they toted over their heads, and finally they moved the heavy one-one-five pod, their only hope for the future, taking care not to jostle or drop it. Every hundred yards, breathless from the exertion, they had to put the pod down and rest.

Kendon was impressed by Laura's physical stamina and determination. She had made up her mind about what had to be done, and now she was throwing herself into the task without reserve. She was so much like her father.

In another river inlet, where the rapids ended, they loaded everything back into the boat. Using paddles, they caught the current but stayed as close to the riverbank as possible. Kendon set up the fishing poles, letting the lines out just enough to drag along the water. Laura had on the straw hat, and Kendon wore the fisherman's hat. The uniforms, the pod, and the weapons were covered by the blankets, but who would they fool? Kendon wondered. The Directorate troops must be searching for the two snipers, and they must realize by now he had slipped through. The lives of the snipers had merely bought time, but how much? Soon the helicopters would search again. If he had to shoot them down, their whereabouts would be known again, and he and Laura would be back to square one.

They drifted for about five miles. Up ahead, he heard motorboats. As they got closer, he saw they were approaching a recreational area with a boat launch. The river had been widened into a small lake, and a dozen boats were out on the water. A cluster of boats was stopped in the middle of the artificial lake.

Set back in the woods was a campground, with tents, trailers, and RVs scattered under the trees. Plumes of wood smoke rose through the branches. Children were splashing in shallow water along the riverbank.

Laura said, "Maybe we should ask if someone's got a cell phone. We'll tell them it's an emergency."

Kendon lowered the outboard motor to the water and started it. He headed for the cluster of boats, but when they got within fifty yards, Laura suddenly pointed back up the river. "Look behind you, Michael. A helicopter!"

He heard the rotors and felt a chill run up his spine. He reached down and gripped the beam weapon, but kept it under the blanket. He wondered what to do. If he got close to the boaters, he would endanger them. But there was safety among them, too. With any luck, he and Laura would be taken for campers.

He turned to look. A Black Hawk was moving slowly down the river, only a hundred feet off the water. Its movement was steady and deliberate, as if searching for something. The helicopter got closer—too close to launch rockets, but close enough to open up with machine guns.

Kendon let his mind relax, and he tried to pick up on the psychic environment. He felt the presence of danger, disturbances in the ocean of mind like large waves roiling and crashing, but he did not sense the adrenaline spike that would signal imminent hostility. He guessed the helicopter was searching for the missing snipers.

He shouted to be heard above the chopper noise. "Act like you think they're friendly. Wave to them."

Laura smiled feebly and waved. The Black Hawk swooped overhead and continued up the river. Kendon sped toward the cluster of boaters, in a half-dozen small boats with outboard motors. Most of them were occupied by adults, but in two of them were small children who had a look of fright in their eyes.

Kendon cut the motor and drifted up. Men from several of the boats were shouting to each other while pointing at the water. Kendon couldn't hear what they were saying because of the helicopter, but he soon saw why the boats were clustered together: Floating in the water was a body, face down, dressed only in a sleeveless undershirt and shorts. The hair was dark and short, with a balding patch at the back of the head.

It was Viktor's body.

The Black Hawk abruptly stopped, hovered above the water, and turned in place.

After hanging in the air for a moment, it slowly headed back toward them.

Chapter 16

While waiting for a call back from the trustee, Tepler felt like a death-row inmate hoping for a last-minute reprieve from the governor. He was at the kitchen table, with Gabriela on one side of him and Maria and Marcelo sitting across. He had placed the silver cell phone in the center of the kitchen table, and they were waiting for it to bring news of hope.

All of them were fidgety, especially Tepler. He kept getting up, pacing the kitchen floor, then sitting down again, all the while cradling his bandaged arm. He couldn't get the image out of his mind of the people massacred at Arecibo, or of the black-clad men who tried to kill him at the observatory.

Who were those people? he wondered. What motivated them to do such terrible things?

Gabriela's mother finally got up and set about preparing a meal of soup and banana croquettes stuffed with beef. The kitchen soon filled with the aroma of food, as if it was a normal Saturday afternoon and soon friends and relatives would arrive with other dishes to share a pleasant evening on the patio.

Gabriela pitched in to help while Tepler and Marcelo stared at each other across the table. They ate in silence, heads bowed, avoiding eye contact. Following the meal, Marcelo proposed a game of Scrabble, but the game was listless.

"Shouldn't we tell all of our friends and relatives what we know?" Maria asked.

"We should wait until we know more," Gabriela said.

After Marcelo put the game away, Maria began to cry, and he touched his wife on the arm to comfort her. He was a solid man, a square-faced merchant who spoke little, but when he did, people listened. As he patted her arm, he said softly, "I don't think God went through all of the trouble to create our world only for it be destroyed by these soulless creatures that Eric told us about. We have no reason to give up hope."

At one point, Gabriela went to fetch her violin and attempted a Paganini sonata, but it was without spirit and ended when she, too, broke down and cried.

An hour later, the doctor returned to check up on Tepler's shoulder and gave him an injection to ease the pain. Tepler found the drug calming, but he didn't want to be calm. He wanted to throw himself into the center of action, but he was frustrated by the fact there wasn't any center to throw himself into. There was only the cell phone. Finally, not able to stand the wait any longer, he dialed Mortimer Barclay's number.

Barclay answered just before the call transferred to voice mail. "This is Mortimer Barclay," the trustee said in his usual imperious voice.

"So what's happening, Mr. Barclay?" Tepler said hotly. "How come we haven't heard back from you?" He pressed the phone tightly against his ear and surveyed the anxious faces around the kitchen table.

"I'm sorry to say this, but there's nothing to report yet."

"Haven't you tried contacting the daughter?"

"Yes, and in fact she tried calling me, but she called while I was on the phone with the hospital in Austin where she works. She left a message."

The trustee didn't continue with an explanation of the message, leaving Tepler hanging. It was one of the quirks that Tepler had put up with over the years. The trustee would lead people up to a certain point, engaging their interest, then he would stop talking, forcing them to ask follow-up questions.

"And what was the message?" Tepler asked, unable to keep impatience out of his voice.

"She said she had something urgent to tell me, but she couldn't leave a callback number. Apparently, she no longer has her cell phone. She said she would contact me later and for me not to tell anyone about her call. I got the impression she was in trouble, maybe on the run."

"What makes you thinks so?"

"She said something about news reports that she was being held hostage by terrorists. She said, and I quote her, 'In case you've seen the news about me being kidnapped by terrorists, put your mind at ease. It's completely false.' I hadn't heard anything about it, so I turned the TV on and flipped through all the news channels. There were reports of a possible terrorist on the loose in Texas, someone with connections to a Chechen terrorist organization who is in possession of stolen nuclear materials. A massive manhunt is under way. They showed a photograph of him on television."

Barclay stopped, again leaving Tepler hanging.

Tepler was barely able to hide his impatience. "What's that got to do with Donald Meller's daughter?"

"The reports say it's the same person Laura Meller was last seen with at the hospital. What's most curious is that the house Donald Meller used to own was blown to pieces two hours after she left the hospital. Such a shame, too. It was a magnificent home. Haven't you been watching the news, Tepler?"

"All we get is local news here and some Latin American channels. I don't get it. How is a suspected Chechen terrorist connected to Laura Meller?"

"The reports say this person went to the hospital in Austin last night, and she was seen leaving with him. Police assumed she didn't leave with him voluntarily. However, in her call to me, she implied she wasn't taken against her will."

"Something's missing, Mr. Barclay. It doesn't add up."

"I didn't think so, either. I called the hospital after we spoke earlier today, and I was told that Laura Meller wasn't in and nothing more. That's when I turned the TV on. I called the hospital back, but it was a difficult getting connected to someone willing to talk. After I identified myself as the trustee of an account that funds pediatric cancer research, I was finally put in touch with the head nurse of the cancer ward."

Again the deliberate silence.

Tepler sighed. "Okay, and what did you learn?"

"The man she left with last night was, in fact, the same person on television. But he spoke English well, and he performed a 'miracle' while he was there. That's the nurse's word, not mine. While he was waiting for Laura to meet him at the hospital, he healed a child of a brain tumor with his hands. X-rays were taken this morning and the tumor had vanished."

"That doesn't sound like a terrorist," Tepler said.

"Oh yes, and the nurse said that UFOs were seen in the sky above the hospital. A lot of the hospital staff observed them."

"What kind of nuclear materials were stolen?"

"There was nothing about it on the news, except that it was nuclear material taken from a research facility somewhere in New Mexico."

"Didn't you say Donald Meller worked for a defense contractor in New Mexico?"

"Yes, as a matter of fact. Bach-Merling had a major involvement in nuclear research at Los Alamos and at Sandia Laboratories, among others."

Tepler began to grasp the situation. If there was nuclear material in possession of someone accompanied by Donald Meller's daughter, then it had to be the power source needed to fuel the weapon. Meller's daughter had to know about the weapon, and she and this alleged terrorist were trying to reach it with the fuel. But they were being pursued.

It was clear that somebody wanted to prevent their success. Tepler didn't understand it. Who could possibly have an interest in a dead planet?

"The people who shot me and who killed all those people at Arecibo were wearing black, like commandos. Has anything about them come up in the news?"

"There have been various reports. The nurse in Austin said some people in black overcoats showed up in the hospital parking lot and took away an X-ray technician. Others arrived later by helicopter, but were soldiers in black uniforms who claimed to be federal agents, although federal authorities have denied any knowledge of those people."

"At Arecibo, I saw people being forced onto black buses, some at gunpoint. Has there been anything in the news about black buses?"

"Why, yes. In fact, there's been quite an uproar. There are reports from across the country about people being taken away against their will. The black buses supposedly belong to the Office of Naval Intelligence, but the federal government denies this."

"Somebody in our government has to know about all of this," Tepler said.

Barclay said, "I think the general feeling is that we're facing a nuclear attack, and that authorities are responding with massive preparations, including the evacuation of key people from Washington and from around the United States. The National Guard has been called up. Do you know that the president will address the nation tomorrow morning?"

"No, like I said, we only get local news here. I haven't had time to watch TV, anyway. I've been too busy just trying to stay alive."

"From what I've learned so far, Tepler, I'm inclined to believe authorities think we are facing a major terrorist attack. There hasn't been any mention of an asteroid anywhere. If what you're saying is true, we should have heard about it by now. You can't sit on something like that for long."

"You can if you kill or kidnap everyone who knows anything about it."

"I hope you're telling me the truth, Tepler. If you're making this up, you're going to face serious consequences."

Tepler wanted to strangle the trustee, but said calmly, "I have to talk to Laura Meller. She knows what's going on."

"I'm trying."

"Call me immediately when you hear from her, Mr. Barclay. Tell her what I've told you about Cabo Rojo, but don't tell anyone else about this. You don't know who you can trust anymore."

Tepler's voice had taken on an authoritative tone, and he could sense that the trustee resented it. Tepler smiled and added, "Have her call me immediately. Here's the cell phone number."

He gave it to Barclay and asked him to repeat it, number by number, then hung up.

Gabriela and her parents had heard only half of the conversation, but it was enough for their faces to brighten. Tepler filled them in on the other half.

"*Gracias a Dios, gracias a Dios,*" Gabriela's mother said, her hands clasped. "God has heard our prayers."

Tepler knew first hand that if Laura Meller and this alleged terrorist were able to reach Cabo Rojo with the nuclear fuel—assuming they actually had it—they were going to run into a final obstacle. The killers in black uniforms were in control of the observatory, in possession of the weapon.

"We've got to get the observatory back," Tepler said. "But how?"

Gabriela said, "Maybe my cousin could help. You met him—Nestor Estrada. He's the commander of a National Guard infantry battalion. The soldiers are from around here. I went to school with some of them."

Tepler thought about it. It was clear it was going to take force to oust them. At last count, there were at least a dozen black Humvees at the observatory, and then there was the helicopter that he had seen land. That meant twenty, thirty—maybe even forty of them.

The National Guard had soldiers, vehicles, and weapons, everything they would need, and they had already been mobilized. Tepler suspected it had to do with the asteroid. If so, that would make it easier to get help.

"How can I get in touch with him?

"I imagine he can be reached through his wife."

He handed Gabriela the cell phone.

"We don't have any time to lose."

Chapter 17

The Black Hawk helicopter bobbed back toward the floating body like a tiger ready to pounce. Kendon said to Laura, "Ignore the helicopter. Stare at the body." He paddled alongside the boat that was closest to the sniper's body and acted like he wanted to help.

Leaning over the side of the boat was a beefy man in cutoff pants, a yellow T-shirt, and a baseball cap who was trying to reach the body with an oar.

"What happened?" Kendon shouted in order to be heard over the roar of the approaching helicopter.

The man shrugged. "Looks like he's been shot."

"Anyone call the police?"

"Not yet."

The helicopter reached them, hovering forty feet overhead. The rotor blast flattened the water and sent hats flying from various boats. Kendon and Laura pushed down on their hats to keep from losing them.

A voice with a distinctive Eastern European accent barked over the helicopter's loudspeaker, "All of you. Move away, now!"

Kendon re-started the outboard and followed closely behind the other boats as they distanced themselves from the body. Kendon watched as a Directorate soldier was lowered by cable to the water. While dangling above the body, the soldier deftly looped a rope around the torso, under the armpits. Then, with the body hanging beneath him, the soldier was lifted back to the helicopter. With the sniper's body dangling below, the Black Hawk banked, flew over the trees to the road, and headed back in the direction of the cabins and the small town of Madison.

Several minutes later, the shoulder mike on one of the sniper's uniform squawked. A voice in Russian said, "Viktor, report your position." A minute later, Volodya's shoulder microphone sounded as well, with the same command.

Kendon smiled and thought they must believe he was stupid or that he was unaware they had recovered Viktor's body. He knew if he pressed the transmit button, they would be able to pinpoint where the broadcast emanated from.

Laura looked at him quizzically.

"They don't have a clue where we are. For all they know, we went back to that little town or fled across the river into the hills."

Over the rumble of the outboard motor, Laura said, "We have to call Mortimer. Someone here must have a cellphone."

Their boat was close to the shore, not more than fifty yards from a picnic table where three men, middle-aged and wearing tropical patterned shirts and straw hats, were drinking beer.

Kendon wondered if the sunglasses, fishing hat, and two-day growth of beard were sufficient to keep him from being recognized. All Laura had to hide behind were the sunglasses and the hat.

"We better not chance it."

While he was thinking about what to do, one of the men at the picnic table stood up and point excitedly at the sky. Other people nearer to the campgrounds began pointing up, too.

When Kendon looked up, he saw several disks clearly profiled against the clouds. He immediately understood why they were there: The Breeders had used their powers to locate the body. All of the Directorate agents and soldiers were implanted. Even though Viktor was dead, the implant would continue to function until the body decayed, relentlessly broadcasting coded information unique to him. They must have pinpointed Volodya's body, too.

The disks were hovering at several thousand feet, but soon moved north in the same direction as the helicopter. Kendon found their presence worrisome. Even though they were now free of implants, Kendon knew firsthand of the alien ability to probe the mental landscape until latching onto a psychic clue.

Laura was staring at the sky, a worried look on her face. Kendon shouted over the noise of the outboard motor, "Close your eyes, Laura. Block your thoughts. Think white, think bright. Picture the sun in your mind. Don't let anything else enter your head."

Kendon revved up the motor and zoomed downriver where the stream narrowed and the current quickened. The disks kept moving north, away from them, and after a few minutes he could no longer see them.

Soon it would be dark.

Only one more day left, Kendon thought, and they were boxed in, somewhere in Texas, far from a destination they still didn't quite know. He knew that to keep from falling into despair he had to focus on little steps; he had to take care of one task, and then move on to the next, and from there go on to the one after that: find a place to hide the boat, steal a car, transfer everything from the boat to the vehicle, get to a phone, contact the trustee, locate an airplane, find someone to fly it, make it to Puerto Rico, locate the beam weapon, insert the one-one-five pod, deflect the asteroid. And, at last, defeat the Breeders and everything they represented.

You can do it!

As the boat sped down the stream, he kept repeating it to himself: *You can do it!*

He gazed at Laura, at the floppy hat partially covering her face, at her closed eyes and partly opened mouth, at her rhythmic breathing as she forced herself to think of nothing but swirling whiteness.

He knew he would gladly sacrifice his life if it meant she would go on living.

I am fulfilling my purpose. If the world lives, you live. I will make the world live for you.

Ahead, the land flattened on the other side of the river into farm country, with a two-lane road paralleling the river. Farmhouses were scattered here and there. On the campground side of the river, it was still hilly and the road to Clifford had disappeared behind hills. Kendon veered to the farm side of the stream and looked for a secure place for the boat. Soon, he found a wide creek mouth, hidden under trees and dense foliage.

In the twilight, Kendon could see they had discovered a perfect hiding place. The creek was deep enough for them to paddle in near the road, almost as far as the culverts that allowed the creek water to flow under the road.

They pulled the boat into the brush and covered it with branches and leaves. Kendon checked the clips of the two side arms he had confiscated from the snipers. They were fully loaded. They now had four semi-automatic pistols, plus a sniper rifle and an M-16. Quite an arsenal, he thought. They were nothing like the portable beam weapon, but it was great to have conventional weapons, too.

For the moment, all they needed were two handguns. He stuffed his pistol into the backpack and handed Laura hers.

"I'll be back with a car."

She shook her head. "I'm not staying by myself again."

Kendon was torn by the idea of leaving the one-one-five and beam weapon unattended. On the other hand, he feared not being able to protect her if Directorate troops came searching the riverside.

"Okay, then let's go," he said.

As they trudged up the embankment to the road, Kendon looked back at the creek and felt anxious about leaving the one-one-five pod and the beam weapon. The boat was well hidden, but what if someone stumbled on it? He knew they didn't have any choice. They needed a vehicle.

He made note of landmarks so they would be able to find the boat again. Guardrails had been installed where the road crossed the creek. It would be easy to find the boat later, even in the dark.

They walked for fifteen minutes, passing by two farmhouses set far back from the road. Cars were parked at each and the homes were lit up. Not good candidates.

A car swooshed by, slowing as it passed by them, but then continued on.

"We need to hitch a ride into town," Laura said. Kendon didn't understand the expression, so Laura stuck her thumb out to show him what she meant. "We flag someone down, like this."

A few minutes later, a second car approached, headlights bright.

"It doesn't look like a Humvee," Kendon said, but held the automatic against his leg.

Laura waved at the driver, her thumb out. The car, an old, boxy Ford four-door, slowed until it was even with them and stopped. The window rolled down. The driver, an older man wearing overalls, with gritty fingers and a weathered face, leaned toward them. "Ya'll going to town?"

Laura smiled brightly. "Yes, to Clifford."

"Well, hop in then."

They slid into the wide front seat, Laura in between.

"Clayton's my name," he said once Kendon closed the door "Car trouble?"

"Actually, boat trouble," Kendon said. "We hit a rock and put a hole in the bottom."

"Seems like there's no end to troubles folks can have."

Kendon was eager to pump him about Directorate activities.

He waited a couple of minutes and said, "We heard there's a terrorist on the loose up in the north end of the county. Any truth to that?"

"There's been a lot on the news. People think we're gonna get attacked again, this time with a nuclear bomb."

"Oh?"

"The president's going to say something about it at ten o'clock tomorrow morning."

Kendon and Laura glanced at each other, believing instead he would reveal the truth about the asteroid. Too bad he hadn't already gone public with it, Kendon thought. They could get all the allies they needed at the snap of a finger.

"We saw black helicopters, black Humvees, men dressed in black," Kendon said. "They looked military, but nobody knows who they are."

"Well, you know, there's been a lot of speculation in these parts. Seems the sheriff isn't too happy about it, with them running all over his county. They stopped my nephew this morning on the road to Madison and made him turn around. They said they were with the Federal Emergency Management Agency."

"Never heard of it."

"They're the folks who're supposed to help people where there's been a disaster."

"Has there been a disaster around here?"

"Not yet, but I suppose there's gonna be if a nuclear bomb goes off."

"Have they been in your part of the county?"

"Some road blocks. Helicopters flying over. And those black Humvees."

"Any around here?"

"Well, there's a checkpoint up ahead, at least there was one earlier when I was driving out of town. But they're letting locals through."

Kendon could feel his blood freezing. Laura squeezed his hand.

"How far?"

"Couple miles, I suppose."

"Any other way to get into Clifford?"

"Farm roads."

"Take the farm roads then." Kendon said it with vehemence, frightening the driver.

"Why, I don't know, Mister. Maybe I just better let you folks off."

"Listen to me," Kendon said. "Those people aren't who you think. They're not from any of your federal agencies. They're not even from your country."

Laura intervened. "We're not bad people, Clayton, but they are. Where can you turn to avoid those men?"

The old man stopped on the shoulder. It was dark all around, with lights from isolated houses in the distance. Kendon was afraid the farmer was going to jump out of the car and run off.

From the moment he had gotten into the car, Kendon sensed the man was deeply troubled about something, and had picked them up mainly to share his burdens but he had not gotten around to it yet. Kendon leaned his head back and closed his eyes and repeated out loud what came to his mind about the man: "Your wife had a stroke and had to be in the hospital for two months. The insurance policy doesn't cover the medical costs completely, and as a result you are going to lose your farm."

Clayton looked astonished. "You aren't from these parts. How can you know that?"

"I just know," Kendon said. "You've lived in the country all your life, and now you're afraid you're going to have to move into town, into some cramped apartment."

Kendon reached into the backpack. He put his hand around the bundle of what was left of the stolen ATM money. "There's about fifteen thousand dollars here. It's for you if you help us out."

"I think you oughta just get out."

"You said a minute ago there's no end of trouble folks can get into. You couldn't have said it better. You're going to find out to-morrow morning from the president what kind of trouble is on the way, and you're not going to like what you hear. We have a way to keep it from happening."

Kendon handed the bundle of money to the man.

"If it's that important, then forget the money."

He made a U-turn and drove back up the road a half mile, then turned down a side road. Kendon thought a moment about re-cruiting him and making use of his car and maybe his home telephone, but a good look at the man made him decide against it: He was on the verge of panic Decent, but overwhelmed with per-sonal problems and without nerve. A spent man.

The city lights grew brighter as they approached, and soon they were in town. As in Madison, campaign posters were everywhere, as were groups of people on street corners holding signs and wav-ing at cars.

Kendon had never liked the neon ugliness of the towns he had seen in his upper-world forays. This town wasn't any different: commercial streets lined with brightly lit stores, the streets heavy with traffic.

Kendon pointed to a shopping center with a cinema at one end. Clayton stopped in the middle of the parking lot, and Ken-don and Laura slid out. Kendon realized that if he had been on his own, he would have to consider killing the man to ensure silence, but he couldn't take such a drastic action with Laura present.

He peeled off several hundred dollars from the bundle to keep some cash on hand, then leaned in the door and dropped the bun-dle on the front seat.

He said, "With that money, you can keep your farm, but don't say anything to anyone about giving us a ride. Tomorrow, listen to your president and then remember what I told you. We have a way to do something about it, but if you talk about us to anyone, you'll ruin it. Tomorrow you will understand."

The man nodded, eager to get away. As the car sped off, Laura said, "We've got to call Mortimer."

Kendon looked around the busy shopping mall. At one corner was a gas station with a telephone booth, but it was too brightly lit and would call attention to them. As they walked along the storefronts looking for a telephone, Kendon realized someone was staring at them. Even though he couldn't see him, a clear image of the man had formed in his mind.

"There's a man carrying a shopping bag who thinks he's seen us before, but he can't place us. Don't make eye contact, just stare straight ahead."

As they walked farther down the sidewalk amidst a bustle of shoppers, his mind became filled with intrusive images, as if he was suddenly immersed in a sea of thought and emotion. As they walked, he closed his eyes. "That old man sitting alone on the bench is praying for people who look troubled. The man over there in the white T-shirt is looking for someone to have sex with. The woman in the blue dress at the entrance to the Target store lost a child several months ago. She just saw a boy who reminds her of the dead child, and she's struggling not to cry."

Kendon tugged Laura from the sidewalk into the parking lot. He wanted to flee. What had started as flashes of insight at Carlsbad Caverns into the dentist's life had turned into a relentless assault on his psyche. He rubbed his forehead and groaned. Laura placed her hands comfortingly on his arm.

"You know how to keep it out of your mind," she said. "If you can keep the Breeders out, you can keep anything out."

He nodded and let the image of brilliant whiteness consume his mind. When he was in the cocoon, curled up in a center of brightness, the crush of thought and emotion ceased.

He let his breath out. "Okay, I'm better."

They were in the middle of a vast parking lot. In an area farthest from the stores, Kendon spotted a Ford Explorer similar to the one he had stolen at Carlsbad Caverns. It was parked halfway between lampposts, partly hidden on both sides by other parked cars. He slipped the screwdriver from the backpack up his sleeve and pointed to a spot fifty yards away for Laura to wait.

Glancing casually around to see if anyone was coming, he walked up to the vehicle. With the palm of his hand, he rammed the screwdriver deeply into the lock. With a twist of the handle, he popped the door open and repeated the maneuver with the ignition switch. A few seconds later, he backed the vehicle out of the stall and drove to where Laura was standing. She got in, eyes downcast.

"Look for a cell phone. Sometimes people forget them," Kendon said as he rummaged around.

They patted the interior down and felt under the seats, but didn't find one. Kendon eyed the glove compartment, which was locked. While steering with one hand, he jammed the screwdriver into the lock and forced the door open. They smiled with relief when they saw a cell phone inside.

"Oh, thank God," Laura said.

Kendon found a darkened parking lot sheltered from the street by trees and bushes. Laura turned the phone on and dialed the trustee's number. It rang several times. At each ring, they glanced nervously at one another. It kept ringing until finally someone answered.

Kendon felt his heart leap when he heard the voice say, "Mortimer Barclay here."

"Mortimer, this is Laura Meller."

Kendon leaned toward to phone to listen better.

"Are you safe?" Mortimer said.

"Yes, I'm fine."

"I watched the news after getting your message earlier today. I don't know quite what to make of it."

"Ignore the news. I'm with the man they're looking for, Michael Kendon. He used to work with my father. He's not a terrorist. We're safe for the moment, but we're being hunted. Michael wants to talk to you."

She handed the phone to Kendon.

"This is Michael Kendon. Is it safe to talk right now?"

"I'm home alone," Barclay said. "I don't believe anyone is listening in. Before you say anything else, please tell me where Laura's father is. I lost contact with him ten years ago."

"He died two days ago."

"I'm so sorry. How did it happen?"

"It's too complicated to explain right now," he said and gave the phone back to Laura.

She said, "I've got a lot to talk to you about, Mortimer, but I don't know where to begin."

"It might simplify things if you first answer a question. Are you by chance in possession of a device of some kind that could fuel a powerful weapon?"

"Yes."

"Good, then I think we're on the same page."

Laura held the phone between them so that Kendon could hear. "What do you know about it?" Laura said.

"The news reports claim it's stolen nuclear material. Is that true?"

"Yes and no, depending on how you look at it. It was something my father created."

"Well then," Barclay said. "I have some extremely interesting information to pass on to you."

Kendon could hear every word. He could tell from his voice that the trustee had become excited.

"Go on," Laura said.

"I'm in touch with someone in Puerto Rico who knows about your father. He is the resident astronomer at an observatory your father had built on top of what used to be a lighthouse. He told me that two days ago he discovered an asteroid that is heading for Earth and predicted it will strike on Sunday night. He also said he discovered what looks like a weapon hidden underneath the telescope. He's convinced your father built it specifically to divert the asteroid. All it lacks to function is a power source. Is there a connection here, Laura?"

Kendon could feel the hair standing up on the back of his neck. He took the phone from Laura.

"This is Michael again. Yes, we have the power source for it, but we don't know where in Puerto Rico to go. We had an idea it was hidden inside a lighthouse somewhere in southwestern Puerto Rico, but we don't know anything more than that. Who is this astronomer? Where is he?"

"His name is Eric Tepler, and the observatory is at Cabo Rojo."

"Where's that?"

"It's at the southwestern tip of Puerto Rico, on a cape. It was an unusual place to put a telescope, but that's where Donald Meller wanted it built."

"I have to talk to Tepler. What's his phone number?"

Barclay gave it to him. Kendon repeated it to Laura, who wrote it down, then repeated it to himself several times.

"There is a complication, however," Barclay continued. "Tepler's on the run. He said men in black uniforms took over the observatory and shot him in the arm when he tried to get away. He jumped over a cliff into the sea and swam to safety."

Kendon's heart sank. He glanced at Laura who had heard every word. She looked crushed.

"Where are you?" Barclay asked.

"Somewhere in Texas. The next step is to get an airplane."

"I will put the financial resources of the trust fund at your disposal."

"There's no time for that now. We're near an airport, and we'll get an airplane one way or another."

"Who are those people in black?" Barclay asked.

"They're Directorate troops. It's a paramilitary organization. They think they're going to rule over what's left of the human race."

"I have to confess that the more I hear about this the more

confused I get. Would someone please explain what is going on?"

"There's no time, Mortimer, and I don't think you'd believe me if I told you."

"Well," Barclay said, "if you told me the Tooth Fairy was involved, I think I would be inclined to believe you at this point."

Kendon's mind was racing at hypervelocity. What had gone wrong? What had led the Directorate to the observatory? He reviewed the steps he and Laura had taken that day. The weak link lay in communications. Laura had called Barclay from the river cabin. It was an outgoing call, but it would still leave a trail. In their searches, the Directorate soldiers must have found his Jeep Cherokee hidden in the garage under the cabin. Did they then check to see if any calls had been made from the cabin? The Directorate had access to all phone records indirectly through NSA and CIA computers. If they had determined there was a connection with Barclay, they could have monitored his telephone activity. All of the incoming and outgoing calls would tell a story and could have led them to Eric Tepler.

Kendon said, "You need to go into hiding immediately, Mortimer. You're in danger. If they think you could help them capture us, they'll come for you."

The voice at the other end gasped. "Tell me what I should do."

"Grab some clothes and get out. Sleep in your car if you have to. Don't use your cell phone anymore, but keep it with you and charged in case we need to call you. Keep it off, but check now and then for messages. They can pinpoint your location when you're using it, but if you're mobile, you can get away quickly."

"Is that absolutely necessary?"

"Do you want me to tell you what they'll do to you if they get their hands on you?"

"No, I heard enough from Tepler."

Laura took the phone. "Good luck, Mortimer."

"Thank you, and good luck to you, too. I'm terribly sorry about your father."

After turning the phone cell phone off, Laura smiled, "We guessed it right—a lighthouse."

"Your father was a very clever man. He was afraid to tell me where the weapon was located out of fear the Breeders could pick up on it. But he told me exactly what I needed to know: Go to Puerto Rico, go to the lighthouse."

Chapter 18

*T*he cell phone was again the center of the universe. It lay in the middle of the kitchen table, cruelly silent, the only object on a fresh cloth Gabriela's mother had thrown over the table after the meal.

Tepler and Gabriela sat quietly staring at it, feeling exhausted from the strain of waiting for it to ring. They were expecting two telephone calls now, one from either the trustee or Laura Meller, and another from Nestor Estrada, Gabriela's cousin.

Gabriela had left a message with the colonel's wife for him to call, saying it was extremely urgent, that she had information regarding the reason the Puerto Rico National Guard had been mobilized. But an hour and a half had gone by and he hadn't called. Nor had Mortimer Barclay or Laura Meller.

Finally, the phone rang. Tepler grabbed it before it could ring a second time, noting as he picked it up the New York telephone number that appeared on the caller screen. He said hurriedly, before the trustee could speak, "What have you heard?"

"I have good news for you," Barclay said in a rush. "I just spoke with Laura Meller. Unfortunately, her father died two days ago. However, she's with Michael Kendon, the one they're calling a terrorist, and they have what you want. They're going to contact you in a few minutes and fill you in on the details."

The trustee's voice sounded nervous, even panicky.

"What's the matter?" Tepler said.

"I have to get out of here. This Kendon fellow warned me that the same people who shot you and who are pursuing them could come for me."

"You better get out fast, then. How do I contact you?"

"I will have this cell phone."

"Good luck," Tepler said.

"One thing before I go," Barclay said. "I want to congratulate you. You have done remarkable work, Eric. And you're a very brave man."

"Thank you, Mr. Barclay. I appreciate that very much."

When Tepler filled Gabriela in on the conversation, tears of relief welled in her eyes. He put his hands over hers.

Several minutes later, the phone rang again and the sound ran through Tepler like an electric shock. He knew this was going to be the most important telephone call of his life. His hand was shaking as he pressed down on the talk button.

"Hello."

"Are you Eric Tepler?"

"Yes," Tepler said, his voice strained.

"This is Michael Kendon. I'm with Donald Meller's daughter, Laura. I believe you know who she is."

"We have a lot to talk about," Tepler said.

"Yes, we do. But we can't stay on this line very long. It may be compromised. The important thing for you to know is that we have the one-one-five pod—the power source for the weapon. The trustee told us you discovered the asteroid and that you also found a weapon underneath the observatory. Tell me about the asteroid first."

"It's massive, five or six miles in diameter. It will hit tomorrow night at eight thirty-five off the southwest coast of Puerto Rico. I was able to detect what looks like an enormous lenticular object that's traveling alongside. The asteroid changed course about three days ago, but the object is still with it. My guess is that it's guiding the asteroid in."

"That's correct," Kendon said.

"I found the weapon hidden in a cylinder that supports the telescope. The cylinder is eight feet in diameter and forty feet high. My friend Gabriela and I were able to deploy the weapon using the electrical power of the observatory. When it's deployed, it interlocks with the telescope. My impression is that the telescope is the tracking and aiming mechanism for the weapon. At the base of the cylinder is a removable panel that gives access to a horizontal hollow tube. Once the weapon is activated, the tube is drawn upwards. That tube has to be where the power source is inserted. I think I can make the weapon work once it has the power it needs."

"What are the dimensions of the tube?" Kendon asked.

"About a foot in diameter and five feet long."

"Those are the dimensions of the one-one-five pod."

Tepler felt electricity running up his back to his neck. "There's only one thing wrong. Barclay must have told you I don't control the observatory anymore. It was taken over by people in black uniforms. Who the hell are they?"

"They belong to a paramilitary force that controls underground facilities where research is done on alien technology. They kill anyone who reveals anything about it, and they will kill anyone who gets in their way. I know what they're capable of because I used to be one of them."

"I've seen what they can do. They slaughtered more than a dozen people at the observatory at Arecibo. Then they shot me when they took over the Cabo Rojo Observatory. I barely escaped. My shoulder is ripped to shreds."

Kendon said, "When I heard about what happened to you, I wondered if it's already too late to do anything about the asteroid. If they know about the weapon, they could have removed it or destroyed it by now. What's your assessment?"

"I'm not sure they know about it. They've been kidnapping or killing anyone who could know about the asteroid, particularly targeting astronomers. Cabo Rojo was one of their objectives because it's an observatory. We made sure the weapon was folded back into the cylinder, and the access panel is hidden. If they find the weapon, it will be accidental. And even if they do discover it, I don't think they would understand what it is."

"Why are they still there?"

"It's on an isolated cape. The support building is big, with a lot of rooms, so I imagine they're using it as a command post. I saw a helicopter fly in."

There was a long pause again. Finally Kendon said, "I think your assessment is correct. We'll have to proceed on the assumption they don't know about it."

"Why are they doing this?" Tepler asked. "The asteroid will kill them, too. It's going to kill everyone."

"It's too complicated to explain right now. I'll tell you everything when we meet. Laura and I have to find a fast airplane and get to Puerto Rico, but we need to know where to land."

"Mayaguez is the biggest city on this side of the island. It's about twenty-five miles north of here, and it's got a pretty big airport."

"Too big, too dangerous. Anything smaller and closer? Even a dirt runway will work if it's long enough."

"There's a private airfield not far from the cape, the Lajas Valley Air Park. I've been told the runway is three thousand feet long. I've seen it. It's got a grass runway."

"That will have to do. See if you can get coordinates."

"Even if you get here in time, there are at least twenty heavily armed men holding the observatory. Maybe as many as forty. What do we do about them?"

"We'll have to organize an attack. We have the upper hand with the weapon I've got, and we'll have the element of surprise. But we're going to need manpower. What are your ideas?"

"I'm at the house of my friend, Gabriela. Her cousin is a colonel in the Puerto Rico National Guard and commander of an infantry battalion with urban combat experience in Iraq. They were called up for duty yesterday, and I'm convinced it's because of the asteroid. I'm waiting for a call from him. I don't intend to tell him too much, but I want to feel him out about his capabilities and where his troops are going to be tomorrow."

There was a long pause again. Tepler wonder if the connection had been lost, but after a moment Kendon said, "You've got the right instincts, Eric. I'll figure out how to get them out. Ask the colonel to put together an assault team, soldiers with experience in house-to-house, room-to-room fighting. No more than thirty soldiers, but with backup. We'll need a couple of snipers, too, and troops to control access to the observatory. Tell him to have his people prepared and on standby and to keep this request to himself, to keep it outside of his chain of command. That's important. We don't want to lose control of the operation. Appeal to his self-interest. Make it clear to him that if we fail, he and his family are going to die tomorrow night."

"The president is supposed to speak tomorrow morning," Tepler said. "I'm betting he's going to go public about the asteroid."

"I think so, too. That should convince the colonel to cooperate. He has nothing to lose."

Tepler nodded. "Okay, I got it."

Kendon added, "Another thing: Tell him to paint two Humvees to look like Directorate Humvees—dull black inside and out. I believe you know how they look. We're going to need them."

Tepler tried to picture the man he was talking to. The voice was deep, assured, and commanding. A clear image of Kendon didn't form in his mind, but he sensed that he couldn't have wished for a better ally. He gave Kendon two other cellphone numbers to call in case a problem arose with Gabriela's phone.

Kendon said, "I'll call you as soon as we're in the air. And one last thing, Eric. As a precaution, you should move to a different location. The Directorate has the ability to trace phone calls. If they haven't already, sooner or later they're going to catch up to this phone and the calls I've made from it. I don't want any harm to come to you or your friend."

"Okay, we'll get going right away. There are lots of places we can stay."

After he hung up, Gabriela threw her arms around his neck. "Oh, Eric, I'm not so afraid now."

They held each other tightly and soon were kissing with abandon. They were interrupted when Maria came into the room. She cleared her throat to get their attention and smiled when they looked up at her, embarrassed.

"While you were on the phone, Eric, I received a call from Nestor. He is in San Juan for meetings with his superiors. He will be back early tomorrow morning, and he has agreed to meet with you then."

Eric nodded and said, "We've got to get out of here, all of us. We could be in danger. We need to find somewhere else to stay for the night."

Maria said, "I will go and tell Marcelo."

Chapter 19

After Kendon turned the cell phone off, Laura said, "It sounds like he knows what he's doing. What's your impression?"

"Brave, intelligent, resourceful. He's someone who can be counted on. But I don't think he's ever killed anyone. He's a scientist, not a warrior. Like your father."

Kendon drove several miles outside of town. Campaign posters lined the road. Posters showing the ruddy, round-faced sheriff of Clifford County were everywhere and were bigger than all the other signs, leading Kendon to deduce that the race for sheriff was the most important of the lot.

"Before she moved to Europe, my mother was active in regional politics," Laura said. "She used to host fundraising events at our home. I remember seeing the sheriff at some of those events when he first ran for office."

"That's not good. That means he knows who you are, and he has to know we're on the loose somewhere in his jurisdiction. On a personal level, he would be eager to rescue you from the terrorist who abducted you. But he's also a politician who wants to be re-elected. That means we've got more than the Directorate and the Breeders to worry about."

During preparation for his undercover role, Kendon had been

allowed to study the political structure of the aboveground world and its popular culture so that he could blend in with the captive scientists and technicians of Meller's research group. It occurred to him that the democratic process was remarkable, but that it had been betrayed by the group of men who established the Collaboration. They had made important decisions in total secrecy, decisions that were now leading the human race to its extinction at the hands of an enemy most people knew nothing about.

Kendon spotted a sign saying "Clifford County Airport." The access road was well lit with amber street lamps. As he drove toward the airfield, he surveyed the road, but he didn't detect any danger. Dozens of airplanes were parked at one end of the runway near a line of hangars. Some of the buildings were lit up inside.

Kendon didn't know much about airplanes, but it was logical to assume the bigger the better, the sleeker the faster. That ruled out most of the aircraft there, small single-engine planes. After parking and walking to the tie down area, they found a half-dozen twin-engines and three turboprops. Two of the turboprops had "For Sale" signs on them. Farther away, near a huge Quonset hangar, were three executive jets.

He pointed first to the jets, then to the turboprops. "A jet would be the best, but they're not for sale. One of these will have to do."

"What do you have in mind?"

"We pass ourselves off as potential buyers to get the owner to show us the plane, then we make him fly us to Puerto Rico."

Before leaving the airport, Kendon wrote down the contact information and the make and model of the airplanes. He drove back the way they had come, but once in Clifford he chose a route through tree-lined neighborhoods to avoid potential trouble in case the theft of the Ford Explorer had already been reported.

He stopped under a tree on a quiet street lined with bungalows and turned the motor off. Light from a street lamp filtered through the leaves. Somewhere in the distance a dog barked.

Indistinct voices could be heard somewhere up the street and then a door slamming shut. On the other side of the street, a woman and a small child got into a car and drove off.

He scanned the neighborhood to be sure they were not being observed and said, "What names do we use when we call about the plane?"

"Mr. and Mrs. William Heath," Laura suggested. "William and Laura Heath."

"How about William and Connie Heath?"

The bigger of the two turboprops was a 1984 King Air 300. Kendon dialed the number for that airplane. A man answered immediately and said his name was Bob Sagecroft, the name on the "For Sale" sign.

Kendon identified himself and explained that he and his wife had seen the airplane and were interested in hearing more about it, especially the asking price.

"Well, she's in mint condition," Sagecroft said. "Customized interior, engines recently overhauled, all the inspections up to date. She's got a lot of add-ons, including extra fuel capacity. We're asking $1,250,000."

Kendon turned to Laura and said loudly enough for the seller to hear, "What do you think, Connie?" He repeated the asking price.

"That sounds rather high, darling," she said. "But it's worth a look."

Kendon turned again to the phone. "I'm more familiar with the B200," he said, referring to the other aircraft for sale. "What's the range of the 300 model? What does she cruise at?"

"She'll take you from here clear to Alaska at 340 knots. You can push her a little faster, up to about 365, but your range will drop. If you're serious, I'd be happy to take you and your wife up to show you what she can do."

"We're only in town for the night. When can we see it?"

"Well, it's too late right now. You're not gonna see what you need to see in the dark. Will the morning work for you folks?"

Kendon was eager to get on the way, but he realized the late hour and the darkness was a problem. He didn't want to appear overly eager. "Eight o'clock?" he suggested.

"Eight it is," the voice said. "Be prepared to fall in love."

If they left at eight, Kendon calculated, they would be in Puerto Rico in less than six hours. That would leave enough time to take back the observatory before dark and to ready the beam weapon.

When the phone clicked off, Laura threw her arms around his neck. He put his arms around her, too. He didn't want to move, but then he thought of the one-one-five pod and the hidden boat and became nervous. It had been painful to leave everything behind at the creek, particularly the beam weapon, although he realized there was no choice.

He started the motor and quickly found his way to the outskirts of town, following farm roads until he finally reached the river road. The closer they got to the river, the more his anxiety grew about the boat. What if someone had stumbled onto it?

The river road was dark. Black clouds obscured the moon, and the landmarks Kendon had noted when they came up from the river had been swallowed by the blackness. He drove several times up and down the road without finding the creek.

Finally, Laura pointed excitedly, "That's it. There's the guard rail."

Kendon bounced the vehicle down the slope into the brush, under the thick canopy of trees. He stopped at the edge of the creek, near the boat. When he got out, he heard the rush of the river and felt the chilly breeze that rustled the trees.

Kendon led Laura through the underbrush to the boat. It was just as they had left it. In the dark, nearly slipping in the cold wetness of the creek bank, they first transferred the sleeping bags and other light gear to the Ford Explorer, then the rifles and food. Kendon kept the beam weapon slung over his shoulder like a rifle.

The final trip they reserved for the one-one-five pod. After removing it, Kendon tipped the boat until it filled with water and sank. They each grabbed an end of the heavy cylinder, careful not to stumble and send it rolling into the creek. They lugged it toward the vehicle, but before they reached it, Laura stopped.

"Wait, I hear something."

"Helicopters! Quick, under the brush."

Two Black Hawks, one flying low over the river, the other flying above the road, were scouring the riverbank and roadside with searchlights.

How foolish could the Directorate be, Kendon wondered? They had to know he was able to shoot down helicopters easily. Maybe they *wanted* him to shoot one down in order to give himself away. That was something Bogdan would do: send men to their death in order to flush out a target. Did the Directorate pilots suspect they could be so readily sacrificed?

They slid the red pod under brush and huddled next to it. Kendon slipped the beam weapon from his shoulder and flicked the selector switch to high intensity, then shoved the weapon out in front of him, ready to grab it if needed. But when the green light switched on, he was surprised to see the front end of the weapon lift off the ground. The turquoise field emanating from the barrel had a repelling force, and the weapon now rested at an angle, propped up like a field mortar.

"That glow will give us away," Kendon said as he rushed to turn the weapon off.

Once off, the barrel lost its support and the weapon dropped to the ground.

The Black Hawk that was over the river was in the lead, its bright searchlight sweeping the riverside foliage. When the spotlight came to the creek entrance, the helicopter abruptly turned and hovered over the river, aiming the spotlight into the woods. Points of blinding light splashed through the leaves onto Laura's arm. The other helicopter hovered over the road, low enough to be able to spot the Ford Explorer hidden under the branches of the creek trees. Kendon pulled the beam weapon close to him, one finger on the selector switch.

His mind seemed to see inside the helicopter. The copilot had seen the vehicle and was reading the license plate number through binoculars, relaying the information into his mouthpiece. The helicopter remained hovering over the road while the other Black Hawk stayed over the river, keeping the searchlight on the woods.

"If it touches down, I'm going to shoot," Kendon said. "Stay behind me. The weapon will shield us."

Laura nodded.

While the Black Hawk over the road focused on the Ford Explorer, the other swept its spotlight up the creek and into the trees along the bank. What were they looking at, Kendon wondered? Had they detected the scuttled boat?

Both helicopters had to contain troops. If the one over the road landed, he and Laura would be quickly surrounded. The beam weapon would be difficult to use in close quarters. Kendon could see that he would have to level the floodplain for half a mile in each direction, but even then some of the Directorate soldiers could survive if they were in ditches or other low spots.

He flicked the switch to low intensity just as the helicopter began rocking in a slow descent to the road. He was in a dilemma about which to shoot at first. The river chopper was the most dangerous because its nose was pointing right at them. If it opened fire with its rockets, they would be finished in seconds. But if he shot at it first, the other helicopter would touch ground and a dozen men would leap out.

He aimed at the helicopter over the road.

Four . . . five . . . six . . .

The green light went on. Kendon stood up and fired, and the gravity beam struck with its awesome kinetic force. The Black Hawk exploded, shooting flames in every direction. He swept the road with the beam, then swiveled in place, making sure Laura was behind him.

Just has he turned, the second helicopter fired a volley of rockets. Kendon furiously swept the sky in front of him, up and down, right and left. The beam caught the rockets just as they closed in.

The rockets exploded. The helicopter exploded. Flaming, it fell into the river.

"Quick, grab one end of the pod," Kendon said as he flicked off the beam weapon.

They carried the heavy cylinder to the back of the vehicle and slid it in. Kendon slammed the gears into reverse and backed up the slope to the road. What was left of the first helicopter had dropped into a field on the opposite side of the road and was burning fiercely.

He sped away, relieved there weren't any soldiers left to hunt them down. Headlights off, Kendon turned down a farm road and drove as fast as he could in the dark. He spotted taillights in the distance and used them to guide him. Very soon, the region would be swarming with Directorate helicopters and troops, not to mention local law enforcement.

It had cost them lives, but the Directorate had gotten what they wanted: They had him localized. Distance and more distance, that was all that would save them now.

He drove for ten minutes at breakneck speed, quickly catching up to the car that had at first appeared as distant as a star. But he decided not pass it and instead tailed it by a dozen car lengths.

In the rear view mirror, Kendon could see lights appearing high over the river. Helicopters? Breeders? Probably both.

The lights soon moved away from the river, some in his direction, some toward Clifford, some back upriver. Up ahead Kendon spotted a crossroad. He swerved left onto it and followed it up a hill. In the faint moonlight that broke through the clouds, he could see the hill was covered with trees. Near the top was a gravel road, the entrance to a farm. Kendon shined a flashlight on a "For Sale" sign posted on the gate. The gate was closed but unlocked. Jamming the accelerator to the floor, Kendon rammed the gate and drove up the bumpy road a hundred yards to the farmhouse. The house was two stories with a wrap-around porch. Kendon aimed the headlights on the house and saw it was vacant.

Fifty yards behind the farmhouse stood a barn with a silo. It leaned a few degrees to one side, but it didn't look like it was in danger of tumbling down any time soon. Kendon drove up to it and jumped out of the car to look inside. Other than a few rusting plows and stacks of hay in a corner and in the loft, the barn was empty.

"This is where we'll have to stay for the night," Kendon said. "If anyone comes up the road, they'll go to the house first."

Kendon backed the Ford Explorer into the barn and swung the large wooden doors shut. The barn smelled of manure, hay, and motor oil. Except for moonlight coming through knot-holes and cracks in the shrunken sideboards, the barn was dark. He pulled down bales and cut the bindings so the hay scattered, forming a soft fresh layer against the bare ground. He unfolded the sleeping bags, then stacked bales of hay next to a window that looked out at the barnyard. With the beam weapon leaning within reach against the bales, he sat and stared out of the window.

For the first time since the morning, Kendon felt at ease. How could anyone, Breeder or human, find them now? Laura sat next to him on the bale, gripping the M-16 Kendon had taken from one of the snipers. They leaned against each other.

"You better get some sleep," Kendon said. "We've got a long day tomorrow. I'll keep watch."

"I'm not sleepy." She put the stock of the M-16 against her shoulder and aimed at the barn door. "How does this work?"

Kendon took the rifle and tapped the selector switch with his forefinger. "Push the lever forward to free up the trigger. The 'semi' setting is for single fire, the 'auto' setting is for three-round bursts." He showed her how to eject and re-insert the magazine.

"Do you think you could shoot someone?" he asked her.

"I don't know. Maybe if I had to."

They sat quietly, staring out of the window, keeping their minds enshrouded in whiteness. Ten minutes went by and neither said a word. Then Laura said, "You haven't told me much about my father or how you got involved in the resistance."

He stared out at the barnyard, listening to the sounds of the night and scanning the sky. He didn't want to answer. He didn't want to think about Donald Meller because he would have to think about what he had done to him. If he began talking about it, he would have to tell her about her father's last moments.

She put her arm around his neck and kissed him.

"I want to know everything. I hadn't seen him for ten years, but you were with him only three days ago."

"It would be better for you to tell me what you remember about him," Kendon said.

She was quiet for a moment, immersed in thought. "He was very funny. He always had a twinkle in his eye. He had such a vivid imagination. When I was young he used to make up stories about trees and boulders. He could give them their own thoughts and personalities. He made them come alive."

Kendon remembered the merriment in those eyes, even when there wasn't anything to be merry about.

Laura continued, "What stood out the most about him was his kindness. It wrapped around you and protected you. That's the feeling he gave."

Kendon felt his heart sinking at the memory. Even as Meller died, asphyxiated under Kendon's hands, his eyes were kind, smiling at him, loving him like a son, rallying him to carry on the struggle.

Several minutes more went by in silence while Kendon stared quietly through the window.

Finally he said, "Go on."

"When I was older, we had disagreements over his defense work. I couldn't understand how someone like him could be involved in that kind of work. He had a saying, 'Good people who are weak invite tyranny. To prevail, the good must be strong.' That was his philosophy."

Meller's eyes were never merry when he spoke about the Breeders. Kendon remembered those were the only moments when his eyes glowered.

They think they are gods. They think they have the right to destroy us and replace us with their own creation. We will stop them. We will prevail.

"Did he change?" Laura said.

Kendon shook his head, but then realized Laura couldn't see the gesture in the dark.

"No," he said, his voice catching in his throat. "He was just as you described. To the very end."

"Tell me about him. Please."

Kendon's head began to ache. He closed his eyes and rubbed his forehead. "I think it would be better for us to get some sleep. We're safe here."

He lay down on one of the sleeping bags. It was soft on top of the hay. Laura lay down on the other sleeping bag and propped herself on an elbow. "I want to hear about my father. Please, tell me about him."

Staring up at the rafters, Kendon told her about the day he was first introduced to Meller and his research staff. He was already a defector in his heart, a rebel in search of allies. He had sickened of his role as assassin. Its ruthless demands had violated his essence. Meller had greeted him with the polite coldness reserved for outsiders, even though he was introduced as a captive like them.

At first, he only fit in on a professional level. In preparation for his undercover role, the Directorate had given him intensive courses in mathematics, nuclear physics, and materials science. He had a quick mind, a retentive memory for equations and formulae, and an intuitive grasp of science. But it wasn't until an accident occurred that he was able to earn Meller's trust and was brought into the resistance. One of the engineers had cut himself in the palm of his hand badly enough to require stitches. Kendon, however, told them stitches weren't necessary and used his healing ability to mend the wound.

"That was the turning point," Kendon said. "Your father was convinced that such an ability had to be a spiritual gift, and he believed someone with such a gift was worthy of trust."

Meller then taught him breathing and meditation techniques necessary for mind control. When Kendon was finally as adept as the other members of the group at shielding himself from psychic intrusion, Meller briefed him about the true Breeder objective and about the weapon he had built to deal with the asteroid, and that all it needed to work was the ununpentium power source that he had been working on. Meller revealed the chief problem revolved around a practical matter: Now Directorate captives, they had to find a way to escape with the one-one-five pod and get it to the weapon.

Once he began talking about Donald Meller, Kendon felt that mental dam had been broken and a flood of memories poured through the breach. He knew he could talk for days and never reach the end of what he could tell Laura about those few precious years.

He told her he had once suggested sharing the secret technology with the Committee. They had an interest in defeating the aliens, he argued, and it was their goal to challenge the Breeders militarily once they possessed advanced weaponry. But Meller said the Committee couldn't be trusted. Some of the members were thoroughly evil, and they were not as capable as the conspirators at shielding their minds from Breeder scrutiny. If shared, Meller's secret work would certainly be discovered.

Laura put an arm over Kendon's chest and nestled closely to him. He turned to face her and held her tightly and felt the warmth of her body against him.

He knew he loved her and wanted to tell her so, but he found himself facing the same dilemma he had faced when he decided to reveal his undercover role to Meller. The secret had created a separation between them as great as the distance between planets, just as the secret he had killed her father now created an unbridgeable chasm with Laura.

He thought about the ironies of it. He had been truthful with Meller about his undercover role, and as a result he hadn't been trusted with the details of the final phase of the conspiracy. Yet his direct involvement in the end phase would likely have assured its success. And when it failed, he was thrust into a position both to make it succeed but also to end Donald Meller's life, an act of mercy to spare him the agony of prolonged torture.

Now he was with Meller's daughter with this grim truth churning inside of him, not knowing what the consequences would be if he revealed it to her, but knowing that he had to tell her no matter what.

He leaned on an elbow and stared at Laura's face. His eyes had adjusted to the feeble light, and the soft contours of her cheeks and mouth and chin were visible. Her hair was brushed back except for a few strands crossing her forehead. Her eyes were wide open, staring back at him.

"I haven't told you everything about his final moments," Kendon said.

"You told me he was killed."

"I left out something important. I didn't know if you could understand it."

"What is it? You can tell me."

"They had tortured him. He was in a lot of pain and knew they were going to torture him again. He was afraid he might reveal where the one-one-five pod was hidden and the location of the beam weapon."

"I understood that from what you told me."

"There's more. After he revealed what I needed to know, he begged me to end his life."

"And you did?"

"Yes."

"How?"

"I suffocated him."

Laura didn't say anything. He saw that her eyes had closed and he felt a change in her body. She had moved close to him, but now her body seemed to melt away. She turned over on her back and stared at the rafters.

He rolled onto his back as well. He felt both relieved and anguished. Laura didn't speak, and he didn't dare touch her. He heard her breathing deeply and slowly and wondered if she had taken refuge in sleep. But then he felt her roll back onto her side facing him. He felt her staring at him, then her hand slid across his chest, her fingers seeking the buttons of his shirt. She pulled toward him and their mouths locked.

For an hour, the world beyond them ceased to exist. Kendon had never known such a feeling of bliss.

Laura lay with her head on his chest. "We've only known each other for two days, but it seems like there's never been a time when we haven't been together."

"I feel that way, too," he said.

Kendon wanted the closeness to last forever, but he realized that making it last even beyond the weekend was going to depend on him.

He stared at the rafters and at the moonlight through the cracks in the barn. He heard helicopters far in the distance. They were together, they were safe, and they needed to rest.

He kissed Laura's ear. "Go to sleep. At least for a few hours."

She was soon asleep, nestled in his arms. He drifted into sleep as well. He dreamed they were back on the river. The sunlight beamed through the trees and splashed onto Laura wearing the floppy straw hat and she looked so beautiful. Then it was night and they were caught in the rapids, and in the moonlight he could see that she was terrified.

"Laura! I'm here. Don't be frightened."

He held out his arm to her, but she was looking up at the moon. *The moon was full and round and bright and it burned through his eyelids.* He heard a familiar noise, the faint buzz of a Breeder disk. He dreamed he was awake and then realized it wasn't a dream.

He struggled to open his eyes, but the light was too intense. He felt pinned to the ground, unable to move. The pressure in his head made him squeeze his eyes shut. It was a familiar pressure, the probing once again of mental fingers slithering into his skull and wrapping around his brain.

They're here!

He fought to assert his will, to regain control through the strength of his own mind. He imagined a ball of intense light, hot and round and brilliant. He forced it to grow more and more intense, changing it from hot yellow like the sun to pure white like the radiance of the galactic center.

The brighter the image in his mind became, the more he felt the fingers receding from his brain and the pressure lessening. Soon he was able to move his arms and open his eyes. The barn was filled with creamy luminescence that came from outside the structure, lighting up the loft, the rafters, and the ceiling.

A high-pitched humming was coming from in front of the barn. Kendon pushed himself up onto one elbow, but covered his eyes with the back of his hand against the blinding light that radiated through the rectangle of the open barn doors.

He felt panic when he realized Laura wasn't beside him. He shouted, "Laura! Laura!"

She was walking toward the doors, toward the light, her naked form silhouetted against the brilliance. She was holding the M-16, but it was being pulled forward as if by a magnetic force and finally flew out of her outstretched arm. Her arm still outstretched, she kept walking slowly toward the light.

"Don't let them take you!" Kendon cried with all his strength.

"You're stronger than they are. Your mind is brilliant. Fight them, Laura, fight them with your mind."

He struggled to get to his feet, but he was unable to stand. He could feel the ground shaking. The Ford Explorer, with the one-one-five pod still in the back, was rocking and moving slowly toward the door, the braked wheels dragging across the hard-packed earth of the barn floor.

Next to Kendon, the portable beam weapon was shaking and moving forward, too. He grabbed it with both hands. He tried to pull it to his shoulder, but the traction was too strong. He struggled to keep it from flying out of his grasp.

"Fight them, Laura!" he shouted. "You're stronger than they are."

He said to himself, *I love you Laura. I won't let anything to happen to you, Laura. You are my world, Laura.*

Then the words burst out of him. "I love you, Laura. I have always loved you. Even before I met you I loved you."

He felt the whiteness of his mind growing, expanding, pushing back the brilliance coming through the door.

He jumped to his feet and roared at the light, "I am Kendon! I am human! I will defeat you!"

Again and again, the words ripped upward from his solar plexus. With every shout of defiance, the brilliance in his mind expanded until exploding like a supernova, sending its light through the universe.

The beam weapon yielded to his pull. He shoved the selector lever forward to full power and jammed the weapon to his shoulder and aimed it at the spacecraft.

Beneath the exquisite light emanating from the upper section of the craft was a kaleidoscope of flashing lights, red, blue, and yellow, spinning around the base, bright and mesmerizing.

The craft was hovering just above the ground. It was a Breeder command ship, fifty-two feet in diameter, twenty-seven feet from top to bottom. He knew its every dimension.

He aimed at the upper lights, but Laura was directly in his line of fire.

He counted: "Four . . . five . . . six . . ."

He stepped to one side, but still she was too close. He ran toward the barn entrance. Laura suddenly collapsed, crumpling to the ground on her side.

". . . seven . . . eight . . ."

The Ford Explorer was directly behind her. In only seconds, the traction from the spacecraft would drag its wheels over her body.

". . . nine . . . ten . . ."

He could feel fear. *Their fear.* They knew what he was about to do. They had counted upon the superiority of their mental abilities, amplified by their technology, to dominate and control them, but they had locked themselves into place by their own tractor beam.

Mentally, he could see them now scrambling inside the craft, their bony fingers with suction cup ends frantically tapping lights on a flat panel.

Kendon pressed the trigger. The turquoise beam flashed, striking the bright light emanating above the kaleidoscope. The huge craft flipped backwards, hitting the ground and rolling on its edge like an enormous hubcap before coming to rest against a knot of trees. The brilliance of the machine faded and then went out completely.

He aimed at the upturned craft and fired short bursts to knock it farther and farther away. Then he fired one long burst.

The spacecraft exploded.

He lifted Laura from the ground and carried her into the barn and left her lying on the sleeping bag. He ran back outside and scoured the skies, but he couldn't detect any other alien craft, nor could he hear the sound of helicopters.

He rushed back into the barn and cradled Laura in his arms. He was in agony until she opened her eyes.

"I fought them," she said weakly. "I heard you shouting to me. I fought them with my mind."

"You were stronger than they were. They couldn't control you."

When he pulled her to her feet, they both became conscious of their nakedness. They dressed hastily and threw everything into the Explorer. They jumped in, slamming the doors after them.

Without even a glance at the remains of the spacecraft, Kendon swerved out of the barn and sped down the winding gravel lane.

Chapter 20

Kendon couldn't figure out how they had been detected in the barn. Perhaps the Breeders had gotten lucky, or perhaps they had zeroed in on them by picking up on subtle body signals, on coded energies emanating from their DNA. Who could really know the extent of their capabilities? But then he realized that for an hour, he and Laura had let down their mental shields. The barriers that separated them from each other and from the universe had fallen. Their love had given them away.

Now they were on a mountainside overlooking the airport. Their car was hidden among trees, far off the road at the foot of a sheer granite cliff. They ate canned food, then huddled in the front seat to wait for dawn.

Laura was leaning against him, still trembling from the experience in the barn. "I was so frightened," she said. "It was exactly like when I was abducted."

"They want you. They want your genes. They want you as a genetic resource."

"What good would that do now? You said they already have millions of hybrids."

"In case something goes wrong with what they've created so far and to continue their genetic experiments."

Laura was staring at the sky. The first light of dawn was breaking through the darkness. "Tonight the asteroid will come. It's hard to believe."

"What time is it?"

She looked at her watch. "Nearly six."

"That gives us fourteen hours. Maybe fifteen."

After it became light, they got out to stretch and to make themselves presentable, like big-city folks with more than a million bucks to spend on a spiffy airplane.

Kendon and the portable beam weapon were now inseparable, yet he hadn't had a chance to examine it as closely as he wanted. He had used it in self-defense three times, each time learning something more about it, but not yet knowing its full potential.

He turned it on. As before, after the weapon warmed up a flux of turquoise energy emanated from the barrel and spread outward and down. He placed the weapon on the ground, and as before it rested at an angle on the energy field. He threw rocks at it from the front, studying how they bounced off of the glow. Yet when he threw stones from the opposite side, they flew unimpeded through the field. He also found he could pass his hand through the field while holding the weapon without harm. He imagined that the gravity beam weapon at Cabo Rojo would also emanate a parabolic shield, one immensely more powerful.

At seven thirty, the cell phone rang. Kendon saw it was the same telephone number he had called the night before to contact the airplane owner.

It was the seller. "I just want to make sure you're still interested in taking a look."

"Yes, we'll be there at eight o'clock sharp," Kendon said.

After he turned the phone off, Laura said, "What's the plan once we get to the airport?"

Kendon had been working it over in his mind. They were to meet on the tarmac. He imagined the owner would be waiting close to the airplane, either in his car or standing next to it.

"The key to it is to get him to show us the interior of the plane. Once we're in the airplane with him—"

Kendon showed how he intended to draw the pistol from under his shirt. "We bind and gag him. You watch him while I load everything into the plane. I can handle the one-one-five pod alone if I have to. Then we explain to him why we're doing it. We hold back nothing. We offer him compensation, including for the airplane, but we have to make it clear to him that he doesn't have a choice. He has to fly us to our destination. After we take off, we'll be able to tune in to the president's speech, and long before we get to Cabo Rojo, he'll be on our side."

"What if there are other people with him?"

"Same plan. We get them all aboard so we can talk about the purchase. Then out comes the persuader," he said, lifting the gun again.

Kendon wondered if anything could go wrong, but decided that it didn't seem likely. The owner was eager to show the plane, and it would be fueled and ready for takeoff.

At ten minutes to eight, Kendon drove down the mountain road toward the airport. There weren't many cars around, and he didn't see any police cars. He spotted the turboprop from the airport road. The plane was white, and Kendon admired the sleek beauty of the fuselage. A man was standing near the left propeller. Nearby was a gold Lexus.

"Good, he's alone," Laura said.

The man waved as they drove up. He was tall, with Kendon's athletic build, wearing a Western shirt, gray slacks, an oval belt buckle, a bolo tie, and a cowboy hat. Kendon stopped next to the Lexus. The door of the airplane was open, the steps lowered to the ground.

Kendon sucked in air. He was a cool actor, but he felt a burning in his stomach. He wondered if Laura felt the same. She was wearing sunglasses and feigned excitement as they got out of their vehicle.

"Ooh, I've always wanted a King Air," she gushed.

The man with the cowboy hat and bolo tie stepped up to them with a warm smile, hand outstretched. "Bob Sagecroft," he said.

Kendon shook his hand. "William Heath. This is my wife, Connie."

The seller's gaze lingered on her for a moment, then he turned to the airplane.

"Well now, here she is. She's a real beaut', ain't she?"

Sagecroft spoke with a confusing twang and the clipped words of the South, but Kendon answered what he thought was expected. "She sure is," he said.

They walked to the front of the plane, around the other side, and finally around the tail. The seller ran his hand over the smooth fuselage.

"I don't care what anybody says about the competition, but there hasn't ever been a better turboprop than this here 300 model."

They walked toward the steps.

"I take it you've got the maintenance logs, all the documents?" Laura said.

"Sure do, Ma'am. They're all inside. Why don't you let me give you a tour of the interior? It's mighty comfy in there, all done up in leather."

Sagecroft made a gentlemanly gesture toward the steps for her to go in first, but Kendon felt himself tensing up inside. He was standing near the foot of the short stairway. Laura had already stepped onto the first rung, and the seller was right behind him. Kendon felt there was an imbalance of some kind emanating from the man, but he couldn't put his finger on what it was. He closed his eyes and focused his mind to get a clearer picture. But just as he did, two men in civilian clothes burst from inside the plane, guns drawn, shouting, "Freeze! Don't move!"

Kendon heard people running up behind him, shouting the same commands. Police cars raced out of a nearby hangar and surrounded the plane.

Sagecroft at first had his hands up, too, but as soon as they were surrounded by a dozen armed men, half of them in uniform, he grabbed Kendon by the arm and twisted it to force him to the ground. He frisked him and found the pistol.

Kendon felt cold handcuffs slapping around his wrists. The side of his face was pressed to the concrete. Small pebbles on the ground dug into his cheek, and the odor of concrete moistened by the morning dew filled his nostrils. He looked for Laura. His heart sank when he saw her being treated in the same crude way.

"Leave her alone," he yelled.

He heard her protesting, "You're making a mistake, a terrible mistake."

Kendon shouted to her, "Tell them everything, except about Virginia Woolf," hoping she would understand not to reveal their destination.

He heard some doors slam and someone say, "The sheriff's here."

Two plain-clothes policemen pulled Kendon to his feet. A tall, heavyset man in uniform wearing a brimmed hat walked up. It was the same ruddy face as in the campaign posters for Alvin Bamford. Three uniformed deputies stood close behind the sheriff. Kendon quickly understood he was political booty.

The sheriff looked around at the assorted policemen. "Well now, what'd I tell you all? Didn't I tell you they'd be looking for an airplane?"

Heads nodded.

Kendon didn't recognize the insignias on the uniforms of the three deputies surrounding the sheriff, but it was clear from the way they echoed him that they were underlings of rank. He scanned the faces of the other policemen. Some showed curiosity, others dripped hatred. He was the enemy, someone who wanted to destroy them.

"Now, I know this is Laura Meller, so that means you have to be Michael Kendon, also known as Arkady Semyonovich Vitrikov, also known as the terrorist everybody's been looking for these last couple days. The voters of Clifford County are going to be mighty pleased their sheriff was able to take out somebody like you. That'll put Clifford County on the map, right where it belongs."

"I want to make a statement," Kendon shouted for everyone to hear. "Right now."

"There'll be time for that later," the sheriff said. "Put the woman in the back of my car."

"There's no time," Kendon insisted. "By tonight, it will be too late. You will all be dead."

"You making terroristic threats against police officers?" the sheriff said.

"I want to confess to everything. Those helicopters—I shot them down. I killed those people at Carlsbad Caverns. I'll tell you everything that happened, and more importantly, why. I have only one thing to ask in exchange for my confession."

"I don't cut deals," the sheriff snapped.

Kendon knew that if anything about his arrest became public, the Directorate would descend upon Clifford within minutes, and there could be a blood bath. He and Laura and the weapons would be taken away, then nothing would stand in the way of destruction.

"All I ask is that you don't broadcast anything about this arrest, not even to other police agencies. Don't let anyone know about this. There are men wearing black uniforms who now have the run of your county. They claim to be American federal agents, but they're not—they're not even American. They're searching for me and Laura Meller. If they find out about this arrest, they'll come for us. And they will kill anyone who stands in their way."

"You don't say," Bamford said.

"They're after me because of what I know and because of what I possess. It's in the Ford Explorer, in the back. They want it. It will prevent the calamity that is going to happen tonight, and they must not get their hands on it."

The sheriff said, "Is that so?" and rolled his eyes at one of his subordinates. All of the deputies surrounding the sheriff grinned from ear to ear.

"Your president is going to speak about it this morning at ten o'clock. Listen to what he has to say."

The sheriff bellowed, "He's going to be talking about a terrorist on the loose with a nuclear bomb, that's what he's going to be talking about. And right after he gives his speech about you on national television, I'm going to be making a public announcement: The Clifford County Sheriff's Department has captured the terrorist and his bomb."

Kendon could see the Ford Explorer. Plainclothes deputies had opened the door but were keeping back, made nervous because of their belief they were only a few feet away from a nuclear bomb. The deputies holding Kendon pushed him toward an unmarked vehicle with short antennas jutting from the rear roof. Kendon struggled to break free, but too many hands were on him.

"Be careful handling what you find in the vehicle," he shouted as they dragged him to the car. "The red cylinder isn't a nuclear bomb. It's a fuel source invented by Laura Meller's father to power a beam weapon that he created. The other device in there *is* a beam weapon. It's what I used to shoot down those Black Hawk helicopters. It was also invented by Laura Meller's father, and it's very dangerous. It could take off the top of that mountain."

He pointed with his chin to the mountain where he and Laura hid that morning. "Listen to your president. And for your own sake and for the sake of everyone you love, do not let anyone know you have us or those devices."

Kendon didn't resist as one of the deputies pushed down on his head and shoved him into the back of the unmarked vehicle. It was now in the hands of fate.

In front of the vehicle were two city police cars; in back were two unmarked sheriff sedans. As the caravan sped into town, Kendon looked out of the windows for signs of the Directorate and the Breeders. Ten minutes after leaving the airfield, the caravan arrived, tires squealing, into a garage underneath the county jail.

Five minutes later, Kendon was in a concrete cell not much larger than the one in Alamogordo. Still handcuffed, he sat on a concrete bench with his back to the cold wall, anguished that the world could now be doomed because of a publicity-seeking, small-town politician.

He didn't know the time; it had all happened so fast, but he guessed it was eight thirty, maybe a quarter to nine. He realized the only hope now rested with the president of the United States. Would he tell the truth?

A half an hour went by before the cell door swung open. The sheriff stepped into the cell. He wasn't wearing his hat, and Kendon thought he didn't look so stupid with it off. The sheriff motioned to two subordinates to remain at the door.

He sat down on the concrete bench opposite Kendon, leaning forward with one arm resting on his leg, and stared at Kendon.

"Well, you sure got Laura Meller brainwashed. It's like Patty Hearst all over again."

Kendon didn't understand the allusion. He said coldly, "Whatever she told you is the truth."

"I knew her mother. She was an upstanding woman who was active in Texas politics. I'd been to her home a number of times for fundraisers."

"It was a nice house. I hated to destroy it."

"Who are those men in black?"

Kendon explained, not holding anything back. He explained the Collaboration, and he told him about the origins of Directorate agents and soldiers in Eastern European orphanages and how they were indoctrinated in underground facilities in the United States. "The Directorate is not under the control of your elected government. I know about it because I used to be one of them."

"How do you know Donald Meller?"

Kendon explained that, too.

"Where were you at five o'clock this morning?"

Kendon wondered if Laura told him about the Breeder ship. "In a barn. With Laura."

"Where?"

Kendon named the road and described the area.

The sheriff abruptly stood up. "You've gotta be the best bull crap artist I've ever come across. And I hope to God that's all it is, pure bull crap."

"You don't have much time to make up your mind about it."

The cell door swung shut behind the sheriff. Kendon sat there as before, handcuffed and leaning against the bare cell wall. He couldn't tell how much time went by. A little time, a lot of time. One thing for sure was that Puerto Rico was getting farther and farther away, perhaps now unreachable even if a miracle happened.

He thought about Eric Tepler, waiting vainly for the one-one-five pod that would make the beam weapon work. He wished he could call him.

Finally, the jail door swung open again and two deputies walked in. They grabbed Kendon by the arms and escorted him down a corridor, through thick doors with remotely activated locks, and finally to an elevator. The elevator went down several floors. The deputies escorted him along a corridor lined with offices and stopped at a door with a nameplate that said "Sheriff Alvin Bamford."

Bamford was sitting behind a massive executive desk. He pointed to a chair, but Kendon remained standing. "Remove these handcuffs," he said.

The sheriff shook his head. "You've admitted to killing more than fifty people in the last couple-three days. Personally, I'd feel safer setting my fanny down on a rattlesnake than cutting someone like you loose. Just set your butt down in that chair. We've got some talking to do."

Kendon sat down and glared at him. "You're time is just about up, Sheriff. Where I need to go with the red cylinder is a long way from here."

Bamford leaned back in his chair. "I listened to the president." He cocked his head to one side, but didn't say anything more.

"Then what are we waiting for?" Kendon said. "You know about the asteroid. Release me, and give me back the one-one-five pod and the beam weapon. And get me an airplane."

"The president said it wasn't for sure it's going to hit. Possible, but not for sure. He said for everyone to stay calm and stay put. He's going to set an example by remaining in the White House with his family."

"He didn't tell the truth. It's definitely going to hit, and six billion people are going to die. It's being guided in."

"Oh? Who's guiding it in?"

"I'm sure Laura has already told you what's involved."

"What's in it for those people in black uniforms—the Directorate folks you told me about?"

"They will survive in underground facilities along with the people that the Breeders and the Directorate have been rounding up. The Directorate will control what's left of the human race."

The sheriff nodded. He picked up the phone and barked, "Bring it in."

Two deputies came through the door carrying a twisted, charred metal object. Kendon recognized it as the archway to the control room of a Breeder ship. It had what looked like hieroglyphic inscriptions etched along the side of the arch.

"What's all these chicken scratches?"

"They're ideograms. It's the alien slogan: 'We are gods: We create, we rule, we destroy.'"

Bamford snapped his fingers. Two more deputies came in, one holding a metal rod with what appeared to be melted glass at one end. The other deputy was carrying a stainless steel tray.

The sheriff pointed to the rod. "What the hell is that?"

"It's a symbol of power carried by the Breeder commander.

The crystal at the tip is a device that amplifies mental energy a hundredfold. That's what they use to incapacitate people before abduction."

The deputy placed the tray in front of the sheriff. On it was a folded white cloth with a bulge in the center. The sheriff pulled back the top of the cloth, exposing a grayish-blue hand that was torn off at the wrist, with four long bony fingers, each with suction cups on the tips. A dark blue liquid had congealed at the severed wrist and gave off an odor of ammonia.

"What's this?"

"That's the left hand of a Breeder. If you found it near the barn I told you about, then it comes from the spacecraft I destroyed this morning. They were trying to abduct Laura and seize the one-one-five pod."

The sheriff stared at the hand in disgust and said, "It was holding the rod."

"Then it's the left hand of the commander of the ship that I destroyed this morning."

Bamford folded the cloth back over the hand. "So what you're telling me is that these aliens—the Breeders—are the ones that diverted the asteroid and are guiding it in."

"It's going to hit tonight."

The sheriff leaned backward in his oversized chair, the fingertips of his hands joined together. "Now, I want you to tell me the rest of the story, son, and I want you to be truthful with me. Where did Laura Meller's father build the beam weapon?"

Kendon smiled in disbelief. The moment he entered the room, he had picked up on some kind of ulterior motive to the interview. Now he could clearly see the motive: Armed with that information, the sheriff intended to get to the weapon himself, thinking he could deflect the asteroid and claim credit for it to further his political ambitions.

Kendon said, "Even if you were able to get to the weapon, it's not likely you could figure out how to work it—at least not in time to stop the asteroid. But I doubt you could get that far. You would have to fight your way through as many as forty Director-ate soldiers who have taken over the facility. They're trained killers. You could take your entire police force with you and you wouldn't stand a chance."

Bamford huffed, "What makes you believe I had that in my head?"

"We're running out of time, Sheriff. Get me back to the plane. Give me back everything you seized. And Laura Meller comes with me."

The sheriff paced back and forth. Finally, he grabbed the phone and shouted, "Call in every available deputy. Send five cars with lights flashing but no sirens to the west side of town and have them stop at the river and wait for further instructions. I want the SWAT team and ten deputies at the airport, ready to block the roads. Get them there in fifteen minutes. Keep them back and out of sight."

Kendon said, "Don't dispatch by radio. Your transmissions can be monitored."

The sheriff bellowed into the phone, "And by God, don't do any of this by radio. Use the telephone. I want strict radio silence."

The sheriff said to Kendon, "Stand up and turn around."

Kendon stood up.

The sheriff pulled out keys and unlocked the handcuffs. While he was doing so, Laura rushed into the office and threw her arms around Kendon. They held each other tightly.

"Forget the turboprop," the sheriff said. "I've got something a lot faster—an executive jet. It happens to belong to one of my campaign contributors, and his pilot is standing by."

Chapter 21

*A*t eight in the morning, two hours before the president's televised speech, a National Guard Humvee pulled up in front of the modest house in La Parguera where Tepler, Gabriela, and her parents had taken refuge. Through the front window, Tepler saw Nestor Estrada, dressed in combat fatigues, signal to the driver to remain in the vehicle.

Estrada was a short, well-built man. In civilian life, he was regional manager for a telecommunications company. When Tepler met him two days earlier at Gabriela's home, he had been smiling, relaxed, and pleasant. But now, as he marched up to the front door, his face was grim.

Gabriela opened the door for him before he could knock. Rather than hugging Gabriela, Estrada saluted. He was stiff and professional—a soldier now, not a family member. He stared for a moment at Tepler's arm, which was cradled in a sling.

"My men are deploying in San German and Mayaguez. I don't have much time. Why have you requested my presence here?"

Tepler couldn't remember ever feeling so tense. He wondered if he would be able to convince the colonel not only to retake the observatory, but to do so without seeking clearance from his superiors.

Gabriela led her cousin into the living room. "We have

something extremely important to talk to you about. It's related to the reason you were mobilized," she said.

"How could you know anything about it?"

"It's because of the asteroid, isn't that true?" she said.

The stocky battalion commander looked surprised. "Where are you getting this? Nobody is supposed to know about it until the president speaks this morning."

"Eric was the one who discovered the asteroid."

Estrada glanced at Tepler, then at the sling. He nodded at Tepler, as if to congratulate him.

Tepler said, "I discovered it three days ago and passed the data on to other observatories to verify. It's huge and it's going to hit tonight at exactly thirty-five minutes past eight. The devastation will be global."

Estrada shook his head. "I was briefed last night in San Juan. I was told it's not certain it will hit. When the president gives his speech this morning, he will ask everyone to remain calm and to stay indoors. We've been called out to maintain order. Nobody can predict how people are going to react to the news."

"If that's what the president intends to say," Tepler said, "then he won't be telling the truth. There's no question about it. It's going to hit just off the coast of Puerto Rico, southwest of Cabo Rojo."

"How can you be so certain?"

"Because it's being guided in like a missile. It's supposed to hit."

Tepler realized that if it weren't for Gabriela's presence, Estrada would likely turn on his heels and leave. The battalion commander glanced impatiently her.

Tepler nodded at her to explain.

"It's being guided in by a spacecraft," she said. "I saw it myself through the telescope."

Estrada's eyes narrowed. He squeezed his lips together and said, "I came here out of respect for your mother, because she asked me to, Gabriela. I wasn't expecting to hear such nonsense." He turned toward the door. "I'm sorry, but I have to go."

"Wait," Tepler shouted. "What Gabriela says is true. I don't have the evidence with me. It's at the observatory, and that's the reason we asked to see you. The observatory was taken over by men in black uniforms." He pointed to his shoulder. "This is what they did to me. They tried to kill me."

The mention of soldiers dressed in black seemed to click with Estrada. "When was that?"

Encouraged, Tepler said, "It happened the night before last, after I met you. I drove to Arecibo because I wasn't able to get through to anyone there. I wanted to find out why I couldn't communicate with them, and I wanted to get them to use the radio-telescope to track the asteroid."

He told Estrada about the massacre and about his narrow escape later from the Cabo Rojo observatory.

Gabriela said in a rush, "Have you been told anything about those people?"

"We have intelligence about their activities in Puerto Rico. They've been rounding up people in black buses. Our information is that their activities are related to national security, and we are under orders not to interfere with them."

"Is it national security to massacre people? I saw what happened. They're not what you think. They were speaking an Eastern European language of some kind. I have it from a good source that they're part of a paramilitary organization."

Estrada scoffed. "Police received an anonymous tip about Arecibo, but they didn't find any bodies when they went to investigate, only a parking lot full of cars but no people."

"I *saw* the bodies," Tepler replied. "Fourteen of them. They were lined up and machine-gunned to death. I *witnessed* the murder of another person, one of the program coordinators. He was trying to run away and was shot in the back."

"What do you want of me?" Estrada asked.

"We have to take the observatory back. Our survival depends on it. Hidden under the telescope is a weapon that was intended to be used against the asteroid. It was built by the same scientist who built the observatory, and I now know it was built specifically to deal with this asteroid."

"How could a scientist know about the asteroid so far in advance?"

Gabriela stamped her foot, surprising Tepler. He could not have imagined Gabriela angry. "You already know the answer to that, Nestor. Your own uncle predicted it fifteen years ago. The scientist visited Miguel. He believed in him when no one else did, and he built the weapon underneath the telescope. That is the real purpose of the Cabo Rojo observatory."

Tepler worried that his worst fear was about to be realized. Before the colonel arrived, Gabriela had told him about the ridicule that surrounded her uncle's prediction and how it had divided the family. Some family members had also been humiliated and had sought to distance themselves from their uncle. Nestor's family had moved to San Juan.

"I would show you the weapon," Tepler said, "but the paramilitaries have it. There are at least twenty of them—maybe twice as many—and they're killers. They have to be driven out."

"Where is this scientist?"

Tepler said, "He's dead, but the weapon is intact. He created it in two parts. The weapon itself is hidden in a very large cylinder that supports the telescope. The second part involves the power source. Someone is coming with it from the States. Once we have the observatory back, we insert the power source, which slides into a tube at the base of a cylinder. The tracking and firing systems of the weapon are integrated with the telescope. I've checked out the controls. Once the weapon has power, I'm confident I can deal with the asteroid."

Estrada sat down and held his head. "I don't know what to tell you except that I don't have the authority. My orders are to not interfere with them. My orders are to deploy my men and deal with any civil unrest that breaks out following the president's speech."

"Then we are all going to die tonight," Gabriela said.

Gabriela's parents appeared in the kitchen door, looking somber. Gabriela's father said, "It was the fate of our family to be drawn into the center of this, Nestor. It was your destiny to be in the center of it, too. I can now see that it was the reason you became a guardsman and distinguished yourself in Iraq and became a military leader. It was in preparation for this moment. The fate of your wife and your children, the fate of Puerto Rico, the fate of the entire world is now in your hands."

Estrada stood up and paced back and forth.

"I have to obtain permission from my superiors. I can't act on my own authority in any matter involving the use of force."

Tepler said, "That would be a tragic mistake. Who would understand? Even if your superiors could be made to understand, it would take too long. We only have half a day. You *have* to take matters into your own hands."

"I don't understand any of this," Estrada protested. "What would be the motive for destroying this world?"

"I don't have the answer to that," Tepler said, "but the people who are coming with the power source do. One of them is the daughter of the scientist who built the weapon. The other is someone who used to be part of the paramilitary group, but who defected."

"Who are you talking about?"

Tepler didn't want to give him Kendon's name in case the battalion commander had heard something about him. The hunt for a terrorist in the United States suspected of possessing a nuclear bomb had to be big news, if only in San Juan where the colonel had been the previous night. If he made the connection, that would only create another complication, another obstacle to overcome.

"Would you be disobeying orders merely by making preparations for combat?"

Estrada shrugged.

"Could you have thirty men with house-to-house combat experience and two snipers standing by, and also have sufficient troops in reserve to control the roads to the observatory? You don't have to make a final decision until these people arrive with the power source. Then you can decide what to do."

"I don't have a problem with that."

Tepler said, "This man knows how the paramilitaries operate and I think he has a plan. He asked to have two Humvees painted black so they resemble the ones they drive. Can that be done?"

"I can have them painted at the motor pool. When do your friends arrive?"

"I don't know yet. They're going to call me when they're on the way."

Estrada looked at his watch and shook his head. "They don't have much time left, do they?"

"No, they don't."

Chapter 22

Kendon and Laura were snug but tense in the back seat of the sheriff's unmarked car. He was thrilled that at last they were on their way, but he couldn't shake the feeling that something was wrong. In the last twelve hours, he had blown two Directorate helicopters out of the sky and had demolished a Breeder command ship, all near the city of Clifford, yet there were no challenges now from the ground or the sky.

The Breeders had to know he and Laura were there; they had to realize they were on their way to the airport. Were they now wary because of the beam weapon?

Kendon gripped the weapon tightly, ready for action. Before leaving the county jail, he had insisted on carrying it with him. It was now like a third arm. The one-one-five pod was safely in the trunk, as were his dress uniform and the black uniforms and the weapons he had taken from the snipers.

The sky was overcast and the air chilly. Two unmarked police cars followed them at a distance, and several other unmarked vehicles drove toward the airport on side streets. As their car sped down the road, Kendon and Laura kept watch, searching the streets and the skies for anything suspicious.

The sheriff spoke over his shoulder, keeping one eye on the road. "You're still not going to tell me where you're heading?"

"I'll tell the pilot once we're in the air," Kendon said. "It's better for no one else to know."

As they drove through town, Kendon was struck by the almost complete absence of people. The president had given his televised speech half an hour earlier. Had everyone now taken refuge at home?

Kendon had known about the Breeder intention for years, and he had had time to adjust to the knowledge and to make secret plans with the other conspirators. Participating in the resistance had given him energy, direction, and hope. He felt sorry for the billions of people worldwide who, only that morning, had learned they could die before the day was over. The president had spoken not just to the American people, but to the entire world, and Kendon seethed at the lie. The president had given them hope, yet he had to know there was absolutely no hope. If he didn't know before, he had to know now about the Collaboration, and he had to be privy now to the secret decisions made decades before by a cabal of politicians, bureaucrats, industrialists, and military leaders that had sealed the fate of humanity.

If the president had chosen to stay at the White House, it was because he knew what was in store for survivors. He had chosen death.

Kendon's mind screamed: *We are not going to die. We will defeat them. I will expose the lie. Today, the world will know the truth.*

The sheriff turned onto the airport road. Kendon couldn't see any of the security arrangements. The police had hidden well.

As they zipped along the road, Laura pointed to the mountains where they had taken refuge that morning. A chunk was missing not far from where he and Laura had been, giving it the look of a volcano after an eruption. Kendon was appalled. The mountaintop must have been thrown hundreds, maybe thousands of yards away. If there were people on the other side, they would have been crushed by falling rocks.

He noticed the sheriff was looking at him in the rear view mirror. "I warned you about the beam weapon," Kendon said.

The sheriff grinned. "I had to see for myself. That's one of the reasons you're now a free man."

"What's on the other side of the mountain?"

"Not a soul, if that's what you're thinking."

The massive explosion would have drawn attention. It was something more to worry about.

"We still have to get out of here safely," Kendon said. "We need to come up with a diversionary tactic."

"Like what?" Bamford asked.

"Can you get other planes in the air? Send them in different directions."

"Too late for that. There's only one pilot out there that I know of, the one that's waiting for us."

Laura leaned forward. "Why not announce you captured us? As soon as we're airborne, go public with the arrest. Tell it like it happened. We were caught when we tried to steal an airplane."

Kendon thought about it. As a diversion, it could work except that the Directorate would go looking for them at the county jail. "You would have to say we were already being transported under heavy security to some big city like Austin, or Dallas, or Houston."

The sheriff nodded. "Yeah, like we're turning you over to the feds. I can talk a good line."

"There's something else you need to do. The debris from the Breeder ship has to be secured. It's evidence, and a lot of people are going to want to get their hands on it and make it disappear."

"What do we do with it?"

"Have your trusted personnel take as much of it as they can and hide it. Give it away, truck it away, bury some of it. The same with the Breeder body parts. They need to be secured and kept from decaying. Store them in refrigerators if you have to."

"Folks might think twice about that, but I'll see what I can do."

They entered the small airport. The sheriff drove up to one side of a closed hangar and honked. A garage door rolled up, revealing a Learjet, sleek, white, and beautiful, with engines mounted on each side of the fuselage near the tail. The sheriff drove into the hangar and parked behind the plane.

A tall man wearing a white shirt with epaulettes stood next to the stairs to the cabin. He had a pleasant smile and the friendly, easy-going manner Kendon had noted among many of the upper-worlders in his hunter-killer days. Back then, he had thought it was a trait of shallow, pampered people. But now he understood: It showed the trusting, open nature of people who had not been raised in fear.

Bamford introduced the tall man as the pilot, Mark Owens.

"She's fueled up and ready to go," Owens said. "If we can get there in under five hours, we won't have to refuel."

Kendon said, "We have some things to load."

Just as he turned toward the car, three of the undercover cops from his earlier arrest walked up to him. One of them was Sagecroft; the other two were the deputies who had been hiding in the turboprop.

"I hope there's no hard feelings over the rough treatment," Sagecroft said.

Kendon shrugged. "You were doing what was expected of you."

Sagecroft introduced the other two men, Kraemer and Hendricks, and said, "We've been thinking you might need some help at the other end. We want to volunteer. The sheriff's got no problems with it."

Kendon thought about it. They looked rugged and reliable. They had been trained in the use of firearms and were skilled at role playing. They could be useful, Kendon realized. It was clear he would need all the help he could get to dislodge the Directorate troops from the observatory.

He nodded at them. "I'll brief you when we're on the way. Give me a hand with the gear."

"You're the boss," said Sagecroft.

They transferred the weapons and equipment from the trunk of the sheriff's vehicle to the jet, saving the one-one-five pod for the last. Kendon and Sagecroft lugged it into the jet and set it down in the aisle in the back. The undercover agents took seats near the rear. One of them rested his foot on the pod.

The cabin smelled of leather upholstery, and Kendon was pleased with the luxury of the plush carpets. It was the perfect airplane for a woman like Laura. She was waiting with the sheriff next to the stairs. Kendon stepped out of the plane and said to Bamford, "If we succeed, you're going to have six billion friends."

The sheriff touched two fingers to the brim of his hat. "You're running out of time."

Kendon took Laura by the hand and led her up the stairs. He admired how even under duress she was graceful and serene. He hoped for the future, but it was possible they had only until the night to live. He wanted to savor every moment he had with her. He led her to the forward compartment and held her hand lightly as she sat down in one of the cushy seats. He sat next to her while she snapped her seat belt in place.

He looked at Laura tenderly. He felt a mixture of joy at their being together and the thrill at last of being on their way. Now there was at least a chance to defeat the Breeders; now there was hope for the future of the world and for their own future.

Kendon went to the cockpit and strapped himself into the copilot's seat. Through the window, he saw the sheriff twirl his forefinger in the air. The hangar door opened and a tractor backed up to the airplane. The driver hitched the tractor to the jet and towed it to the runway.

The sky was overcast, but free of rain. It looked free of everything. But was it? Perhaps the Breeders were waiting in the distance, beyond view, intending to follow. All they could do now, Kendon realized, was to proceed and hope for the best.

The jet engines whined as the pilot checked instruments. He turned to Kendon. "Where are we heading?"

"Puerto Rico."

The engines whined louder and louder. The jet pushed forward and straightened on the runway. The pilot released the brakes. As it gained speed, the plane shook and vibrated. Finally, the nose lifted up, the ground fell away, and the jet streaked upward into the clouds and soon climbed above them.

It was eleven o'clock in the morning. Kendon calculated the time left before impact: nine-and-a-half hours.

He took out the stolen cell phone, but decided against using it, instead walking to the rear of the plane to the undercover cops. "Any of you gentlemen have a cell phone?"

Sagecroft offered his. Kendon returned to the cockpit and dialed a number. A man answered.

"Is this Eric Tepler?" Kendon said.

The voice said, "God, am I glad to hear from you. Where have you been?"

"We had some problems, but we're on our way. What are the coordinates of the airfield?"

Kendon repeated them to the pilot.

"How long before you get here?" Tepler said.

Kendon turned to the pilot. "What do you estimate?"

The pilot punched some numbers into a calculator and said, "Depends on the wind. Four hours, give or take twenty minutes."

Kendon repeated the information and said, "You can breathe easy, Eric. We've got the missing piece with us."

Tepler said, "And you can breathe easy, too. I've got some help lined up. The National Guard commander has prepared his troops, and he's willing to listen once you get here."

"What about the Humvees?" Kendon asked.

"They're going to paint them just like you want."

"I'll call you when we're approaching," Kendon said.

He left the cockpit to sit next to Laura. As he held her hand, he stared out of the window at the sky above and the clouds below.

What could go wrong, he wondered?

Chapter 23

*T*epler, Gabriela, and the National Guard commander were waiting for Kendon in a battalion Humvee parked behind the small Quonset hut at the entrance to the Lajas Valley Air Park, the only building at the small airfield.

"You can't see them, but my troops control the airfield," Estrada said as he explained the security measures he had taken.

Tepler nodded to the colonel, who was in the front with a driver, and strained to force a smile despite the throbbing pain in his shoulder. He wanted badly to take some of the painkillers the doctor had given him, but they were opiates, and he was afraid they would dull his mind at a time when he needed to be at his sharpest. Instead, he had opted for aspirin and ibuprofen, but their effect on the pain was hardly noticeable.

Their Humvee was hidden from the road, but they had a clear view of the runway, a grassy strip that ended three thousand feet north at a line of trees. Beyond the trees were low hills covered by the lush foliage of the region. Tepler strained to detect Estrada's men, but he couldn't see anyone from the platoon that had been deployed behind the tree line and on the adjacent properties.

He thought it was a good idea to keep out of sight, but in fact there were hardly any vehicles on the road. Normally on a Sunday, the two-lane country roads were full of cars. He and

Gabriela had listened to the communications between Estrada and his company commanders and knew that none of the feared disturbances had happened. After learning about the asteroid, people had stayed home, huddling together indoors. Even the big cities were like ghost towns. If there was any unrest, it was among the guardsmen, who wanted to be with their families.

Tepler looked at his watch. It was nearly three o'clock. The jet would arrive soon, but he wondered if there would be enough time left to organize an effective assault. Not even six hours remained before the asteroid was going to slam into the Caribbean.

Estrada got out of the Humvee and scanned the sky with binoculars, then lowered them and shook his head. "We're running out of time fast."

Just then the cell phone rang, causing Tepler's heart to leap. He hit the talk button.

"We're approaching," Kendon said.

Estrada raised his binoculars again. After a few seconds he said, "There it is!"

Tepler and Gabriela jumped out of the vehicle and looked up. "We see you!" Tepler said into the cell phone, unable to contain his excitement.

Gabriela squeezed his good arm and shouted joyfully, "At last!"

The jet was a dark dot against the clear blue sky, but it quickly got bigger, and soon details of the plane were visible. It seemed to drop out of the sky. Tepler held his breath as the jet touched down and bounced slightly. Then came the roar of the thrust reversers. It didn't seem like the jet would ever stop, but it slowed and came to rest barely a hundred feet from them, the twin engines still whining.

A National Guard truck came out of nowhere and drove up to the jet. A dozen guardsmen in full combat gear and carrying M-16s jumped from the rear of the truck and surrounded it, their rifles hugged to their bullet-proof vests, the muzzles pointing at the ground, their eyes alert.

Tepler, Gabriela, and the colonel ran to the plane, arriving just as the engines shut down.

The passenger door opened. Tepler watched as a man about five years older than him, tall and with an athletic build, stepped down from the plane. He was carrying a boxy weapon that didn't resemble anything he had ever seen before.

Tepler assumed that it was Michael Kendon and was pleased to see that his physical presence matched the voice he had heard. Even though he was in civilian clothes, Kendon had a military bearing and exuded an air of self-assurance. The woman with him also had an impressive presence.

Kendon thrust his hand out, first to Gabriela, then to Tepler and Estrada. He introduced Laura, then the undercover police whom he described as "volunteers from Texas."

Kendon said to Tepler, "I brought you a present."

Sagecroft and the other two Texas lawmen went back into the airplane, then returned a minute later carrying the blood-red cylinder. They backed out of the plane with it, one man on each end. Sagecroft had one arm wrapped around the middle.

Since he was familiar with the dimensions of the hollow tube at the base of the cylinder, Tepler knew what to expect, but he was still surprised at how small the one-one-five pod appeared. It was barely larger than an industrial cylinder of acetylene or oxygen, and somewhat narrower in diameter than the typical home water heater.

He touched it, as if not yet fully trusting his eyes. "God, I can't believe it's finally here," he said.

"It's heavy," Sagecroft grumbled. "Where do want us to take it?"

Estrada pointed to the Quonset hut. "We'll talk inside," he said as he marched toward the building.

The front part of the building was used for business, with a small, enclosed office on one side. In the back was an open storage area with a sofa dividing the office from stacks of cardboard boxes. Empty brown beer bottles, evidence of a recent party, were sitting along the top of the sofa, leaning against the boxes stacked right behind it.

The Texas lawmen lugged the one-one-five pod in and gently put it down on a table where Kendon had placed the portable beam weapon. The lawmen left and came back a few minutes later with the weapons and uniforms Kendon had seized from the snipers.

By the time they were inside the Quonset hut, Kendon had grasped a great deal about the National Guard commander. He sensed he was high-minded and brave, but, as a soldier, he had been conditioned to obey, to take action within the context of plans conceived by a large military organization. He was a cog in the machinery, yet now he was being asked to take drastic action on his own, to commit his men to lethal action, and he was deeply troubled.

Kendon was pleased that the commander had at least made preparations and that he was willing to listen. A detailed military map of the region was tacked to the front wall along with photographs of the lighthouse-observatory and a floor plan. One of the photographs was a grainy blowup showing black Humvees parked in front of the observatory.

Kendon tapped the photo. "How did you get this?"

"I sent a recon team in this morning. They're still out there."

Estrada pointed to the map of the peninsula. It showed the lighthouse-observatory on one bluff and a second bluff across the inlet to a small bay where the reconnaissance team was located. Kendon had seen the peninsula from the air and thought the layout vaguely resembled the boot of Italy. The two bluffs, separated by the inlet, formed the bottom of the boot.

Kendon examined the recon photos, absorbing every detail. The hexagonal lighthouse tower, capped by the dome of the observatory, stood above a large, rectangular, colonial-style building, painted gray with white trim, maybe twenty-five feet high and eighty feet long. The roof was concealed behind a three-foot parapet that he knew could hide snipers. The tower jutted from the rear of the building, a hundred yards from the edge of the cliff and a calm Caribbean Sea. Directorate Humvees were scattered in front of the building, inside the wrought-iron fence that surrounded the facility. The photographs showed seven vehicles as well as two Directorate soldiers on guard. They were leaning against the iron bars of the fence, facing the road leading to the observatory. They were smoking and their machine guns were slung loosely over their shoulders.

Kendon was impressed by the photographs. "What other preparations have you made?"

Estrada balked. His hands were on his hips. "Before I tell you anything more, I want to know what I'm getting my men into. And I want to know who the hell you are. I don't have a clue about you."

Kendon stood next to the one-one-five pod and said, "I am only the bearer of a gift that was created by Laura's father, Donald Meller. The gift is what it's all about, not me. This is what will save the human race today."

He gripped the handles welded to the cap of the red pod and turned it counterclockwise. Soon the cap unscrewed completely. The sharp point of the orange rod jutted out.

Kendon stepped back for everyone to get a look at it and said, "That is ununpentium, Element 115. It was mined somewhere in the universe, maybe a million light years from here, maybe even ten million. I don't really know. It's the element that fuels the alien spacecraft, and it's the only source of energy powerful enough to divert the asteroid. The rod weighs forty-two pounds, but it contains more energy than the combined power of all the nuclear weapons in the world. The technology of the weapon is complex, but basically it transforms the potential energy of ununpentium into a focused gravity beam. Short bursts won't have much of an impact, but a sustained application of the beam against the asteroid will push it far enough off course to keep it from hitting Earth."

Kendon handed the portable beam weapon to Estrada. "This is a miniature version of the weapon that's hidden in the observatory. The ununpentium fuel rod in here is about the size of the tip of your little finger, but it's powerful enough to blow away a mountain."

Estrada examined the boxy weapon and then looked at Kendon. "Okay, it runs on ununpentium. Now I want to know who the hell you are. And who are those people who took over the observatory?"

Patiently, Kendon explained. He covered it all clearly, concisely, and quickly—the Collaboration, the Directorate, the creation of the hybrid race to replace the human race, his role in the Directorate, his secret defection while still in the underworld, and, finally, his work with Donald Meller. He told them as much as he knew about the human-sized Breeders and their extraordinary mental capabilities, and about the child-sized Clones, one of their creations.

He didn't hide the fact that he had been an assassin and had killed people to keep them from talking about what they knew. Kendon spoke directly to the colonel, but kept glancing at Tepler and Gabriela and the undercover officers. They needed to hear it, too.

"Laura's father envisioned an alternative to a no-win military confrontation with the aliens and what he knew would be a lose-all collaboration. He saw there had to be a third alternative, one of resistance to both the Breeders and the Collaboration. He learned about the asteroid fifteen years ago from someone here in Puerto Rico and had the observatory built as a cover for the weapon. He also engineered the fuel source. Unfortunately, he's not here to see his work completed."

Estrada said, "If they took over the observatory, they must know about the weapon."

Tepler interjected, "I'm not sure about that. They're silencing astronomers to keep the approach of the asteroid a secret."

"Then what are they doing at the observatory?" Estrada asked.

Cradling his wounded arm and wincing from pain, Tepler said, "It's out of the way. I suppose they've turned it into command center."

"The asteroid is supposed to hit in five hours," Estrada said. "Are they going to die, too?"

Kendon said, "An hour before, they'll send helicopters for them. There are underground facilities in Puerto Rico, too, in the central mountain range, and even closer—deep inside Sierra Bermejo."

Estrada stiffened and looked over his shoulder, as if glancing in the direction of the mountain range. "That's just up the road from here."

"Midway up the north face is a portal overlooking Laguna Cartagena," said Kendon. "It's one of the Breeder bases secured by the Directorate. It's connected to subterranean waterways that lead to the sea. I didn't realize it's so close."

Estrada said, "There have been a lot of UFO flaps in the area. I always thought it had to do with advanced U.S. airplanes operating in secret."

Gabriela turned to Kendon and Laura and said, "There's something you should know. Nestor and I are first cousins, and it was our uncle who told your father about the asteroid fifteen years ago. Eric and I only learned about Donald Meller two days ago. We visited my uncle, and he told us about him. That's when it became clear that the machine underneath the telescope is a weapon."

Laura smiled warmly at her. "Fate has brought us together, Gabriela."

Estrada said, "It wasn't possible to believe my uncle fifteen years ago, and it's hard for me to believe what you're saying now. I listened to the president this morning. He said it isn't certain it's going to hit."

"He wasn't telling the truth," Kendon said. "He couldn't. He would have to tell the world about the Collaboration and the fact that a handful of people more than half a century ago made decisions in total secrecy that are now about to cause the end of the human race. If we have to, we'll try to take the observatory without your help, Colonel. If we fail, you will die tonight along with everyone you love. It's that simple."

Estrada didn't respond. He stood there rubbing his neck, unable to make a decision.

Gabriela finally said, "My father said it better than anyone. He said that it was the fate of our family to be drawn into the center of this. Nestor, you really have no choice except to act."

Estrada paced back and forth, rubbing his neck. Finally, he cursed and said, "Okay, I will take full responsibility. But we need to work out a plan."

"What preparations have you already made?" Kendon said, relieved by the decision.

The colonel pointed to the map. "A mile and a half from the observatory is a walled tourist inn. It's on the shore, the last building before you get to the lighthouse. They don't have much business this time of the year. This morning, I sent two platoons there hidden in civilian vans and SUVs. My men are combat ready and are waiting at the inn for orders. Both platoons have had house-to-house combat experience in Iraq. One platoon will proceed hidden in boats around the bluff for the assault. The second will remain at the inn to secure the road to the observatory and will serve as a reserve force, if needed. I will have another hundred men controlling the roads as far north as Boqueron."

Kendon nodded. "Before you attack, I need to secure the tower and the observatory in order to protect the telescope and the beam weapon. Where are the Humvees that were painted black?"

"At the armory. What do you have in mind?"

Kendon picked up his wrinkled gray dress uniform and the two black assault uniforms and spread them out on the table next to the one-one-five pod.

"I hold the rank of major in the intelligence branch of the Directorate. This is my dress uniform. I can bluff my way in. I'll need two volunteers wearing these black uniforms to go with me, and another two who will pose as Nomenklatura prisoners."

He saw that everyone except Laura was confused by the term so he explained the word.

"Once in the observatory, I'll have the element of surprise and can take control of the tower. At my signal, you will launch the ground assault."

Gabriela said, "You're not going to fool anyone with those uniforms. They need to be cleaned, mended, and pressed. The belts and boots need to be polished."

"How long would it take?" Kendon said.

"A little more than an hour." She turned to the colonel. "I need to get to La Parguera to take care of it."

Estrada called for a Humvee. A few minutes later, a soldier entered the Quonset and saluted. Estrada pointed to Gabriela and said, "Take her where she needs to go and stay with her."

Tepler said, "I'll go, too."

Kendon said, "No, you stay here. You're the key to making the weapon work, but you're not going to be of much use with that shoulder. I have a way to heal you quickly."

Gabriela scooped up the uniforms and left with the soldier. Kendon pointed to a couple of chairs. Tepler sat down, looking confused.

Laura said, "He has a remarkable ability to heal with his hands."

Kendon was about to sit down next to Tepler when a thought occurred to him. He turned to the colonel, "How many men do you have under your command?"

"About six hundred."

"I didn't realize Sierra Bermejo is so close. It's possible the

Directorate will launch a counterattack. Where are your men now?"

"One company is on patrol in Mayaguez, another in San German. A third is broken up into platoons and squads for duty in smaller communities."

"How far away?"

"The farthest are only an hour away."

"What about surface-to-air missiles?"

"We have shoulder-fired weapons, but they're at the armory."

Kendon strode up to the map and studied it for a moment. "You need to position all of your troops within a few miles of the cape. We need to set up a perimeter against a possible helicopter attack. The Directorate has plenty of Black Hawk helicopters that carry door-mounted 50-caliber machine guns, and also rockets. All it would take to destroy the tower is a single rocket."

"So now you want me to shoot down helicopters?"

"We have to do whatever it takes."

"This is more than we talked about."

"It's a matter of the world living or of the world dying. Take your pick."

The colonel rubbed his forehead. His face was drawn and lined, as if he hadn't slept for a week.

"Anything else?" he said finally.

"What about radar? Does your battalion have any mobile radar?"

"Not as a part of our mission. We do have obsolete trailer-mounted radar units in storage at the armory. I train my men on them to help them get better jobs in the civilian sector."

"How many?"

"Eleven. Why?"

"I think we're going to get visited by every Breeder spaceship in the solar system. Breeder and Clone ships have beam weapons which aren't particularly powerful, but at close range they can be devastating."

"So you want us to track them?"

"No. In the early days of combat with the Breeders, before the Collaboration began, several of their ships were downed by high-powered radar, particularly when the radar came from several sources simultaneously. It disrupts the control of their ships, and they crash. I don't know much about the technology, but maybe you can replicate that with high-powered bursts. You're the one who knows the capabilities."

Estrada took his cap off and scratched his head. "There's something odd about those radar units. They weren't regular army hand-me-downs. They were donated specifically to the battalion by a private foundation ten years ago. They have a lock-on-target capability and are much more powerful than they look."

Tepler jumped to his feet. "What's the name of the foundation?"

"I haven't looked at the file in a long time, but I remember the initials: TAF."

"That's the Third Alternative Foundation," Tepler said excitedly, "the same foundation that built the Cabo Rojo observatory and the weapon—Donald Meller's foundation."

Kendon said, "Laura's father thought of every angle. If nothing else, they'll keep their ships off balance until we get the beam weapon working. When it's working, it should emit a protective shield. The tower isn't going to be safe until we have the shield in place."

Kendon turned on the hand-held beam weapon and set it on low intensity. "Watch this," he said.

When the green light went on, the translucent field of turquoise energy emanated from the barrel, visible even in the harsh fluorescence of the overhead lamps. Kendon placed weapon on the ground. It sat at an angle, like an open umbrella.

"I suspect we'll see a similar effect at the observatory. I hope so, because it could mean the difference between success and failure."

He picked up the weapon, holding it forward to keep the parabolic shield from touching anything, then turned it off. The turquoise shield vanished in an instant.

Estrada paced back and forth. Finally, he picked up a radio transmitter and seemed about to speak into it. But after staring at it for a moment, he put it down and pulled out his cell phone.

"If they've been monitoring our radios, they will think we're still out patrolling to deal with civil unrest." He held up the cell phone. "This is how we communicate from now on."

Estrada punched numbers into the cell phone and soon was giving orders to re-deploy his troops. He gave a strict order to limit communications to cell phones and couriers.

Kendon sat down next to Tepler. He placed his hands a half-inch above Tepler's wounded shoulder. "I want you to close your eyes. Part of the healing process is in your mind. I want you to imagine your wound healing. That's important."

Tepler nodded.

Kendon leaned his head close to the wound. He closed his eyes and repeated the same healing process he had used on himself, on Molly, and on Laura. He blocked out everything else from his mind, including the sound of the National Guard commander giving orders, and plunged his thoughts into the subcutaneous world of the young astronomer's ripped shoulder. His eyes closed, he felt a stream of energy flowing from his hands into the wound.

Laura watched the healing, amazed once again at Kendon's ability. But her attention soon drifted to the weapons on the table, first to the sniper rifle, then to the M-16 and the automatic pistols. She picked up one of the Directorate side arms, removed the clip, then re-inserted it and chambered a round. She flicked the safety switch on and off. She removed the clip again and ejected the chambered round by moving the slide. She repeated the process again and again until even the coldness of the gunmetal felt comfortable in her hand. She aimed at the beer bottles lined up along the top of the sofa, at the far end of the Quonset hut. She wished she could shoot to get a feel for the recoil.

Kendon's concentration was only broken when Gabriela returned with the spruced-up uniforms. She had a puzzled smile when she saw Kendon with his hands hovering just above Tepler's wounded shoulder. It looked like both men had dozed off. Laura put her finger to her lips as a sign not to disturb them, but at that same moment Kendon opened his eyes and stood up.

Eric opened his eyes, too, and smiled at Gabriela.

Kendon said, "Move your arm."

Tepler removed the sling and lifted his arm, gingerly at first, then with ease, as if nothing was wrong with it. He let it swing loosely.

"It's still a little sore," he said as he rubbed his shoulder. "But the throbbing pain is gone."

Gabriela removed the gauze. The wound had shrunk to half its previous size, and the yellow and purple bruises had disappeared.

Estrada said, "Is there anything you can't do?"

"It would take a couple more hours to heal you completely," Kendon said. "Unfortunately, we don't have any more time."

"At least I can use it again," Tepler said.

Kendon grabbed his cleaned-up dress uniform and black boots and disappeared into the side office. When he stepped out a few minutes later, his new appearance caused a stir. Wearing a uniform designed to project power, he was like a different man. He placed the black beret of a Directorate intelligence officer on his head and adjusted it.

"There's no getting away from Arkasha," he said to Laura.

Laura was fingering the smaller of the black uniforms, the one that had belonged to Viktor. "Do Directorate women wear these uniforms, too?" she asked.

"Yes, ranking officers will sometimes have a female aide dressed in a black uniform. Basically they're status symbols and sexual playthings for the powerful."

"Then I'm going with you."

Kendon protested. "I can't allow it. I need someone with military training, someone who won't hesitate to shoot. You're a doctor, a pediatrician."

He knew there was a deeper reason for not wanting her with him. He didn't want any harm to come to her. If she were to die and he were to live, he would feel emptiness for the remainder of his days.

"I know how to shoot."

Kendon was about to say, "This is a man's job," when Laura said, "I know what you're thinking, and you're wrong. My father started this, and I'm going to finish it."

"I'm sorry," he insisted. "I can't allow it."

Laura grabbed the Directorate pistol from the table. Holding it like a pro, she suddenly swiveled her body toward the storage end of the Quonset. The blast of three rounds was deafening, masking the sound of three beer bottles shattering, one after the other.

Estrada said, "If you don't want her with you, I'll take her with me."

Without a word, Laura grabbed the smaller of the two black uniforms and disappeared into the office. She came out a few minutes later as transformed by the uniform as Kendon had been. Her hair was tied neatly in the back, her head covered by the purple beret.

Kendon pointed to the nametag sewn on the upper left breast of the shirt.

"That says Viktor on it. You don't look like Viktor."

A clipboard was handing from a nail on the wall. Laura grabbed it and held it close to her breast, covering the nametag.

"I am your female aide. I am your sexual plaything."

Kendon realized it was useless to protest. She was as strong-willed as her father and as determined. He stepped out of the door of the Quonset and motioned to the Texas policemen, who had gone outside to smoke, to come back inside. They looked at him as if they didn't recognize him at first.

"I've got a job that requires your skills," he said when they entered.

He handed the second black uniform to Sagecroft, who was about the right build. "Go into the office and get dressed. From now on, you are Volodya."

Kendon said to Kraemer and Hendricks, the other two Texas sheriff deputies: "Sagecroft is going to drive you in the back of a Humvee. You are my hostages and your hands will look like they're cuffed behind your backs, but you will actually be sitting on your guns. I'm going to leave you in the custody of these guards."

He showed them the grainy reconnaissance photo of the observatory grounds, explaining the plan and tapping his finger on the two guards. "When the assault begins, you take them down. That means you shoot to kill. If you don't, they won't hesitate to kill you. You will have M-16s and plenty of ammunition hidden in the back of the Humvee. Your job will be to cover the side entrance. Anyone in a black uniform who comes out of that door dies. Is that understood?"

They nodded.

Kendon picked up the portable beam weapon and showed Estrada the selector switch. He turned the weapon on and flicked the switch to low intensity.

"It takes six seconds to warm up on low intensity, ten seconds for high intensity. Low intensity is more than you'll need."

He handed Estrada the weapon. "I am entrusting this with you and only you. You will initiate the assault either at my signal, or after exactly ten minutes if you haven't gotten a signal from me, by blowing away the wrought iron fence and the Directorate Humvees. The two Humvees that we go in will be parked to one side, out of your way. Remember that the beam destroys everything it touches, so you don't want to touch the building. Fire one-second bursts, starting with the wrought iron fence just to get the hang of it. Then fire again to sweep away the vehicles. The beam will throw everything for miles, that's how powerful it is."

Tepler was surprised when Estrada sheepishly took the beam weapon and looked at the map where Kendon was pointing. He had been expecting the colonel to rebel at being given orders. He was, after all, the commander of the men who were going into combat, but it was clear he accepted that Kendon had taken charge.

Estrada said, "That means my troops approach from the same side after I've cleared the way for them."

"Yes," Kendon replied. "I suggest you have a fifty-caliber machine gun positioned exactly opposite the main entrance. A half dozen men are likely to spill out of the building to see what happened when you sweep away the Humvees. It will make an incredible noise. The gunner must ignore them and shoot directly through the door into the building. That will take out anyone inside who happens to be in the line of fire. Your troops will take out the ones who come outside. You also need snipers positioned to cover the windows and the roof. I've got an extra sniper rifle if you need it. The machine gunner should continue firing into the door until your men are positioned to go in."

"I get the picture."

"Have some of your men take control of the other side of the building where the tower is. For the rest of your soldiers, it's going to be room-to-room combat. But you'll have the advantage, since by then a third, maybe even half of their people will be out of action. The rest will be in a state of shock. They're not expecting any opposition—they're not even wearing body armor."

Estrada nodded.

"One more thing," Kendon said. "Don't use any grenades. The concussion could harm the mechanism of the weapon underneath the telescope. And no firing in the direction of the dome—that's where we will be."

Chapter 24

Kendon maneuvered the black Humvee along the road leading to the observatory, feeling the vibration of the powerful motor in his hands and arms. Laura was in the passenger seat, staring ahead in silence, and Estrada and two soldiers were hiding under a tarpaulin in the back.

Driving close behind them was the second Humvee with a black-clad Sagecroft at the wheel and the two undercover lawmen in civilian clothes. They were seated in the rear with their hands tied loosely behind their backs, their buttocks concealing automatic pistols.

The sun had fallen in a blaze into the sea. Here and there, men, women, and children stared at the black vehicles from doorways or windows of the pastel-colored homes that lined the road, their faces full of fear and suspicion. Kendon was certain they had made the connection between the menacing presence of the black-clad soldiers and the news they heard that morning about the asteroid.

When they were two miles from the cape, Kendon spotted the lighthouse-observatory on the high bluff, at the far end of the peninsula, a lonely sentinel against the approaching asteroid.

He glanced over at Laura. The assault uniform clung to her figure as if it had been molded onto her. On her, the beret had a stylish flair. She smiled back at him, but in her eyes he saw steely determination. He wondered if she was afraid.

He wasn't afraid for himself, but he felt fearful for her. He had sensed the moment they met at the hospital that they would meet their fate together. If they succeeded, they would succeed together; if they died, they would die together. But he prayed that if they were to die, she wouldn't suffer.

He reached over and gently put his hand on hers. "A part of me didn't want you to come, but I'm glad you're with me."

She lifted his hand and put it to her lips, then kissed his hand. It was then that he realized she was trembling.

"You give me courage," she said.

"You give me strength," he said.

They had gone over the plan again and again. Kendon had instructed everyone in the basic technique of mental control because it was important for the success of the operation to create a psychic shield against the Breeder mind. Estrada had passed the information on to his commanders as well. It was difficult to master true mind control, Kendon knew, but even a clumsy effort was better than no effort. He was encouraged by the near certainty that none of the soldiers were implanted.

Up ahead were the high walls of the salmon-colored tourist inn where Tepler and Gabriela had taken refuge with the one-one-five pod, guarded by an entire platoon of reserve troops. The assault team had already been deployed, hidden in fishing boats, and the soldiers were now positioned at the far end of the bluff.

The Humvees whizzed by the tourist inn onto the unpaved road through the salt marshes. The air was filled with the odor of marsh water and super-concentrated salt. Tall bushes that thrived on salt water grew in thickets. The winding road was full of deep potholes, but the Humvee drove over them as if they weren't there.

Estrada had sent another recon team into the marshes to

monitor the road where it led up the bluff and to search for a secure spot where he and his two soldiers could jump out unobserved. Kendon realized the skill of the guardsmen because he could not detect them.

The closer they got to the observatory, the more the dome-covered tower dominated the skyline and stood out against the orange sky.

After a few minutes of slow driving through the marshlands, Kendon came to the base of the bluff and the access road that led to the observatory. He drove slowly up the slope. At a low spot where the Humvees were hidden even from the observatory, Estrada and the two soldiers jumped out.

Clutching the beam weapon, Estrada disappeared into the brush, followed by the soldiers.

Before the colonel jumped out, Kendon said to him, "Remember, under no circumstances do you abort the mission. If you don't hear from us in ten minutes, begin the assault. It will mean we are dead, wounded, or taken prisoner, and you will have to take the tower the hard way."

"Good luck," Estrada said.

Without slowing, Kendon continued up the hill. When they got to the crest of the bluff, the observatory came into full view. It was even more imposing than in the photographs. The hexagonal walls of the old lighthouse tower shouldered the oversized dome. Inside the compound created by the wrought iron fence were the Directorate Humvees, parked closely together near the main entrance.

Two sentries were outside the fence, slouching against the fence at the side of the building. When Kendon drove up, they stood stiffly at attention and saluted. Kendon parked along the side of the building to keep the vehicles out of Estrada's line of fire.

One of the soldiers rushed to open the door for Kendon. He knew from the nametags—Fedya and Vadik—that the guards were Russian speaking.

"Where is your commander?" Kendon said in Russian. "I have orders to inspect the telescope for possible removal."

They were young, low-ranking soldiers, in the first stage of their Directorate careers, just as Kendon had been fifteen years earlier before being recruited into the intelligence service. The soldiers pointed to the tower.

As planned, Sagecroft parked to the right of Kendon's Humvee, also to keep it out of the line of fire of the beam weapon.

Kendon snapped his finger at Sagecroft and said in Russian, "Volodya, you are to come with me."

Sagecroft, who had practiced until pronouncing it perfectly, replied in Russian, "Yes, sir."

Kendon pointed to the undercover officers in the back seat and said to the guards, "They're Nomenklatura. They're handcuffed to the seats, but keep an eye on them."

Kendon, followed closely by Laura and Sagecroft, marched through the cluster of Directorate Humvees to the main entrance. He glanced toward the wrought iron fence, knowing that a machine gun had been positioned in the brush below the crest of the bluff, ready to be moved forward once the fence and vehicles had vanished under the fury of the gravity beam.

The high arched door was wide open. As he stepped inside, Kendon reviewed in his mind his pretext for being there and the authority he was acting under. He imagined the small contingent was under the command of a lieutenant—at best, a captain. He was a major and in full dress uniform. Directorate troops had obedience literally beaten into them; even minor infractions could lead to severe punishment. The commander would do as requested and lead them to the tower.

Kendon noted the exterior walls were three feet thick, while the interior walls were two feet thick. He regretted forbidding the use of hand grenades. He was expecting to see more than a dozen soldiers loitering in various rooms that were connected by wide, arched doorways. But there was no one.

Kendon sensed trouble, but the trouble did not have a face yet. They readied their weapons and checked two side rooms, one that Kendon knew was a rarely used office; the other, Tepler's private quarters, but both were empty. They walked back into the main room. All of the windows were shuttered, and it was dark except for the light pouring through the main entrance.

At the back of the main room was a wide opening to yet another room. At the far end, in the darkness, Kendon saw the entrance to the tower. It was up a short flight of stairs leading to a set of massive double doors, and it made him think of the entrance to a temple.

Just as Kendon walked toward the stairs, a man stepped out from behind a wall. He was in the darkness and Kendon couldn't distinguish his features, but he could see that his head was bandaged and that his sidearm was holstered. His heels clicked with each step on the hardwood floor.

Kendon aimed his pistol. "Where is your commander?"

"I am in command here," the man said.

"Show yourself."

The man stepped partly out of the darkness and stopped. Kendon could see a Directorate dress uniform like his, the uniform of an intelligence officer. He again heard the familiar click of boot heels.

"More," Kendon ordered.

The man stepped completely out of the shadow. Kendon's heart leaped when he recognized him. "Bogdan!" he said, his voice betraying astonishment.

The top of Bogdan's head was wrapped in gauze. From his bearing, it didn't appear that he had suffered any other injuries from the cavern explosion. Kendon surmised the stalactites must have fallen around him, but not directly on him. Otherwise, he would have been crushed to death.

Bogdan smiled. "Don't do anything stupid, Arkasha. There are six machine guns pointing at you and your companions. Lower your weapons."

Kendon could hear movement behind him. He lowered his pistol, and Laura and Sagecroft followed his lead. Immediately, three Directorate soldiers ran up behind them, stripped them of their weapons, and searched them. One of them found Kendon's cell phone and handed it to Bogdan.

Bogdan approached Laura. His smile had the temperature of liquid nitrogen. She turned away from him with a look of disgust. He grabbed her jaw and twisted her face toward him.

"So this must be Donald Meller's daughter."

"Leave her alone. How did you find out about Cabo Rojo?" Kendon demanded.

"You were good at hiding your trail, but not that good." Bogdan looked toward the spiral staircase, the nitrogen smile warming up slightly. "I'm in a boastful mood. Come with me. I'll show you how I found out."

Before reaching the stairs, he pointed to Sagecroft and said to a Directorate lieutenant, "Have your men guard this one. If he gives you any trouble, shoot him."

Soldiers marched Kendon and Laura up the spiral staircase at gunpoint. Bogdan followed. As they started up the staircase, Kendon glanced under the lower rungs where Tepler had told him to look. His heart sank when he saw that the access plate had been removed. It meant they knew about the beam weapon.

As if reading his thoughts, Bogdan rapped the metal cylinder with his knuckles and said. "It's a marvelous invention. It's actually an improvement over Breeder technology. Not even they possess anything this powerful."

Midway up the stairs, Kendon noticed a door, which had to be the access door to the roof of the main building. He resisted the urge to shove the door open in an attempt for him and Laura to escape. He knew they would be shot down in seconds.

Kendon was the first to enter the observatory. With the barrel of his rifle, the soldier guarding him shoved him into the room. Kendon gazed first at the squat green telescope that aimed at the heavens through the opening in the dome. The cannon Tepler had described was not there, so it had to be back in the cylinder.

There weren't any other soldiers in the small observatory. As he stepped farther in, he saw an older man tied to a chair. He was heavyset, with a fringe of gray hair and a jowled face. He had been badly beaten. His head was hanging down and his body was leaning as far forward as the ropes would allow. Kendon couldn't see his hands, but he was certain fingernails were missing. He wondered if he was dead, but then saw the man's head turn slightly at the sound of people entering the room.

Laura entered the observatory next, a soldier directly behind her. When she saw the man, she gasped, "Mortimer! What have they done to you?"

Mortimer tried to look up at her, but didn't appear to have the strength to lift his head. He said in a weak voice, "Forgive me, Laura. I tried not to say anything, but I couldn't take the pain."

She swung around toward Bogdan, who was the last to enter the observatory.

"What have you done to him, you animal?"

His face had the smugness of someone in total control. "Your telephone calls led right to him. It didn't take much to get him to talk. One fingernail gave me Cabo Rojo, another gave me the technical drawings."

Bogdan pointed to cardboard boxes piled in a corner. "Everything having to do with the design and construction of the beam weapon is in those boxes—of the weapon in the tower anyway. I seized them last night at an engineering company in New Jersey along with the computer files. The only things I don't have are the stolen ununpentium pod and the portable beam weapon that you have caused so much havoc with. Where are they?"

Kendon's mind was racing at full velocity. What else did Bogdan know? He clearly hadn't gotten a fix on Tepler, who was safely hidden at the tourist inn with the one-one-five pod. But had

Bogdan been able to link cell phone calls to the Puerto Rico National Guard? Had he deduced from the electronic trail that an assault was imminent? He had to know something was in the works. He would certainly know Kendon wouldn't risk entering the observatory without backup, that there had to be a bigger plan. Where were all of the Directorate soldiers, Kendon wondered? There had to be at least twenty of them and maybe twice that many. Mentally, he felt their presence. Had they set up an ambush?

Bogdan touched the gauze wrapping his head. As if remembering what Kendon had done to him at the caverns, his eyes became inflamed. He shouted, "I don't intend to be patient about this. Where are they?"

Something was about to give. Bogdan was clearly on the verge of violence, but there was some other tension in the air that Kendon could sense. He glanced at the soldiers to see where they were standing, but also to size them up. The one who had roughly marched Kendon up the stairs had stepped back and was waiting with machine gun pointing it at the floor but finger on the trigger. He had the dull face and opaque eyes of a gooney, and Kendon sensed that he had already been corrupted by acts of violence committed in the name of the Collaboration.

But the soldier who had marched Laura up the staircase was different. Kendon saw the nametag: Sergei. Kendon could sense the turmoil of a young soul trapped by fear. It was like reading his own soul years earlier, that of an intelligent and sensitive young man thrust by circumstances into situations that conflicted with an innate sense of right. Sergei was also holding his rifle at the ready, with finger on the trigger. He returned Kendon's glance, and Kendon grasped instantly that the soldier was at a turning point.

Kendon said to Bogdan, "I can give you everything you want— if you join us!"

Bogdan sneered, "Join you? What on earth for?"

"The Breeders don't have to succeed. The world doesn't have

to end. They can be defeated, right here, right now. There's no reason for you to continue with their program. Think about it, Bogdan. You were raised in circumstances you hadn't chosen, and you were indoctrinated and given no alternative. But now you have an alternative. With the weapon under the telescope, we can deflect the asteroid. You and I, Bogdan. We can defeat them. We'll be heroes. Even the most heinous things we've done in the name of the Collaboration will be forgiven."

"Heroes to whom? To the vermin that populates the world? The asteroid will cleanse the planet. The best and the brightest around the world are being spared thanks to the Collaboration. With these technical drawings and with the portable beam weapon, I will be able to deal with the Breeders and their hybrids."

"You're implanted. They know everything you think and everything you do. They will kill you and strip the survivors of all hope. At least Meller and his group were able to keep it a secret. They knew how to control their minds."

"Do you think you were the only ones who achieved mind control? I wouldn't be in this room if they knew my thoughts."

Kendon was taken back. It had never occurred to him that anyone outside of Meller's group had been able to develop such an ability.

Bogdan sneered. "You should have shared this technology with the Committee. We could have turned it on the Breeders already."

"They couldn't be trusted."

"You had your plan, and it failed. I have my plan, and it won't fail."

Bogdan's eyes became inflamed again. His chest heaved up and down, as if deliberately pumping himself into a lethal fury. He shouted again, "Where is the pod? Where is the portable beam weapon?"

Instead of waiting for an answer, Bogdan put his pistol to Mortimer's temple and fired. The bullet went clean through the skull, sending a spray of blood, brain tissue, and bone fragments against the telescope.

Bogdan put the gun to Laura's head. "Tell me, or she's next."

Laura's eyes were squeezed shut, and she was biting her lips as if to keep from screaming. Kendon glanced at the soldiers. Neither had moved, but their eyes were eloquent: The gooney was staring at Mortimer's body with morbid fascination, but Sergei's eyes showed barely disguised revulsion.

Kendon said, "I'll tell you what you want to know, but we need to work out a deal."

"The deal is, I don't shoot her in the head. Start with the ununpentium."

"In the second Humvee we came in. Under a tarpaulin in the back."

"What about the hand-held beam weapon? Is that in the Humvee, too?"

"No, it's down the road—in case any helicopters come."

"I figured you had some help. The local militia? I've got a surprise waiting for them. Tell them to surrender the weapon and no harm will come to Laura."

"I can't. You have my cell phone."

Still holding the gun to Laura's head, Bogdan reached into his pocket with his free hand to retrieve the cell phone. He tossed it to Kendon.

Kendon flipped the cell phone open. "If he agrees, and I don't know if he will, I'll have him put it down in the middle of the road." Kendon pointed to the gooney. "Have your soldier watch out the window."

Bogdan motioned for the soldier to stand at the window. Kendon caught Sergei's eye and held his gaze for a second.

Kendon dialed. When Estrada answered, Kendon turned the phone toward Bogdan to show him that a connection had been made.

Kendon wondered what he should do after giving the command to attack. All he could think of was to fling himself at both

Laura and Bogdan to knock them down. That might give Laura and him a chance to escape down the spiral staircase. Perhaps Sergei wouldn't shoot, or would shoot high. It wasn't likely, but Kendon didn't see any other choice.

"What's going on?" Estrada said.

"I'm in the tower with Laura."

"Do I start the attack?"

Kendon said, "Yes . . ."

The phone clicked off, but Kendon continued speaking, as if Estrada was still on the line. ". . . yes, everything is under control. We have an agreement so there won't be any bloodshed. But as a gesture of good faith, I want you to lay the beam weapon down in the middle of the road. We won't need it. Don't ask questions. Just stand in the road with it so we can see you."

Turning to Bogdan from the window, the gooney said, "I see someone in a uniform holding a weapon."

Bogdan said to Kendon, "Tell him to put it down in the middle of the road."

Kendon repeated into the dead phone, "Put it down in the middle of the road and walk back down the hill."

The gooney continued describing what he was seeing: "He's kneeling down. He's aiming it in our direction."

Bogdan shouted, "What?"

At that instant, Kendon heard the familiar roar of the gravity beam when it touched something solid. He could imagine the pulverized Humvees and the wrought-iron fence flinging at hypervelocity across the bay.

Bogdan exploded. "Shoot Arkasha! Kill him!"

The two soldiers raised their rifles, but Sergei suddenly spun in the gooney's direction and fired two quick bursts. The bullets hit him in the chest, flinging him backwards. Sergei swung the rifle back in the direction of Bogdan, but by then Bogdan had grabbed Laura by the waist and had swung her in front of him as a shield.

Kendon took advantage of the distraction to dive at them, but just as his body collided with theirs, Bogdan fired at the soldier, hitting him twice in the abdomen.

Kendon's weight sent Bogdan tumbling backwards, causing him to lose his grip both on Laura and on his pistol. The two men grappled furiously on the floor, each grabbing for a chokehold on the other. Though thinner and lighter than Kendon, Bogdan had sinewy strength and a crushing grip. He managed to roll on top, seizing Kendon by the throat with one hand; with the other hand, he reached down to his leg and pulled out a knife strapped inside his boot.

Kendon struggled to loosen Bogdan's fingers and to ward off the knife that Bogdan raised over his head, ready to plunge into his face. Bogdan screamed, "I should have killed you back at Alamogordo."

A gunshot rang out. Bogdan's head snapped back. A trickle of blood oozed from a hole in his forehead just below the gauze. His grip on Kendon's throat relaxed. He slumped to one side. Kendon pushed him off.

Laura was standing two yards away with Bogdan's pistol gripped in her two hands. Her eyes were as cold as gunmetal. She lowered the gun when Kendon got to his feet. Bogdan lay on his back, his mouth and eyes frozen wide open as if astonished that he was now dead.

Sergei was holding his abdomen. Blood was oozing from between his fingers. Kendon knelt beside him and put his hand gently on the wounded man's shoulder and said, "If we are successful today, it will be because of you."

"They're on the roof," the soldier groaned. "They have grenades. They were expecting an attack."

"How many?"

"Seventeen, maybe eighteen."

"Are there others like you?"

"It's possible, but I don't know who. It's not safe to talk about such things to others. And you have to be careful about your thoughts so that the Breeders don't know."

Kendon pointed to Laura. "She's a physician. She will help you."

Kendon ran to the window, furiously dialing Estrada's number. The guardsmen had already begun their attack. The 50-caliber machine gun had opened fire and was hammering at the main entrance.

Down below, he could see the roof of the lighthouse building. At least a dozen Directorate soldiers were hiding behind a thick, three-foot high parapet along the entrance side of the building. Another half dozen were hiding along the parapet that faced the road. Kendon couldn't see the entire roof—possibly there were more.

The colonel finally answered.

"Keep your men back," Kendon barked. "The roof is crawling with soldiers hiding behind the parapets. It's a trap."

"It's too late. My men are already moving in."

"They're going to lob grenades at them."

"What do we do?"

"Blow away the parapet along the entrance side of the building. That will take out everyone hiding behind it."

Kendon heard hand grenades detonating. He grabbed Sergei's M-16 and rushed halfway down the spiral staircase to the door leading to the roof. He opened the door slightly to look out. Just as he did, he saw the turquoise beam lick the edge of the building. In less than the blink of an eye, the parapet and the dozen Directorate soldiers who had been hiding behind it vanished amidst a tremendous roar.

He estimated another six men remained along the parapet that faced the road, but it would be too risky to have Estrada aim the beam weapon at that part of the building. It was too close to the tower.

Readying the machine gun, Kendon stepped out, looking first

to see if there were any soldiers anywhere else on the roof. The only ones he saw were shooting from the parapet, or were lobbing grenades over the wall.

Kendon fired burst after burst at them, and they fell one by one. A live grenade rolled from the hand of the last fallen soldier. Kendon leaped back through the door just as it exploded. He managed to kick the door shut with his foot, but the blast flung it back open. Shrapnel threw the wooden door off its hinges and peppered the cylinder, but the shrapnel impacts were not powerful enough to penetrate the steel.

Downstairs in the main building, the battle was furious. Kendon heard the confusion of machine-gun fire and the screams and shouts of men in close combat.

He wondered how many of the guardsmen had survived the hand-grenade assault. Were there enough to take on the remaining Directorate soldiers? How many were down in the main building? He remained half way up the tower, just above the door to the roof, his machine gun pointed down. He had to guard the tower at all cost. He edged farther down the spiral staircase, knowing that he needed to keep the fighting away from the exposed access door. A bullet, either directly aimed or stray, could ruin the beam weapon.

Down below, the shooting raged and subsided, moving to one area of the building then to another, then back again to where it had been before.

After about five minutes, he heard boots clambering up the metal stairs. Kendon yelled in English, "Halt! Identify yourselves!"

"Guardsmen."

"Who is your commander?"

"Capt. Jose Luis Beltran."

"Who is your battalion commander?"

"Lt. Col. Nestor Estrada."

Kendon said, "Show yourselves, but slowly."

He saw the barrel of an M-16 first, then the camo sleeve of

the soldier holding it, then the grease-painted face of a guards-man.

The soldier smiled and saluted. His nametag said Lt. Orozco. "The colonel warned us you were up here. We've secured the main building, sir."

For the first time since driving up the road, Kendon felt the tension draining from him. He led the soldiers to the door to the roof and said, "The observatory is secure, but I'm not sure about the roof. I think we got them all, but you need to make sure."

The lieutenant used his hands to give orders, using rapid finger codes indicting the number to go through the door, who would go first, and which sides they would fan out to. In a rush, they poured through the door, Orozco first. Kendon was impressed. "Citizen soldiers," Estrada said when explaining the National Guard to him.

Machine guns rattled and a couple of minutes later, the lieutenant came back onto the staircase. "All clear. I'm leaving four men on the roof."

Kendon went back up to the observatory, followed by the National Guard lieutenant. Laura was bending over the wounded Directorate soldier, stanching the bleeding, oblivious to the other bodies. Sergei's eyes were closed, his face drawn in pain.

As Kendon and the lieutenant entered the room, Laura looked up. "He's in a state of shock. He needs medical attention immediately."

Orozco said, "We have medics on the way. We took a lot of casualties."

Kendon pointed to Sergei. "I understand how you feel about your men. That is how I feel about this man. All of us owe our lives to him. Please give him the same attention you would give your own."

Kendon was certain they weren't out of danger. He tried calling Estrada, but his call was transferred to voice mail. After dragging the body of the gooney out of the way, he looked out the window and saw the National Guard commander standing in the road at the crest of the hill next to a Humvee, talking on his cell phone. A soldier was holding the beam weapon. Estrada spotted Kendon and waved. Kendon pointed to his cell phone to show him they needed to talk.

Kendon's phone rang.

"Any action anywhere else?" Kendon said.

"Nothing on the ground yet," Estrada said. "The sky's clear, too."

"That's not going to last for long."

"I don't think so, either."

Kendon said, "We need to get Tepler and the pod here fast. We don't have any time to lose."

"My troops are bringing them now."

Chapter 25

*I*t was already dark when the first vehicles of the convoy escorting Tepler and the one-one-five pod cleared the crest of the bluff, headlights off but visible in the moonlight. Bristling with soldiers outfitted with combat gear, bullet-proof vests, and machine guns, the convoy was made up of the private trucks and SUVs that had secretly taken the soldiers to the tourist inn earlier that day.

Standing near the rubble in front of the main building, Kendon watched the vehicles approach. His eyes nervously shifted from the convoy to the skies, searching the darkness for any evidence of a counterattack.

He neither saw nor heard anything. Nor were there reports from the National Guard troops positioned farther inland or the radar units Estrada had deployed in an arc several miles from Cabo Rojo.

Not yet, anyway, Kendon thought.

Superimposed in his mind was an image of the asteroid, streaking closer every second. How far away was it now? How much time was left? He forced himself not to think about it. It was more important to focus on the task at hand, at getting the weapon up and running and the shield in place.

Think only about the shield. The shield is the priority.

Kendon watched as the guardsmen removed the last of the dead Directorate soldiers from the main building, lining the bodies near the edge of the bluff. They had already cleared the observatory and the roof of bodies and had set up an emergency room inside the main building to treat the wounded, with Laura in charge.

Other than the wounded soldier in the tower, only four Directorate soldiers had survived. They were kneeling on the ground facing the wall near the main entrance, their hands cuffed behind their backs, guarded by the three Texas lawmen.

Tepler and Gabriela were in the back seat of a Chevrolet Suburban. Gabriela jumped out first and rushed up to Kendon.

"Where are the wounded? I want to help."

He pointed inside. "Laura's with them," he said as she ran inside.

"Where's the pod?" Kendon said as Tepler slid out of the vehicle.

"In the back."

They rushed to the rear of the Suburban. Tepler flung the back door open. The red cylinder lay on the floor.

"It's time to see if this thing really works," Kendon said as he dragged the pod toward him.

With Kendon on one end, Tepler on the other, they carried the pod into the lighthouse to the base of the tower. At the foot of the spiral staircase, Tepler steadied the cylinder while Kendon grabbed the handles and deftly unscrewed the cap, exposing the tip of the orange ununpentium rod.

When the cap came off, Kendon felt an electric thrill running up his spine. "I've waited a long time for this moment."

Together, they pushed the pod into the hollow tube. It slid in as easily as a battery into a flashlight.

It took ten minutes of flicking the fuse box switch back on after each power failure, but as soon as the one-one-five pod had been drawn upwards into the accelerator, the weapon came to life with whirs of massive gears engaging. At the first sign the weapon was at last self-powering, Kendon and Tepler broke out in broad smiles.

"By God, it works!" Tepler said.

Kendon said, "I want to see the beam weapon."

He followed Tepler up the spiral stairs to the observatory. The bodies were gone, but the blood was still there—pools on the floor, splashes on the walls, and streaks and spots on the telescope. It didn't bother Kendon, but he could see that Tepler struggled not to look, as if trying to deny what had happened only fifteen minutes earlier in the place he had called home for the last five years.

The cannon now dominated the domed chamber, dwarfing the squat but impressive telescope. Kendon ran his hand over the thick green tube, and stooped to examine where it came out of the floor. He was reminded of the sketch Donald Meller had drawn of the beam weapon. Somehow he had imagined it much smaller, but the cannon was three feet in diameter, fifteen feet in height, just touching the base of the dome. He knew it was filled inside with powerful coils that ensured a focused gravity beam.

Meller had never once mentioned a telescope, and Kendon understood now that it was part of Meller's security concerns. It would have given away too much to a man he had not fully trusted. How he wished that Meller had had total confidence in him. If he had gone along with them, he was certain he could have ensured Meller's survival and that of the other conspirators. Meller would be there now, working with this young astronomer to get the weapon ready to challenge the asteroid and defeat the Breeder's scheme. He imagined Meller in the room, with his white hair and stooped shoulders, bending over the control panel, scrutinizing images on the monitor, finally able to savor victory.

A call on the cell phone interrupted Kendon's thoughts.

Estrada spoke rapidly. "Where are you?"

"In the observatory with Eric."

"We've got trouble. You better get down here."

Kendon rushed down the spiral staircase and joined Estrada outside the main building. The colonel was shouting into the phone, "Hold back. Don't do anything unless you're attacked, but under no circumstances do you let any of those helicopters go south of Highway 303."

"What's happening?" Kendon said.

Estrada pointed to the northeast. "An entire squadron of helicopters came out from behind Sierra Bermejo. There's a cluster of disks in the sky, but so far, the helicopters and the disks are only hovering.

Kendon looked in the direction Estrada was pointing and became worried. That could be worse than an actual attack. The fact that they were holding back meant he was missing something. But what? He put a hand over his forehead, in part to suppress a headache, the result of unrelenting tension. He closed his eyes to see what images formed in his mind. Soon, a picture emerged of a soft, doughy substance with a fuse sticking in it.

"Explosives! The tower is rigged to explode. That's why they're holding back. They're waiting to see if the observatory blows up. If it does, they won't need to take any further action."

Kendon glanced at the captive Directorate soldiers, who were still on their knees facing the wall. He marched up to them and shouted in Russian, "Where are the explosives? Where were they planted?"

Three of them had blank looks, and it was clear they knew nothing. But the fourth, a man whose thin, crafty face reminded him of Viktor, looked at him with a sneer. Kendon quickly sized him up as irremediably hard core.

Kendon grabbed the soldier by the shirt, lifting him to his feet. He screamed in his face, "Where are the explosives?"

"You will not find them in time. You are doomed."

Still gripping the man, Kendon closed his eyes and let his mind relax. The image of the explosives was freshly stirred in the soldier's mind. He was thinking about it now, and Kendon saw it as clearly as if looking at a photograph—a long box covered by a panel with inset gauges. Kendon thought about where he had seen such a panel and then remembered it was in the observatory. It was the telescope's control panel. The explosives were rigged to the switch!

Kendon shoved the Directorate soldier to the ground and sprinted into the building and up the spiral stairs, shouting, "Eric! Don't touch anything! Do you hear me? Don't touch anything!"

The staircase was forty feet high, laborious to climb one step at a time let alone to run up. Kendon kept shouting as he sprinted up the stairs, not knowing if his voice could carry clearly all the way to the top. Nearly out of breath, he burst into the room and saw Tepler leaning across the control panel, his hand only inches away from a red switch next to the main monitor.

"Don't touch it!" Kendon cried. "It's rigged to explode!"

Tepler drew his hand back as sharply as if he had just touched something hot.

Kendon said, "They've got the place wired. The explosives are under the control panel."

The panel, with its dials and monitors, was exactly what he had seen in his head. He pointed to fresh scratches in the grooves of one of the screws holding the panel in place.

"See, it's been tampered with."

Tepler grabbed a screwdriver from a drawer, and Kendon carefully removed all of the panel screws. With the tip of the screwdriver, he lifted one side free and shined a flashlight into the box underneath. He could see wires and electrical gear, but he could also see something white and doughy wrapped inside like a coiled snake.

"C-4," Kendon muttered.

"What's that?" Tepler said.

"Plastic explosive. Very powerful. Be careful not to touch the switch."

They lifted the panel. A tangle of wires attached to instruments and meters prevented them from moving the panel more than six inches from the box, but it was enough for a clear view the malleable explosive packed inside. The fuse, a two-pronged electrode with wires leading to the switch, had been jammed deep into the explosive.

While Tepler held the panel upright, Kendon ran his fingers gently over the soft material and searched for other suspicious connections. When he didn't find any, he slid his hands back to the fuse. With the thumb and forefinger of one hand, he grasped the electrode. Slowly, with one hand pushing down on the C-4, he pulled the fuse out. He peeled the explosive from the panel box. When it was entirely removed, he bunched it together and held it between his hands.

"There's enough to blow away the entire observatory and the upper half the tower."

Tepler went pale. "What other surprises have they got for us?"

Rigging the telescope controls was something Bogdan would have thought of, Kendon knew, and it would have appealed to the Breeder's malevolent nature. They had prepared the trap in case they had to abandon the facility before the conspirators arrived.

The observatory and tower could easily be destroyed with a volley of rockets from one of the departing Black Hawks, but that wouldn't show any imagination. A rigged tower, on the other hand, would be a cruelly clever way to dispose of the conspirators if they were able to get there after the Directorate evacuated its troops. The tower would explode precisely at the moment the rebels thought they had succeeded.

Even though he was dead, Bogdan had come within seconds of succeeding. With fingers trembling, Tepler detached the electrode and rewired the switch. Together, he and Kendon set the panel back in place.

Kendon called Estrada on the cell phone. "We found it. We're safe."

Estrada said, "We've got another problem. You better get down here."

"Are they on their way?"

"Yes, but there's something else. Hurry."

Kendon's head throbbed painfully just above his eyebrows. He wanted to appear calm and self-assured, but the tension was building explosively inside of him.

He shoved the cell phone back into his pocket and said to Tepler, "I have to go. For you, getting that shield up is the priority."

Tepler looked at the wall clock. Only thirty-six minutes were left before impact.

"I could use your help," he said.

"Get the shield up," Kendon said. "Until then, the only purpose I have is to keep you alive. You are now the most important man on Earth."

Kendon could see Tepler's fingers were still trembling.

"You can do it, Eric. I know you can do it."

Chapter 26

*E*strada pointed to the portable beam weapon and said, "Something's wrong with this." He turned it on and waited the usual time for the green light to switch on. When it finally lit up, Kendon could barely see the turquoise shield coming from the barrel. Yet in the darkness, it should have been brightly visible.

"What's the problem?" Kendon said.

"I think it's running out of power."

Ever since first seeing the flash of the weapon, Kendon had thought about energy depletion, realizing that like any other source of energy, ununpentium had to have its limits. But not having any experience with it, he didn't have any way to predict the life of the weapon.

Kendon glanced up at the dome, wondering how close Tepler was to getting the shield to work. He looked north toward the Bermejo mountain range as the sounds of furious combat reached them. Machine guns rattled and explosions on the ground and in the air flashed in the darkness.

High in the sky above the mountains he saw an irregular formation of disks.

Kendon said, "Maybe the accelerator got damaged when you jumped from the Humvee."

"I was careful. It worked perfectly when I took out the Humvees and the snipers. I noticed the power started dropping just a few minutes ago." Estrada pointed to the sky. "I tried taking some of them out. That's when I noticed the problem."

Kendon stared at the stationary points of light and wondered why the Breeders didn't attack.

"They knew before I fired I was going to shoot," Estrada said. "The instant I pulled the trigger, they vanished, then they reappeared even closer than before. It was like they were taunting me to get me to shoot at them."

"They knew the ununpentium was depleting," Kendon said. "They were getting you to shoot at them to deplete it even more."

"It still has something in it. Not much, but it's still useful—see the glow?"

"We can't count on it any more," Kendon said.

He stared into the distance, at the flashes of light that were followed by booms seconds later.

"How long can your soldiers hold off the helicopters?"

"I don't know. Not long."

Estrada's cell phone rang. He answered, listening for a minute, then hung up. "The helicopters are retreating to the east and are heading for open sea. We've got them on radar. They're going to come at us over the water."

"How many?"

"Seven."

* * *

Two things greatly bothered Tepler: First was all the blood. As he worked the keyboard furiously trying to figure out how to get the shield to work, he tried to ignore the pools of red on the floor near the entrance and below one of the windows. He forced himself not to look at the splashes of blood, brain tissue, and cranial fragments on the side of the telescope. Kendon told him what had happened to Mortimer, and he was certain that what was on the telescope could only have been sprayed there by the bullet that killed the trustee. He tried to concentrate, but the bloodiness of the observatory was too distracting. The smell of it was in the air. It was cloying, causing him nearly to vomit. Soon, it became unbearable. He became obsessive about it: It was the blood that was keeping him from figuring out how to get the shield to work. He was sure of it! He had to do something about the blood.

Tearing himself away from the control panel, Tepler ran to a locker where he kept cleaning supplies. Inside was a bucket with a mop, but there wasn't enough time to fill it with water. Instead, he grabbed rolls of paper towels and a bottle of Windex and wiped as much of the mess as he could from the telescope, then sprayed all the surfaces. He had never liked the smell of ammonia, but now he breathed it in deeply as if smelling a bouquet of flowers.

He knew it was insane to take the time with the asteroid screaming toward Earth at twenty miles per second and the booms and gunfire of combat closing in, but he had to get rid of the blood! He threw paper towels over the red pools on the floor. When they were soaked, he balled them up and threw them out of the dome opening. He poured Windex on the floor and used up an entire roll of paper towels cleaning away the last traces. Finally, he threw all of the soaked paper out of the dome. What was left of the Windex he poured over his hands, then he sat back down in front of the keyboard, relieved that the blood was gone and that all he could now smell was the odor of window cleaner.

But now the other thing that was bothering him began to paralyze him: fear that he didn't really know what he was doing. He had boasted that he had the weapon figured out, and it was true to the extent that he was able to call up and understand the program. He could see from the display how the accelerator was controlled, and therefore the power output of the beam. He could tell from his experience with the telescope how the targeting of the beam was integrated with the telescope. Once he found his target, firing the weapon would be as simple as pushing a button. But he couldn't get the accelerator to perform. It seemed locked into the minimal mode that had been initiated by the insertion of the ununpentium pod, and that had merely allowed the weapon to come alive, deploying as it did into the observatory and mating itself to the telescope.

He glanced around the observatory and found the emptiness unbearable. He wished Gabriela were with him, if only to put her reassuring hands on his shoulders, to stand by him as he struggled to figure out what kept the weapon from working, to cheer him on with words of encouragement.

Tepler remembered Kendon's parting words as he left to engage Breeder and Directorate forces: *"You are now the most important man on Earth."*

The thought that everything depended on him made his face sweat and his shoulders ache. He was on a stage and six billion people were watching him, and he was frozen with fright that he wasn't up to the performance.

He looked at the wall clock: Twenty-nine minutes left before impact.

Somewhere down below he heard Estrada shouting orders for his men to set up machine gun emplacements along the cliffs. He heard him yell something about shoulder-fired missiles. What about the portable beam weapon? Tepler wondered.

The more he obsessed about not being able to figure out the problem, the more a children's song took possession of him: *Row, row, row your boat gently down the stream. Merrily, merrily, merrily, merrily, life is but a dream.*

He didn't know why it popped into his head. He thought it was a stupid song to have running in his mind at a moment like this. Life was a hardly a merry dream anyway—it was more like a nightmare. He was in the middle of a nightmare where nothing worked.

His cell phone rang, and he grabbed it, hoping it was Gabriela.

It was Kendon, asking about the shield.

"I'm working on it," Tepler snapped.

"They're coming over the water. I can keep you alive maybe five more minutes."

Row, row, row your boat.

Tepler remembered singing the song with his grandfather. He was from Hungary and had a thick accent, and it was always funny when he sang children's songs. Once when Tepler was six years old, not long after his father had taken him to an observatory and he had been able to see the moon close up, his grandfather asked him what he wanted to be when he grew up. When he said an astronomer, his grandfather asked him why, and he replied, "I want to see where God lives."

He remembered how his grandfather made a big fuss over his cleverness, but then said, "You don't have to become an astronomer to see where God lives." He pointed to the sky, "Look up, young man. You can see it with you own eyes. Up there."

As if reliving that happy moment, Tepler looked up and saw the sky through the opening of the dome and the familiar splash of stars. He could see the telescope aiming through the vertical opening and how the weapon straddled the telescope, the cannon barrel touching the edge of the dome.

Touching the edge of the dome!

He had a flash of insight: *Of course! Why didn't I see it before? The shield isn't working because the weapon isn't fully deployed.*

He had only assumed it was fully extended, but he could see the problem clearly now. The lip of the cannon was touching the underside of the dome, and the contact had caused the deployment to shut down. It had to be a built-in safety feature. Were the protective shield to function when the cannon was still underneath the dome, it would blow off the top of the observatory and possibly take some of the support building, too. The dome had to be opened more to let the cannon fully deploy.

"God, how dumb can I be?" Tepler said as he leaped from his chair.

On the wall was a large red button mounted like a light switch that controlled the retraction of the dome. It was a complex dome for a small observatory, because, in addition to being able to swivel in any direction, the dome could also be retracted by almost 180 degrees.

Nearly flying across the room, Tepler slammed the palm of his hand against the button and held it down. The dome panels lurched slightly as gears engaged. Two quarter sections of the dome slid backward, freeing the lip of the cannon, exposing it completely to the sky.

When the dome was fully retracted, the cannon emerged even farther out of the floor, pushing it far above the top of the dome, reaching out to the sky, toward the abode of God.

* * *

Kendon and Estrada were standing near the edge of the cliff and could hear the helicopters before they could see them. Nearby were two soldiers with shoulder launchers, each with a heat-seeking missile. Their range was only slightly better than the range of the air-to-ground missiles the Black Hawks were armed with.

The light of the moon glimmered on the water and gave the helicopters away.

"Fire!" Estrada shouted.

Two missiles streaked over the Caribbean, then two explosions lit the sky in the distance. By then the other helicopters had approached even closer, enough to fire their rockets. Using the cell phone, Kendon tried calling the tower, but Tepler didn't answer.

He cupped his hands to his mouth and shouted, "Eric, the shield! The shield!"

The guardsman reloaded the missile launchers with their last rockets. They fired again. One missed, one hit.

The disks hadn't moved from their position far above the ridge of the Bermejo mountains, but Kendon could see there were now at least thirty of them, scattered against the blackness and giving the appearance of a bright constellation in the night sky.

Kendon was certain they were deliberately holding back, waiting to see if their surrogates could do the job. Perhaps they were still fearful of the hand-held beam weapon. There had to be some residual power in it. He turned it on and saw that it was even weaker than when Estrada showed him the problem.

Kendon aimed at the advancing helicopters and fired. The beam was barely visible, but he could see the rotors of his target breaking off. The helicopter spun out of control and spiraled into the sea.

"Three to go," Estrada said.

Kendon looked again at the observatory. Something was different. The cannon had emerged beyond the dome, maybe by a dozen feet. He caught a glimmer of turquoise swirling at the mouth of the weapon, but still there was no sign of the shield. It had to spread out and cover the entire facility to be effective.

The helicopters fired, and a volley of rockets streaked toward the tower, closing in as fast as a bullet.

Kendon screamed in his mind, *No! You will not succeed!*

The rockets were inside his mind, encompassed by his energy. As they streaked over the sea, he visualized them changing course, shooting upward instead of straight forward. He focused his mind on the lead rockets, on the air that sustained them, on the circuitry that guided them.

Spin, spin out of control!

Two of the lead rockets began wobbling, then shot upward at the last moment, missing the observatory. But four others were only seconds behind. Kendon poured his energies on them, spinning them in his mind.

The rockets followed his mind, spinning crazily in the air. In the last second of their trajectory, they suddenly shot downward, exploding thunderously but harmlessly against the side of the cliff. Dizzy from the exertion, Kendon staggered close to the edge, but Estrada's firm grip pulled him back.

The remaining helicopters fired again.

"I don't have the strength to stop them," Kendon groaned.

"You don't have to," Estrada said. "Look!"

The turquoise glow from the cannon had spilled farther out than before and now extended half way to the ground, parabolic in shape. Just as Kendon thought that is still wasn't enough, it flared out like an enormous shell, spreading outward from the building a hundred yards in every direction, an energy shield of unparalleled power. All of the guardsmen were beneath it, inside a protected zone that nothing could penetrate.

Only seconds later, the rockets slammed into it, sending ripples of colorful energy throughout the field. Even the sound of the explosions was absorbed.

The helicopters fired rockets again and again. Circling furiously in the distance like stirred up bees, they aimed lower to get under the shield, hoping to destroy the base of the tower, but the shield now extended to the ground.

The missiles exploded harmlessly, their power swallowed by unyielding energy.

Chapter 27

*E*lated he had at last gotten the shield to deploy, Tepler climbed to the opening of the dome and flashed a thumbs-up sign to Kendon and Estrada.

He was already back at the control panel when he heard Kendon shout from the grounds below, "Great work, Eric, I knew you could do it!"

There was no time to lose. He had to find the asteroid, aim the weapon, lock it on target, and fire. And at last shove the asteroid off course, back into the solar system where it belonged, out where it could do no harm.

Tepler was pumped up with excitement at having gotten the shield up, but he quickly broke out in a sweat when he couldn't find the asteroid. The telescope had been programmed to track it, but either the alignment had been disrupted when the beam weapon coupled with it, or the path of the asteroid was now different.

With quick keyboard commands, he tried every search technique he could think of to bring it into view, but still without success. He wondered if the force field had something to do with it. Perhaps it was distorting light, throwing off the sensors. He knew the shield was able to block sound—he had just witnessed the brilliant flash of rocket explosions through the shimmering turquoise shield, but he hadn't heard a sound. He didn't know enough about the properties of the shield to say what effect it would have on light, but wouldn't Donald Meller have anticipated the problem and found a way to compensate for it?

Frustrated by his inability to locate the asteroid, he set up a pattern of grids and then began laboriously searching the grids one by one.

He worked feverishly, unaware of a presence in the room. He tensed but then relaxed when he felt soft, reassuring hands slide onto his shoulders. He glanced up at Gabriela.

"I want to be with you, Eric. I don't want to leave you."

With her touch the oppressive feeling of aloneness vanished. He pulled her hand forward and kissed it.

"Put your arms around me, Gabriela. Please, put your arms around me."

She leaned forward and draped her arms around his neck. She kissed him on the cheek and looked over his shoulder at the monitor.

"You can do it, Eric. Keep looking."

Energized by Gabriela's presence, he continued the grid search. She watched intently and soon pulled up a chair next to him and encouraged him to talk about what he was doing. For him, it was a relief, helping him to work off nervous energy and focus his mind.

Finally, he spotted an object of interest. It was a point of light, but larger and brighter than any in the surrounding cloud of stars, too large to be anything other than a hurtling mountain of destruction. After watching it for a minute, Tepler and Gabriela could see its swift movement across the motionless backdrop of stars.

"That's it, that has to be it," Gabriela said.

He studied the image. It was much larger than when they had last seen it. Before it had been millions of miles away; now it was less than an eighth of the distance between the Earth and the Moon, and it was closing in fast.

The computer made calculations and projected the trajectory onto one of the monitors mounted above the control panel. The asteroid was coming in at the anticipated angle. He wondered how much force it would take to budge it. He had no way of calculating the power of the beam, the X factor of the equation, but a sustained application of its tremendous energy on the underside of the asteroid would surely push it sufficiently out of the way to cause it to bypass Earth. That's what Donald Meller had intended. He regretted that the inventor of the weapon was not in the observatory in command of his creation, or at least present to witness its performance.

Tepler prepared to fire. Once the target was located, the weapon was almost as simple to operate as the hand-held version. Instead of a trigger was a toggle switch. Instead of lifting and aiming, it was a matter of tapping the directional arrows of the keyboard, which controlled the upward, downward, and sideways movement of the beam in whatever increments he programmed them for.

He knew they wouldn't be able to see the beam in contact with the asteroid. They would only be able to observe the effects indirectly, through the change in trajectory shown by lines on the monitor. He checked his computations one more time and was certain that the moment he fired the weapon the beam would strike the asteroid.

Tepler looked at Gabriela. "We're locked on," he said. "All I have to do now is throw the switch."

She nodded encouragement and said, "Do it, Eric. Do it now!"

His hand trembling, he put his finger on a toggle switch, eager to unleash the full power of the gravity beam, but then he pulled his hand back. "I want you to do it, Gabriela."

She reached for the switch. Her violinist fingers were not trembling as she said, "God help us all," and pressed down.

They heard what sounded like both a sizzle and a hum.

Looking up, they saw the thick turquoise beam shooting from the mouth of the cannon, a stream of raw, focused gravitational energy that was now mankind's last hope.

* * *

Minutes before the beam weapon fired, Kendon observed the futile actions of the Directorate helicopters with pleasure and wondered when they would give up. After firing all of their missiles, the helicopters circled a hundred yards above the protective shield. The door gunners unleashed the fury of their 50-caliber machine guns, but bullets were even less able than rockets to penetrate the shield. The helicopters finally left, heading back the way they had come.

When they were gone, Kendon turned to go up to the observatory, but he stopped when he heard what sounded like an electrical discharge. He looked up and his heart jumped at the sight of a turquoise beam shooting from the cannon, a stream of energy that was thick, focused, and fierce.

Tepler and Gabriela appeared in the dome opening and gave them the thumbs up. The guardsmen broke out in cheers.

Tepler shouted, "It's locked onto the asteroid. We've won!"

An ecstatic Estrada grabbed Kendon's hand and shook it vigorously. "We've done it! By God, we've beat them!"

Kendon was swept up by the same emotion, but he knew it was too soon for shouts of triumph. Victory could only be declared once the asteroid had missed.

He was about to head up to the observatory when he heard soldiers near the cliff shouting and pointing to out to sea.

"Colonel, look!"

Illuminated by the bright moon, three large disks emerged from the water. Huge columns of water swirled like twisters beneath them. The disks were clearly visible even through the turquoise shield. They hovered above the sea only a few hundred yards from the coast. As with Breeder ships, intense light radiated from them, but Kendon could tell from their shape that they were Clones.

As he watched them hover, two huge spacecraft, each a hundred yards across, came out of the water. As if choreographed, they did elegant, slow motion flips and then shot at fabulous speed into the sky.

It was only the beginning of an exodus of spacecraft from the water. Within minutes, possibly a hundred more emerged and flew straight up at dizzying velocity. Kendon lost count at seventy.

"What do you make of that?" Estrada said.

"They're convinced the asteroid will hit, and they don't intend to be in the water when it happens."

The last craft to leave the water was a Breeder command ship with the distinctive circular lights swirling at the base. It climbed above the three smaller Clone ships that had remained hovering over the sea and stopped. Then almost simultaneously, from devices mounted in their domes, the four spacecraft fired white beams at the turquoise force field. The beams were as ineffective as the rockets. The energy was absorbed by the shield, causing ripples that quickly dissipated, yet they kept firing.

Estrada screamed, "Get lost, you lousy bastards!" He shook his fist in the direction of the disks. "Go back to wherever you came from! Leave us alone!"

"They're up to something," Kendon said.

"Michael!"

Hearing Laura's voice, Kendon turned. She ran to his arms, and they held one another tightly. It seemed like ages since they were last together, yet only a half-hour had gone by. He kissed her.

"I'm afraid, Michael. They're coming for me. They want me. I can feel it."

"We're protected by the force field. Nothing can harm you here."

Yet he felt uneasy, not knowing why he should feel that way.

He looked at the shield. It covered the facility like an inverted bowl, projecting beyond the bluff into the salt marshes on one side and beyond the cliffs out to sea on the other. The shield was thick and impenetrable. He looked up at the fierce energy streaming from the cannon and was confident Tepler knew how to keep it targeted on the asteroid. But still he felt uneasy.

Beyond the cliffs, out to sea.

In an instant, he realized where they were vulnerable. He flicked the portable beam weapon on and turned to face the sea. He had quickly understood, as if grabbing the information from the minds of the Breeders: The attack on the shield by the four spacecraft was merely a diversion. Rising underneath the shield from the bottom of the sea was a Breeder command ship. The force field didn't extend down to the seabed, and the craft had maneuvered underneath it.

Kendon knew the spaceship was there even before it rose seconds later to the top of the cliff. He could see it clearly in his mind.

"Get back," he shouted to the soldiers nearest the cliff.

He didn't think the hand-held beam weapon would work, but he had nothing else to defend the tower with. Even before the green light went on, he saw the top of the craft rise above the cliff line. A dozen guardsmen aimed their machine guns at it, but they froze as if paralyzed when the hull of the craft came into view.

The ship kept rising until it cleared the cliff. The light emanating from it was nearly blinding. The spacecraft floated toward the observatory, then hovered silently about a man's height above the limestone bluff.

Kendon fought against the controlling energy coming from the craft, as forceful and potent as physical energy. Reflexively, he created an intense counterforce within his own mind. Yet he still felt its power.

He struggled to raise the beam weapon, praying that it had to contain some residual energy. It would be like attacking a tank with a sledgehammer, but at least it was something.

The spaceship's beam weapon slowly arched upward from its cradle next to the dome. It aimed at the tower.

Kendon counted desperately, "Four . . . five . . . six . . ."

The green light switched on. He fired. A feeble turquoise ray slammed the dome of Breeder ship. The force was powerful enough to shove the craft several feet backward, toward the inside surface of the force field. But then the craft sprang back to where it had been hovering before. The beam had hit the ship's weapon, and it lay to one side, bent and nearly detached from its mounting. Kendon fired again, jerking the Breeder ship and tearing off what was left of the weapon.

As he took aim again, a creamy light filled the air, washing out everything in whiteness. He could see the blurred forms of Estrada and the guardsmen standing frozen, facing the Breeder ship with their arms dangling loosely at their sides, unable to move.

He pulled the trigger again, but this time nothing happened. The weapon was dead, its fuel completely spent.

Kendon struggled against the creamy light, shutting his mind to the powerful psychic pull, fighting against it with the force of his will. Laboriously, he looked around. Laura was only a few yards away. She was struggling to free herself, fighting the power of the Breeder mind. She was being drawn in the direction of the ship, walking slowly toward it, her face full of terror.

In his mind, Kendon could hear her screaming, *Don't let them take me, Michael! Don't let them take me!*

"Fight them, Laura. You can do it."

She stopped and thrust her arms forward as if to push back whatever force was pulling her. Then she dropped to her knees and scrambled on her hands and knees to where one of the guardsmen stood frozen. With trembling hands, she detached a hand grenade from his belt. She stood up, but then seemed to freeze. The grenade dropped from her hand and Kendon watched helplessly as she struggled to bend down to grab it again. But she was now unable to bend her body.

At that moment, a panel in the side of the spacecraft slid open. A shimmering stairway appeared out of nowhere and unfolded to the ground. An image slowly formed inside the glow emanating from the door. The image grew larger, humanoid in form, but the intense light behind it kept the outlines indistinct. The form appeared in the rectangular opening with brilliant light streaming over its shoulders and around its head.

Kendon reached for Laura, grabbing one of her hands, but a force locked him in place and he was unable to pull her toward him.

The apparition seemed more to float down the shimmering staircase than to walk. It was a Breeder of rank with a long headdress of golden material with black horizontal lines folded back so that it draped over its shoulders, and it was wearing a bronze-colored tunic that nearly touched the ground. When it was standing at the foot of the craft, Kendon could see the features typical of the Breeder Grays: grayish-blue skin, an angular face with high cheek bones and a pointed chin. It had to be the commander, because in one hand it was holding a spear-like rod with a crystalline tip that glowed, the symbol of authority as well as an instrument for enhancing mindal energy.

The Breeder took a single step toward Kendon, its large dark eyes staring at him. It stood silently, holding the rod upright, the bottom planted on the ground like a staff. Under the Breeder's gaze, Kendon felt a powerful urge not only to bow, but to fall to his knees.

He couldn't see them, but he sensed that Estrada and the other guardsmen had dropped to their knees. The urge to bow down had the force of absolute necessity, as though no other possibility were open to him.

He heard a voice in his head:

Bow to me. Bow to my power.

He felt his grip on Laura's hand weakening. Her hand slid from his, and like the soldiers, she fell to her knees. She struggled to get back to her feet, but it was as if some invisible hand was pushing her down.

The Breeder didn't speak, yet Kendon heard commands for him to submit. He could feel its desire to control him, as if its primary goal in coming out of the spacecraft was to demonstrate its power over him. He could sense that the Breeders were fascinated that such an inferior creature could resist them and overcome every obstacle that had been put in his way.

Before he died, they were going to force him to submit to them. It was a matter of pride.

And he sensed, too, that they wanted Laura. She had been an abductee of whom they had made use in their hybrid program. She was their property, and she was also a prize: They understood the connection between her and the creator of the beam weapon. They wanted her genes.

Kendon filled his mind with swirling whiteness, with a brilliance even more intense than the light emanating from the Breeder craft. He drew on his experience of years of enforced mental vigilance that had been necessary to keep the Breeders from knowing about the longings for freedom, from penetrating the plots of resistance, from discovering the plans for escape.

The image of his dead comrades filled him. He saw again the look on Meller's face as he died. He experienced once again the sordid underground existence imposed by the Breeders with the goal of bringing about this final hour of destruction. He became enraged, and filled with the energy of his rage, he straightened his body and stared at the Breeder, into its opaque eyes, into its darkened soul.

His mind screamed, *I am Kendon! I am human! I will defeat you!*

The creature lowered the rod slowly in Kendon's direction until the glowing tip pointed directly at him. In his mind, he heard a voice: *Bow to me. Bow to the ones who create, who rule, who destroy.*

Kendon felt a blow to his solar plexus, as if a powerful fist had slammed him in the gut, causing him to stagger backward. He could feel the muscles of his abdomen and legs losing their strength, as if the connective tissues were dissolving, leaving him unable to stand. He fought the urge to drop to his knees. He breathed deeply, again and again, imagining his solar plexus as a brilliant white ball as radiant as the sun.

It was the sun and it rose in him and he was the sun.

In his mind, the words exploded again:

I am Kendon! I am human! I will defeat you!

He made two labored steps toward Laura and was able to put himself between her and the spacecraft. He made another two molasses steps toward the Breeder, his arm brushing against his holstered sidearm.

Only ten steps now separated them. The creature stepped backward, its glowing rod leveled in its hand like a spear, its elongated dark eyes reflecting the glow.

The rod amplified the creature's mind, but also Kendon's. He entered the creature through its own device and became one with it. His mind was filled with images that told of a mortal experience differing only in detail from the human, but overlaid with corrosive hubris. He saw the fleets that held the millions of hybrids awaiting the extinction of the life of the world. He saw the asteroid. He saw four huge ships, and his heart felt crushed at what he observed: They were firing beams at the asteroid, and the combined power of the four spacecraft was neutralizing the singular power of Meller's weapon.

He heard the Breeder gloat: *You are defeated. Give us the female. She will be spared.*

He thought of Laura and felt his love for her. He felt the same love now flowing from him to the entire human race, to every being whose life was now was at the verge of extinction. He felt the life of the world flowing back into him, amplifying his power. It was life formed in love, nurtured by hope, propelled by enthusiasm, worthy to be part of the universe adventure.

Bow to me. Bow to humanity.

The creature stood before him, loveless and cruel, motivated only by its desire for control. Kendon took two more steps toward it, now freely and easily, his arms loose, his legs springy. The creature stepped backward. Kendon felt himself growing while it shrank.

His mind commanded: *Bow to me. Bow to humanity. Bow to the life of this world.*

Mentally, Kendon imagined the rod growing hot, as if heated in a forge until it glowed to flesh-searing orange. He saw the creature's grip loosen. The rod dropped from its hand, and the glow in the pointed crystal went out even before it hit the ground.

Kendon imagined a mountain of weight bearing down on the creature. A landslide of boulders crushed it, an avalanche of snow buried it, a hail of stones pelted it. The creature fought to remain erect, but slowly it bent its torso, as if yielding a weight greater than it was capable of bearing.

The Breeder fell to its knees, bending far forward and extending its arms until its fingers touched the ground. It remained in prostration, unable to do anything else.

Kendon knew the Breeders had the ability to mimic human sound. It was a hiss, but it was understandable:

"Hail, Man-God."

The creature fought to free itself. Kendon felt the struggle and in turn he struggled to maintain his control. He felt it surging to collect its own power, drawing on the energy of its humiliation, at the shame of being forced to prostrate itself before a creature it considered not only vastly inferior, but worthy of extinction.

There were more of the creatures inside the craft, and Kendon could sense their confusion. They knew they were in a dangerous position, but they were unable to leave without their commander.

Something was about to give. Kendon was sure of it. He moved his hand slowly down to the holster and the pistol grip, careful not to telescope his intention through his motions or in his thoughts. He felt the rage of the Breeder exploding as it tapped into the most primitive layers of its three-lobed brain, long dormant but still potent. He felt its thirst for vengeance; he tasted its lust for his blood.

"You would slay Man-God?" Kendon taunted.

He pulled the pistol out just as the creature lunged at him, the rod in its hand like a spear. He fired once at its head, hitting it, but he was not able to sidestep the forward thrust of the rod. With searing pain, the sharp crystal point sank into his abdomen.

Struggling to remain standing, Kendon fired once more at the creature's head. Its cranium shattered, the Breeder crumpled to the ground.

Kendon had never before felt such pain. It burned and cut through his being with ferocious stabs. With one hand, he grabbed the rod where it entered his body and tugged, but he could not pull the spear out. It had gone right through him, the crystal point sticking out of his back.

The pain caused him to stagger, and he fought against the blackness that was enveloping him.

"Laura, help me. I need you, Laura."

Controlling energies still emanated from the craft. Laura struggled fiercely to free herself.

"The grenade," Kendon shouted, "Give me the grenade."

With superhuman effort, Laura reached for the grenade. Her hand shaking, she slowly closed her fingers over it. She held it out to him. Grabbing it, Kendon staggered to the opening of the craft. He could sense the door was about to slide shut. He pulled the pin and tossed the grenade through the opening, barely a second before it closed, leaving not even a trace a door had been there.

Kendon stumbled backward, holding the rod with both hands where it entered his abdomen and feeling hot blood oozing between his fingers.

An instant later, a muffled explosion ripped through the craft, and the powerful light emanating from it went out. Its anti-gravity reactor destroyed, the spaceship dropped to the ground, bounced slightly, and then rocked slowly on one of the directional pods before finally coming to rest.

Freed of the controlling energies, Laura, Estrada, and the guardsmen quickly came to their senses. They scrambled to their feet and gasped in horror at the sight of Kendon with a spear through his body.

With one hand, Kendon reached out toward Laura, his eyes pleading, his lips trying vainly to warn her about the Breeder ships near the asteroid.

He pointed to the sky and tried to speak, but the words would not come out of his mouth.

Blackness grabbed his mind. He fell onto his side, into the darkness.

Chapter 28

Kendon struggled against the seduction of darkness, against the figure with indistinct features that beckoned him to follow to where there would be no more suffering, to where there would be no more pain.

I can't die yet. I have a purpose. I haven't accomplished my purpose. I must fulfill my purpose.

He forced his eyes open. Laura was bending over him. He reached up and touched her cheek where tears rolled down. Estrada and a dozen guardsmen had crowded around and were looking down at him, their faces drawn. He felt their sadness, he felt their compassion, he felt their love.

He struggled to speak. He wanted to say, "Eric needs my help." But the words would not leave his lips. He knew with certainty the asteroid was on course, that the energy of Meller's beam weapon was being neutralized by the concerted power of four huge Breeder ships. Eric had to know it was happening, too, but he was powerless to do anything about it.

Kendon had to speak. Marshaling his energy, he was able at last to gasp, "Pull it out. Help me to me feet."

Laura said, "It's too dangerous. It needs to be removed surgically. Medics are coming with a stretcher."

"There's no time. The Breeders are pushing the asteroid back.

It's still on course. It's still going to hit. Eric can't do anything about it. Only I can."

Laura looked up helplessly at Estrada. The guard commander stepped forward. He stood over Kendon and gripped the shaft a few inches above where it penetrated Kendon's abdomen. He glanced at Laura, then at Kendon, who nodded at him to proceed. After hesitating a moment, Estrada placed his foot on Kendon's abdomen and yanked on the shaft, ripping the crystalline tip from him.

Kendon's body contracted into the fetal position. He put both hands over the wound and fought once more against the darkness.

Laura cried, "You've healed others, Michael. Heal yourself."

Kendon gasped, "There's no time. Help me to my feet. I have to get to the observatory."

He felt hands under his armpits. He felt himself being lifted up and then he was on his feet, supported on one side by Laura.

"Give me the rod."

Using his shirt, Estrada wiped the blood from the crystal and handed the shaft to Kendon.

The Breeder commander's rod in one hand, his arm pressing down on Laura's shoulder, Kendon hobbled toward the entrance to the main building. He understood the amplifying power of the crystal, and he channeled his healing energy through it, swirling it downward to his wound, deep into his gut.

The guardsmen, helmeted and in full battle gear, were lined up along the path. As Kendon limped by, they snapped salutes.

Laboriously, with Laura's help, he climbed the spiral staircase. When they reached the observatory, he saw Eric and Gabriela seated at the control panel, peering intently at the monitors. When they turned as he came in, he knew their look of fright had as much to do with what they were seeing on the monitors as with the sight of his blood.

Eric and Gabriela rushed to help bring him into the room.

"We saw what happened to you." Eric said. "You'd better lie down."

"No, I have to stand. If I lie down, I won't be able to get up again. What I need is something to lean against."

With Laura's help, Kendon hobbled over to the telescope and leaned his back against it.

Straining against the pain, Kendon gasped, "Tell me what's happening."

Tepler's bulging eyes revealed his desperation. "The asteroid is still on course. The beam isn't having any effect."

"What is your explanation?"

"There are spacecraft behind and to one side of the asteroid. They're enormous, about fifteen hundred feet in length, like the one that was guiding it in. They must have powerful beam weapons of their own, because they're countering the energy of our weapon."

"There are four of them, aren't there?"

"Yes, how do you know?"

"From the Breeder commander. I saw it in his mind."

The anguish was visible on Tepler's face. "I don't know what to do about it."

Kendon spoke between spasms of pain ripping through his gut. "What have you tried so far?"

"I boosted the power, but they boosted theirs, too. I tried to shoot at them. I programmed their coordinates into the computer and then diverted the beam, but they moved out of the way. It's like they know in advance what I'm going to do."

"How far away did they move?"

"Maybe ten miles."

Laura had unbuttoned Kendon's coat and loosened his shirt. She was holding a cloth against the abdominal wound to stanch the loss of blood. He had already lost a lot of blood, and he was beginning to feel cold. The bleeding was internal as well as external, and he worried he was going to pass out.

To ease the pain, Kendon rested as much of his weight against the telescope as he could. "How much time is left?"

Tepler looked at the clock. "Ten minutes to impact, but we only have five minutes to shift the trajectory of the asteroid. After that, the Earth's gravitational pull will be a factor, maybe the decisive one."

The monitor displayed the trajectory, showing the asteroid's approach at a sharp angle.

"Are you operating the beam at full power?"

"No, at slightly more than half. I'm worried about the asteroid breaking up. Then we would have hundreds of lethal meteors coming at us."

"Can't you spread out the beam? Can you distribute its energy over a wider surface?"

"Yes, I can try that."

His vision blurring, Kendon said, "Show me where they are."

Tepler adjusted the image on the monitor to include the space occupied by the asteroid and the Breeder ships. The four spacecraft were elongated splashes of light, slightly above the more distinct image of the asteroid. "They're clustered at these coordinates, separated by only twenty miles."

"Try hitting them again," Kendon said.

Tepler furiously typed in commands.

"Don't fire until I tell you."

Kendon had propped the Breeder's rod against the telescope. On its own, it was inert, a long shaft mounted by a crystal, long and sharp, and of no more importance than a staff. Once held, however, it transformed and gave its holder immense power.

Kendon grabbed the rod, the crystal tip pointing upwards. As he held it, the crystal point glowed.

His mind powerfully shielded by years of practice, he was confident his thoughts were his own. He wanted to share his intention with Laura, Nestor, Eric, and Gabriela, but he feared revealing anything. They were not as capable of shielding their thoughts as he was, and if he tried to communicate anything to them, the Breeders would pick up on it.

"They know what we're doing," Tepler said.

"Try it anyway," Kendon said. "Maybe we'll get lucky."

He leaned against Laura and looked deeply in her eyes. "You give me strength," he said softly.

She said, "You give me courage. I'm not afraid when I'm with you."

He pointed to the cannon. "Help me move over there."

It was only two yards away, but it was an extremely painful two yards. He breathed deeply from the exertion and fought the desire to grab his belly with both hands.

Instead, he placed the palm of one hand on the cannon and leaned forward, steadying himself. With the other, he held the Breeder's rod.

Kendon cleared his mind of the confusion of thoughts and emotions and even of the awareness of the fire in his gut. He touched the crystal to his forehead and felt his mind leap outward. He experienced it roaming freely in the universe, exulting in its liberty. Where his mind went, he went. What his mind saw, he saw.

He struggled to control his own joyful freedom from his physical being. Focusing his mental self, he saw the asteroid as if it was a huge mountain across a flat dark plain. He saw the four lights above it, and immediately he was inside one of the lights. He felt the collective mind of the Breeders, cocky, certain of victory, triumphant in their belief the humans were making one last futile attempt to stop them.

"Fire!"

Tepler pressed a button. The beam bypassed the asteroid, and at light speed intersected the coordinates of the Breeder ships. As happened earlier, they scattered before it could touch them. Kendon focused his amplified powers on the course of the gravity stream. Now he flowed with the beam. Now he was one with the beam.

In an instant, responding to his will, the beam bent a fraction of a degree. The first of the Breeder ships was caught in it and vanished. A second was caught, too, ceasing instantly to exist, but the remaining two were able to escape as they shot at hypervelocity to a safe distance.

"How did you do that? You hit two of them!" Tepler said.

Mentally and physically, Kendon was drained. Already weakened from the loss of blood, he began to slump. Laura and Estrada grabbed him just in time to keep him from falling.

"The asteroid," he gasped, "Aim for the asteroid. Give it full power, but broaden the beam."

It only took seconds for Tepler to make the adjustments. They watched the monitor to see if the gravity beam was having an effect. Slowly, incrementally, over the course of the next minute, the asteroid altered course, curving slightly upward, though not yet enough to avoid impact. But it was definitely moving from its previous trajectory.

"Two more minutes, that's all it will take to push it safely away," Tepler said.

Nestor, Gabriela, and Laura cheered.

Kendon tried to say, "It's not over yet," but he couldn't muster the energy. He knew the Breeders could not contemplate failure. They had never failed in their stratagems of creation, destruction, and control, and they would not give up. Like the Breeder commander outside the lighthouse, they would come out in challenge.

Laura pointed to the monitor, "Look, they're back. Four of them are near the asteroid."

Kendon could see them on the monitor, too, and also in his mind.

Tepler said, "If I can hold it on its current trajectory, it will strike in mid-Atlantic now. That will cause enormous tsunamis, but it won't bring an end to the world."

"That's not good enough," Kendon said.

"I can't give it any more power," Tepler cried.

Kendon knew it would be futile to try to destroy them again by bending the beam. They knew the tactic now. Only a few precious minutes remained. He looked at the tense and sad faces of Laura, Gabriela, Eric, and Nestor and sensed they were all but resigned to die. He couldn't let it happen. They couldn't die. They had the right to exist. The human race as it had evolved had the right to be. It had the right to take its place in the universe, to be second to none and equal to all.

The image of Donald Meller was again in his mind, urging him with his dying eyes to go forward. Oh, those kind eyes! He felt a tidal wave of love sweeping over him, filling him with its power as it surged in him.

The rod firmly gripped in his hand, the crystal almost touching his forehead, Kendon closed his eyes. He went again out of his physical body, plunging like a diver into a unique energy whose existence had been barely grasped by the human race, but which the Breeders understood and had mastered.

He rejoiced as he streamed into the universe, and he exulted as he merged into the currents of mind. Soon, he was among them—in one of their ships, in the command room, with the commander, in the commander.

His mind was now one with the Breeder and he saw what it saw and understood what it understood: The four ships were about to become eight as four more of the huge craft positioned themselves, their combined power intended to ensure Breeder victory.

Kendon looked at his hands and saw they were grayish-blue and bony, each with four fingers with suction cups on the tips. He moved these agile fingers over the ship's beam-weapon controls, as familiar with them as if he had trained on them for millennia.

He entered new coordinates and gave himself the luxury of looking to the right and left, scrutinizing the startled faces of the commander's subordinates. They understood what was about to happen, but they were powerless to stop it.

Kendon-Breeder fired.

Almost instantly eight ships became six, and six became four, and four became two. The remaining ship understood only too late that it was also being targeted. It fired in self-defense at the same moment it was destroyed.

Seconds later, Tepler exclaimed, "They're all gone! I don't understand how it happened, but they disappeared from the screen. Have they given up?"

Kendon felt his body sliding, stopped from falling to the floor only by Laura's desperate embrace. He could hear Gabriela and Nestor shouting encouragement for Tepler to keep the gravity beam focused on the asteroid.

The asteroid was approaching at an angle, and now only two minutes remained before it would slam into the Caribbean. Earth's gravity was already pulling at it, negating some of the power of the beam weapon. Was it too late? Kendon wondered. Would the Breeders still have their victory?

He tried to project his mind into the beam, thinking maybe he could augment its force, but his physical energy was depleted from his wound, and the loss of blood was making him feel cold. He was certain he was dying, and he despaired that he could do nothing more to help.

With his eyes, Kendon could see the beam streaking from the cannon, and with his ears he could hear the fierce sizzle of turquoise energy leaving the barrel. With his mind, he saw the beam slamming into the underside of the asteroid, spreading out powerful energy flanges like strong fingers gripping a ball.

"You can do it Eric," Kendon yelled as loudly as he could. "You can do it!"

Seconds later, Eric shouted joyfully, "I think I've got it up! It's lifting up. Look, everyone! Look at the monitor! It's going up!"

In his dimming mind, Kendon saw the massive mountain moving slowly upward, away from Earth, flinging back out into the solar system where it could do no harm. He saw thousands of chunks of rock, large and small, that had broken free by the impact of the relentless energy of the beam weapon. As the asteroid swung upward and away, the fragments shot downward, streaking into the atmosphere, blazing from friction, striking harmlessly far out to sea.

He heard cheering voices, first of Eric and Gabriela, then of the guardsmen on the grounds below after Estrada shouted down to them of their victory.

The rod fell from Kendon's hand and slammed against the floor. His body was like a stone, heavy and solid, and it was shooting downward, too, down to the floor, the impact only softened by Laura's grip on him.

As he sank into darkness, he heard footsteps running up to him, and he heard Laura crying, "Don't die, Michael. Don't leave me. Oh, please don't leave me!"

Chapter 29

*L*aura walked across the bluff carrying a tray, her hair blowing softly in the wind. Even in the fading evening light, her smile was apparent from a hundred feet away. Behind her was the converted lighthouse, with the dome of the observatory standing out against the orange sky.

Kendon was sitting in a reclining chair a dozen yards from the edge of the cliff, enjoying the breeze coming off the Caribbean. He watched Laura approach with a mild feeling of guilt. Four days had gone by since the Breeder defeat, and he was as good as new, yet he was allowing himself to be pampered like a man on his deathbed. Surgery had repaired the worst of the damage to his abdomen, but his own healing abilities had restored the rest. Hardly a trace was left of the wounds, inside and out, prompting one of the doctors to say, "You've got to show me how you do that!" But Laura had insisted that he was still in recovery and that he needed to be specially cared for by his own personal physician—her.

While she was at the lighthouse preparing something to eat for her "patient," Kendon watched the sun set and contemplated the tight security that had been set up around the cape. Only a few miles offshore, American warships formed an impregnable cordon around the peninsula. On land, an entire regiment of Puerto

Rican guardsmen blanketed the region. Naval jets routinely flew over the cape.

He smiled at the thought of all the attention Cabo Rojo was getting. The cape was swarming with journalists from around the globe. He had never imagined that this would be the consequence of success—an onslaught of aggressive media, but it was happening, and he understood how important it was to carry the struggle forward. An asteroid and an evil agenda had been defeated, but the powers behind them were still at large, still capable of striking back. What could be better to mobilize a global defense than photographs and videos of crashed spaceships, of aliens both dead and alive, and of captured Directorate soldiers?

The powerful radar units Donald Meller donated to the National Guard had proven especially effective. They had caused sixteen crashes, twelve of them on land and four into the sea. Most of the spacecraft were still intact and had been moved to the edges of the salt marsh for safekeeping. One Breeder Gray and four Clone Grays had been captured alive and more than seventy alien bodies recovered. The live ones were being held at the National Guard armory.

At news conferences, Kendon revealed the truth about the Breeders and the Collaboration. Gabriela spoke about her uncle's prediction and even managed to convince the painfully shy man to give interviews.

In a few short days, the cover-ups, the lies, the denials, and the disinformation of the previous seven decades had been exposed. It was the beginning of the end of a vast mechanism of secrecy that had nearly resulted in the death of the human race.

That morning, Nestor Estrada, now a lieutenant general in command of the newly-formed First Planetary Defense Brigade composed entirely of Puerto Rico National Guard volunteers, had led an assault on the underground facility inside the Bermejo mountains. Just after Laura had gone to the lighthouse to prepare something to eat, Nestor called to brief Kendon about the results of the operation. The Breeders and the Clones were gone, but they had abandoned seven spacecraft that were under repair. After minimal fighting, the guardsmen obtained the surrender of three hundred and ninety seven Directorate soldiers and freed more than fifteen hundred Nomenklatura captives, including all of the people taken from Arecibo. Additionally, they uncovered a small hybrid colony, mostly of children and young adults, whom the Breeders had left behind.

"It was heartbreaking to see how scared they were of us," Nestor said.

Kendon was eager to share the news with Laura. He watched her walk up the path with the tray, enjoying the way her hips swayed and sight of her hair rustled by the breeze.

On the tray were a pot of tea and a plate of hors d'oeuvres. She placed the tray on the small table next to Kendon's recliner and poured tea while he helped himself to some to some food.

"And how is my patient holding up?" she said.

"To tell you the truth, after you left, I had this terrible ache right here." He grimaced and tapped his heart. "But now that you're back, I'm all better."

"You're easy to cure."

He lifted her hand to his lips and kissed it. He told her what he had heard from Nestor Estrada. "He's planning on bringing the media down into the facility tomorrow."

"I feel sorry for the hybrids. They're victims, too."

Nestor had also discovered what looked like a cache of ununpentium—more than two hundred pounds of it.

"If it really is ununpentium, then that's the best news of the day," Kendon said.

They had already discussed the need to create more beam weapons. Asteroids were convenient tools of destruction and readily available. Earth needed protection, but it would take a minimum of three such weapons strategically placed to give adequate coverage. Six would be better.

"The Collaboration is finished," Kendon said. "The entire network of underground facilities will soon be under the control of your elected government, and the hundreds of thousands of the Nomenklatura who are still missing will be liberated."

Laura looked out to sea, and the outline of her face stood out in the moonlight and made Kendon think once again how much she resembled her father. The resemblance was in the intelligence of her eyes and in the determination in the shape of her jaw and chin. She smiled at him, her eyes showing the warmth that he had found so appealing in the photo her father had shown him.

Kendon said, "I've been giving a lot of thought to your idea of opening a clinic here. It's a great location with healing energies of its own, and your research institute could be relocated into town. We could both do our work here."

After he had regained his strength, she had suggested the idea of turning Cabo Rojo into a healing center for children with cancer and other life-threatening diseases. After all, the foundation owned the cape, and control of the foundation would fall to her, so why not make use of it?

Letting his imagination sink into the idea, he had visualized busloads of sick children arriving. He would cure them one by one, giving them back their birthright—a chance to live out their lives, to fulfill whatever destiny had been granted to them by virtue of being born into this world.

Kendon had quickly become dizzy with ideas. Among other things, he imagined opening a school to teach what he knew about healing. But after thinking about it, he decided a school wouldn't work because he really didn't know anything about healing except that he had this unusual ability. So what was there to teach? But then it occurred to him that other people must have the same ability. The old Cabo Rojo lighthouse tower would serve as a beacon, attracting healers from all over the world. They would come to Cabo Rojo to perform their miracles.

Holding Laura's hand, his mind running wild at the thought of the healing adventure, Kendon said, "Being healers has always been our purpose—you as a physician and me with my strange hands. It just took us a long time to get to Cabo Rojo."

When it became dark, they stood up and walked hand in hand along the cliff, enjoying the refreshing breeze and the sound of waves crashing against the cliffs below.

They stared out at the moonlit sea, at the glow and glimmer of the rippling water, and at the line of warships in the distance. After a while, they turned toward each other and suddenly burst out laughing. They embraced, then laughed again, not really knowing why they were laughing, but enjoying every second of it.

Holding hands, they looked up at the sky and gazed at the heavens. The sky was now full of stars. Raised in the underworld, Kendon had rarely had the opportunity to go aboveground and stare at the heavens, but he was a free man now, and he had eyes to see and all the time to look. There they were, billions and trillions of stars, the nighttime ablaze with points of light.

He thought of the beings who had warned the fisherman of the asteroid, thereby setting in motion the chain of events that led to the defeat of the Breeder agenda.

"You know what?" he said.

"What?"

"I think we're on the verge of discovering something incredible. We are about to learn just how metropolitan the universe really is. We're going to find out it's teeming with intelligent life, most of it good, and it's eager to embrace us once we've achieved a better world."

As he gazed at the stars, he imagined they were musical notes, and in his head he heard a lovely melody, at first faint but then louder and distinct. The more he listened, the more he became certain it wasn't his imagination. Then he heard words, too, as if the universe was singing to him.

"Do you hear something, Laura?"

"Yes."

"What is it?"

"A song."

"Can you make out the words?"

"Yes."

"What do you hear?"

"From the shores of a calming sea, I go forth to heal my world."

"Yes," Kendon said. He lifted her hand to his lips. "That is what I hear, too."